MARK OF CHAOS

THE BLOODY INCURSIONS by the dark forces of Chaos call for mankind to defend its lands to the last man. When a young Empire commander is caught up in this carnage of war, he must prove his honour by tracking down and destroying one of the most feared enemy leaders.

The action-packed novelisation of *Namco Bandai's* smash-hit fantasy computer game is set against a backdrop of war on an epic formidable scale.

D1272677

MARK OF CHAOS

ANTHONY REYNOLDS

To my mum, the most generous-natured person one could meet.

A BLACK LIBRARY PUBLICATION

First published in Great Britain in 2006 by
BL Publishing,
Games Workshop Ltd.,
Willow Road, Nottingham,
NG7 2WS, UK

10 9 8 7 6 5 4 3 2 1

Cover illustration by Gergo Sziptner.
Map by Nuala Kinrade.

With thanks to Namco Bandai and Black Hole.

A CIP record for this book is available from the British Library.

ISBN 13: 978 1 84416 396 0
ISBN 10: 1 84416 396 2

Distributed in the US by Simon & Schuster
1230 Avenue of the Americas, New York, NY 10020.

Printed and bound in Great Britain by
Bookmarque, Surrey, UK.

See the Black Library on the Internet at
www.blacklibrary.com

Find out more about Games Workshop
and the world of Warhammer at
www.games-workshop.com

Find out more about Mark of Chaos at
www.markofchaos.com

THIS IS A DARK age, a bloody age, an age of daemons and of sorcery. It is an age of battle and death, and of the world's ending. Amidst all of the fire, flame and fury it is a time, too, of mighty heroes, of bold deeds and great courage.

AT THE HEART of the Old World sprawls the Empire, the largest and most powerful of the human realms. Known for its engineers, explorers, traders and soldiers, it is a land of great mountains, mighty rivers, dark forests and vast cities. It is a land riven by uncertainty, as three pretenders all vye for control of the Imperial throne.

BUT THESE ARE far from civilised times. Across the length and breadth of the Old World, from the knightly palaces of Bretonnia to ice-bound Kislev in the far north, come rumblings of war. In the towering World's Edge Mountains, the orc tribes are gathering for another assault. Bandits and renegades harry the wild southern lands of the Border Princes. There are rumours of rat-things, the skaven, emerging from the sewers and swamps across the land. And from the northern wildernesses there is the ever-present threat of Chaos, of daemons and beastmen corrupted by the foul powers of the Dark Gods. As the time of battle draws ever nearer, the Empire needs heroes like never before.

BOOK ONE

THE YEAR 2302, *two hundred years before the reign of Emperor Karl Franz, was a time of horror. It was the Great War Against Chaos, and it was the largest attack from the forces of Chaos in the far north that the world had ever seen. The Empire was fractured and divided, with the different states battling each other in bitter civil war. It was only thanks to the efforts of the great leader Magnus the Pious that the Empire was not overrun. Magnus united the states, and led a grand coalition to the north to face the enemy in Kislev. The battle raged for several years, yet the forces of the Empire were at last victorious. The forces of Chaos, led by the warlord Asavar Kul, were shattered. With the death of the Chaos leader, the tribes were split, and they began warring on each other once more. Many tribes were destroyed in the great battles, but others were scattered. Many retreated back to their traditional homelands in the north, to resume their constant warfare against their own, but others entered the forests and mountains around the Empire itself.*

The Empire was victorious, but it was a broken land. Decades of civil war had ensured deep-seated enmity amongst the states, and many nobles slipped back into their old, petty rivalries. Plague was rife, and the populace was on the point of starvation. The Great War had bled the coffers dry, and many of the standing armies of the elector counts had been decimated. The Chaos threat had been pushed back, but scattered tribes continued to raid the northern towns and villages, and there were not enough soldiers to defend against these attacks. It was a grim time for the people of the Empire. There was always the threat from the north − for if any of the Chaos-worshipping chieftains grew powerful enough to unite the scattered tribes, then a new era of warfare would be unleashed, resulting in a war that the Empire would be unable to endure.

CHAPTER ONE

His eyes flicked open, but all he could see was darkness. A foetid stench filled his nostrils and he gagged, his stomach heaving. He could taste bile on his lips. His arms felt leaden and weak, the muscles aching and sore, but he pushed up with all his might at the weight pressing down upon him, crying out with the effort. Red light reached his eyes and he blinked painfully. With the last of his energy, he surged upwards, rolling the weight from his chest. It flopped beside him, and he found himself staring into a pair of cold, dead eyes. He cried out in horror, pushed away from the staring cadaver, and found himself looking at another corpse, its face obscured by long black hair. Pushing himself away again, he scrambled back, onto the chest of another corpse. Half its head had been cleaved away. Panic filled him – he was on the top of a great pile of the dead.

Then the drumming started. An infernal sound, like the heartbeat of an evil god, it reverberated around his head, coming from everywhere and nowhere. He could feel the sound beating at him, hammering down upon him like a weight, eroding his will to live. He curled up in a ball, head in his hands, trying vainly to block out the monstrous sound. Tears ran down his face, and he felt his insides twist and knot. He thought he heard laughter, swords clashing, the roaring of daemonic hounds, and the screams and shouts of the dying and the victorious. He was dead, he thought, and this was the hellish afterlife.

His eyes were closed, yet he saw flashes of hateful, violent, maddening images. He saw the daemon with the eyes of fire staring into his soul, muscles rippling and flexing over its massive red, ritually scarred chest. The hateful creature's lips drew back, exposing fangs stained red with gore. Blood slid in thick rivulets down the massive curving horns on its head. He felt that blood drip onto his face, and felt the heat emanating from the creature as it reached for him.

WITH A TORTURED gasp, Hensel awoke. His body was slick with sweat and his flea-ridden bed sheets were wrapped around him tightly – he felt like a corpse, freshly wrapped by the priests of Morr. Thrashing his limbs frantically, he kicked the covers away, trying to dispel the disturbing thought from his mind. The chill night air cooled his body almost instantly.

Sitting up, Hensel placed his feet on the freezing floorboards and rubbed his callused hands over his unshaven face. His heart still beat frantically in his chest, and he breathed in deeply, trying to calm himself. He had been having the nightmares for over a year. Not a single night would go by without the terrifying visions plaguing his sleep. The only time that he could get any blessed dreamless sleep was after he had drunk himself into a stupor – something that he had been doing ever more frequently in the past months.

Hensel wished that he had got drunk that night, but drink cost money, something he was particularly short of. The goodwill of the Cock-eyed Firken, the cheapest pub in Bildenhof, had also dried up. Not that he could blame them, because he'd been penniless for weeks.

Resigning himself to not getting any sleep that night, Hensel arose from his vermin-infested pallet and dressed quickly, throwing on a dirty shirt and belting his most valuable possession, his sword, at his side. Pulling on his heavy greatcoat, he yanked open the door to his room and stepped into the night.

Looking up, Hensel saw that the glow of the silver moon, Mannslieb, was high in the sky, partially obscured by wispy clouds. It was not yet midnight, and he had slept for little over an hour. Trudging through the clinging mud, he walked down the deserted main street of Bildenhof. Dark houses lined the street. A rolling low fog hugged the ground, slipping under doors and seeping through cracked windows. Its touch was cold and wet. He looked up at the dark windows, jealous of the sleep the townspeople were getting.

The buildings of Bildenhof were dirty and mis-shapen, their timbers cracked and warped. Not a window or doorframe was even, their angles skewed and twisted. The roofs were uneven and ramshackle, and you always had to be careful walking under their drooping eaves for there was a very real threat of falling tiles.

Like the Empire itself, thought Hensel, the town was rotten and decaying, just about on the point of collapse.

He made his way over the covered bridge that crossed the pitiful muddy stream passing through town, his footsteps echoing loudly within the enclosed space. Trudging up the small rise beyond the bridge, he neared the watch post.

It was a crude affair, having been hastily erected some months earlier. Little more than a wooden box built atop the thick, twisted trunk of an ancient oak tree, it allowed a sentry a clear view of the northern hillside leading up towards the dark tree line. The beasts of the forest had attacked three nearby villages over the last months, and, in response, the council of Bildenhof had ordered eight of these watch posts to be built along the outskirts of the town. A score of sharpened stakes had been driven into the ground around the base of the watch post, and a shaky ladder leant against it. Hensel shook his head.

He climbed the ladder stealthily, reaching the top with barely a sound. Gingerly he raised his head to look inside. There, with his back to him, he could see a motionless crouching figure, looking out to the north. A pair of crossbows leant against the wall next to him.

'Evening,' said Hensel. The sentry started visibly, a strangled yelp escaping his lips at the unexpected voice behind him. 'You should really pull this ladder up, you know. It would stop people catching you unawares.'

'Sigmar above, man! What the hell is wrong with you?' the man asked. 'Creeping up on a man like that!'

'I'm sorry, Mathias,' said Hensel, his dark-ringed eyes glinting with humour. 'It was too good an opportunity to pass by.'

'Yes, I bet it was,' said Mathias, shaking his head.

'You alone here? Who's meant to be on watch with you?' asked Hensel as he crawled over to take a seat next to the sentry.

'Konrad. He slipped off about an hour ago – to warm his body a little, if you know what I mean.'

'Ah. Who is it this time?' asked Hensel.

'Magritte.'

Hensel guffawed. 'Damn, but she's a popular one with the men of this town!'

'Aye, she is. She won't be if her father ever catches her. He'll pack her off to the temple in Wolfenburg if he ever hears about what she's up to in the darkening hours.'

'Lucky for her he's a heavy sleeper, eh?'

'Aye, indeed it is,' said Mathias. He paused for a moment, and frowned. 'How do you know he's a heavy sleeper?'

'How do you?' asked Hensel, with a grin.

Mathias laughed out loud, and slapped a meaty hand on his thigh. The pair sat in silence for a minute, staring out into the night.

'Couldn't sleep again, huh. The nightmares?' asked Mathias.

The older man nodded slowly in response. 'Ever since Kislev,' he breathed. Mathias didn't ask anything more, which Hensel appreciated. The pair fell into silence, each engrossed in his own thoughts.

A sharp noise echoed through the night, breaking the quiet – a bell was ringing frantically. *An attack.*

Lights flared to life in the houses of the town, and Hensel could hear muffled shouts as people moved onto the streets in fear.

Hensel and Mathias grabbed the crossbows, loading them hastily, and stared out into the night. Minutes passed, and Hensel began to think that it had been a false alarm, until Mathias stiffened at his side.

He looked over at the younger soldier, and saw that his eyes were wide and filled with dread. He followed the youngster's gaze to the tree line, peering into the darkness. At first he saw nothing, just a vague movement in the darkness.

Then he saw them. The dark figures were almost completely hidden in the gloom beneath the trees. There were scores of them.

It was then that the drumming started.

Deep and powerful, the rhythmic pounding of the drums rolled out over Bildenhof. Beating slowly, like the giant heart of some ancient, monstrous creature, the sound reverberated off the high hills surrounding the town, so that the thumping sound seemed to come from all around.

The infernal sound brought Hensel's nightmares to life. For over a year, this same hateful drumming had haunted his dreams, accompanied by images of slaughter and bloodletting, of corpses lying atop corpses, and of giant piles of skulls that reached up to the heavens. The sound struck at him like hammer blows. His whole body flinched with every pounding beat.

At the top of the rise, a single figure stepped from the tree line. Even from this distance the man was clearly massive, and Hensel stared at him in utter horror. He recognised the creature. This was the vicious, hateful daemon-kin that hunted him in his nightmares. He knew every turn of bronze that bedecked the creature's blood-red armour, and instantly recognised the massive re-curved ebony horns that sprouted from the daemon's full-face helm. Heavy, ornate armour covered all but his massively muscled arms, which were decorated with bronze ring piercings and crude tattoos. Chains were wrapped around his forearms, and Hensel recognised the thick, black-furred cloak draped over the daemon-kin's giant shoulders, hewn from the flesh of some Chaotic beast of the north.

Though he couldn't see the creature's eyes from this distance, he knew that hellfire burned in those cruel orbs, and he knew that its sharp teeth were stained red with blood. This being had seen thousands slain beneath its axe, and would see thousands more. A massive bald figure stood behind the fiend, holding aloft a rough cross-posted banner. Heads hung from the banner by their hair, and skulls hung in great strings, held together by loops of sinew tied through the eye-sockets.

Hensel's gaze flickered from the banner bearer back to the red-clad warrior. The daemon-kin raised its massive double-bladed axe into the air, and bellowed a savage, challenging roar. That roar contained the hellish promise of butchery and bloodshed to come. It was joined by screams and guttural shouts from hundreds of throats, and Hensel knew that both he and Bildenhof were doomed.

CHAPTER TWO

SOLDIERS DRESSED IN the purple and yellow livery of Ostermark stepped hastily out of the way of the stocky captain as he stalked up the hill, his horribly scarred face thunderous. He stomped through the mud, past hundreds of tents and pickets, through the vast throng of the army of Ostermark. Laughing and joking stopped abruptly as the captain came into view, and men lowered their eyes and turned away. One soldier saluted briskly, but the captain took no notice.

He marched past row upon row of limbered great cannons, their gleaming barrels being meticulously polished and oiled by their dutiful crews under the watchful eye of a frowning, middle-aged engineer. His helmet grasped tightly under his left arm, his right hand resting on the worn pommel of his sword, the captain stomped onwards. His eyes were set grimly on the massive purple and yellow tent that sat on the peak of the hill, elegant tapering pennants at its tip waving lazily in the gentle breeze.

A pair of guards stood at the entrance to the tent, halberds held to attention before them. One of them nodded to the captain as he approached.

'The Grand Count of Ostermark has been waiting some time for you, Captain von Kessel.'

'Good,' the captain replied curtly. He swept aside the heavy cloth flap and entered the grand tent.

The tent was gloomy and poorly lit. The grand count was an ill old man, and bright light hurt his cataract-ridden eyes. A thick, cloying fug hung in the air. Censers swung slowly from side to side by faceless robed figures exuded sickly smelling smoke. The movement of von Kessel as he entered the tent disturbed the hanging smoke, sending it swirling in eddies.

'Stefan? Is it Stefan who enters?' enquired a voice, reaching out across the dim, smoky tent.

'Aye it is, my lord,' the captain stated sharply. He marched into the middle of the grand tent, and slammed his helmet down on a map-strewn wooden table, making the goblets and writing instruments on its surface jump.

Grand Count Otto Gruber, flanked by a score of advisors and courtiers, was propped up in his leather chair. He stared at von Kessel with his wet eyes, unfazed by the glowering gaze of the captain. The count was an enormous man, big in every sense of the word. His bulk filled the massive leather chair, so that it looked ludicrously small for him, and he shifted his weight uncomfortably every few seconds. His face was bulbous and fleshy, and he wore a wig, tightly curled and powdered, upon his pallid head. He was sweating profusely, and a young man dabbed at his face and neck with a damp cloth. Several years previously, the count had suffered a virulent skin disease, and open sores could be seen upon his pudgy hands and on the rolls of fat of his neck. Blisters, some that had burst and spilt their contents, clustered around his left eye, which was partially closed, gummed-up and red.

'Where were my damn reinforcements?' asked von Kessel bluntly. He hated the sickly stink of the tent.

The count began to speak, but succumbed to a hacking, wet cough. Going bright red in the face, the veins of his nose and cheeks swelling alarmingly, the count hacked and spluttered, and spat into a bowl offered by a manservant. Another servant dabbed at his slack mouth, wiping the phlegm from his lips.

A figure that had been standing in the shadows behind the count's chair stepped forwards. He was a fierce-looking, rake-thin man in his early twenties. He wore simple, but obviously expensive, black clothes, and had a small beard on his chin that was neatly trimmed to a point. Stefan recognised him as Johann, the count's great-nephew and sole living relative. Gruber had married twice, although neither wife had borne him children, and as such, Johann was the count's sole heir.

'Your orders were to hold the pass. You disobeyed the elector's direct order, *captain*,' said Johann, just about spitting the last word.

Not taking his eyes off the count, von Kessel bit back a sharp reply, before he answered. 'I was speaking to the grand count,' he said, icily.

'You disrespectful wretch,' snarled the black-clad young man, stepping forwards, his hand gripping the ornate hilt of his rapier.

'Stop, stop,' rasped the Elector Count of Ostermark, waving a pudgy, ring-laden hand in front of him. 'Enough of this, Johann. Back with you.' The glowering young man removed his hand from his rapier, and stepped back, eyes flashing dangerously.

'The reinforcements, yes. What happened to the reinforcements? Andros?'

A copper-skinned Tilean advisor inclined his head towards von Kessel.

'The despatches were sent, my lord, as you requested. Doubtless the enemy intercepted them. An unfortunate and regrettable mishap,' he said smoothly in perfect Reikspiel, with barely the hint of an accent. He blinked as von Kessel snorted in derision.

'Yes, very unfortunate, yes,' said the count. He turned his watery eyes towards von Kessel, 'And so you disobeyed my order. Explain yourself.' All eyes in the tent turned towards von Kessel.

'I took the best course of action under the circumstances,' said the bristling captain.

'Your orders were to hold Deep Pass,' rasped Gruber, 'and to ensure that none of the enemy advanced towards the undermanned city of Ferlangen, or towards the foothills of the Middle Mountains.'

'And no enemy has done so. I routed them at their camp, and slew their war leader personally.'

'Yet you did not hold your post, as ordered.'

'My men would have been slaughtered. We were outnumbered five to one. I had not enough troops with me to hold the pass. We would have been surrounded and butchered. Once I realised that the reinforcements were not coming, I had to improvise, or be lost. I took the fight to the enemy, hitting them before dawn.'

The ageing elector count seemed suddenly distracted. He inclined his head to one side to watch a trio of flies buzzing lazily around the tent above his head. Bubbling spittle welled in the slack corner of his mouth, and his lazy left eye rolled inwards. The young man with the cloth stepped forwards, dipping his head respectfully, and dabbed at the count's mouth. Stefan's revulsion and pity were displayed clearly on his face.

'I did not raise you to improvise,' Gruber said suddenly. 'I raised you to be a loyal subject of Ostermark, despite your treacherous heritage.'

'Ferlangen and Deep Pass are secure,' snarled von Kessel. 'My loyalty is beyond question.'

'So you say, and so you return in triumph, having slain the war leader yourself. The hero once more, eh Stefan? Do you see yourself as the brave, triumphant hero?'

'I am no hero, my lord, and I have not returned in triumph. I have returned to find out why those despatches for reinforcements were never sent!'

'The despatches *were* sent, were they not, Andros?'

The advisor nodded his head. 'That is true, my lord. The despatches were sent.'

'There,' stated Gruber. 'You are mistaken. The order *was* sent. Be careful what you say, von Kessel,' said the elector count dangerously. 'Your future could be bright, and I have protected you as much as I can thus far. You have displayed your skills at war, time and time again, but at times like these, you remind me of your grandfather. Watch yourself. Do not insult me or my grandnephew, or cast doubt upon my word. My word is law, and yours is just the word of a decorated and competent captain, the grandson of a treacherous, daemon-worshipping cur.'

Not a breath stirred in the tent as Gruber's court waited to see the young captain's reaction. His face was grim, and he stared at Gruber.

Apparently unaware of the stare he was receiving, Gruber pulled something from a pocket within his jacket, and began to stroke it. Stefan saw that it was a toad, long-dead and stiff. Gruber stroked its lumpy back tenderly, and began to giggle to himself, a high-pitched, girlish sound. 'Isn't that right, Boris? His grandfather was a daemon-worshipping, treacherous cur.' Several of the courtiers shifted their weight, exchanging glances. One of them stepped forwards and bent to whisper in the elector's ear.

'What? I'm fine, get away with you,' said Gruber, waving a pudgy hand at the attendant. He looked back at Stefan. 'Do you know where my physician is?'

The captain looked at the count's advisors, but they were refusing to meet his gaze. 'No, my lord, I do not know where Heinrich is. He has been missing for some weeks, has he not?' asked von Kessel, warily.

'Ah yes, he has, hasn't he. Never mind. The old fool is probably lost somewhere.' The sick man coughed. 'I could have had you strangled at birth, you know, for your grandfather's crimes. They wanted it so. People were afraid that you would turn into a traitor too, that you would have infernal dealings. You do not, do you?'

'No, my lord. I pray to our Lord Sigmar every dawn for his protection.'

'Good, good, that is good, but prayer is not always enough. Always remember that it was I who saved you, Stefan.' Gruber paused to cough before continuing. 'If only I had been able to save your dear grandfather. He was a good man, a dear friend, and a proud and noble elector count. The people of Ostermark loved him, and I loved him too,' said Gruber wistfully, smiling weakly. Then his smile faded.

'It only goes to show that the taint of Chaos is seductive, dangerous. The taint must have been in him from birth, but it was hidden well. Always be wary of it, Stefan, for it may also be in you.'

'I will, my lord,' said Stefan, uneasily. He said nothing for a moment, the silence feeling awkward and tense to him. 'By your grace, I shall take my leave.'

Stefan, his scarred face dark, turned on his heel and left the tent. He cursed himself inwardly – he had not left with any of his suspicions confirmed. Johann's acid gaze followed him as he walked out.

CHAPTER THREE

'THE LADDER, MATHIAS! Pull up the ladder!' Hensel shouted, loading the heavy crossbow with shaking hands. The enemy was streaming from the trees, their war cries filling the night. Fur-clad warriors raced down the hill through the coiling fog that swirled around their legs. The giant red-armoured warrior of Hensel's nightmares led the charge, roaring as he ran, his massive axe held in two hands over his head.

Raising the crossbow, Hensel aimed it hurriedly at the blood-red figure. The bolt hissed towards the warrior, flying towards his chest. Impossibly, the warrior swatted it aside with a sweep of his axe. Hensel's eyes widened and he swore, scrabbling for another bolt. 'The ladder, damn it!'

Mathias tore his terrified gaze away from the approaching marauders, and scrambled towards the ladder. An axe, spinning end-over-end through the air, slammed into his back. The force of the blow knocked the young man out of the back of the watch post, and he fell to the muddy ground below, dead.

Hensel swore again, and dropped his weapon, scrambling back to pull up the ladder himself. As he gripped it, a gauntleted fist smashed into his face, and he was knocked backwards, blood spurting from his nose. A sneering warrior appeared at the top of the ladder, his teeth bared in a vicious snarl.

Drawing his short sword, Hensel lunged forwards, plunging the steel blade deep into the marauder's throat. Blood bubbled up the blade of the sword, but the warrior did not fall. His eyes gleaming hatefully, the marauder reached out and gripped Hensel around the throat. The strength of the man was astounding, and Hensel struggled frantically against the crushing power. Straining, he twisted his sword, and a great gush of blood spurted from the fatal wound. Still the warrior did not release his death-like grip, and Hensel's vision began to blur. His life slipping rapidly from his body, the fatally wounded Chaos tribesman fell backwards off the ladder, pulling Hensel after him. They fell fifteen feet, striking the ground with bone-shattering force.

All the breath was knocked from Hensel's body, and he struggled to dislodge the grip around his throat. The warrior beneath him was dead, the fall driving the sword deeper into his neck, almost severing his head from his shoulders, but the warrior's death-grip was still strangling him. Managing to pry the fingers loose one by one, Hensel gasped for breath, sucking in deep lungfuls of air. Pulling his sword from the dead warrior's neck, he rose unsteadily to his feet.

A massive axe smashed into his chest, shattering ribs and embedding itself deep in his body. Blood rose up into his throat, and he dropped to his knees, staring into the eyes of his killer. The massive red-clad warrior stood before him, the pitiless orbs of his eyes rippling with inner fire. He bared his pointed teeth, and his face twisted with savage joy as blood gushed over him. He wrenched the axe clear of Hensel's chest, and the Empire soldier crumpled to the ground.

The warrior raised his axe to the heavens, and roared in his ungodly tongue. The words were incomprehensible to the dying Hensel, lying broken in the mud. Lightning lit up the night in a series of bright flashes. As darkness consumed Hensel, it seemed to him that the flashes were the Dark Gods expressing their pleasure at their minions' work.

'BLOOD FOR THE Blood God!' Hroth roared to the heavens, raising his bloodied axe high in the air for the gods to witness his tribute.

His heart was pumping with excitement, and he relished the surge of energy and power that suffused him now that battle was joined. Hroth knew that the great god Khorne, Lord of Battles and Collector of Skulls, was gazing down upon him, and he could feel that the god was pleased. The veins in Hroth's bulging arms strained with power as the rage grew within him.

Turning his fiery gaze upon the doomed Empire town, Hroth saw people running from their homes, their faces full of terror and their wails reaching up to the sky. The gods would enjoy that sound. With a roar, he broke into a run, heading straight down into the town. Dozens of his warriors ran a step behind him.

They were all of the Khazag tribe, hailing from the far
north-east, months' upon months' ride away, and all
had sworn oaths of blood to him as their chieftain.
The massive, bald figure of Barok loped along, to his
left, holding Hroth's banner high, and to his right ran
Olaf the Berserker, a pair of swords grasped in his
meaty fists.

Surging down the hill through the clinging mud,
Hroth saw that enemy warriors were moving through
the chaos, roughly pushing the frantic commoners out
of their way. As they saw Hroth and his warriors storming down the hill towards them, they halted. The front
rankers dropped to their knees, raising handguns to
their shoulders. Those behind wielded halberds, lowering them as one to create a rippling wall of spiked
steel. Other soldiers joined them so that they blocked
off the entire street.

Hroth growled in pleasure at seeing enemies that
would stand and fight, and picked up his pace. His
warriors ran at his side, screaming and shouting. Shots
rang out, and Hroth felt a burning lead ball scrape his
left cheek, drawing blood. Several Khazags fell under
the first volley, but he did not care.

Racing closer, he saw the puny enemy warriors frantically trying to reload their cowardly weapons. Several
of them raised their guns once more and fired point-
blank into the Chaos warriors, and then Hroth was on
them.

With a sweep of his axe, he smashed aside three halberds aimed at him, the blow knocking the weapons
from numbed hands. Reversing his strike, he cleaved
his axe into the neck of one soldier, decapitating him
cleanly. The axe blade carried on into the head of

another, crumpling the steel helmet he wore in a spray of blood and bone.

Backhanding his fist into the face of another, feeling the skull crush beneath the blow, Hroth began to laugh. He waded into the midst of the enemy's formation, swinging his axe before him. With each blow another enemy died. In these close quarters, the enemy's halberds were useless, and they reached for short swords and daggers. Each blade that flashed towards Hroth was met with brutal force – arms were hacked from bodies, chests caved in and heads smashed to bloody ruins. Those weapons that did reach him shattered against his flesh, or were turned aside by his armour. Olaf the Berserker had dropped or lost his weapons, and ripped a man's throat out with his bare hands. The other Khazags laid about them with abandon, their brutal axes and swords carving through the Empire men with ease. Blood splattered all over Hroth, and he felt the hot metallic taste on his lips. He rejoiced at the slaughter, hacking left and right.

With a roar, he raised his axe above his head in both hands and brought it smashing down onto the shoulder of an enemy soldier, the blow carving its way through breastplate and bone, cutting him almost in two. Kicking the body away, Hroth swung around in search of a new enemy, but could find none. He stood, drenched in gore, breathing heavily. The ground was littered with severed limbs and broken Empire soldiers, and the air was heavy with the stink of death. Several dozen soldiers had been slaughtered for the loss of three of his own. He resisted the urge to swing his axe into a Khazag standing nearby.

Hroth stepped over the slain towards the fallen bodies of his tribesmen. One of them was still alive. Hroth knelt before him, seeing the growing red stain at his belly.

'Your blood will feed great Khorne this night, warrior of the Khazags,' said Hroth. The warrior, his face pale and drawn, nodded fearlessly, refusing to utter any sound of pain, for to do so would show weakness in front of his chieftain and the gods. Hroth stood and swung his axe down, hacking the warrior's head from his shoulders. Picking the head up by the hair, he tossed it to a large, bearded warrior wearing a helmet made from a wolf skull.

'Your brother was a brave warrior, Thorgar,' growled Hroth. 'His skull will bring you power.' The bearded warrior raised the bloody severed head of his brother in both hands, touching it to his forehead.

More handgun shots rang out through the night, and Olaf turned towards the sounds snarling, foam dripping from his lips. Without a word, Hroth and his warband broke into a loping run, heading deeper into the town, towards the sound.

CHAPTER FOUR

'So, DID YOU let the fat old man have it? The reinforcements were never sent, were they?' asked Albrecht. The grizzled sergeant was standing just under an awning, sheltering from the drizzling rain. He was smoking a pipe, blue-grey smoke wafting out into the cold evening air.

Stefan, stomping towards the tent in the rain, frowned at his sergeant. 'You'll get yourself hanged speaking of the count like that.'

'Pah, none of the boys round hear would speak out against me. Would you lads?' snarled Albrecht, turning towards the group of Ostermark soldiers playing dice behind him. They muttered under their breaths. 'Course they wouldn't. They know I'd make their lives much more painful if they did. Besides, it was their arses out there on the line with no reinforcements coming as well as yours and mine.'

'Aye, it was. I don't know if the reinforcements were sent or not. The old count's mind is going. Maybe they were sent, but he recalled them. Who knows? But there isn't a damn thing anybody can do about it.'

'His mind's been going for years. He's too old by far. I reckon it's the wasting sickness what's done it – been fighting that since childhood. Weak bloodline. That's what you get when you have nobles marrying nobles for generations. That family's a bit too closely related, if you know what I mean.'

'We lost too many good men out there, needlessly, but what can be done? Call him a liar? Call him an inbred old fool whose mind is going? I'd be strung up before the words left my lips! You know as well as I that his damn courtiers would love to see me swing.'

'Well, it seemed like a bloody suicide mission to me.'

'Why would the old man want me dead after all these years? He could have got rid of me whenever he wanted. I owe him my life, Albrecht.'

'Maybe. He certainly doesn't pass up an opportunity to remind you of it.'

'Well, if the order was recalled, or never sent, it could have been someone else. That Tilean whoreson Andros for one. As trustworthy as a snake, that one.'

'Or Johann. Was that skinny runt there?'

'Aye he was, spoiling for a fight. More than usual,' Stefan said.

'He may be a decent duellist, but that wouldn't count for nought on a real battlefield,' stated Albrecht. 'It wouldn't have helped him in the mountain pass, neither, if he had been there. He would have been one of the dead being picked over by the crows as we speak, Morr save them. Would have done Ostermark a blessing, too.'

'Aye, you are probably right, but he is the count's flesh and blood, and we are but soldiers,' said Stefan, shrugging. 'I am dead tired. I'm heading to bed.'

'Rest well, captain,' said Albrecht, patting the younger man on the shoulder. He watched his captain stalk off, and blew a smoke ring into the air.

'That right, sergeant? You really think we were sent out there to die?' asked a young soldier, looking up from his game.

'Don't rightly know, lad. It's politics. Still, the captain's a canny devil. He'd be a hard man to catch off guard, and not a man I'd like as an enemy,' replied Albrecht, thoughtfully, 'although, it's definitely possible, the count being without child and all. The captain's a rival to any who would claim the throne when Morr takes the count.'

'A rival? How's that, sergeant?'

'His grandfather was the elector. Therefore, if there was no clear heir, he could make a claim. Not that he ever would.'

'Truly? I thought that was just a story! So those scars on his face – they were put there to mark his grandfather's shame?'

'Aye, burnt into him as a babe. Heartless fiend, a man who could hold a white-hot iron to the face of a newborn.'

'Don't that mean that the captain's cursed, sergeant?' asked the young soldier. 'That he's got the taint?' The soldiers he was playing with froze, halting their game. Albrecht turned to stare at him, his eyes narrowing.

'The captain's a better man than any here. There ain't no taint in him, and I'll personally cut the throat of any man who suggests there is,' snarled the sergeant. 'You're new with our regiment, ain't you?' The young soldier nodded, eyes wide.

'The captain has saved the life of every man here with his actions. Most more than once. Not a one of them has any doubt of him. You'd best learn to respect your betters quick smart, soldier, or else you will find life very difficult here. Very difficult indeed.'

Albrecht puffed angrily on his pipe, staring out at the night. 'Sorry sir. I didn't mean nothing by it,' said the young soldier, avoiding the glares he was getting from around the dice table. Albrecht grunted.

What he had said was true. Stefan, through his actions and strategic decisions on the field of battle had saved his men from certain death time and time again. Certainly, last night in Deep Pass they would all have been massacred if not for the bold strike that the captain had ordered.

Albrecht remembered back to the first time he had met the captain. He had been dubious of the man at first. Stefan von Kessel had been young then, and no captain. No, he had been a frightened young man in Albrecht's regiment, and his horribly scarred face made him stick out amongst the other fresh-faced recruits. He was quiet and reserved, and far too sensitive for the life of a soldier. Albrecht had ruthlessly hounded him, trying to find if there was hardness at his core. Either he would quit, or he would find the strength within him to become a successful soldier.

The scars on von Kessel's face were a terrible weight on him then, and Albrecht knew that they were still; although those feelings were hidden deep within the impenetrable barriers that the captain had built over

the years. Three lines crossed von Kessel's face, linked
by a curving line that arced from above his left eyebrow across his forehead, passing by his right eye and
over his right cheekbone, and finishing on his jaw line.
These lines were each half an inch thick, and pale on
his suntanned face. It was a quarter of a wheel that,
had it continued, would have had eight lines bisecting
it. It was an evil mark, a mark of bad omen.

For this reason, the young von Kessel had been ostra-
cized by his peers, and shunned as a bringer of
misfortune. None of them, bar Albrecht himself, knew
of his cursed heritage. Albrecht hounded von Kessel
relentlessly, and finally the day came when the young
man had stood up to the sergeant, punching him
squarely in the jaw. Albrecht had of course struck back,
knocking the young man unconscious. Nevertheless,
from that day forth, nobody gave the young man any
more grief, and he slowly came out of himself, becoming a comrade in arms with the other soldiers.
Although he would always have difficulty expressing
himself, and would have no close friends, von Kessel
became someone that the other soldiers trusted
implicitly, and someone who they came to respect
greatly.

Gradually he had progressed through the ranks until
he had, somewhat reluctantly, become captain.
Albrecht was not upset to see von Kessel overtake him,
for he recognised the brilliance within the younger
man, if only he would accept it. No, he was proud to
serve the captain, and he loved him like a brother.

Stefan had said that he owed Gruber for protecting
him as a babe. Some protection, thought Albrecht. The
fat bastard had been present when the white-hot

branding wheel had been pressed to the babe's face. Stefan had been so young and small that only a quarter of the white-hot brand had marked his face. To be raised with such a mark of shame upon his face was no way to grow up. True, Gruber could have had the babe drowned if he had wished it, all because of Stefan's grandfather's treachery, but no one who burned the face of an innocent babe should be seen as a saviour in Albrecht's book.

He snorted, and took another long pull on his pipe.

'THERE AIN'T NO taint in him', Stefan had heard the sergeant say as he had walked away. He prayed that the sergeant was right.

HROTH SLAMMED HIS axe into the back of another of the fleeing villagers, and the man fell with a tortured scream. The piteous noise was cut short as he slammed his foot down onto the pathetic Empire man's neck. The night was alight with flames – the Khazags had begun to burn the village to the ground. Those who had cowered in their homes had soon come out when the flames began to lick at the buildings. They were cut down as they ran screaming from the burning houses. To Hroth's disgust, many had chosen to burn to death in the flames rather than face his men. There was no glory in that. Facing an enemy head-on in the heat of battle, staring death fearlessly in the face, *that* was the honourable way to die. The Khazags believed that there would be no rebirth for cowards who let their fears dictate their dishonourable deaths.

The streets of the village were chaotic. Terrified men, women and children ran from the Khazags, their shouts and cries filling the air all around. The flames were reaching the upper storeys of the tallest buildings, and several began to collapse in on themselves as their supporting beams burned. The Khazags had run into two isolated groups of soldiers, and had butchered them mercilessly. Hroth himself had slain a dozen of them, but his axe thirsted for more.

A growl came from a side street, and Hroth turned. A massive furry shape leapt at him, a fang-filled maw flashing towards his throat. He swung his axe into the side of the creature mid-air, and it was smashed into the side of a building, yelping piteously. Thick dark fur covered the beast, and a ridge of spikes protruded from its spine. Hroth's blow had crushed the ribs of the creature, and shards of bone protruded from the wound, blood welling around it. Its tongue lolled out of its mouth, and its eyes were dead.

The massive bald figure of Borak knelt beside the creature. Pushing aside the thick fur on its head, he saw a distinctive, coiling marking.

'This is one of Zar Slaaeth's warhounds. He must be near.'

'Good,' replied Hroth. 'That way,' he said pointing, and began to lope down the darkened side street. He passed a corpse that had been ripped apart, its guts pulled from its body. The warhound's prey, he realised.

Hroth grinned as he thought of Zar Slaaeth. He had long yearned for the day when he would cut his head from his shoulders.

CHAPTER FIVE

STEFAN AWOKE INSTANTLY and had a blade at the throat of the figure that knelt above him. He let out a breath as he recognised the man, and moved the blade away from Albrecht's throat.

'Thanks,' said the sergeant. 'I damn near shat myself.'

'What is it?' asked Stefan, pushing himself from his cot and sheathing his dagger.

'Sorry to wake you, captain. You're needed at Gruber's tent.'

'What? Has something happened to the count?'

'No, nothing like that, but they need you up there all the same. Some general has arrived, or something.'

'A general?'

'Yeah. Dunno who he is, but he's arrived with a great number of knights, apparently. Must be someone important. Rode in from Nuln. Rode straight up to the count's tent and demanded a council of war.'

Stefan frowned. 'Demanded? Not many people can demand a council in the middle of the night with an elector count. What time is it, anyway?'

'Just before dawn.'

Stefan rubbed a hand over his face, wiping the last remnants of sleep away. Albrecht could smell alcohol on the captain. He noted the empty bottle of spirits next to the captain's bed. 'I'll wait outside for you,' he said, and left the tent.

The captain emerged a few minutes later, wearing his battered breastplate, greaves and gauntlets, and a slashed jerkin bearing the purple and yellow of Oster-mark. He held his sallet helmet under his arm. A pair of pistols hung at his side, along with his sword. As ever, a pendant of the twin-tailed comet, the symbol of the warrior-god Sigmar, hung around his neck. 'Let's go,' he said.

The two men were silent as they moved through the camp, climbing the hill towards Gruber's tent. Torches shone around the command tent, and they could see two fully barded warhorses. A knight sat in the saddle of one of the horses, a tall banner held aloft in his hands, while a pair of stable boys held the other. The horses were massive creatures, standing some eighteen hands tall. Stefan could not see the design on the ban-ner, for it was hanging loosely and no wind was blowing, nor could he make out the filigree designs on the horses' barding, but if they were truly from Nuln, the seat of the Emperor Magnus, then he believed that he knew who these knights were, and he was awed.

As the pair drew closer, a slight wind touched the banner, and it fluttered in the breeze. In that moment, Stefan saw the design on the heavy banner. It depicted a skull with a wreath wrapped around its crown, surrounded with scrollwork and intricate designs picked out in gold. These were the newly formed, yet already renowned, Reiklandguard[1]. They had ridden at the Emperor Magnus's side during the Great War. These knights had turned the great battle in Kislev and routed the forces of Chaos. Stefan and Albrecht traded a glance, eyebrows raised. Stefan was waved into the tent. Stamping his feet against the cold, Albrecht stayed outside, keeping a wary eye on the massive horses of the Reiklandguard.

The inside of the tent was lit with lanterns and large candles. Gruber and some of his courtiers were there. The count himself had obviously dressed hastily, for his shirt was half unbuttoned, exposing flabby white skin. He was not wearing his wig, and his white hair was thin and patchy. His eyes looked heavy and red, and his deep frown expressed his displeasure at being woken at such an hour.

A large man in full plate armour dominated the room. He turned as Stefan entered, and the captain saw that the knight was of middling age, his long, tied back hair and sweeping moustache touched with silver. His face was angular and stern, and his fierce eyes commanded respect.

'Is this the one?' The knight spoke in a voice that, although not loud, carried absolute authority.

'It is. Reiksmarshal Wolfgange Trenkenhoff, I present to you Captain Stefan von Kessel,' said Gruber. Stefan's

---

1. The name 'Reiklandguard' was later contracted into 'Reiksguard', when the knights were officially formed into an order. They became, in later years, the traditional bodyguard of the Emperor.

eyebrows raised ever so slightly, the only indication of his surprise. The man standing before him was a living hero of the Empire, a man counted as a close friend and supporter of the Emperor himself. He was the man who had personally formed the Reiklandguard knights, and was the one who had commanded the armies that had defeated the forces of Chaos the year before. His word was second only to the Emperor's in matters of war. Stefan's eyes locked on the reiksmarshal's, and he held them there for a moment before bowing his head to the older man.

'It is an honour,' said Stefan, truthfully.

'The Elector Count of Ostermark tells me that you did not hold your post when ordered to,' said the knight sombrely. Stefan felt as if he had been kicked in the stomach, and his anger began to rise; yet he refused to let his emotions show on his face. Without even looking at him, he could feel the pleasure of the count's great-nephew, Johann.

'Is this true?' asked the knight grimly. Stefan licked his lips before he answered, phrasing he words carefully.

'I would not wish to contradict my count, lord knight. I am a loyal soldier of Ostermark and the Empire.'

'Captain von Kessel and the regiments under his command were sent to Deep Pass, were they not?' asked the knight.

'That is correct, Lord Reiksmarshal.' It was the golden-skinned Tilean advisor Andros who smoothly answered. 'The captain was sent to prevent Chaos forces that had manoeuvred around our position from moving into the mountains.'

'What troops does he command?'

The Tilean advisor looked to his count, who indicated impatiently that he should continue.

'Captain von Kessel has under his charge some… two and a half thousand halberd infantry.'

'Two thousand and thirty-seven, after yesterday,' interjected Stefan, 'and thirty-four more may die during the night from their injuries.'

'As well as *roughly* a thousand arquebusiers, eight hundred crossbowmen, and eight cannon from Nuln,' continued Andros. 'Added to this, there are a number of auxiliary irregulars, including scouts, outriders and militia. They're common riff-raff for the most part.' Stefan was irritated by this remark, but kept quiet.

'That should do. Why was von Kessel chosen for this duty?'

'Because he was available, and because the duty was an important one. Captain von Kessel has one of the best military records in all the armies of Ostermark,' the advisor coolly answered.

'So, von Kessel is one of your most commended captains, yes?'

'He is that, yes, amongst other things,' snapped Gruber, growing tired of the conversation.

'So, he disobeyed an order that would have seen his forces slaughtered, and yet returned victorious.'

Gruber's eyes widened in shock, and he began to splutter and cough, the sores on his neck reddening dramatically. Recovering from his coughing fit, he snarled, 'Is this conversation going somewhere? Otherwise I will retire to my bed.'

'My apologies, Grand Count Gruber. I shall endeavour not to keep you long from your rest. As you know, the north is in ruins, count. You also know that the mage-prince of the elf kind, Teclis, is in Altdorf with our good Emperor as we speak.'

'Yes, yes, I do know that,' said Gruber, 'setting up some colleges or some such thing.'

'The Grand Colleges of Magic, yes. Well, as you may not know, the fleets of Teclis's kin have patrolled the Sea of Claws during these last four years of warfare. They have done us a great service by harrying the Norse longships that plague our northern shores, and by lending their aid where they can. They have also, I am informed, been attacking up and down the coast of Norsca. This has had the effect that many of the Norse have been occupied with their own defence, and many longships did not even set to sea this past year to raid. Without the elves, I fear that all of Nordland and Ostland may have been lost. Indeed, elf land forces even now guard our northern coastline. Our alliance with the high elves is vital.

'Heightened aggression from the Norse has forced the elf patrols further out to sea, leaving an important elf noble stranded on our northern coast.

'Now to the real reason I am here tonight. I am here to requisition an army from you, Count Gruber, and I want Captain von Kessel to lead it.'

CHAPTER SIX

HROTH THE BLOODED and his Khazags moved warily towards the town square. The open area was lit with flickering orange light, the buildings lining it were ablaze. A grand fountain sat in the middle of the square, pale stone sculptures sitting in the circular dais in the middle of the water. Hroth wasn't sure if it was a trick of the firelight, but the water seemed to be blood-red. The statue in the centre of the fountain depicted the hated, weakling Empire god Sigmar, standing with his hammer raised. Eleven statues of warlords stood around him. As Hroth watched, a helmeted warrior perched atop the shoulders of Sigmar swung a heavy, double-handed hammer and knocked the head from the statue. A great cheer rang out.

His arms and hands caked in blood and gore, Olaf snarled as he saw the banners that were held aloft by the warriors on the other side of the square. Made from silky black cloth, they bore the markings of the champion of this warband.

'Zar Slaaeth,' hissed Hroth, and began to stalk across the open courtyard. His Khazags fanned out behind him, almost four hundred all told. The cobbles were strewn with corpses, both of commoners and soldiers. Evidently, many of the townsfolk had fled here, and the few remaining soldiers had chosen this place to make their last stand. Hroth felt his anger begin to grow. These should have been slain by him and his Khazags, offerings to great Khorne. They should not have been slain by Zar Slaaeth.

Hroth had hated him ever since they had first met three years before. At the gates of Praag, Hroth and Slaaeth had fought side by side, but that was only because of the power and authority of the High Zar Warlord, Asavar Kul. Hroth had never met the high zar, but just the fear that his name created was enough to hold the champions that fought under his banner from their own disputes. Hroth and Slaaeth had fought ferociously at Praag, slaughtering the Kislev defenders that stood against them. Slaaeth, with his fine voice and charismatic persona, had been the one made zar at the battle's end. There had been no such honour for Hroth, and the fact that Slaaeth was also a Khazag rankled. On that day, Hroth had vowed to great Khorne that the skull of Slaaeth would be his.

The rival warbands eyed each other warily. To an outsider, the two warbands would have looked almost identical. Both tribes being Khazags, they bore similar arms and armour. Only in the choice of ritual tattoos and piercings were the differences apparent. While the

warriors of Hroth the Blooded favoured crisscrossing
scars cut into the flesh of their arms and cheeks, and
many were adorned with blood-red tattoos that displayed their dedication to the Blood God, Khorne, the
warriors of Zar Slaaeth tended towards spikes piercing
their brows, ears and noses, and they had spidery, coiling tattoos on their flesh. In terms of numbers, the
warbands were equally balanced.

A tall figure in black armour rose from where he sat,
trailing his fingers through the golden hair of a
motionless woman. The naked corpses of at least a
dozen men and women were strewn around him. No
doubt, they had sated Slaaeth's desires, but briefly.

Slender for a Khazag, Zar Slaaeth stood half a head
shorter than Hroth, although his slightness made him
look much smaller than the massive Khornate champion. His face was handsome, and his hair was
perfectly white and straight, trailing down his black
armoured back. He bore a small coiling, purple tattoo
on his left cheek – a mark of the god of decadence,
Slaanesh. His eyes were completely black, the pupils
having long since dilated completely.

'Your power is past, Slaaeth,' snarled Hroth as the
enemy champion walked towards him. The two warbands had formed semi-circles around their
champions. They knew what was to come. Both warbands had seen their champions face countless
rivals.

The champion of Slaanesh threw Hroth a disarming
smile, and flicked his pale hair. 'So, you think that your
time has come, Hroth the Blooded.' He opened his
mouth, and ran his long, pointed purple-pink tongue
over his teeth. 'I will feast upon your innards once this

is over. I shall keep you alive for the sensation – you may enjoy it. I know that I shall, dear Hroth.'

'I'm going to hack you to pieces. Khorne likes the blood of Slaanesh's champions,' growled Hroth.

Slaaeth chuckled in response, flexing his hands before drawing a long, single-bladed, curving sword with his left hand and a black, barbed whip in his right. The coiling whip seemed to thrash around with a life of its own, as if it longed to inflict pain. Hroth crouched low, gripping his axe in his hands, and began to stalk towards his foe.

Hroth saw that the zar's shaman stood amongst his warriors, his mouth moving soundlessly. He was a massive bare-chested man, who wore a heavy fur over his shoulders. Every exposed inch of his flesh was covered with intricate black markings. They coiled and writhed across his skin, forming into new and varied forms with every passing second. In his hands, he held a tall staff that looked as if it had been made out of a number of ancient tree roots twisted together. At its top, the roots twisted into the shape of an eight-pointed star, blackened by fire. Hroth realised that the shaman did not really hold the staff. The staff seemed to be holding onto him. Its twisted branches had encircled the hand and forearm of the man, embedding deep into his flesh. Slaaeth saw Hroth's eyes narrow, and turned to see what the Khorne champion was looking at.

'I see you like the staff, eh? Is that why you are here? Come to fetch it, like a hound for your master?' Slaaeth smiled again. 'Yes, I see that that is it. You have been sent like a dog to come and get it for your dear master, Sudobaal.

'I know what it is that your master seeks, but I think that I shall keep this staff for myself.'

'I call no one master,' said Hroth dangerously.

'Of course not, dog,' taunted the zar.

Behind the rival champions, the warbands began to strike their weapons against their shields in perfect unison, grunting each time they struck. The square echoed with the sound, and it got louder and louder as the two rival champions began to circle each other. This was a ritual that had been performed by Khazag champions for countless generations, and each man knew that the gods themselves were looking down, eager for the spectacle to come. Both warriors were chosen of their gods, each having been granted powerful gifts that set them apart from the other tribesmen. Both had slain a dozen other chosen champions in duels such as this.

Slaaeth's whip cracked out, seeking Hroth's eyes. He turned his face, so that the barbed whip merely scored his cheek. He tasted his own blood on his lips, tasted the power within him. With a roar, the Khornate champion leapt forwards, swinging his axe in a murderous arc.

The slender Slaanesh champion danced to the side, moving gracefully despite the black armour he wore. As Hroth's axe hissed harmlessly past him, he lashed out with his curved blade. It bit deep into Hroth's red and bronze shoulder guard, sliding effortlessly through the powerful armour. The Khorne champion snarled in pain. As he stepped away, Slaaeth flicked his whip out, and its barbs nicked at the flesh of Hroth's neck.

Hroth circled back around, eyes fixed on his opponent's every move. Feinting a blow towards Slaaeth's head, Hroth swung his axe low in a strike towards the groin. The zar swayed back out of the way, and swung his curved sword towards the head of his foe. Hroth ducked out of the way of the attack and made to step in to hammer another blow at his foe, but Slaaeth had twisted away, and lashed out once more with his whip. The thong of the whip wrapped around one of the horns of Hroth's helmet, and ripped it away from his head with a yank.

Hroth snarled, his eyes blazing with fire, and he leapt again at the agile zar, axe hissing through the air. Slaaeth stepped neatly to the side, but he could not avoid the return blow. Hroth slammed the shaft of his axe into his opponent's face. The zar staggered back a step, and only his preternatural speed saved him from the murderous attack that sliced through the air towards his neck.

The pair circled each other once more. Blood dripped from the wound on Hroth's shoulder, and the minor cuts on his throat and cheek. Slaaeth's face was bruised and bloody.

The champions stepped into each other, axe and sword flashing. Slaaeth moved effortlessly, always keeping just outside of the reach of the heavier Khornate warrior. He danced in from time to time to strike a blow, but most of his attacks were being turned aside by Hroth, who seemed to be getting stronger and faster as his anger grew. A minute passed. Blood was streaming from a cut to Hroth's side.

Slaaeth slashed a blow towards the wounded side, and Hroth stepped in and grabbed the smaller man's wrist in a bone-crushing grasp, halting the blow mid-swing. Dropping his whip, the zar's free hand flashed down and came up a fraction of a second later

with a barbed dagger that he plunged into Hroth's forearm. Slaaeth's long tongue flashed out, punching
through the flesh of the Khornate warrior's cheek
before flicking back. Hissing, Hroth pulled the zar
towards him and slammed his forehead into the face of
the Slaanesh champion, crushing his nose. Still holding onto the zar's wrist, he brought his knee up into his
foe's groin. Again, he slammed his armoured knee into
his enemy, who slumped. Only then did he let go with
his left hand, swinging his axe high over his head.

The zar rolled backwards, snatching up his whip.
Once again the whip lashed out. Keeping his axe aloft
with just one hand, Hroth grabbed the reaching thong
of the whip in his fist, pulling the zar off-balance. Then
he slammed his axe into the zar's neck. His head, white
hair trailing behind it, flew through the air and rolled
across the ground.

Hroth ripped the dagger from his forearm and threw
it to the ground. Turning, he walked towards the zar's
shaman. The other members of Slaaeth's warband
backed away from the man, who began to speak
quickly, raising his hands defensively before him.
Without ceremony, Hroth slammed his axe down into
the head of the shaman, cleaving it from the crown to
the jaw. The man fell to the ground. The branch-like
tendrils that connected the staff to him drew back,
pulling free of the dead flesh and leaving gaping holes
in the shaman's hand and forearm. Hroth kicked the
twisted staff away from the corpse, and rose up to his
full height, staring venomously around at the warband
of Slaaeth.

'Any man who wishes to join me may do so. Any
who does not, speak now and face me.'

There was silence around the courtyard. Hroth stepped towards the closest of Slaaeth's warriors, a man with the eight-pointed star cut into his forehead. Hroth reached for the man's dagger and drew it from its scabbard. Raising his own hand, Hroth cut into his palm. His blood bubbled as if it was boiling from the cut. He held the wound to the man's face, cupping his mouth and nose. The man started as the boiling blood touched him. Hroth removed his hand.

'You are blood-bonded to me. You have become one of my battle brothers this day,' said Hroth.

The man held both palms upwards and bowed his head to his new chieftain. His looked upon Hroth in awe – the chosen of Khorne knew that the warrior could taste the god's power in his blood.

The other warriors began to gather around Hroth so that they too could become of his tribe.

CHAPTER SEVEN

THE LAST WEEK had been a blur of activity for Stefan von Kessel. He was weary and footsore, but each night he slept better than he had for years. A gruelling fourteen hours of marching each day, followed by setting up camp for the night, six hours of rest with watch duty every third night, and breaking camp before dawn the next day was a demanding task.

The captain's army had expanded, for the reiksmarshal had requisitioned more of the count's troops. These included more of Ostermark's state troops, mainly spearmen and a number of additional bow-armed scouts. They were lowborn, down to earth and simple men, but their hearts were brave, and their hunting skills were welcome, for they brought fresh game to camp each evening.

The reiksmarshal and two hundred of the Reiklandguard knights rode alongside the marching army of Ostermark. These were awe-inspiring figures to the common soldiers, and they were neither aloof nor arrogant enough not to mix with the Ostermark foot troops after a day's march. Stefan was pleased to discover that these were not wealthy, upper class knights who had bought their way into the order for political gain. No, these were hardened warriors, each one a veteran of dozens of battles. Every one of them had fought in the Great War Against Chaos, and all were on the field the day that Magnus rode with them when they had routed the enemy outside the grand city of Kislev. They were earthy men, chosen for their bravery and their skill in battle.

Von Kessel learnt that this newly formed order was unique, for its knights were drawn from the very best of all the other knightly orders to form this elite cadre. Heroes all, he felt honoured to be marching at their side.

His mind drifted back to Gruber's tent a week past. 'I want Captain von Kessel here to lead it.'

The tent had been silent as the words sank in. Johann's face twisted in anger. Gruber's jaw dropped open. It was the count who had spoken first.

'This is, this is... unacceptable,' he stuttered.

'I think you will find it is perfectly acceptable, Grand Count Gruber,' said Reiksmarshal Trenkenhoff coldly.

'But von Kessel is mine! He is unsuitable for the position, surely. No, his place is here.'

'He may be your man, but *you* are the *Emperor's* man, and here and now, *I* am the voice of the Emperor. You cannot defy me, count.'

'Reiksmarshal,' said Stefan. All eyes turned to him – most had forgotten he was even there. 'I am honoured by this, but I feel I am not… worthy of this honour.'

'There! Even the boy doesn't think it's a good idea!' proclaimed Gruber.

Trenkenhoff turned his steely gaze towards von Kessel. 'Why do you feel that you are unworthy of this duty the Empire demands of you?'

'Do you not know of my grandfather?'

'I do. What of it?'

'Well, I thought that the dishonour I bear would–' began Stefan, but the reiksmarshal cut him off.

'I don't give a damn who your grandfather was or what he did. This is not a duty you can decide not to accept. I carry the Emperor's word. I outrank you, count, and I certainly outrank you, *captain*. If your Emperor demands your service, then you will damn well serve. Or you will hang.'

'Ready your men, captain. We leave at midday tomorrow, marching hard. Make sure they are well provisioned.' And with that, the reiksmarshal had turned on his heel and stormed out of the tent.

Stefan smiled and shook his head as he recalled that strange night. The Reiksmarshal Wolfgange Trenkenhoff had spoken to him as the first light of dawn was seeping over the camp. 'I spoke the truth in that tent,' he had said. 'I do *not* care what shame you feel you carry. It is of no interest to me. The only thing I care about is you leading your soldiers well. What you displayed in Deep Pass was initiative and self-belief. You knew that the attack on the Chaos encampment was going to work, did you not?' Stefan had nodded. 'You acted quickly and calmly, evaluating the situation and responding boldly. That is a rare thing, von Kessel. A rare thing indeed.

'The Empire was formed by such bold moves, and its survival rests on them. Had Magnus not taken the bold step of attacking the Chaos forces in the north, but rather done as the electors wished, and waited within our castles and cities like frightened children for the hammer blow to fall, the Empire would, I believe, have been shattered utterly, by now. Had the power of Asavar Kul, curse his soul, not been broken on the plains of Kislev, then he may even now have been storming our capital city, Nuln, and slaughtering our people in their tens of thousands.

'Always remember that, von Kessel. Act thoughtfully, act intelligently, and act boldly, but always remember to act! For to do something, even if it turns out to be the wrong thing, is much less dangerous than to do nothing.' The reiksmarshal paused for a moment before he spoke again.

'And if I ever hear you publicly doubt yourself again, I will kill you myself.'

CHAPTER EIGHT

EIGHT CIRCLES WERE marked on the cave floor in red powder, surrounding the kneeling black robed figure. Each of the circles overlapped with its two neighbours, and an offering to the gods lay in the centre of each. One was a small pile of bones, while another held a blood-red stone riddled with purple-red veins that throbbed and pulsed with light. A skull sat in the centre of another of the circles, horns protruding from its brow and its chin elongated, splitting into another pair of bony horns. The thighbone of some massive beast lay in another, its length covered in intricate, swirling scrimshaw.

In the centre of the circle directly in front of the kneeling figure was a heavy brass icon depicting the eight-pointed star of Chaos, and in another was a small white stone, perfectly round. The air shimmered around the white pebble. The last offering was a beating heart, sitting on a golden plate. One circle lay empty.

Little light entered the cave, and the hood of the kneeling figure was pulled down low, obscuring its face. Its arms hung limply at its side, dead-white claw-like hands touching the cold stone floor. They twitched spasmodically, and the arms began to move. Reaching up, the figure drew its black robe from its chest, exposing a tautly muscled, lean torso covered in scars. The skin of the torso was a sickly pale colour, and blue veins could be seen under the translucent skin.

From the shadows, a grotesque shape moved towards the kneeling figure. Its movement awkward, it slithered across the floor, stopping just outside the red powdered circles. Its malformed, babyish face was perched atop a worm-like tail, and it pulled itself forwards with a pair of tentacle limbs. Its eyes were slitted like those of a snake, and they glittered yellow.

Raising itself with some difficulty, it lifted one tentacled limb over the red powder, and then another. Its face twisted in concentration, it carefully shifted its weight forwards, leaning on the side of its face, and lifted its tail over the circle. Carefully it repeated the manoeuvre, so that it sat before the kneeling figure. It raised itself as high as was possible on its tail, mouth opening soundlessly, exposing small, sharp teeth.

The robed figure reached out and picked up the disfigured creature, turning it around so that its tail touched its belly. The thing squirmed, gnashing its teeth, and its tail began to burrow into the figure's flesh. Its tentacles too began to burrow deep into the pale figure's belly, pulling the creature further and further inside the black robed man's body. Soon all that could be seen was the hideous face of the creature, and then it too was swallowed by flesh. Colour began to return to the kneeling figure's pale body, and the blue veins disappeared.

Closing the black robe, the figure rose to its feet. It swept a hand in front of its body, and a sharp wind entered the cave, scattering the red dust. The circles disappeared, and the figure marched from the cave to meet the victorious champion.

HROTH WAS PLEASED with the new addition to his standard. Slaaeth's head, hanging by its long white hair, stared blankly ahead. The chosen's mouth was hanging open limply, and his tongue lolled from his mouth, almost a foot long. As much as he had disliked the Slaanesh champion, there was no doubting that the gods had favoured him, at least for a time. His head was a worthy addition to the trophies of Hroth the Blooded.

Stomping through the dense undergrowth, swatting twisted, grabbing branches out of his way, he recalled the words of Slaaeth. *Sent like a dog*, he had said, to fetch the staff for his master.

He scoffed. No one was his master, he thought, kicking a rotten log from his path.

He hated the dark, dense forests of the Empire. He knew that they served his purpose, for even when its armies were at full force the weak Empire men could not patrol every square mile of the massive forests that filled their lands. Dark things lurked in the hidden depths where no men trod, and thousands of beastmen infested the deeper reaches of the forests. Still, Hroth loathed feeling so enclosed. The trees were giant twisted things that had grown into all manner of contorted shapes. Their branches far overhead wove into an impenetrable covering, letting no hint of light through. Thick, rotting mulch covered the ground, the thin layer of ice that lay atop it cracking as Hroth stepped through the dark wilderness.

The darkness itself did not bother him. No, he was used to that. In the homeland of the Khazags, months of travel to the far north-east, almost half the year existed in darkness, for the sun rose barely above the horizon. The land of the nomadic Khazags was open, and almost completely free of vegetation. Good horseman land. Craggy dark rock covered its slopes, ragged and sharp. Steaming pools of sulphur-rich water could be found amongst some of the rocky peaks, occasionally bursting forth as towering geysers when the gods were hungry. That was the landscape that he was comfortable in, with the skies open above him, never with a roof over his head.

He also hated skulking around in the shadows. Again, he knew it was necessary, for his warband, though growing, was not large enough for him to march straight through the Empire. Nevertheless, it rankled. Facing the enemy on the field of battle, that was what he longed for. To face the might of the enemy head on, and to triumph, that was the way of Khorne.

Hroth stalked into the clearing. The ground was blackened with fire, and a group of warriors stood at its centre. They saw the approaching Khorne champion and his warband, and turned to face him. One of them, wearing fully enclosed black armour, walked forwards to meet him. A dull red glow could be seen through the slits in his helmet, emanating from within. He halted in front of Hroth, who folded his arms and stared at him hard before nodding his head in greeting.

'I see you, Hroth of the Khazags,' the warrior intoned, his voice muffled.

'I see you, Borkhil of the Dolgans.'

'You were the victor then. I was not so sure that you had the power to take Zar Slaaeth.'

'I am pleased to have proven you wrong,' growled Hroth. 'The Blood God is with me.'

'Just as the Dark Prince was with Slaaeth. Then the Lord of Pleasure is a fickle one, easily bored by those whom once he favoured.'

'The devious one is not to be trusted,' said Hroth.

He had met Borkhil on several occasions, for he was never far from Sudobaal. Borkhil and his ruthless black armoured warriors were utterly dedicated to the sorcerer, hailing from the same tribe, and recognising the power that he wielded. Looking over Borkhil's shoulder, Hroth stared at the other warriors. Two were Kurgan chieftains known to him, powerful warriors both. Another was a tall, broad shouldered chieftain of the Norse, his eyes blue and piercing, and his long blond hair knotted with charms and fetishes. The last was a shorter man wearing heavy furs and no armour upon his chest. His skin was daubed with paint, and a bestial skull obscured his face. Another Kurgan chieftain, Hroth reasoned. He saw that the man's legs ended in cloven hooves.

'Did you find what our Lord Sudobaal sent you to retrieve?' asked Borkhil.

Hroth bit back an angry reply. 'I brought *your* lord what he wanted, yes.'

'This is good. The word can be spread to the scattered tribes. Our grand success and our Lord Sudobaal's ascension grows ever closer.'

'Where is the sorcerer?' asked Hroth sharply. The black armoured figure of Borkhil was silent for a moment, looking at the glowering champion of Khorne before him.

'You are a powerful chieftain, Hroth the Blooded of the Khazags. Your victories are many, and all can see the favour of the gods upon you. You have been blessed, for you have become chosen. You have proven yourself a valuable ally of Lord Sudobaal.

'But always remember that he is *more* powerful. His skill in the Dark Tongue is the equal of the most favoured shamans of the far northern tribes. He surpasses the skill of any witch of the Khazags. When he speaks the Dark Tongue, the gods themselves hear him, for he is their oracle, and they grant him great power. He commands a dozen powerful chieftains. You are but one of them, remember. Never let your foolish pride make you his enemy.'

Before he could reply, Hroth saw the black robed figure of Sudobaal making his way down the rocky rough ground that rose above the other end of the clearing. He felt the hair on the back of his neck rise as the sorcerer approached, and could taste the sharp, electric taste of magic in his mouth. He hated the sensation, but repressed his dislike.

'The sorcerer is powerful, yes,' snarled Hroth at Borkhil, out of the earshot of the approaching sorcerer, 'but one day soon I will be more powerful even than him. On that day I will cut you down, Borkhil, and offer your skull up to the Blood God.'

'If such a day was to come, then I would welcome the chance to face you, Hroth of the Khazags,' intoned the black armoured figure, before stepping aside for his Lord Sudobaal. The other chieftains bowed their heads at the approach of the sorcerer.

The sorcerer threw back his hood, exposing his ancient, pinched face. His features were hard, cruel and fierce despite his age, and he exuded menace. Power emanated from him in throbbing waves, as if the invisible, ever-present winds of magic responded to every beat of his heart. Deep sigils were cut into the skin of his cheeks – runes of power that made Hroth's eyes hurt. The sorcerer's unblinking, snake-like yellow eyes conveyed no emotion, and his mouth was set in a deep scowl.

'You have the staff?' the sorcerer asked, his voice deep and sepulchral. Though Hroth stood almost a full head and a half taller than the sorcerer, the smaller man oozed menace and power. Hroth could feel the power of the sorcerer beating upon him, urging him to fall to his knees. Gritting his teeth, he waved the warrior Thorgar forwards. He bore a heavy fur pelt in his arms. Laying it on the ground, Thorgar drew the furs back, exposing the twisted staff within, careful not to touch it. The inside of the fur was singed, and the smell of burning hair rose from the pelt.

Sudobaal stared unblinking at the staff, and his mouth twisted into a savage grin. He stepped forwards eagerly and crouched beside it, his talon-like hands feeling the air above the staff. The runt can barely contain himself, thought Hroth, as the sorcerer became flushed, and his breathing quickened.

'Yes,' whispered the sorcerer. 'This is it.' He licked his dry, pinched lips, and reached towards the twisted shaft. He picked it up gingerly in both hands, cradling it gently as a mother would her babe. He rose to his feet, eyes shining.

The staff began to move, very slowly, and the uncoiling root-like tendrils wrapped themselves around Sudobaal's hand and forearm. The sorcerer watched transfixed as the sharpened ends of the branches pierced his skin and entered his veins. He felt a pull at his heart as his blood began to flow into the staff, travelling up its twisted length and pumping around the stylised Chaos star at its tip. It burst into flames suddenly, blue and green fire that rippled and flickered along the entire staff.

Sudobaal smiled cruelly as he came to understand and master the staff. With a single thought he made the blue-green flames flare up angrily, changing hue to a deep purple-red, lighting up the entire clearing with the daemonic glow. With another thought, he made the flames dissipate almost completely, their flicker almost imperceptible.

'You have done well, chosen,' said Sudobaal, his features once more set grimly. Turning towards Borkhil and the other chieftains, who were clearly awed by the display, Sudobaal spoke, his deep voice authoritative. 'My plans are soon to be fulfilled. Torben Skull-splitter, take your Norsemen north-west tonight. Travel by road and clear the way of any enemies you discover. Torch any buildings you find, and slay any within. I will send a message to you within the week. Dharkon Gar, you and your cousin will take your tribes south. Plunder and pillage all that you can, be a wound in the side of the Empire that they cannot ignore. They will divert some forces to deal with you, for your warriors are many – too many to be ignored.' The two Kurgan chieftains nodded their heads. Sudobaal turned towards the cloven-hoofed, shorter chieftain.

'You, Ghorbar Beast-kin, will travel the dark paths to the north-east, two weeks' march from here. Seek out the beast tribes hidden there. Prepare the gibbet tree for my coming.'

The chieftain bowed his head, and marched off, barking orders.

Turning back towards Hroth and Borkhil, Sudobaal was silent for a moment. He inclined his head to one side, as if listening to a voice no one else could hear. Then he nodded to himself, and spoke. 'Hroth the Blooded, you and your warband will accompany me. I name you my warlord, chieftain amongst my chieftains. You have proven your worth to me, and the gods favour you.' With that, Sudobaal turned on his heel and moved off, climbing the rocky ground back towards the cave.

Borkhil dropped to one knee before Hroth. 'My blade is yours, warlord,' intoned the black-clad warrior. The other remaining chieftains did likewise.

Hroth the Blooded smiled, exposing his sharp teeth. Flames burnt furiously in the eyes. Yes, he thought, I have proven my worth.

BOOK TWO

CHAPTER NINE

FOR TWO ARDUOUS weeks of hard marching, the soldiers of Ostermark trudged towards the north coast of the Empire. The lands they passed through had suffered much during the previous three years. Although the main force of Asavar Kul's army never crossed the borders of Kislev into the Empire itself during the Great War, hundreds of warbands did, sent to sow terror and dissent amongst the Empire's populace.

While Asavar Kul marched into Kislev at the head of the greatest Chaos force the world had ever seen, these warbands struck at isolated, rural Empire villages and towns, burning them to the ground and sacrificing the inhabitants to their Dark Gods. The Empire, divided by four hundred years of internal struggle and civil war, did not react in any orderly fashion. Deep division between the provinces meant that there was no unified defence, and as each elector acted independently, doing what he saw as best for himself, the forces of Chaos flourished within the dark forests of the Empire.

Over the previous four hundred years, as civil war and unrest plagued the Empire, the elector counts had grown lax at rooting out the evil creatures that lurked in the forests that surrounded their cities, and so when the forces of Chaos began their assault, countless thousands of beastmen from the forests joined them. Their ranks were swollen with those who had been cast out of their homes – for consorting with Dark Powers, or for being unable to hide hideous mutations from the societies they lived in. Many that had slunk away into the darkness now arose, eager to cast down those who had oppressed them. They had been lurking for generations, awaiting their time to rise and slaughter those they had hidden from.

Witchcraft and sorcery had long been forbidden in the Empire, and all who dabbled in its dangerous arts, or were accused of doing so, were ruthlessly hunted down, tortured and burnt to death. Those fearing persecution also fled into the concealing darkness of the forests. Most were slaughtered by the dark things that lurked there, but some survived, for their dark magic skills were true. These magisters and witches also rose up when the waves of Chaos energy rippled from the far Northern Wastes, and they attacked the Empire from within its own borders alongside the Chaos warbands, the mutants, the cultists and the uncountable beasts of the forest.

The lands they had marched through still bore the mark of this devastation. It would take generations before the wounds healed, thought Stefan, although he doubted whether the Empire had generations to spare. The Great War had been won, but in his darker moments, he wondered whether the conflict would ever end. He had never voiced such doubts and never would, but sometimes in the dead of night they crept up on him. Or they came at him when he walked silently through yet another deserted village, the skeletal remains of its occupants nailed to barn doors, long since picked clean by carrion eaters.

The northern lands had perhaps suffered the most of all the lands in the Empire. They were far from any of the great cities, and far from the protection that they yielded. Many of the people that had lived this far north had no idea of what was occurring in the outside world before the hordes of Chaos descended upon them, hacking and slaying, and ravaging and burning.

The villages that Stefan and his army discovered that were still miraculously inhabited were overrun with plague and pestilence. He ordered his soldiers to pass by these infected settlements in wide arcs, not venturing too close. Still, many of the sick and dying villagers would cry out to the men of Ostermark for aid or food, for they were starving as well as plague-ridden.

Many of the men of Ostermark had wished to aid the wretches, but they were sternly ordered not to do so by the sergeant, Albrecht. 'It won't do them or us no good, lads.'

Still, a steady stream of rag-tag hangers-on attached themselves to the marching military force. At first, it was just a few frightened families whose homes had been destroyed, and they quickly made themselves useful around the camp, cleaning and cooking to earn some food. Stefan cast a blind eye to this, for it had no damaging effect. However, the rabble grew steadily as the days passed, and soon there had been hundreds of the pathetic hangers-on following the army. Most could not match the exacting pace set by Stefan and the reiksmarshal, and they were encouraged to head south, towards Wolfenburg. As the days passed, most were left behind to face the dangers of the wilderness. Many took the captain's advice and began to make the perilous trek towards Wolfenburg, but Stefan knew that most would never make it. Still, for every family group that was left behind another attached itself to the cavalcade, and they were joined by more unsavoury elements.

Dozens of doom-laden zealots had joined the mob: men and women who had been driven to the point of madness by the horrors they had witnessed over the last years. They screamed and ranted that the end of the world was nigh, and beat themselves with whips, chains and spiked clubs. They were terrifying to the other hangers-on, and disturbing to the soldiers. Their ranting and raving, proclamations of doom and wanton masochism was bad for morale. 'No man needs to be reminded of his own mortality quite so blatantly,' the reiksmarshal had commented, eyeing the flagellants warily when they had first started to band together behind the baggage trains of the army.

Stefan's face was grim as he and Albrecht marched through the camp, passing by the campfires of his soldiers. The men ate in relative silence, and there was no laughter or mirth. Some soldiers called out to Stefan in greeting, and he acknowledged them with a nod or a word.

Thirty greatswords picked from Stefan's elite bodyguard marched behind the pair as they moved away from camp, heading towards a bonfire that raged some way off in the distance. The greatswords carried their massive two-handed swords over their right shoulders, and wore flamboyant feathers in their hats. They wore heavy armour, and marched in perfect, disciplined unison behind Stefan and Albrecht. They were awesome warriors, fearless and skilled, and they had never faltered in the face of the enemy. Still, even they were uneasy as they marched towards the ranting madmen.

Stefan could hear the raised voices of the flagellants, and could see ragged figures capering around the rising flames. The green moon Morrslieb could be seen hanging high in the sky, much larger than its pure, pale sister moon of Mannslieb. Nights when the green moon hung so large were bad for the Empire, for strange and unnatural things tended to occur. Some said the dead walked the land on such nights, and others that it heralded evil to come. The flagellants were most certainly responding to it, working themselves up into a frenzy as the moon climbed its way across the heavens.

'Damn it, captain, they are pitiful figures, but I cannot hate them,' said Albrecht, referring to the crazed zealots.

Stefan knew what he meant. The hardships of the previous years had made these people what they were.

'Handy in a fight, though,' added Albrecht. Stefan had to admit that this was also true. Having long since confronted their own vision of the world's destruction in their mind's eye, they were fearless of death.

Only two days past, the convoy had been attacked by greenskins. Although essentially stupid creatures, Stefan recognised that they were cunning, for they had

waited in ambush until the Reiklandguard and the
bulk of the warriors of Ostermark had passed through
a narrow valley before launching their attack. The rearguard was too far back to be able to intercept the
whooping creatures as they had sprung the ambush
and streamed from the rocks to attack the seemingly
defenceless artillery trains, baggage wagons and rag-tag
hangers-on who struggled to keep pace.

The first to reach the Empire column were the
vicious, smaller greenskins riding massive, slavering
wolves. The demented flagellants had thrown themselves at the enemy, and proceeded to rip them apart,
ignoring their own often-fatal wounds. They hurled
themselves onto the spears of the foe in order to close
with them and smash them to the ground with their
flails and crude hammers. This assault had so stunned
the ambushers that they had lost their momentum,
and Stefan was able to organise a counter-attack
quickly. The greenskins were slaughtered in droves by
the black powder handguns of the men of Ostermark
and the powerful bolts of their crossbows. Those
greenskins that did manage to survive these lethal vol-
leys, and reach the Empire convoy, were met by Stefan
and his halberdiers, and were cut down with ruthless
efficiency.

As they drew closer to the crazed zealots capering
and screaming around the bonfire, Stefan ordered his
greatswords to a halt. With just Albrecht at his side, he
marched towards the flagellants.

There were about seventy of them, dressed in filth-
encrusted robes and tattered clothing. Several had
ripped the clothing from their bodies, despite the
deepening cold of the approaching winter, and he

could see great bloody wounds upon their backs from their self-flagellation. Some had carved statements of repentance and doom into their own flesh. Others had put out their own eyes, and pranced around the fire blindly, great bronze bells hanging around their necks tolling mournfully. Others wore spiked collars that cut into their necks, their bodies slick with blood. One had a battered parchment nailed into the flesh of his chest, a page ripped from a holy book of Sigmar, which Stefan frowned at. A pair of men cried out ecstatically as they flayed the skin from each other's backs.

A towering man wearing battered plate armour stood in the centre of the group, loudly extolling his vision of doom and despondency. His hair and beard were grey and unkempt, and his eyes were wild. Around his waist he wore a string of skulls. Bizarrely, a dead fish, its mouth incredibly distended, had been pulled over the cranium of one of the skulls. Carved into his forehead was the image of a twin-tailed comet, the symbol of Sigmar, and he stood upon the back of another man lying prostrate in the mud, froth dribbling from his mouth. Stefan recognised with surprise that the breastplate the figure wore was the same as those worn by the Reiklandguard, probably scavenged from the dead, he reasoned. Seeing the two men warily approaching, the madman turned towards them and raised his hands into the air.

'Join with us, my children! Give up yourselves to the end of humanity! The day draws near, the end times are upon us! Abase yourselves before great Sigmar, pledge your soul to him and beat the fear from your bodies!'

Albrecht threw the captain a dark look. Stefan folded his arms and planted his feet firmly, looking into the crazed eyes of the self-proclaimed prophet.

'I am already a devout worshipper of great Sigmar. I have no need to abase myself, nor beat myself to prove it to him.'

'Repent, my child. There is darkness within you. Let that darkness out. Be free. Burn it from your soul!'

A cheer from the flagellants greeted that proclamation, and several of them raised their burning braziers high into the air. Others scrambled over each other to lift burning brands from the fire. The air was suddenly filled with the stench of burning flesh, as one of the zealots reversed his brand and held its flaming end to his abdomen. One of the crazed followers of the doom-laden prophet stepped towards Stefan, holding a burning brazier before him.

'Burn it from your soul!' he shouted, repeating the words of the prophet, and he thrust the brazier forwards. Albrecht stepped in front of his captain and swung a meaty fist into the man's face. He dropped the brazier and fell to his knees, clutching at Albrecht's leather tabard. 'Thank you!' he screeched. Albrecht kicked him away, a look of disgust on his face.

'The end does approach,' said the prophet quietly, his voice sounding more lucid. 'We cut down the Everchosen, Asavar Kul, on the battlefield of Kislev, but it matters not. Another will rise. Even now, another is growing in power. Perhaps he will have the power to unite the scattered tribes. A new era of horror and death is upon us. We will never escape it.' He glanced at his demented followers. 'These men and women have seen that it is inevitable.'

'I do not believe that the end is inevitable,' said Stefan, 'and if it is, it would not change my resolve. Where there is evil, it must be fought. There is always hope. To give up on that is to give up completely.'

'I believed so once myself,' chuckled the preacher humourlessly, 'but there *is* no hope, for I have seen the future. Sigmar has granted me the vision. I see blood and fire and death. There is nothing more. Blood and fire and death.'

'You fought well against the greenskins,' said Stefan, changing the subject as he saw the gleam of madness returning to the preacher. 'Had you and your followers not reacted so quickly, many people would have been slain.'

'There is no future for these people,' said the prophet, indicating the flagellants. 'There is no future for me. In death, we can lend our aid to Sigmar and to the Empire.' He lowered his voice before he continued. 'Their homes have been destroyed, their families slaughtered before their eyes. They have witnessed things that would drive any man insane. They have nothing, nothing but the memories that haunt their every living minute. No, were they to travel to Wolfenburg, or even distant Nuln, they would have no life. Penniless, their minds ravaged by horror, they would die, starving to death and alone in their madness. Together, they are a family, and if we can find death while aiding our Empire, then we have done something.'

'What is your name? You rode with the Reiklandguard once, true?' said Stefan. He had no doubt, now, that this man was once a knight, and had not scavenged the breastplate from a corpse, as he had first thought.

'Aye, I rode with the reiksmarshal, it is true. A fine man. We crushed the Chaos fiends of the north,' he said, 'and I have no name. I gave it up long ago. I have no family, no home, and have no need of a name. I will burn brightly, and kill for the Empire, and I will die nameless.'

'Why do you ride with them no longer?'

'I fell in battle, ambushed. A red devil cut my horse from beneath me, and I was trapped beneath it. The devil had wanted to kill me then and there, I knew, but a vile sorcerer stopped him. I was taken alive. My legs were useless, broken at the hip. For five days and nights I was their prisoner. My head was filled with visions.

My captors changed before my eyes. They grew extra limbs, and tentacles sprang from their bodies. Their faces blurred to those of dogs and lizards, and the grass turned black beneath their footsteps. Their horses changed to giant, slavering hounds of darkness that breathed fire, their eyes glowing red and their long tongues lolling from their mouths. Madness was upon me. The red devil grew wings, and flaming horns sprang from his forehead. Then my madness was broken, for the reiksmarshal appeared, and my fellow knights. I was rescued. My body would heal, but my mind was lost. Blood and fire and death. That has been all that I see when I close my eyes,' he whispered. 'The end is near. Blood and fire and death.'

He raised his arms above his head. 'Blood and fire and death draws near, my children!' he screamed.

Stefan turned away from the man, and began to walk back towards his greatswords.

'The man's insane,' said Albrecht.

'Aye, he is, but I think his crazed brethren may be useful in the dark days that draw near. Every fighting man will be needed.'

'Maybe,' said Albrecht dubiously. 'Do you think he really was a Reiklandguard? Its hard to imagine one of those knights falling so far.'

'I believe he was. The ravages of Chaos can strike down all but the most pure,' Stefan said.

Albrecht saw the captain unconsciously grasp the symbol of Sigmar that he wore around his neck.

'Do you truly think it wise to allow those madmen to keep following us?' asked Albrecht.

'Do you truly think we could stop them?' countered von Kessel.

'No, I suppose that we couldn't,' the burly sergeant admitted.

'He wants to die helping the Empire, Albrecht. He wants to die doing something good before the madness consumes him completely. You saw them fight the other day. We could use men like that.'

Behind them, they could hear the raised voice of the prophet, screaming out his vision of destruction.

'Just keep them the hell away from our men.'

CHAPTER TEN

'WE MUST BE swift, warlord. My time draws near,' hissed
Sudobaal. For two days the Chaos forces had moved
quickly through the darkness of the forest, barely stopping to rest. It mattered not to Hroth. His warriors
were Khazags, well used to such extremes. They could
run for a week fully armoured and still have the
strength to fight a battle. Borkhil's black armoured
warriors too were strong, and they showed no signs of
tiring.

'We will be at the gibbet tree before the day is out,
Sudobaal,' said Hroth.

Most of the warriors were on foot, and Hroth had
set a crippling pace, forcing them to run for the last
two days. The black armoured knights of Borkhil were
spread throughout the trees to either flank of
the running warriors, picking their way through the
trees carefully. Hroth's marauder horsemen, lightly

armed and armoured, and riding stout, hardy horses of the Khazag plains, ranged before the others, scouting out the easiest route through the forest. The sorcerer rode his steed alongside the running Khorne champion, its midnight flanks lathered with sweat. It was an ill-tempered beast, temperamental with all but the sorcerer. It had no hooves, its legs ending in taloned claws that gripped the ground, ripping up clods of earth with every step. The sorcerer fed it hunks of flesh each evening, the creature's sharp teeth ripping the flesh from the bones.

Hroth ran with his warriors, rejoicing in the feeling of power and strength that coursed through him as the miles passed behind him. His axe hungered for blood, but he knew that much blood would soon run. Patience, he told himself. Soon there would be thousands of skulls for him to offer up to his deity. He longed for the day.

As the hours passed, Hroth felt his body changing within his skin. The itchy feeling within his thick flesh was not an unpleasant sensation. He could feel his muscles tearing and reforming, and could feel the blood coursing through veins and arteries to feed his growing power. His bones were straining within his body, and he could feel them strengthening. He could feel them hardening, and knew that soon they would be almost unbreakable.

Khorne was with him, he knew. Khorne, who could see into his heart and mind, and see the plans formulating within him, was pleased.

Fingering his axe, he looked at the hunched figure of Sudobaal crouched atop his Chaotic steed. Yes, he thought, Khorne was pleased by the actions he planned.

'Once we have arrived, I will need to prepare the ritual. It needs to happen tonight, and end precisely when the green moon is at its largest in the sky.'

The Khazags called this moon Ghyranek, the green giver of life. Its appearance was unpredictable, sometimes not being seen for weeks, and other times passing by in the night sky so close that its power could be felt by all beneath it. At these times, the shamans would lead the Khazags in ritual celebrations.

Hroth knew that the moon was powerful. He had witnessed its power several times when it had appeared large in the skies. On one occasion, it had heralded the *change* in the warrior Glukhos, and mouths had appeared on his bare flesh. He had eventually been ripped apart by the mutations that wracked his body. The celebrations had been great the night that the tribe had witnessed the touch of the gods. Hroth knew that the closeness of the moon was bringing about the changes he felt within his own body.

'The Chaos moon will be close, tonight. It heralds our victory,' continued Sudobaal.

'With the ritual complete, I will know the resting place of the great zar, the anointed Asavar Kul. The cursed elf-kin took his body, seeking to hide it from us forever. But I shall learn where it resides, and we shall travel there. The blade of Asavar Kul, the Slayer of Kings, holding the essence of the great daemon U'zhul, lies with his body. Any whom the gods deem worthy to wield the Slayer of Kings could unite the tribes that lie scattered throughout the lands. I shall lift it, and the world will tremble! With you at my side, Hroth, we shall take up the challenge where Asavar Kul failed, and bring bloody ruin to this land!'

'Blood and fire and death,' agreed Hroth, fingering his axe.

CHAPTER ELEVEN

STEFAN FOUND IT hard not to smile, as the comical figure of the engineer berated the soldiers of Ostermark that towered above him. He was a small, balding man wearing clothes far too fine to be travelling to war in, and two pairs of spectacles were perched precariously on the end of his nose. The soldiers of Ostermark were silently ignoring him as they lashed additional ropes around the wagon, while four others hammered wooden chocks under the mired wagon wheels, which had sunk deep into the clinging mud. A thick, waterproof canvas sheet covered whatever was held within the wagon; probably gunpowder, guessed von Kessel.

'Buffoons! Imbecilic, inbred Ostermarkers. Don't tie the rope around that bit – there, put it there, dammit! No, no, no, not there you fool! Around that there –

see, there it is,' flapped the engineer. No one was paying him any attention.

Most of the convoy had halted. Shouts came from behind the mired wagon, urging the soldiers to hurry up. The soldiers shouted back at them good naturedly, swearing profusely and colourfully as only a soldier, or a sailor, can.

'This is precious cargo, you buffoons,' shouted the engineer. 'Pay attention to what you are doing!'

Von Kessel trudged down to the mired wagon, sinking to his ankles in the thick mud.

'Engineer Markus, you seem a little flustered,' said von Kessel amiably.

'Flustered! Damn right I'm flustered. Excuse my crude language, captain, but your men have not been listening to a thing I have been saying to them!'

'I shall listen, Markus. Calm yourself,' Stefan said, trying not to smile. The front pair of spectacles was slipping closer and closer to the tip of the engineer's nose. He was certain they would fall into the mud any second.

'Right, right. Very good of you, captain,' said the engineer. He cleared his throat, as if he was about to start a great speech. 'This wagon contains a most precious and intricate apparatus, one that must be handled with great care,' he began. He cast a venomous glance towards the soldiers straining to pull the wagon from the mire.

The horses strained, a dozen soldiers heaved on the ropes, and another four pushed at the cart from behind it. The wagon moved ever so slightly, inching forwards, before slipping back into the mud with a jerk. The soldiers at the back fell to their knees in the mud, much to the amusement of those behind. 'Gently gentlemen, please!' shouted Markus the engineer. 'If anything is damaged, I'll see you all held personally responsible!'

'Nothing will be damaged, Markus,' assured von Kessel.

'Well, I hope not. That's an expensive and rare piece of field equipment in there, captain,' the engineer said, waving a finger towards the wagon.

Von Kessel frowned. 'Field equipment?' he queried. 'I didn't know anything about any additional cannon.'

'Aha! No you did not! And it is far more than a cannon,' the engineer proclaimed. 'Requisitioned at the reiksmarshal's order, it was. I tell you, the Elector Count Otto Gruber will be upset when he hears that the reiksmarshal took it, he will. A very special piece of equipment, this. The *Wrath of Sigmar*.'

'The *Wrath of Sigmar*?'

The engineer leant in close to the captain, a conspiratorial look on his face. 'It's one of Von Meinkopf's macro-mainsprings of multitudinous precipitations of pernicious lead,' he whispered proudly. He rocked back on his heels and sucked on his teeth, awaiting the astonished gasp from the Ostermark captain.

Stefan looked at him blankly. 'It's a what?' he asked.

'A what?' the engineer scoffed. 'Do they teach you nothing in Ostermark?' The engineer sighed and rolled his eyes at the bemused captain. 'In layman's terms, it's a helblaster volley gun. Ah, yes! Now I see you understand!'

Von Kessel looked again at the wagon with wide eyes. It was a powerful weapon indeed. He waved for more men to come to help the ones struggling to free the bogged-down wagon, and he walked into the middle of the mire to lend his own help. He leant his weight against the back of the wagon, and set his boots in the mud. The call was given, and von Kessel heaved along with all the other soldiers. Straining, he could feel the wagon beginning to move, and redoubled his efforts. Suddenly, with a great sucking noise, the wagon sprang forwards and rolled free of the mire. Von Kessel and the other soldiers pushing it fell face first into the mud.

Laughter rang out. As the captain rose to his feet, the laughter petered out. He spat mud from his mouth, and wiped his hand across his face, clearing the clinging mud from his eyes. Then he began to laugh. The other laughter started up again, and the muddy soldiers slapped each other on the backs, laughing and cursing.

Stepping through the mire, the captain approached the engineer once more. 'There you are, Markus. The engine is free, and no harm came to it. I hope it was worth the effort.'

'Oh, it will be, captain,' said the engineer, offering von Kessel a silk handkerchief, which the captain declined, much to his relief.

'Captain! Our scouts have sighted the coast!' came a shout. Von Kessel bid goodbye to the engineer, and began to make his way to the front of the column, where he found the reiksmarshal. The knight looked at the mud-covered captain and raised an eyebrow.

'I slipped,' the captain said flatly.

A scout could be seen galloping hard down the trail towards them. Thick white froth was on the lips of his horse, and it whinnied and stamped the ground in agitation as he brought it to a halt before his captain.

'What news, Wilhelm?' asked von Kessel.

'Are you alright, sir?' asked the man. The captain waved a hand to dismiss the question, flinging mud as he did so. 'It's bad, sir. Castle Kreindorf is occupied, as the reiksmarshal had said, and I can see white sails out to sea, sir. Elves, I believe.'

'And this is bad news how?'

'They cannot land, sir. The castle is surrounded, and the ships cannot beach.'

'Surrounded? Is it the Norse? Quickly, dammit!'

'Aye, I believe so, captain, and other things too.'

'Other things?'

'They are quite far-off, but there are thousands of them. Furred beasts that walk like men.'

'Beastmen,' spat von Kessel.

'Aye, captain.'

'We must move with haste,' said the reiksmarshal calmly. 'If those elves are slain, it will be very awkward for our Emperor Magnus.'

'I'm sure it would be more awkward for the elves,' said von Kessel. 'What are they doing out here anyway? And why are those ships trying to beach?'

'I fear they are trying to land so that they can pick up one of the elves. Someone very important: an elf mage of the royal bloodline.'

'A what? We came all this way to rescue an elf sorcerer-prince?' asked a stunned von Kessel. The reiksmarshal turned his cold gaze towards the young captain.

'We came all this way to aid our high elf allies, and to secure lasting peace between our people. They are an ancient and powerful race, Captain von Kessel. If ever our friendship with them should falter, then we will be in dire times indeed,' he said curtly, 'and there is an elf mage-*princess* in that castle. The death of a princess of the royal household of Ulthuan on Empire soil would not be a good thing.'

Stefan grunted in response. 'Can we see the siege from the ridge, Wilhelm?' he asked the scout.

'Yes, captain. I will lead you there,' the scout answered, stepping from the saddle of his horse. A young man took the reins from him, and led the horse away.

'Good,' said von Kessel. He turned to a soldier standing nearby. 'Bring the engineer, Markus, up here. Make haste.'

'The engineer?' enquired the reiksmarshal, as the soldier ran off.

'He has an eye-glass.'

The climb to the ridge was steep, and Markus slipped to his knees several times, as he climbed, cutting his fine silver silk stockings and grazing his knees on the rocky ground. He cursed silently, breathing heavily. He looked down the way they had come. He had not realised how far they had climbed. The convoy snaking its way along the road was far below.

'Hurry yourself, engineer,' hissed Captain von Kessel. The engineer, puffing and sweating profusely, climbed the last steep incline to the top of the ridge. He gasped as he reached the summit, and surveyed the scene laid out before him.

He stood on the edge of a great cliff. It dropped off several hundred feet below him, the height making his head spin. The valley flattened off, leading to the rocky coastline of the Sea of Claws, about two and a half miles off, the engineer estimated. He was famed within the Engineers' Academy in Nuln for his skill at judging distances and trajectory.

The northern fringes of the great Forest of Shadows spread out at the foot of the cliff, thinning a mile from the coastline. In the distance, beyond the line of the trees was a crumbling castle, long abandoned by men of the Empire. It perched atop a rocky spur about a mile from the coast. The ground around the castle seemed to swarm and ripple with movement. The sea itself was dark, and the mists over the water disguised where the sea ended and the sky began.

'Engineer, your eye-glass, please,' said the captain. The engineer nodded and gently removed what looked like a leather scroll case from within his fine, embroidered coat. He popped off the lid of the scroll case, and von Kessel could see that inside it was lined with rich, purple velvet. The engineer carefully upended the case, and eased a cylindrical object wrapped in soft cloth from inside. With great care, he unwrapped the brass eye-glass, and handed it gently to the captain.

'Be careful with her, I beg you.' The captain nodded, and raised the object to his eye, squinting into its lens. He had owned such a contraption himself once, but it had been broken during a battle. He carefully turned the knobs on top of the cylinder until what he viewed through the lens came into focus.

Firstly, he turned his gaze towards the castle. He could see glittering figures upon the partly ruined ramparts, dressed in silver and white: elves. An ornate, tapering flag flew from the highest remaining tower, its perfectly white material almost glowing. It was hard to judge from this distance, but he estimated that there were around two hundred figures on the castle walls.

He turned his gaze towards the forces of Chaos that swarmed around the castle. Like a living tide washing up against the castle, the forces of Chaos were innumerable. He saw hundreds of banners topped with grisly trophies, carried by men in horned helmets. They threw themselves at the walls in living waves. A pair of rough, hastily constructed siege engines rolled slowly towards the crumbling castle walls, pulled by massive furred creatures. Even as he watched, he saw one of the siege engines fall soundlessly, surely crushing scores of men beneath it. The elves must have war machines upon the walls, he thought.

Stefan's gaze passed over Chaos warriors until it reached the rocky coastline. There was only one clear landing from the sea, the rest of the coastline being made up of rocky cliffs. Longships had been pulled up onto the land at this one small harbour. The waterfront was swarming with figures. He reckoned that there must be in the realm of a thousand followers of Chaos between the harbour and the castle.

Looking out to sea, five white sailed cutters could be seen, sleek high elf ships that sliced through the water at great speed. In turn, they rapidly approached the harbour and unleashed great bolts from the war machines on their decks, before swinging back out to sea. Clearly, they could not land in the harbour, for there were too many enemies swarming along the coastline. Any attempt to land would be easily defeated. 'Damn it,' swore Stefan. He tossed the eye-glass back to the engineer and began the descent back to his army. Markus gasped and caught the eye-glass awkwardly, breathing a sigh of relief when he did not drop it. 'Thank you, Lady Verena,' he breathed, invoking the name of the goddess of learning and justice.

He glared darkly at the figure of Captain von Kessel, who was already some way down the incline and shouting to his sergeants to join him and the reiks-marshal to discuss battle plans. Markus quickly rewrapped the eye-glass and replaced it in its case, and began his descent. He managed to trip only once on the way down the slippery incline, stubbing his toe painfully. Not for the first or last time, he cursed the war that plagued the lands, and kept him from his quiet life of study.

Still, he reasoned, it wasn't all bad. At least it looked as if he might get to try out the *Wrath of Sigmar* on something other than a practice target. He grinned evilly, his stubbed toe and ripped stockings forgotten.

CHAPTER TWELVE

THE GREEN MOON hung large in the heavens, swollen and emanating dark power, as Sudobaal had predicted. The preparations had lasted almost two hours already, and Hroth was growing impatient.

The sorcerer had spent much of the time chanting incoherently, although the sound of the words had made Hroth's skin crawl. The sorcerer had capered around the tree, dancing from one foot to the other, squeezing the blood from a fresh heart onto the twisted roots of the massive tree towering above them. The heart had recently belonged to a runtish ungor, a stunted lesser beastman.

The creature had squealed like a stuck pig when Hroth had grabbed it by its scrawny throat. Its cries had been cut short when he had twisted the creature's neck sharply, bones crunching loudly. The thing had been weak – he had almost pulled its head from its body, corkscrewing it off its shoulders in that one savage movement. The other larger beastmen had brayed and snorted when the creature had died – what passed as laughter in the crude creatures.

The sorcerer had deftly cut the heart from the ungor, and Hroth had kicked the corpse into the hollow that lay beneath the twisted shape of the gibbet tree. The bones and bodies of hundreds of corpses lay in that hollow, all slain by the beastmen, and all sacrifices to the Dark Gods of Chaos. Scores more corpses hung in the leafless branches of the tree above, strung up by their necks or nailed brutally to the boughs. Other wasted corpses were slumped in hanging metal cages that swayed slowly above, creaking ominously.

Runes of Chaos were carved into the trunk of the gibbet tree, runes that held great power despite the crudity of their creation. These carvings wept red, blood-like sap that dripped down into the hollow, and onto the corpses piled there. A series of standing stones stood around the base of the massive tree, each surrounded by piles of weapons and shields. Heads had been rammed onto stakes and driven into the ground. Cruelly barbed bushes of thorns crept around the stones, and over the twisted roots tree's.

Hundreds of black carrion birds sat perched in the branches and boughs. Earlier, they had been busy flapping from one branch to another, fighting to rip the choicest strips of flesh from the corpses that hung there. The sound of their harsh cawing had filled the evening, but they had fallen silent and settled down as the sun had set, and now they sat motionless as the witching hour drew nigh.

A great many beastmen had gathered around the tree by the time that Hroth and Sudobaal had arrived. They had been greeted by the beastman chieftain, the wargor Gharlanoth, and his bray-shaman. The two powerful creatures had exposed their furred necks to the sorcerer in a show of submission.

The beastmen were true creatures of Chaos, instinctively recognising the power of the sorcerer and responding to it with deference and respect. Two hundred of the wargor's bray-herd were arrayed around the gibbet tree, awaiting the ritual with barely contained excitement, stamping their cloven hooves on the ground. Fights broke out, and several of the gors had raised weapons against one another, snorting and spitting, as they fought for the best places from which to view the coming ceremony. These outbursts were instantly stopped by the wargor Gharlanoth, who roared his displeasure.

Hroth's face clearly showed his impatience. The sorcerer had left the clearing almost an hour ago, and had yet to return. He snarled in irritation.

SUDOBAAL WAS RAVENOUS. Hunger wracked his wiry frame, his stomach gurgling loudly. 'Yes, yes,' he whispered. 'We shall eat now.'

A prostrate warrior, one of Hroth's tribesmen, lay on the ground in front of the black-clad sorcerer. He lay rigid, unable to move, staring up with fearful eyes at the sorcerer crouching above him. 'You should be proud,' Sudobaal hissed. 'Your sacrifice is necessary. It will feed us.'

The warrior struggled to rise, but his limbs would not respond to his urging. 'It's the poison. Don't fight it. Embrace your last moments,' the sorcerer said. He had led the warrior away from the gathering, saying that the man had been chosen by the gods for a special task. He had shoved an upturned skull into the man's hands, dark liquid sloshing within the cranial cavity. 'Drink,' he had urged. The man had looked uneasy, but had raised the skull to his lips and drunk it dry.

Kneeling, Sudobaal opened his robes, displaying his taut, scarred torso. The skin just below the breastbone bulged outwards, and the warrior's eyes stared at it wildly. The creature within Sudobaal, the creature that was a part of him, pushed itself to the surface of the sorcerer's flesh. Its deformed, babyish face grinned as it emerged, exposing dozens of tiny, sharp teeth. Pallid tentacles slid from the sorcerer's torso. One reached out eagerly towards the warrior. The other coiled up over the sorcerer's chest and gripped his shoulder, pulling the rest of the creature's body from its host.

Sudobaal shuddered and closed his eyes as the thing pulled itself from his flesh and dropped clumsily to the ground. The colour began to drain from the sorcerer, his skin turning to grey in seconds. The creature blinked its own yellow slanted eyes, and pushed itself upright.

Reaching across the immobilised warrior, it pulled itself with some difficulty onto his chest and stared hungrily at the man's stomach. A thin, purple tongue flicked out of its mouth, and it lowered its head, biting into the warrior's flesh. Skin gripped tightly between its teeth, the creature strained upwards, shaking its head from side to side, ripping and tearing. It then thrust its tentacles into the wound, and peeled the flesh open, exposing the coiled innards within. It would feed well this night.

HROTH GLARED AT the sorcerer as he returned to the gathering, greeted by the howling and braying of the beastmen. Sudobaal's face was flushed, and he barely leant on his staff as he strode past the towering Khorne champion. He began to sprinkle black powder from one of his pouches in a large circle within the ring of standing stones, creating an unbroken curving line. A stone slab stood in the centre of his circle, its surface a dull red colour. Thousands of sacrifices to the Dark Gods had been made on that slab, for this had been a holy place to the beastmen for centuries.

At the most northerly point on the circle, Sudobaal marked out a smaller circle in the red powder. Moving to the most southerly point, he emptied a purplish powder onto the ground, creating another circle. On the most easterly point, closest to Hroth, he marked out a circle in green dust. The Khorne warlord could smell its putrid stink. On the other side of the tree, the westerly side, Sudobaal laid out a circle of blue.

While Sudobaal was busy with his own work, the beastman bray-shaman began to light the black braziers that surrounded the gibbet tree. Each brazier was made from a human skull. As each was lit, the bray-shaman threw a handful of dried herbs and leaves onto the flames. The orange-red flames flared high, and briefly changed to purple. Then they died down low, and the colour changed once more, this time to a deep, dark red. Acrid smoke began to fill the air, making Hroth feel light-headed. His stomach clenched as he breathed deeply, the thick smoke entering his lungs.

The sorcerer's chanting increased in pitch, and he moved completely around the stone ring three times anti-clockwise, careful not to disturb any of the circles he had marked. He scratched an eight-pointed star in the earth between each of the coloured circles, using the tip of the twisted staff fused to his arm.

Still chanting, he ushered the beastman chieftain's bray-shaman forwards. The massively muscled creature carried forth the offerings to be placed in the circles and Chaos stars scratched into the earth. The scrimshawed thighbone, the heavy brass icon, the small pile of bones and the blood-red, veined stone were placed in the centres of the Chaos stars. Each one of these items had been recovered by Hroth. Many skulls had been offered up to Khorne to retrieve them all. Black, oily smoke began to rise from the items, and Sudobaal's chanting intensified once more. Colours and shapes swirled before the Khorne champion, and he thought he could make out devilish, shadowy faces that snarled and hissed.

Next, the bray-shaman carried forth the shimmering white stone, and placed it inside the purple circle. Its hand brushed the powder as it placed the stone in its place, and Hroth could hear the sound of flesh sizzling. The beastman pulled back its burnt hand quickly, but did not cry out for fear of interrupting the sorcerer's ritual. Quickly, the bray-shaman took the horned skull and placed it in the red circle. The Khorne champion found himself mesmerised by the skull, thinking that he heard a voice from within it calling out to him. The skull lay unmoving, but the Khornate champion could feel its call. He knew that the acrid smoke that rose from the braziers around the tree was truly beginning to affect him, and his vision swam before him. Dark shapes swirled at the corners of his vision, and he felt their icy touch on his neck. He heard them whispering in the Dark Tongue, the language of daemons, and the voices clawed at his sanity. The bray-shaman placed the plate that held the still-beating heart into the green circle. Instantly, the heart began to swell, putrid boils appearing on its surface. The beastman then moved back amongst its brethren.

Sudobaal, his chanting now loud and booming, moved to place himself just outside the blue circle. Screaming his arcane words to the heavens, he slammed his twisted staff into the earth. Flames burst into life around the blue circle. Azure fire licked at the base of the staff, rippling up its surface and covering Sudobaal's arm. The tendrils that connected the staff to his arm retracted, and he released his grip on it. The staff remained standing straight upright, as if held by an invisible arm. Sudobaal had stopped chanting, and surveyed his work, paying no heed to his smoking arm.

The heart in the green circle beat loudly. The pustules over its surface had burst, spilling their putrid contents onto the plate. The air around the pale stone shimmered and blurred, like the horizon on a hot day. A sickly sweet perfumed purple smoke was rising from the stone. The staff in the blue circle continued to blaze with azure flames. In the red circle, blood was dripping from the eye sockets of the horned skull, pooling beneath it.

Sudobaal motioned for Borkhil to approach him. The massive black armoured champion stalked forwards. He was not wearing his helm, and his head was pale and hairless. Hroth's vision swam before him, and he tried to focus on the sorcerer's face. A myriad of other faces just beneath the skin seemed to be trying to push out of the sorcerers flesh. He heard laughter, and felt his stomach contract again. I will not let this sorcery overcome me, he swore, and he tensed his iron-like muscles, feeling the rage building within him.

'I have need of a powerful sacrifice: a sacrifice that the gods themselves will take note of.' The voice of the sorcerer seemed to come from a great distance away. Hroth was not sure if Sudobaal had truly spoken, or if he had imagined it. The words made little sense to him, but his hands involuntarily clenched into fists, and he felt the muscles of his arms and chest straining.

'The fey elf kin have used their understanding of the winds of magic to cloud the resting place of Asavar Kul from my sight. Only with a powerful sacrifice can my vision be cleared.'

The black armoured figure of Borkhil bowed his head to the sorcerer, and turned to face Hroth, his face expressionless. He lifted his massive, double-handed spiked mace from his back, and he took a menacing step towards the Khorne champion.

Eyes narrowing as he tried to focus, Hroth growled deeply in his chest. He tried to move his hands to his axe, but found that he could not. The veins on his neck bulged. Sudobaal grinned evilly, 'You are a powerful champion, but your usefulness has passed.'

Hroth strained against the invisible bonds that held him in place. He struggled against them, willing himself to step forwards, smash Borkhil aside and cut down the treacherous sorcerer. Borkhil, hefting his massive weapon before him, stalked towards the immobile champion of Khorne.

'I am sorry that it has to be this way. It seems that we will never face each other in the combat circle to discover who is strongest,' the big man said blankly. 'Such is the way of things.'

A barbed dagger plunged into the black armoured champion's neck. Dark blood gushed from the fatal wound. The massive warrior dropped his weapon, and put a hand to his neck in a futile effort to stem the bleeding. Blood gushed from his mouth, and he fell to his knees in front of Hroth. Behind him, Sudobaal stood with the bloody dagger held before him.

The beastman shaman trotted forwards and gripped Borkhil's neck tightly in its massive hand. It held a roughly hewn bowl out to catch the blood, which steamed and hissed as it filled the vessel.

'A powerful sacrifice...' repeated Sudobaal, and Hroth felt his invisible bonds disappear. Every instinct screamed at him to step forwards and cut down the sorcerer, but he held back. No, he would learn the resting place of Asavar Kul before that, and so, with difficulty, he suppressed his rage.

'I can see the hatred in your burning eyes, champion. You would dearly love to rip me limb from limb, wouldn't you?' the sorcerer asked. 'It matters not. That rage you have drives you. You are stronger than he was. That is why you are living still, and Borkhil is dying on the ground. That is why his blood will complete this ceremony and not yours. All that was Borkhil's is yours – his tribe, and his skull. Serve me well.'

Sudobaal took the bowl proffered by the beastman shaman, and walked with the hissing, bubbling blood to the circles. Chanting again, he walked around the circles, splashing blood into each of them.

Black smoke began to rise out of the earth in the centre of the large marked-out circle as Sudobaal's chanting continued. Oily and black, it coiled upwards with reaching tendrils, curling around itself. The flames of the braziers and torches arrayed around the clearing spluttered and dimmed, some of them going out altogether. A chill wind swirled through the darkening clearing, carrying whispers and threats. The oily smoke began to take form, roughly creating the shape of a muscular figure with encircling wings and three pairs of horns.

Embers of light appeared in the face of the smoke-figure. Sudobaal's chanting reached a crescendo, and he flung his arms into the air. The creature of smoke solidified slightly, the face gaining features, and it stared around the clearing. Hroth felt the power of the daemon as its gaze passed over him, and he almost staggered back from it. Its mouth opened, exposing dagger-like fangs, and it began to speak. A second or two later, the sound of its voice issued forth, out of sync with the movement of its lips. The sound was like a thousand voices screaming in a howling gale, and the words made no sense to Hroth, although they scratched at his sanity. The daemon reached out with long arms of smoke towards Sudobaal, but jerked its hands back as it touched the barrier formed by the sorcerer's careful preparations, and electricity sparked.

The daemon roared in sudden rage, its maw opening impossibly wide, and its eyes glowing intensely. It grew larger, swelling to over fifteen feet in height, and it spoke quickly, anger evident in its tone. Sudobaal shouted back at the daemon. Blood had begun to trickle from his ears and nose. The daemon was silent, and the sorcerer screamed out again, speaking the true name of the creature.

'Yyfol'gzuz'cogar!' screamed Sudobaal at the towering daemon. 'Yyfol'gzuz'cogar!'

The daemon struggled against its bonds, roaring and thrashing about madly. The swirling wind that whipped around the clearing intensified, throwing sticks and branches through the air. One of the braziers grazed Sudobaal's head as it was hurled through the air, knocking him closer to the circle and the daemon. Regaining his footing, the sorcerer shouted again. The daemon began to speak, compelled by the foolish mortal who had learnt its true name, each word dripping with evil and malice.

The swirling wind intensified as the daemon was once more silent, and a sudden gust burst past Sudobaal's defences, scattering the powder that marked out the circles surrounding the daemon.

The daemon's scream of triumph turned to rage when Sudobaal threw the last remaining contents of the bowl over the creature. The boiling blood dispersed the figure of smoke, and with a word of banishment Sudobaal sent the raging creature back to the Realms of Chaos. He slumped to the ground, black blood dripping from his nose and ears and eyes. Silence filled the clearing.

Hroth stepped towards the crumpled figure of Sudobaal. 'You know where it is?'

It was a long while before the sorcerer answered. 'I know where we must go,' he breathed finally. 'Gather the warbands. We move for the coastline this night,' he managed before falling into unconsciousness.

CHAPTER THIRTEEN

A SHARP HORN blast sounded. Stefan von Kessel swore. The horn was echoed by another, further off.

'They know we are here,' said Albrecht.

Stefan had directed his army to the east onto the top of a plateau, where the height and angle of the hills had hidden its approach towards the besieged castle. They were close to the tops of the plateau, and would soon be able to see down onto the castle and the coastline. Sounds of battle could be heard in the distance.

'There is nothing for it. Double-time march. Make sure the cannon are set quickly once over the brow of the hill,' Stefan ordered. His sergeant nodded and moved down the line of soldiers, shouting orders.

The plain of the plateau was almost bare of trees, and the army of Ostermark marched towards its peak in a long battle line. Rank upon rank of halberdiers, swordsmen and spearmen marched steadily, increasing their pace at the sergeant's barked commands. Regiments of crossbowmen and handgunners were interspersed with the halberdiers, jogging lightly, unencumbered by the breastplates and heavy helmets worn by the other soldiers. Far out on the right flank was the mob of flagellants, working themselves up into a crazed frenzy. The Reiklandguard, their armour shining brightly and pennants flapping from their lance tips, cantered behind the ranks of state troops, and behind them, the artillery moved forwards, pulled by heavy draught horses.

Stefan kicked his steed forwards, galloping the final five hundred yards towards the brow of the hill. Before reaching the top, he dismounted and dropped to his stomach, crawling forwards the last yards and looking down. He surveyed the scene for some time, before remounting his horse and galloping back to his army.

He rode along the front of the marching columns, and reined in beside the reiksmarshal.

'The enemy are some eight hundred yards distant once we pass the summit, reiksmarshal.'

'Good,' his commander said. 'We will unlimber the cannon once we move over the ridge, and ready them to fire. The enemy will close on our position quickly. Ensure your troops are ready. When we defeat this first attack, leave two full regiments to protect the cannon, and drive your foot soldiers towards the castle. Be wary, and do not let yourself become surrounded. I will lead my knights towards the north after the first attack, and strike from there. We must clear the beaches.' Stefan nodded. 'And captain,' said the reiksmarshal, 'Sigmar guide your sword.'

'He will,' said von Kessel with certainty, and he turned to his sergeants to relay his orders. He stepped from the saddle and gave the reins to a waiting boy, who took the horse away from the battlefield. He pulled his sallet helmet onto his head, and strode in front of his army to join his regiment of greatswords. The battle-hardened warriors occupied the centre of the Empire line, their massive two-handed swords held over their right shoulders.

Albrecht, marching with a regiment of halberdiers, crested the brow of the hill, and his eyes widened.

'Sigmar save us!' exclaimed one of the halberdiers. Other soldiers swore as they too saw the battlefield arrayed before them.

The crumbling castle was about a thousand yards off, and completely surrounded by the besiegers. The clash of weapons could easily be heard, together with the roars of charging men and the screams of the dying. A living sea of Chaos surrounded the besieged castle, hundreds upon hundreds of savage Norsemen struggling to breach the defences of the defenders. Furred beastmen fought alongside the Norse, each taller than a man, with curling horns growing from their bestial heads.

Arrows descended from the walls in great clouds, cutting down swathes of the attackers with each volley. Those that fell were trampled underfoot by the press of the Norsemen, but there were dozens left to fill the gaps where their kinsmen had fallen.

Hundreds of Norscans were gathered on the beach-head, waving their axes and swords at the elf ships that skimmed across the water just outside the small bay. Massive cliffs towered up on either side of the bay, and rocks jutted from the water at their base, sharp and treacherous.

Figures could be seen on the crumbling castle walls, wearing tall gleaming helmets and spotless white robes. Their weapons flashed as they struggled to repel the waves of attackers that surged up the steep hills surrounding the castle. Ladders were hoisted up against the walls, and ropes thrown over its walls. Many were cast down, sending those warriors climbing them tumbling into their comrades, but the walls were too low, and the defenders too few, for the siege to last much longer.

The south-east wall was little more than a crumbled pile of stone, and here the battle was at its most fierce. The Norse were scrambling over the piles of rocks, and being cut down in their scores by the archers on the intact sections of the wall on either side of the gap. Those few warriors who did manage to survive the hail of death were met by elf warriors artfully wielding massive blades that they swung around them with deadly efficiency, and were cut down mercilessly.

As he watched, Albrecht saw a massive bull-headed creature, standing easily twelve feet tall, leap into the breach, clambering swiftly over the boulders, desperate to kill those before it. Arrows streaked down into the beast, and soon dozens of shafts protruded from its thick, furred hide. Uncaring, it carried on, intent on slaughter.

A slight figure stepped into the breach alongside the warriors, wearing a long flowing robe and cloak of pale blue. The figure held a tall staff in its hand, which it pointed towards the charging bull-headed minotaur. Flames, bright and searing, burst from the tip of the staff and hurtled towards the creature, which exploded into flames. Bellowing in fear and pain, the creature stumbled blindly for a few steps, before falling to the ground, a blackened, smoking corpse. Several of the halberdiers around Albrecht made signs of protection.

'Was that a woman?' asked one man.

'Dunno,' said Albrecht. 'Can't always tell with those elves.' He shouted for a halt, the call echoed by the other sergeants up and down the line. The army of Ostermark came to a stop, looking down upon the chaotic battlefield before them. Men below were turning to face this new threat, and shouts and horns could be heard, the sounds carried up to them on the wind. A group of about fifty lightly armoured horsemen, armed with bows and spears, peeled off from the rest of the force in a wide arc, and began to ride to the south.

'They're trying to get around our flank,' muttered Albrecht.

With a braying roar, three hundred beastmen, led by a giant bestial creature with three arms, began to run up the hill towards the Empire force. Their cloven hooves pounded the ground, making it tremble. Huge, slavering hounds ran at their sides, massive creatures the size of small ponies. Behind them, several hundred Norse warriors turned and began to trudge up the hill. Many carried round shields with flayed skin pulled taut across them. Cursed symbols were painted onto this flesh, and Stefan gripped the twin-tailed comet talisman hanging around his neck tightly, muttering a prayer. Others of the Norse had no shields at all, and loped up the hill carrying massive axes, requiring two hands to wield them.

A second group peeled off from the mass below, and began to march up the hill just behind the others. There were around a hundred warriors, and they wore fully enclosed plate armour over long chainmail. Like the other Norse warriors, they wore heavy helmets topped with rising horns and heavy cloaks thrown over their shoulders.

'Fire!' screamed one of the Ostermark sergeants, and the air was filled with the cracking fire of hand-guns. Dozens of the charging beastmen fell to the first volley, to be trampled by those behind. Another shout sounded, and black bolts from hundreds of crossbowmen hissed through the air, driving into the enemy with sickening force, punching them from their feet and sending them sprawling to the ground.

A booming sound echoed across the battlefield, quickly followed by another, as the Empire cannon, now readied, fired their first shots. The sounds rever-berated in Albrecht's ears, and smoke rolled from the massive barrels. The cannonballs streaked through the air, ploughing into the enemy with deadly force. Albrecht saw a massive, bestial warrior's head taken clean off by a cannonball, before it continued on into the press, killing dozens. Each cannonball ploughed through the enemy, kicking up clods of earth, and driving great furrows through the ground where they bounced and skidded. Legs were ripped from hips as cannonballs screamed through the foe. Warriors raised their shields helplessly, and arms and shields alike were shattered. A second volley of handgun fire tore threw the enemy. Dozens more dropped at this close range.

'Right lads, here they come!' shouted Albrecht.

CAPTAIN STEFAN VON Kessel stood calmly facing the approaching enemy. Another volley of black crossbow bolts hissed through the air, cutting down great swathes of the beastmen. Still others came at them, although their numbers were less than half of what had started the charge up the hill.

Captain von Kessel cocked one of his pistols with his right hand, his left hand holding the comforting weight of his shield. A litany of Sigmar was written on the inside of the shield, painted on with intricate calligraphy. He knew the words off by heart, but having them before him was still a comfort. His faith would protect him against the evil of Chaos.

The slavering hounds that ran alongside the beastmen were loosed, and they launched themselves at the lines of Ostermark state troops, growling and roaring. They were hateful creatures of Chaos, mutated and deadly. Although their sheer size was enough to indicate their twisted Chaotic breed, many of them bore mutations. Massive tusks curled from the maws of many of the beasts, while others had long bony spines that erupted from their backs. One had hands instead of front paws, and Stefan wondered in disgust if it had once been a man.

Raising his pistol, he aimed it at the head of a charging beast, a massive wolf-like creature with a tail that curved over its back and ended in a huge poisoned tip. Pulling the trigger, he saw the creature's wide head explode in a satisfying spray of bone and blood. Holstering the ornate pistol, he drew his sword. More hounds raced over the ground, and launched themselves at the greatswords. Dozens of other hounds reached the line of the Ostermark army at the same time, intent on the kill.

With a shout, Stefan von Kessel raised his sword and shield in front of him, and leapt forwards to meet the beasts. His greatswords moved with him, shouting as they heaved their massive blades.

Stefan plunged his sword into the throat of the first creature, and it fell, blood gurgling from the wound. He smashed his shield into the face of another, before its head was cleaved from its body by the sweep of a greatsword. The warriors wielded their massive weapons with brute strength, cleaving and slaying with every powerful swing.

Cannon boomed again, along with the sporadic crackling fire of handguns as they were reloaded and fired. The last of the hounds were cut down by the greatswords, and Stefan saw that the beastmen were all but broken, countless bodies littering the hill. The last of them charged recklessly against the halberdiers to his right, running straight onto the sharpened points of the tall weapons. Those that were not slain instantly were impaled by more of the weapons as those behind drove their halberds forwards into the bodies of the beastmen.

The Norsemen advancing behind the beastmen were trudging over the bodies of those beastmen who had fallen, and they readied themselves for the charge, shouting out incoherent challenges and threats. They raised their weapons to the heavens, as if imploring their gods for strength, their voices harsh and ugly-sounding to Stefan. Horns blasted out across the battlefield, and drums pounded. Dozens of the warriors fell, black crossbow bolts in their throats or chests pierced by handgun shot.

'For Sigmar!' shouted Stefan. 'For Sigmar!' roared his army in response, and the two battle lines charged towards each other.

Stefan roared wordlessly as he ran, sword held high over his head. He blocked a descending axe with his shield and swung his sword down into the warrior's neck. Blood spurted and the blond-haired Norseman fell. The greatswords swung their massive weapons into the foe, using the momentum of the charge to make their blows even more powerful. One warrior raised a shield to deflect a strike, but his shield was hacked in two by the force of the blow and he went down, clutching the stump of his arm.

Stefan used his shield to batter another warrior off balance before plunging his sword into the warrior's gut. He deftly turned aside the thrust of another attacker, and his return blow cut a bloody trail across the warrior's face, smashing his helmet loose. A blow from a greatsword took him in the chest, cutting apart his chainmail and carving into bone and flesh. The weapon was embedded deep in the warrior, and as the greatsword struggled to pull it free an axe smashed into his face.

The screams of the dying cut across the clash of weapons and war cries. A tall warrior, his blond beard braided and decorated with black iron skulls and beads, bellowed as he struck at Stefan with a two-handed axe. He turned aside the blow with his shield, his arm jarring with the impact. He hacked his sword into the warrior's leg and he fell with a curse. Von Kessel kicked the downed warrior in the jaw, sending him sprawling backwards, and struck out at another Norseman.

Reiksmarshal Wolfgange Trenkenhoff surveyed the battlefield with a seasoned eye. The Ostermark infantry were engrossed in the melee, their ranks blurring with those of the Norse as they battled furiously.

With a shout, he ordered the handgunners and crossbowmen further out onto the flanks, as the bustling melee threatened to enfold them. Von Kessel's aides nodded, and the sharp notes of bugles rang out over the field. The sergeants of the regiments heard the sounds, and swung their troops away from the expanding battle line. The cannon fired again, aiming over the top of the fighting and into the ranks of the fully armoured Chaos warriors who were drawing near to the battle.

Out on the right-hand side of the battle line, von Kessel saw the disorganised rabble of flagellants hurl themselves into the fray, screaming and chanting. On the extreme right-hand flank he could see a small group of handgunners, smoke rising in front of them as they fired upon the horsemen who were drawing near. Many of the horse warriors were punched from their saddles, but they continued on. The reiksmarshal was not concerned. The engineer with his beloved volley gun, *Wrath of Sigmar*, was out on that flank. He had seen the devastation that could be wreaked on the enemy by those powerful weapons countless times, although he doubted that the Chaos horsemen knew the danger that they approached.

The fully armoured Chaos warriors were just entering the fray, and he could see the halberdiers lined against them begin to falter under their assault, their line beginning to buckle. That was where the danger was, he knew, and he shouted to his Reiklandguard. With another shout, he kicked his powerful destrier forwards. As one, the knights galloped down the hill, angled so that they could pass through the gap formed by the handgunners pulling back. The earth rumbled beneath them.

THE ENGINEER, MARKUS, chortled in triumph as he knocked another two horsemen from the saddle with a pair of quick shots. He lowered his repeating handgun, marvelling at its accuracy and distance. Only on the practice fields of Nuln had he used this weapon, and he had longed for the day when he could test it in earnest. He was not displeased. The clockwork cogs smoothly rotated the barrels of the gun into the firing position, and he was pleased that the sight of the handgun was perfectly adjusted. The horsemen were close now, however, and he gave the *Wrath of Sigmar* a final look over with his trained eye.

The horsemen, galloping hard and guiding their steeds skilfully with their knees, unleashed a volley of fire from their short, powerful bows. Markus heard the groans of pain as arrows struck the handgunners. He tutted in irritation as an arrow clanged off one of the barrels of the *Wrath of Sigmar*.

'Heathen barbarians,' he snarled, and ordered the crew of the war machine to rotate the weapon to face the horsemen. He grinned as the horsemen drew even nearer. An arrow pierced his flamboyant, feathered hat, knocking it to the ground.

'Fire!' he screeched, and all hell was unleashed. The three firing mallets struck, and three gouts of flame burst from the ends of the uppermost barrels. They boomed loudly, smoke spewing from the chambers. Working smoothly, one crewmember rotated the crank wheel, and the next three barrels swung into position.

Again, the three mallets struck, and three more gouts of flame accompanied the booming as they fired. The other crewmembers were hastily reloading the weapon even as the last shots were fired. Markus was grinning like a maniac.

The smoke began to clear, exposing the devastation that the weapon had wreaked. The field was strewn with horses and men, and their screams filled the air. Severed limbs and bloody torsos were scattered across the ground.

The handgunners drew long daggers and ran towards the fallen horsemen, stepping over the gory remains, and seeking out any survivors. They dispatched the living with cuts to the throat. Soon, the screams were silenced. Markus rubbed his hands with glee.

THE GROUND POUNDED beneath the hooves of the heavy warhorses as they charged across the field and into the fight from the flank. The knights lowered their lances as one as they closed on the foe. Many of the fully armoured Chaos warriors turned to face the charge, holding their shields up defensively. Picking out his target, Reiksmarshal Trenkenhoff aimed his lance tip at the warrior's chest. As the warrior raised his shield he altered his aim slightly, and the lance punched into his throat, driving through the plate gorget there. Impaled, the warrior was lifted from his feet and driven backwards, the lance tip bursting from the back of his neck. The reiksmarshal's well-trained and battle hardened steed lashed out with flailing hooves, crushing another, and he continued the charge deep into the enemy formation.

The Reiklandguard ploughed through the enemy, smashing them aside with their sheer bulk and momentum, lances embedded in the foe. They discarded their lances and drew their sabres, hacking down at the foe milling around them.

The reiksmarshal drew his own blade, a beautifully crafted and potent weapon. Runes ran up its perfect blade, and he could feel the power contained within those runes as he held it. It was one of the twelve Runefangs forged by the dwarfs for the leaders of the Empire, the weapon of Emperor Magnus himself. The Emperor had presented it to the reiksmarshal just before he had left Nuln and ridden north.

Striking down with the Runefang, he cut through a helmet as if it was paper, splitting the warrior's head from crown to jaw. The standard-bearer of the Reiklandguard was at his side, holding the embroidered flag high, even as he drove his sword down, cutting the arm from a warrior that reached for his reins. The knights drove deep into the enemy formation, hacking and slaying.

Stefan could see the banner of the Reiklandguard, and could feel the desperation of the Norscans building. With renewed vigour, he smashed the pommel of his sword into the face of an enemy, and then slashed his sword across his throat.

'For Sigmar!' he shouted again, and drove forwards into the enemy. The greatswords pushed forwards with him, hefting their deadly weapons, although they were already tiring. Still, the greatswords were the toughest and bravest of Stefan's troops, and they took strength from the sight of their captain fighting by their side, cleaving into the enemy fearlessly.

A Norse warrior at the back of the press of men, seeing the knights driving through the flank of the warriors in front of him, turned and fled. The warriors

on either side of him saw him run, and thinking that
they had not heard the order to pull back, turned to
run with him. Soon the Norsemen were streaming
from the battle in an unstoppable rout.

Stefan cut down a warrior as he turned to flee,
feeling the other Norse running behind him. The
greatswords leapt forwards and hacked down countless others as they ran. The only warriors who did
not flee were the fully armoured warriors, who
closed ranks and stood fighting defiantly, shoulder
to shoulder. They were soon surrounded on all sides
by halberdiers, knights and greatswords, but fought
on still, exacting a terrible toll on the warriors of
Ostermark. The captain saw several of the glorious
Reiklandguard fall, dragged from their saddles as
their horses were slain beneath them. The knights
were much more vulnerable now that they had lost
their forward momentum. The Chaos warriors were
cut down one by one, but each one that fell slew two
or more of the Empire troops. Finally, they were all
slain.

Stefan roared for his troops to regroup. Short horn
blasts sounded, and the Empire troops, flush with victory, moved back into formation. The cannon boomed
once again, firing at the enemy that was now several
hundred yards down the hill.

Responding instantly to the shouted commands of
Stefan and his sergeants, the battle line condensed its
ranks, and began to march to the beat of drums, down
the hill towards the besieged castle below. Two regiments of spearmen held back, and reorganised
themselves upon the hillside to guard the cannon that
continued to fire down into the maelstrom of battle

below. A pair of smaller detachments of handguns and crossbows arrayed themselves on the flanks of larger formations.

To the south, he could see the tattered mob of flagellants running at full speed down the hillside towards the castle. He could also see the figure of Markus moving towards the other cannon, his pride and glory, the *Wrath of Sigmar*, being dragged along the ridge by a pair of draught horses. He was glad that the engineer had survived the first stage of the battle.

'We have weathered the first attack, men!' roared Stefan as he marched. 'Now let's finish this!'

THE NAMELESS self-proclaimed prophet of the end times screamed incoherently as he ran towards the forces of Chaos. He blinked blood from his eyes, caused by the twin-tailed comet freshly carved into his forehead. His Reiklandguard breastplate was covered with parchment scraps nailed through the steel and into his flesh. Each of these was covered in his scrawling writing, descriptions of his visions of madness and death. Above his head he brandished a scythe, a weapon that he had found just days before at an abandoned, smoking farmstead. Sigmar himself had guided him to it, he knew, for it was a fitting weapon with which to cut down the enemies of the Empire.

'Sigmar is with us, my brethren!' he screamed as he and the other crazed flagellants raced towards the enemy running up the hill to meet them. 'Our time has come! Purge the evil from them, as we have purged the evil from ourselves!'

A flaming figure ran past him, screaming in joy as he burnt to death, swinging a long chain above his head.

'See the dedication of our martyr brother! Honour him with death and pain!' screamed the nameless prophet, and the flagellants screamed their praise. The flaming martyr was the first to hit the enemy lines, smashing his chain across the face of a Norscan, ripping his helmet from his head. Another man rammed a sword into the flagellant's guts, and the nameless prophet saw it rip out of the man's back, splashing blood. The burning man wrapped his arms around his assailant, thrashing and screaming, and the pair fell to the ground, both ablaze. They were trampled beneath the press of bodies as the Norscans and the flagellants smashed into each other.

The Norse were better armed and armoured, and were skilled warriors. Most of the flagellants wore little but tattered, bloody robes, and wielded only crude weapons. Most were no more than farmers driven to madness by the horrors of the war, and knew nothing of fighting skilled opponents. Nevertheless, the flagellants embraced death, and threw themselves at their enemy with crazed intensity, hacking and smashing at the Norscans without any regard for themselves. Their limbs were hacked from their bodies, but they fought on, madness lending them incredible strength and endurance. One flagellant, a scrawny, malnourished man of middling years had his legs hacked off by an axe; he fell to the sodden ground, but fought on, plunging his dagger up into the groin of his killer and dragging him to the ground. He stabbed the man in the chest over and over again, foam dribbling from his mouth.

The nameless prophet laid about him with his scythe, cutting down Norscans as he screamed of redemption and eternal fire. The scythe broke as a warrior raised his shield against it, but he cared not, and leapt upon the man to rend him with his hands. He thrust his thumbs deep into the man's eyes, and he fell screaming. Taking up the man's axe with his bloodied hands, he threw himself deeper into the thick of the fighting, hacking left and right.

'Salvation! Salvation has come to you heathens!' he screamed as he killed. 'Forsake your Dark Gods and give yourself to Sigmar!'

A spear was hurled through the air and struck the nameless prophet's chest, knocking him to the ground, although it did not pierce his breastplate. From the ground, he lashed out with the axe, cutting the legs from a man. The Norscan fell to the ground, roaring in pain, and the nameless prophet leapt onto his chest, holding him around the head.

'Darkness comes for you!' he screamed in the man's face as he rammed his head into the ground again and again. Leaping to his feet, blinking blood from his eyes, he screamed wordlessly and smashed the axe into the face of another Norscan.

Swords cut him, axes grazed his bones, and spears pierced his limbs, but he did not notice them. All he could feel was the warmth of Sigmar's anger within him, strengthening him. He killed and killed and killed, and when there were no more to kill, he led the bloodied rabble that remained of the flagellants in a crazed charge down the hill towards the bulk of the Norscan army.

CHAPTER FOURTEEN

THE TALL ELF stepped lightly onto the battlements, her ghostly white waist-length hair flowing around her in the breeze. Her skin was pale, almost translucent, and utterly flawless. She cast her icy gaze across the battlefield that raged below her.

The arrival of the Empire troops had been timely. She knew that they had been coming, but had feared that they may have arrived too late. They may yet be too late, she thought, but did not truly believe it.

'You should step down, Lady Aurelion. It is not safe,' said a soft voice at her side. She turned towards Carandrian, her personal bodyguard. He stood at her side, dutiful as always. He was a proud warrior, and wore a tall gleaming silver helm, as did all the Swordmasters of Hoeth.

'We are besieged, Carandrian. Of course it is not safe,' she said, and continued to survey the battlefield.

The Empire soldiers had swiftly reorganised themselves after their initial foray, and were on the move. They marched down towards the castle to engage the rear of the besiegers. Their wide battle line would overlap the enemy on the north side of the castle, she noted. That should draw the Norsemen away from the gatehouse, which was the only exit from the castle. The Empire knights had cantered along the hillside to the north, and were charging down from the headland onto the beachfront, slaughtering everything in their path.

The dull thud of cannon fire reached her, accompanied by puffs of smoke that obscured the Empire war machines from even her sharp sight. Crude, dirty machines, those cannon, barbarous and dangerous, and as deadly to those using them as to the enemy. She could not understand why anyone would wish to use the black powder favoured by the humans, for the risks were great. They have a different regard for life, she reminded herself. Their lives were so short that they did not see how valuable life was. Still, she thought, the life of a human was nothing to her. They were crude creatures, as likely to tend towards evil acts as good. She found it ironic that her forces were besieged by humans, and that humans had arrived to aid her.

The proud warriors of Ulthuan stood all along the battlements. Many had fallen, and Aurelion grieved for them, but many remained, defiant and honourable. They fired their gleaming white bows smoothly, mindful that they were short of arrows, and each carefully targeted shot slew one of the attackers. Even before the Empire forces had arrived over the brow of the hill, they had fought without fear, killing efficiently and ruthlessly with cold pride and nobility: true warriors of Ulthuan.

She glanced seawards, and saw the gleaming dragon ships cutting across the water. If the ships could land, the siege would be broken.

She stepped lightly down from her exposed position on the walls, and called across to Arandyal, the leader of the Silver Helm knights. Their steeds were standing still in the courtyard below, untethered – the steeds of Ulthuan needed no such crude methods to keep them from running away. The knights had joined the other warriors on the walls, lending their swords to aid the defence. Arandyal broke off from the combatants he faced, and ran lightly along the walls.

'My Lady Aurelion?' he called.

'Ready your Silver Helms, Arandyal. You must aid the humans to clear the beach.'

The elf signalled his understanding, and ran back into the melee. His men began to pull back along each side of the wall, fighting as they retreated towards the crumbling stone staircases at either end. The enemy swarmed over the unprotected wall.

Drawing power into herself, Aurelion began a softly sung incantation, the intricate and difficult words rolling off her tongue effortlessly, musical and beautiful. Raising her staff, she pointed it at the midpoint of the wall, where the enemy gathered in the greatest numbers. Searing flames burst at their feet, and they shouted in shock and pain. The flames took hold of the warriors, their cloaks, hair and flesh burning and melting. Screaming, the warriors stumbled blindly, falling from the walls and setting their comrades on fire. Aurelion extended the spell outwards, so that the flames ran left and right along the wall until the whole area blazed with roaring flames. With every second that passed, the flames roared hotter and higher. She could feel the heat on her face, flushing her icy pale cheeks red.

She turned back to look over the crenellations once again, and saw the warriors swarming below her. 'They come again,' she said as ladders were thrown against the wall. She stepped back, behind Carandrian. Many of the ladders were pushed backwards by the warriors on the walls, to fall amongst the tide of evil that swarmed at its base. Norsemen swarmed up the others, and the wall was suddenly the stage for vicious, close-quarters fighting once again.

Carandrian stepped forwards, moving like a dancer, and swept the head from the first attacker to leap over the crenellations with a sweep from his two-handed sword, the blade humming through the air. The warrior fell from the walls without a sound. Another fell to the blade of Carandrian as he plunged the weapon into its chest, the thin blade sliding through the ribs to pierce the warrior's heart.

Glancing down, Aurelion saw that Arandyal's warriors were nearly ready. Most were in the saddle, their long lances held aloft. She signalled to the eagle claw bolt throwers on the roof of the keep to direct their fire outside the gatehouse. They reacted instantly, swinging their war machines around lightly, and began to fire down into the masses. Each bolt fired was four feet in length, and the machines had a phenomenal rate of fire. Dozens of the bolts streaked down, skewering the warriors beyond the gatehouse.

'Have the Empire soldiers engaged fully?' she asked Carandrial. The tall warrior dispatched another foe, his blade first slicing across its stomach and then back across its throat in a smooth motion.

'They have, Lady Aurelion. Now would be a good time for Lord Arandyal to sally forth,' he said calmly, the point of his blade piercing another warrior's neck. With a deft movement, he ripped his victim's throat out.

The elf mage signalled to Arandyal, who raised a hand in recognition and, perhaps, farewell. The warriors atop the gatehouse increased their rate of fire, sending arrows streaking down into the foe, clearing the immediate area around the gates. With a groan, the portcullis was raised, and the heavy drawbridge was released. Chains rattled as the bridge was dropped, striking the earth with a heavy thud.

A note from a horn was blown, clear and high, and the Silver Helms galloped from the castle and onto the battlefield.

'Prince Khalanos, cousin,' said Aurelion quietly. 'Where are you?'

CHAPTER FIFTEEN

CAPTAIN STEFAN VON KESSEL slew another Norseman, and seeing that no other enemy was immediately before him, took a deep, shuddering breath. His hand was slick with blood, and his sword was beginning to slip in his grip. Wearily, he wiped a hand across his blood-smeared brow. He winced as pain flared up his side. He could feel the scrape of bone as ribs rubbed against each other. He knew that he had been lucky, but it didn't feel like it. He ordered his greatswords to the north, to aid Albrecht's halberdiers still battling there.

The attack towards the castle had gone well. Caught between his advancing army and the walls of the castle, the Norsemen and the last of the remaining beastmen had been cut down without qualm or mercy. The impact of the halberdiers and the greatswords had been great, and the enemy had buckled in front of them. Those at the back were being peppered by the arrows of the elf defenders. Occasionally, magical gouts of flame would roar forth from the white haired sorceress on the battlements. Charred corpses fell to the ground, but continued to burn, the flames seeming to grow hotter as the minutes passed. Stefan was wary and suspicious of magic generally, but he was glad that the sorceress was on his side.

The men around him were bloody and bone-tired, and all sported minor wounds. Many of their number had fallen, for the Norse were savage warriors, their skills honed by lives of constant warfare and battle. They were big bastards too, thought Stefan, generally standing a full head taller than the men of Ostermark. Despite this, his men had fought well, and at first had inflicted far more casualties on the foe than they had received themselves.

As the battle played out however, the greater numbers of the Norsemen began to take its toll. The Empire line had been pushed back at its wings. The only part of the battle line that had continued to make ground against the Norse was Stefan's greatswords. Even then, their forward momentum had gradually been halted, and they had fought desperately for some time not to be pushed back. For all that, Stefan was proud of his men, and none of them had fled in the face of the terrible enemy. Brave men, Ostermarkers, he reminded himself.

The enemy had been unable to move around the flanks of the Empire army, despite their greater numbers. The handguns and crossbowmen back on the hill had advanced, and their fire, together with that of the cannon, had kept the flanks clear.

Stefan prayed that the reiksmarshal was faring well, and that the attack towards the castle itself had drawn most of the Norsemen away from the beach. He had heard a clear, high note blown from a horn that was clearly not a human instrument, followed by the thunder of hooves, but that had been almost an hour ago.

A flood of Norsemen raced into view. He wondered if Albrecht had routed them, just as the Norse threw themselves at Stefan and his soldiers. They seemed desperate to break through the greatswords, and lashed around them wildly. Wearily, Stefan raised his sword and shield, feeling more tired than he could ever remember. You are getting old, soldier, he thought.

He blocked a strike with his shield and struck back, but his attack had little strength behind it and was easily knocked aside by the large Norseman.

'You are weak, little man,' said the warrior in broken Reikspiel, and stepped forwards to knock the captain aside. He stopped abruptly as an arrow took him in the neck. He stood for a moment, before tumbling forwards onto the ground. Suddenly, arrows filled the air, and the Norsemen looked around in confusion. A group of elf horsemen thundered by, firing their arrows with unerring accuracy into the Norse. The arrows dropped dozens of them, and Stefan shouted loudly, gathered his strength, and launched himself at the remainder. He cut down two of the warriors, plunging his sword into the chest of one, and the groin of another. Suddenly he was faced with men in purple and yellow.

'Albrecht!' called the captain. 'I'm glad to see that you have avoided Morr's touch.'

'Aye captain, I ain't ready for him to come for me yet.'

A deep roar echoed across the battlefield, louder than the sound of any cannon.

'What in Sigmar's name is that?' said Albrecht, and he shouted to his troops to about face, ready to confront whatever new threat was approaching from the direction of the beach. Leaving his greatswords to aid the other regiments of state troops to the south, Stefan moved alongside Albrecht, the halberdiers stepping aside to let them through. They could hear another sound – it sounded like the canvas sails of some massive ship flapping in a heavy wind. Air buffeted around Stefan and the halberdiers, who looked around uneasily. They were as exhausted as him, their faces pale and drawn, as they awaited this new horror.

The roar sounded again, much closer this time. Von Kessel could feel the sound reverberating within him.

'Sigmar save us,' breathed Albrecht as he saw what approached. Abject terror rippled through the halberdiers.

A massive shape closed on them, swooping down from the clouds and plunging hundreds of men into shadow. With a beat of leathery wings, the dragon roared towards them, flames blazing from its nostrils.

It was the colour of the sea, a faraway sea that was warm and filled with life, not the cold, black sea that lay off the coast where the fighting was taking place. It was a massive beast, almost as long as a ship from nose to tail, and its wings seemed to cover the sky. Great spines projected from its curling, flexible backbone, extending up its neck and forming a spiked mane behind its head. Its strong, sinuous limbs were powerful enough to rip a castle apart, and its jaws could crush stone. Its serpentine eyes blazed with an ancient, feral intelligence.

Though it seemed a futile gesture, Stefan drew and cocked the one pistol he had not yet fired, and levelled it at the monstrous creature diving towards them. Its mouth was wide, and its reptilian lips curled back, exposing countless massive teeth, each as large as a greatsword. It breathed in deeply, sucking up a huge amount of air. Any second now, Stefan expected a great gout of flame to engulf him, yet he stood, unafraid. He just hoped he could hurt the creature before he was slain, and he aimed at one of its baleful eyes.

Just as he was about to pull the trigger of his pistol, he relaxed his grip and pulled his arm back.

'What are you doing?' asked Albrecht through gritted teeth, but then he saw it too.

A figure, wearing ornate armour of glinting dark green, straddled the back of the blue-green dragon. The armour was shaped to mimic the dragon he rode upon, dark green wings extending from his artfully crafted helmet. In one hand he held a long lance that glowed with golden light and in the other he bore a shield that was unscathed by any mark or dent.

'It's an elf,' breathed Stefan. The dragon roared over-head, throwing dust and debris up in its wake. The men of the Empire turned, as one, to watch the mas-sive creature hurtle past. Great gouts of flame suddenly roared from the creature's mouth, roasting alive dozens of Norsemen, their weapons and armour melt-ing instantly under the heat. The dragon disappeared from sight for a moment, before soaring high into the sky once again, already hundreds of yards away. A pair of Norse warriors was clutched in the claws of the dragon, and as the stunned men of Ostermark watched, they were crushed in the powerful grip and dropped lifeless to the ground. Another figure hung, impaled halfway down the shaft of the dragon rider's glowing lance. With a dismissive movement, the Norscan chieftain was thrown to the ground.

A great cheer went up as the dragon wreaked havoc upon the remaining Norse, burning and rending. The battle was won.

CHAPTER SIXTEEN

WARLORD HROTH STOOD on the high rocky headland, staring out to sea, fingering his axe. The setting sun made the water look like a sea of blood. In the distance, he could see dozens of Norse longships ploughing through the sea towards the beach, mighty sails billowing in the strong winds. Hundreds of oars plunged into the water, drawing the ships forwards at an impressive rate through the rough sea.

Tall figureheads could be seen on the prow of each vessel, each unique to its ship. Some of them featured carefully crafted dragon heads, baring their fangs and curling tongues extending from their gaping maws. Others bore carved torsos and heads of daemonic entities, the gods worshipped by the Norse. Curving horns spread from the heads of many, and some had massive carved bat-like wings that spread behind them and onto the hulls of the ships. Hroth recognised many of them, although he was unfamiliar with their Norse names.

He was pleased to see that various visages of Khorne featured prominently on the prows of many of the longships of the flotilla. The Norse might call him different names, but it mattered not. Great Khorne cared not what name he was known by, only that skulls and blood were delivered to him in great abundance. One of the carvings showed him as a dog-faced bestial god of pure rage, the unmistakable symbol of Khorne engraved onto his forehead. Another showed him as a massively proportioned warrior, a sword and an axe crossed over his barrel chest, skulls hanging from his intricately carved armour.

The ships had strange mechanical apparatus built into their hulls that Hroth imagined must be machines of war and destruction. Massive spiked bolts protruded from the sides of some ships; others had rotating spiked drills that could just be seen below the surface of the water, while others had wheels with massive chains wrapped around them, which fed into the mouths of carved daemons. What these actually did was beyond him.

The longships were drawing near, fearlessly riding the massive waves that drove them towards the beach. Most of the ships had about thirty rowing benches, but there was one ship amongst the others that was truly immense, holding at least seventy – around three hundred Norsemen pulled hard on the massive oars of this giant of a ship as it powered towards the sand. This ship clearly belonged to the powerful warlord of this Norse tribe. It also bore the symbols of Khorne, the Lord of Skulls. The prow of the ship bore a bestial bronze face, and red flames smouldered in the vicious eyes of the beast. Hroth realised that the entire ship was made of beaten bronze, and he wondered how it stayed afloat.

Dozens of corpses were suspended on gibbets lining the sides of the ship. They were strung up and pierced with massive spikes that had been hammered into their bodies while they were still living. There was a slopping trough beneath the cadavers, running to the front of the ship, and feeding into the mouth of the bestial figurehead. When these unfortunates were first strung up, their blood would flow down the gore-troughs, to feed the creature.

Hroth could feel the power of the Blood God within this ship. He could feel the favour of Khorne upon the warlord that rode within it, even though he could not see the man; but the power emanating from the ship was more than just this: it came from the ship itself.

The massive, bronze face on the prow of the ship strained to one side, and its mouth opened and closed as it searched for enemies. Hroth knew that the essence of a daemon was bound within the very body of the ship. Powerful sorcery indeed was needed for such a feat, and his respect for the warlord grew. Clearly it was the power of this daemon that kept the bronze vessel afloat. Turning, he climbed down the rocky goat path to greet this warlord and his tribe.

Hroth's army was arrayed just beyond the sandy beach, and he smiled as he saw its size. On the march to the coast, he had encountered warbands that were roaming the countryside raiding and pillaging. He had slain the champions of several and taken their warbands for his own, and his banner hung with the heads of his most worthy opponents. Other, wiser champions had instantly sworn allegiance to him. Other warbands had sought him out, throwing their lot in with him, eager to gain his respect. The warriors of his initial warband, Olaf the Berserker, Barok the standard-bearer, Thorgar Skull-splitter, and the other surviving Khazags occupied a powerful position within the army. They had been at the fore of every battle, their armour stained red from the slaughter.

The sorcerer Sudobaal was waiting for him on the sand. With a claw-like hand, he motioned impatiently to Hroth.

'Come, we must meet with Ulkjar Headtaker of the Skaelings. Call forth my army. A show of my power is needed,' hissed Sudobaal.

The chosen of Khorne glared at the sorcerer. 'I shall call forth *my* army,' he growled. Sudobaal glanced at him sharply. The ever-present flames that rippled over the staff that was once again fused with his arm flared brightly, showing the sorcerer's anger.

'Call my army forth. Remember that it was *I* who made you, chosen. I can just as easily dispose of you.'

Hroth wanted to smash his axe into the sorcerer's skull. This was not the time, he told himself, as he felt his anger building. Cutting down the cur, as pleasing as that would be, would avail him little – the runt was the only one who could locate the resting place of Asavar Kul. His fiery eyes blazing, he swung away from the sorcerer and stalked across the sand to summon his army.

'Bring the warbands forwards,' he growled to the towering, bald-headed Khazag Barok. 'Let us show these pale-haired Norscans what real warriors look like.'

THE LONG OARS drove powerfully into the icy black water in perfect unison with each pounding beat of the giant brass drum. Each oar was held by four of Ulkjar's strongest Skaeling warriors, and his flagship vessel powered through the swell towards the beach.

Ulkjar Moerk the Headtaker, like most of his kind, was tall and blond, with piercing blue eyes, yet he stood a full head taller than the largest of his warriors. His armour was black and rimmed with bronze, and he bore the symbols of the Blood God on his shoulders so that none could doubt his allegiance. A twin pair of short, wide-bladed swords hung at his belt. They had been enchanted by the greatest of all the Norse shamans, and thousands had fallen beneath them, their blood let in sacrifice to the Blood God.

His ship closed on the beach, but the beating of the drum did not relent, instead picking up pace as the breakers began to buffet the vessel. With a surge of energy, the Skaelings heaved at their heavy oars, and the daemon-infused ship hurtled towards the sand. It was lifted by the huge swell, and with a surge was driven down into the trough of the wave. White foam washed over the rear of the ship as it neared the beach. At the last second, the beating of the drum stopped, and the Norsemen lifted their oars high into the air as the ship hit the sand. The power and momentum of the ship drove it high onto the beach, cutting a furrow through the black sand. It ground to a halt, and Ulkjar leapt over the railing, landing lightly fifteen feet below.

Ulkjar walked around to the front of the ship, and looked up at the daemonic bronze face. Its metal neck strained, rippling with muscles as the daemon within tried to tear itself loose of its prison. Its face was over twenty feet from one side to the other, and it bared its teeth at him, a low growl echoing hollowly from deep within. It was large enough for a man to stand inside its maw without being able to reach the roof of the mouth. It was capable of ripping apart the hulls of enemy ships, and the creature's smoking red eyes regarded Ulkjar with hatred.

'Thank you for the safe crossing once again, Dweaor-jner,' said Ulkjar, meeting the gaze of the angry daemon and speaking its true name. The creature, compelled by the power of its master, lowered its gaze in submission.

Ulkjar pulled off one of his brass gauntlets, stepped close to the metallic daemonic face, and ran his hand across a jagged metal tooth. Gripping his hand into a fist, he held it inside the massive bestial maw of the daemon, allowing his blood to drip onto the bronze tongue. He removed his hand, and licked the residue of blood from it. The wound had already closed.

The other Skaeling longships had beached, and their crews were pulling them higher up on the sand. Ulkjar gestured to his two younger brothers, and they fell in behind him as he marched across the sand towards the pair of figures waiting for him.

An army was arrayed behind them, drawn from dozens of tribes. It was a large force, over five thousand strong, he guessed. He cared not. An army was only as strong as its warlord, and although his Skaelings were only two thousand in number, he was the strongest

Skaeling warlord that had ever lived, and would not be cowed by any man, even one who boasted a force as large as this. Only one man had ever truly impressed Ulkjar, and he had been slain the previous year. One such as Asavar Kul was rare.

The pair stood motionless, awaiting his arrival. One was stooped and cloaked in black. A twisted staff was fused to his right arm, and his skin was an unhealthy shade of grey. His features were pinched, and deep lines furrowed his face, but there was power in this one. His eyes were unblinking and yellow, cold as a serpent's. Sigils and runes of power were carved into his leathery cheeks. A sorcerer, thought the Skaeling dismissively. He had no time for such.

His gaze moved to the other man, sizing him up. Now this was a true warrior, he knew. He was shorter than Ulkjar, but was, nevertheless, a big man with massive, powerful shoulders: a warrior born. He wore blood-red armour, and a helmet topped with curving horns. His eyes were no normal eyes – flames flickered in his orbs, smouldering dangerously. Ulkjar could feel the favour of the Blood God on this man, and he knew that this warrior was one of the chosen, just as Ulkjar was.

'My shamans heard your call,' said the Norscan bluntly to the sorcerer. 'The omens showed that Kharloth, the Blood God, wished that I answer it.'

'Indeed he does, Ulkjar Moerk, Headtaker of the Skaelings,' hissed Sudobaal. 'My name is Sudobaal.'

'I know what your name is. And you,' he said, turning towards the chosen of the Blood God. 'You are Hroth the Blooded. I heard of your defeat of Zar Slaaeth. I had wanted to kill that one myself, but it matters not. Word of your growing power precedes you.'

The armour-clad chosen of the Blood God folded his arms across his massive chest.

'And I know of you, Ulkjar. You led the Norse in the attack against Praag. It is said that you clashed swords with Asavar Kul himself, and that he spared your life. Is that true?'

'It is the truth, chosen. I am not ashamed to have been bested by him,' said Ulkjar. 'None other has ever faced me and survived. None ever will.' The two chosen of Khorne regarded each other dangerously.

'It is good that you have come. The gods will it,' said Sudobaal. 'They have shown me a powerful vision, Ulkjar. The pitiful Empire believes they have won, that their lands are safe, now that Asavar Kul has fallen. They are mistaken.'

'They are never safe,' barked Ulkjar. 'They know this, and choose to live lives of fear and weakness. They know that their lands will always be raided and under the sword, for as long as Norscans plough the seas.'

'There is truth in what you say, Ulkjar, but you miss my point. The Empire believes that they have time to lick their wounds. I can make sure that they do not have this time. Aid us, and together we will gain the power to crush the Empire utterly, to finish what was begun by Asavar Kul.'

'Kul was the Everchosen. None doubt this. All the followers of the true gods swore themselves to him – Kurgan, Norscan and Hung. With his fall, the tribes of the Norse were fractured. Now we battle each other to assert dominance. There is none who can claim it. No Norscan can stand against me, but even I cannot unite the Norscans. It is the same for the Kurgan, no?'

'This is true.'

'Many powerful warlords, but none who stands above them all. You,' said the Norscan, nodding his head towards Hroth, 'I have heard of. But neither you, nor I, can unite the scattered tribes. We would need to spend our lives slaying champions to prove our worth. There will always be those who think they can overcome us. The battles would never end.

'Asavar Kul came to Norsca. None challenged him but me. All knew his power, and none would contend it. Such a warrior comes but once every ten generations.'

'This is true,' said Sudobaal slyly, 'but I know where his sword is.'

The Norscan snorted.

'It is lost. Any who bore that blade and overcame the daemon bound within it would be truly favoured by the gods. None among the Norscans would dare to challenge such a one. But it is lost.'

'And few amongst the Kurgan or the Hung would contend with the one who wields it, either,' said Sudobaal. 'It is lost no more – I have been shown where it resides.'

Ulkjar frowned. If the sorcerer spoke the truth, then he had much to gain. If he held the sword, none could stand against him.

'My shamans, powerful as they are, cannot see it. How is it that you claim to know of its whereabouts when my shamans do not?'

'Enough of this,' growled Hroth, staring up at the taller warrior. 'Too much talk. We have need of your ships, Norscan.' Ulkjar regarded him coldly.

'Your name is spoken of in all of Norsca, chosen,' said the Skaeling, 'but so too is mine. Your power is rising like the dawning sun, but mine is at its peak – it is the sun high in the sky, bright and strong. You cannot match me.' Hroth growled and gripped his axe tightly.

'You know I speak the truth. The Blood God has seen power and greatness in us both – but do not demand anything of me, whelp. I am your better.'

As the Norscan spoke, the flames in Hroth's eyes blazed brightly. Uncaring, Ulkjar raised himself up to his full height. He knew that the eyes of the Blood God were upon the two champions, and that he looked down upon this battle of will with interest. Ulkjar also knew that the eyes of all his Skaelings and the warriors of Hroth watched the pair. He had led his tribe for two decades – he knew well the power that a great leader could inspire in his men, but also that it was a fickle thing if one did not work at it constantly.

Ulkjar was careful whenever he was under the scrutiny of his followers – always he was conscious to give off the aura of power, and of being the one in control. If he was not, then he knew he would constantly have to watch his back, and fight the inevitable challenges to his position from amongst his own tribe. He would have none of that. No, he would exert his dominance over this warrior before him, in front of both their tribes. If he could provoke Hroth, draw him into a conflict and defeat him, then those tribes must submit themselves to him.

'I will take your head, Norscan filth,' growled Hroth.

'Will you indeed, whelp?' answered Ulkjar. He was comfortable and relaxed. How many times had this same encounter played out in the past? He had long since lost count of the enemy champions he had slain. This would be no different. The chosen was powerful, true, but that would just make this victory that much sweeter. He would claim the chosen's army once he was done with him, and force the sorcerer to take him to where the sword of Asavar Kul resided. Then, none could stand against him. The days of blood would begin once again. Truly he was blessed in the eyes of the gods, he thought.

'I will cut you limb from limb, Kurgan,' said Ulkjar. 'I will feed your blood to the daemon within my ship. I will take your army from you. A new era of blood-shed and terror will begin, and you will not be a part of it,' he said matter of factly, and drew his pair of swords.

'Less talk. Let your blades speak for you.'

'As you wish, whelp.'

Sudobaal smiled as the two warriors readied themselves for battle. He cared not who won this contest, and he had known that it was going to happen as soon as he had made the decision to contact Ulkjar's shamans in his dream-journeys. He had never had any doubt that Ulkjar would challenge Hroth. He was too proud and too successful a warlord to willingly submit to anyone, let alone a Kurgan. He would not care if Hroth was cut down. Ulkjar was strong-willed, but Sudobaal knew that he would be easier to manipulate than the Khazag chosen. Hroth was just too damn stubborn. He had no doubt that the Norscan was more subtle and devious than Hroth – certainly he knew how to impress his followers. Hroth's stubbornness was also his strength, however. The chosen of the Khazags did not know how to back down to anything, and he was completely single-minded in his determination. His lack of subtlety, his straightforward directness, was a powerful thing.

It was probably for the best, thought Sudobaal, that he would be slain. He wondered if he had misjudged Hroth – would he have become too difficult to handle, had his power continued to grow? Certainly Sudobaal had already found it increasingly difficult to influence the champion of Khorne. The sorcerer pushed the thought from his mind, and focused back on the contest.

Sudobaal remembered some wise old warlord saying that a battle between sword and axe was a contest that could never last long. As the warriors began to trade blows, he knew that this would hold true today.

Ulkjar was faster than Hroth, and had a longer reach. Hroth was shorter, but more powerful than the Skaeling. Where the Norseman fought with a slow-burning, cold fury, Hroth's anger was hot and fiery, and his fighting style reflected this. Every blow was filled with the power of his anger. Each of his attacks was intended to end the fight. Ulkjar moved with fluid grace, like a mountain lion. He blocked the lethal attacks of his foe and lashed out with lightning-fast counter-attacks, each cutting deeply. He intended to cut his enemy down piece by piece, wearing him down slowly until he could make the killing blow.

A vision flashed into Sudobaal's mind, and he dropped to his knees clutching at his temples. The two warriors battled on, ignoring him. Searing pain stabbed at him as the vision unfolded. He saw a battlefield littered with corpses. He saw the walls of a mighty city of the Empire falling. He saw a laughing daemon picking the eyes from a corpse. He saw Ulkjar and Hroth, fighting back to back. A dark robed figure was there. Himself. There was a glowing figure that hurt Sudobaal's eyes to gaze upon, a burning hammer held in its hands. Fire surrounded the hammer as he wielded it, and twin tails of flame followed in its wake. A black arrow came streaking through the press of battle, heading straight towards the vision of himself. Sudobaal screamed a warning, but his double could not hear him. He was about to witness himself being slain. He screamed again, but there was no reaction, no sound. As the arrow homed in on its target, scant feet from striking him in the back of the head, the vision of Ulkjar stepped forwards, inadvertently stepping into the path of the missile.

Sudobaal snapped out of the vision. Blood was dripping from his nose and his ears. He knew what the vision had shown him. Whatever occurred here, Ulkjar must live, or else, he himself would die.

Ulkjar plunged one of his blades into Hroth's side, the sword punching through armour and flesh. Seeing an opening, he thrust his other sword at the exposed throat of the Khazag. Realising his error a fraction later, he tried to reverse the thrust and step back, but it was too late. Hroth was already dropping to one knee as the Norscan surged forwards, swinging his axe around horizontally in a vicious arc. His other sword was stuck in the Khazag's side, so he could not defend against the blow, and Ulkjar knew that Hroth had taken that injury deliberately.

The axe smashed into Ulkjar's belly as he moved forwards, and the force of the blow was enough to cleave a horse in two. Ulkjar felt the axe blade cut through his belly, passing through his armour and flesh before hitting his spine. To Hroth it was like hitting stone, and the axe jarred in his hands, unable to hack through the iron-like bone. Still, the Norscan sank to the sand, awash with blood.

The two thousand Norse stood motionless. On the other side of the beach, thousands of voices erupted, chanting Hroth's name over and over again. All of them knew of Ulkjar, and to see him humbled by their champion was a sign of the god's favour.

Hroth, his eyes flaming, stepped forwards to finish the Norscan. Already, Ulkjar was pushing himself to his feet, his wounds closing. He stood tall, although he carried no weapons, and regarded the victor coldly.

'Truly you are the chosen of the Blood God,' he said, his head held high, waiting for the blow that would end his life.

Sudobaal staggered forwards, stepping in between the two warriors. Hroth's eyes blazed.

'Step out of my path, sorcerer. His skull belongs to me,' growled the chosen of Khorne.

'His skull belongs to the gods of Chaos, and the gods of Chaos demand that he lives; for now,' said Sudobaal, wiping the blood from his nose. 'He has a role to play yet.'

'What is this madness?' barked Ulkjar. 'You bested me, Hroth the Blooded. Finish it now. Give me that honour.'

'Do not do it, Khazag. It would anger the gods,' snarled Sudobaal, 'and it would anger me.'

Hroth battled with himself. He wanted to smash the sorcerer aside and claim the Norscan's skull. It was his right.

He swung away from Sudobaal and the Norscan, and he heard Ulkjar curse him. Rage boiling within him, he stalked towards the two brothers of Ulkjar who were standing nearby, their faces pale. Seeing the fury within the chosen of Khorne, they made to draw their swords, but they were too slow. In a moment, they were both dead, their bodies falling to the ground, pumping blood across the sand.

Hroth continued forwards, stalking across the sand towards the two thousand stunned Norsemen. Breathing heavily, Hroth glowered at them.

'You men, Skaelings of Ulkjar,' he roared. 'You are my men now. You live or die as I wish it.'

'You!' he shouted, pointing out one particularly large, bearded Skaeling. 'Pick out one man from every ship, and bring them to me.' The man hurried to his task. Within minutes, there was a line of almost fifty men standing before Hroth. None of them would meet his gaze. He stood before the first man in the line.

'Kneel,' he snarled. The man dropped to his knees before Hroth. Without ceremony, and using all his immense strength, he smashed his axe down onto the man's neck. The man's head rolled across the sand, spraying blood. Hroth stepped before the next man. 'Kneel,' he snarled. Leaving the man kneeling before him, Hroth strode back to Ulkjar and stood glaring up at him.

'Ulkjar Headtaker, you are a dead man. Your skull belongs to me, and I will claim it,' Hroth snarled. He stepped forwards, biting his thumb between his sharp teeth. He pressed the bloody thumb hard into the taller man's forehead, making the flesh hiss. The

Norscan did not flinch. Removing his hand, Hroth held Ulkjar's gaze. 'You are marked. Your skull *will* be mine.'

Hroth swung to glare hatefully at Sudobaal. The sorcerer returned the stare, saying nothing. Without another word, Hroth stalked back towards the kneeling Skaeling warrior and hacked his head from his body. Hroth lifted the head by its hair, threw it alongside the first, and moved to the next man in line. 'Kneel,' he snarled.

Two hours later, the Norse ships were being pushed back into the icy black sea, and the pale moon of Mannslieb rose high in the sky above. Hroth stood on the deck of the largest ship, his arms folded across his chest. Sudobaal and Ulkjar stood at his side. Most of the army had been left behind, all bar Hroth's Khazags and Ulkjar's Norse, waiting for their return.

Hroth watched the land slip into the darkness, his eyes locked on the flames blazing high on the sand. Fifty skulls were piled in the centre of the massive pyre, and the flames were mirrored in the flames in his eyes.

CHAPTER SEVENTEEN

STEFAN VON KESSEL stood before the small mirror in his tent, a bowl of warm water placed on the table in front of him. He was stripped to the waist, and he looked at the wound on his side. The chirurgeons had stitched it as best they could, but blood seeped from the wound. It mattered not, he thought. Countless other scars were etched on his chest and stomach. He bore no scars on his back, he noted, with a certain amount of pride.

Dipping his blade into the warm water, von Kessel continued to shave his face. The scars he bore on his face made shaving difficult and time-consuming. The scars were ugly, three thick lines that crossed his face linked together with an arc running from above one eye across his forehead and down the side of his face, ending on his chin. Albrecht had once asked him why he shaved at all. A beard would cover up much of the scarring, he had remarked. Von Kessel had answered that he had nothing to hide. He wondered if that was really true.

Every time he looked in a mirror, he was reminded of his grandfather's shame. He would carry this shame to his deathbed, he knew, but at least he was alive. He wondered if the same could be said for his father. His mother had died giving birth to Stefan, but his father had lived on. When the treachery of Stefan's grandfather had been discovered, his father had been cast out of Ostermark. His face had been burnt, and the witch hunters had put out his eyes. They had given him thirty days to leave the Empire altogether. If he was discovered within its borders after that time, he would be slain as a traitor.

Stefan had no brothers or sisters. He was the last in his family line. *The merciful elector*, Gruber had been called by the people of Ostermark once he had been chosen to take up the position. It was his mercy that had spared the life of Stefan and his father. He had argued passionately for their lives with the witch hunter, who had wished to burn all the bloodline of the treacherous previous elector. It had been part of Gruber's duty to care for the young Stefan, and raise him within his own household. Every couple of years, the witch hunter would check in on Stefan, examining his body for signs of the taint, and speaking to him endlessly, assessing his state of mind. It was only through von Kessel's faith in Sigmar that he had been spared.

Pushing such thoughts from his mind, Stefan finished shaving and dried his face. Dressing quickly, he buckled on his armour, doused the lantern and left his tent. It was dark, and the camp was lit with countless burning torches. Moving through the camp, he walked purposefully to the tent of the reiksmarshal, Wolfgange Trenkenhoff. A pair of the legendary Reiklandguard knights, standing guard, nodded at him as he approached. He waited outside the tent until the reiksmarshal emerged, and saluted his superior.

'Let us meet with these elves, then,' the reiksmarshal said, and they began the walk through the camp towards the crumbling castle perched on the hill.

'These are important allies of the Empire, remember,' continued the reiksmarshal. 'They are haughty and arrogant and proud, but always remember that they are important allies. As you know, we would have been overrun and destroyed had they not aided us in the Great War.

'You are blunt and straightforward, von Kessel,' said the reiksmarshal, and Stefan felt his face burn. He felt like he was back in his classes. 'I value these qualities in you; but you are also quick to anger, and speak your mind, often without thought. You will not do so today. The elves are not human; they have a different set of values than our own. They are easily offended, and we cannot afford to alienate them here today.

'Watch what you do, and for Sigmar's sake think about what you say before you say it,' said the reiksmarshal as they neared the gatehouse. 'Actually, don't say anything much at all, captain.'

A pair of elves stood by the entrance to the gatehouse. The castle was lit up, but not with the orange light of torches. Delicate lanterns hung beside the gate, and cold blue light emanated from within them, although Stefan could see no flame. The drawbridge was lowered, and the portcullis raised. Stefan stared at the elves, having never seen one of them up close before.

They were tall and slender, taller than he was, but far lighter and more delicate. They looked as if their bones would shatter under a heavy blow, he thought. Their limbs were long and elegant, and their faces were slender, with high cheekbones. Their eyes were almond-shaped and sharp. They wore long scaled armour that hung almost to the ground, and elongated silver helmets covered their heads. Tall shields emblazoned with green dragon heads rising from turbulent water were strapped over their left arms, and in their right hands they held long white-hafted spears. The shield tips were teardrop-shaped. All the metal that they wore and carried was a strange white-silver, unlike any metal that he had ever seen before. The elves glared coldly at the approaching humans, but let them pass without a word.

Von Kessel and the reiksmarshal passed through the gatehouse, under the murder holes and hanging portcullis, marching purposefully towards the courtyard, which was also lit with cold blue light. The reiksmarshal and Stefan froze mid-stride as they came out of the gloom of the gatehouse.

The great dragon they had witnessed that afternoon filled the space in front of them. It was sitting like a cat, its rear legs folded beneath it and its front legs straight. Its massive tail, easily thirty feet long, curled around its legs. The thin tapering tip of the tail flicked back and forth angrily. Its wings were folded on its back, and its head was held high and proud, almost as high as the gatehouse itself. It glared down at the two humans maliciously, its eyes narrow, a deep hiss slipping from its serpentine throat. It tensed its claws, ripping up the massive flagstones of the courtyard.

Two figures moved into view. One was the female sorceress that Stefan had spied upon the battlements earlier that day. The other was the tall dragon rider, still dressed in his battle gear. They walked across the courtyard, moving gracefully, like dancers. The woman said something to the man, who did not respond. She spoke again, more sharply, and he replied softly.

She walked towards Stefan and the reiksmarshal, while the man turned and spoke in a sing-song voice to the dragon. It was still glaring balefully at the two humans, smoke rising from its nostrils and a dull rumble emanating from deep within its chest, like the growl of a hundred angry dogs.

The dragon rider spoke a word sharply, and the dragon turned its gaze to him. It blinked its eyes and growled, before unfurling its giant wings and springing high into the air. Beating its wings powerfully, sending leaves and wind swirling around the courtyard, it flew off into the night.

'Greetings, men of the Empire,' said the female elf in perfect Reikspiel. Her voice was clear and crisp, and she enunciated her words carefully. She was beautiful, in a ghostly, haunting way. Her eyes were the softest violet, and her skin was flawless white, almost translucent in its perfection.

'Greetings, my lady,' spoke the reiksmarshal, bowing low to her. Stefan too bowed, somewhat stiffly.

'I am named Aurelion. This is my cousin,' she said, motioning towards the tall dragon rider who was now at her side, 'the prince Khalanos.'

'I am Wolfgange Trenkenhoff, reiksmarshal and commander of the armies of the Empire, my lady. This is Captain Stefan von Kessel.' The lady Aurelion nodded her head gracefully to the two men of the Empire. The tall prince stood impassively, no emotion or recognition of the two men showing on his cold face, his eyes steely grey.

There was an awkward silence, and Stefan felt incredibly uncomfortable. The steely-eyed dragon rider, Prince Khalanos, regarded first him and then the reiksmarshal. Von Kessel did not know whether he should hold eye contact with the elf. He didn't know whether that was considered rudeness, or if it was a sign of weakness if he did not. He glanced at Aurelion, found her coolly regarding him, and flicked his gaze back to the icy prince. He decided that he would rather be seen as rude than as weak, and held the prince's gaze.

'It was a pleasure to fight our mutual enemy on the field of battle with you, once again, Prince Khalanos,' said the reiksmarshal, breaking the silence. Stefan was grateful that the prince switched his gaze to the reiksmarshal. 'As always, your skill and bravery do your people proud.' The prince did not respond, but bowed his head in acknowledgement.

'And we thank you, reiksmarshal and captain, for your efforts this day. Without your arrival, many more elves would have lost their lives and would be making their journeys to the realms beyond this one.'

'It is our pleasure and duty to have lent our aid, my lady Aurelion, although I am sorry that we did not arrive sooner, so as to have saved any elves from losing their lives on Empire soil. I extend my deepest sympathies and condolences to those that have survived, and my utmost respect and gratitude to those who passed from life today.'

'Your lands are in ruin, it would seem,' said Aurelion. 'The war may have been won, but your people suffer.'

'They do indeed,' said the reiksmarshal. 'It is a hard time for us. Warbands of Chaos roam our lands slaughtering and burning. Plague spreads amongst our populace. Many are starving. We are most grateful for your aid in combating this evil today.'

'There is more evil to come before your land can begin to heal,' said Aurelion. 'A time of great darkness draws near. The enemies of the Empire are many and powerful, and your land lies defenceless.'

'Not defenceless, my lady. Even now, our armies scour the forests, rooting out the Chaos worshippers that have hidden themselves there. The warbands are many, but they are scattered and disordered. They are self-destructive, and have fallen into their usual habits, now that their leader has been slain. They battle each other, slaughtering their own kind as much as they fight us.'

'One has risen who could unite the scattered warbands. He has gathered almost nine thousand warriors to him and they are not in the far north – they are within the borders of the Empire as we speak.'

'Nine thousand? Gathered in one place? Surely that is not possible.'

'Nevertheless, it is true, I fear. A time of darkness grows near.'

'Tell me where you have seen this army, my lady, and we shall raise our armies to fight it. Tell us where this warlord is hidden.'

'He has taken to the seas. He seeks an ancient power: a power that he cannot be allowed to find.'

'He has left the Empire?' asked Stefan, the first words he had spoken since meeting the elves. The mage Aurelion turned her slanted, violet eyes towards him.

'He has, captain.'

'Then surely this is a good day for our lands, lady?'

Aurelion stared coldly at the captain. 'No, it is not a good day. If the enemy is allowed to retrieve what it seeks, then the truly dark days will return, for your Empire and for all enemies of Chaos.'

'What is it that they seek?' asked the reiksmarshal, throwing a sharp glance towards the captain.

'Something that would grant them much power. Something that they cannot be allowed to possess.'

'What would come to pass if they manage to retrieve this thing?

'Darkness, fire and death. I cannot stress enough the importance of this in the... the language of your people.'

'If that is so, my lady Aurelion, then we must stop them. We of the Empire have always trusted the council of the elves of Ulthuan. We will trust it now."

'Indeed it would be unwise for you to ignore my warning.'

'Do you know where the forces of Chaos seek this source of darkness?'

'I do.'

'And what, do you propose, is the best way for us to combat this foe? The Empire port of Marienburg is some days' travel. It will take nigh-on a week for a message to reach it, and for ships to be sent. We will have lost the scent of our quarry by then.'

The mage Aurelion turned towards her companion, the dragon rider Khalanos, and nodded almost imperceptibly to him. The muscles in his jaw twitched, and his eyes narrowed.

'It has been many years since I had need to converse in your crude tongue,' the prince said curtly. 'I shall speak but briefly. More of the ships of my fleet will arrive in the night – I sent them to engage the cursed Norse. Already I have lost many elves to them. They will be mourned in Ulthuan. At the height of noon tomorrow, my ships will leave this shore to seek our foe. There will be room for two thousand of your men below decks. There is room enough too for your horses, reiksmarshal, for I lost many silver helms this day. Two thousand more men can ride on the decks of my ships if they have no fear of the seas.'

'You are most gracious, Prince Khalanos, to allow us aboard the vessels of fair Ulthuan,' said the reiksmarshal. Prince Khalanos merely nodded.

'You will bring none of your foul black powder cannon aboard the ships of Ulthuan,' said the prince. 'Dwarf inventions have no place on elf ships.'

'Truly, I am loath for my soldiers to leave the soil of the Empire when it is at its most vulnerable, but if that is what must happen, then so it must be.'

'You are wise for one of your kind, Reiksmarshal Wolfgange Trenkenhoff,' said Aurelion.

'However, I am the supreme commander of the armies of the Empire. I cannot leave the Empire without the consent of the Emperor Magnus. I will not lead the Empire forces that accompany you, Prince Khalanos. Captain von Kessel will lead in my stead.'

'As you wish it,' said Aurelion. Stefan felt the cold eyes of Prince Khalanos regarding him. 'Neither shall I be joining the pursuit,' continued Aurelion. 'I am to travel to the city of Altdorf and join with Lord Teclis. I am to aid him in his teaching your people of the ways of magic.'

Stefan cleared his throat, and everyone turned towards him. 'Is it wise, my lord, for our soldiers to be leaving the borders of the Empire at this time?' he asked. The reiksmarshal regarded him impassively, but anger flashed in his eyes.

'Long have we trusted the council of the elves, captain,' said the reiksmarshal diplomatically. 'You are right to be concerned for your Empire, as ever, but this is the course of action that we must take. I will send a messenger to the Emperor Magnus this night, informing him of this new development. Now, my lord and lady, we shall bid you goodnight, and leave to ready our troops.'

'Why do you bear those scars upon your face, human?' It was Prince Khalanos who spoke, and silence greeted his question. Stefan's face darkened. The reiksmarshal looked at him, frowning.

'It... I received them as a babe. My face was burnt,' he said finally.

'Burnt?' asked Khalanos coldly. 'An accident?'

'No,' said the captain. 'I... my grandfather brought shame upon my family. He was burnt at the stake for his crimes. It is this shame that I bear.'

The elf dragon prince frowned. 'You are a barbaric race,' said the elf, his mouth curled in distaste.

'Burnt at the stake... Is that not the manner of death within the Empire for those who consort with the powers of darkness?' asked Aurelion.

'It is, my lady,' said the reiksmarshal quickly, 'but von Kessel is utterly dedicated to the Empire and our cause, and a fervent follower of Sigmar, I assure you.' The reiksmarshal's words were dismissed with a slight shake of the head from the mage.

'No, I doubt that not,' she said, a slight frown creasing her delicate mouth. She regarded Stefan evenly, her eyes unblinking. He found himself unable to tear his eyes away from her gaze, both beautiful and uncomfortable. 'There is no taint in you, captain, nor is there any in your family.' With that, she turned on her heel and left, the stunned human trying to understand what her words meant. The dragon prince nodded to the reiks-marshal and left the two humans standing alone.

The older man slapped the captain on the shoulder with a heavy hand. 'Come,' he said, 'this is not the time to dwell on the words of an elf seer.' Von Kessel nod-ded dumbly, and the pair walked from the castle to rejoin their army.

'THEY ARE A barbaric race,' the dragon prince Khalanos repeated, this time in the elegant language of his race.

'They have a certain... vitality about them,' said Aurelion.

'It is their short lives. Why did you tell the human that he had no taint in him?'

'He feared that he harboured the seed of Chaos within him, yet he does not.'

'But why tell him? What does it matter to us?' asked Khalanos. The elf mage shrugged her shoulders.

'He has a right to know,' she said. 'Will you be able to stop the enemy from discovering the body of the Chaos warlord?'

'We will stop them or we will not,' said Khalanos simply. 'The human warriors will help, but will it be enough? I know not. The humans must not learn that it was the duty of the elves to protect the body of the Chaos warlord, no matter what happens. None must learn that our wards have failed.'

Aurelion's eyes met with those of the dragon prince. She understood his words, and they saddened her. If word escaped that their wards had failed, then it may be discovered that the wards set on blessed Ulthuan itself were close to faltering. They needed Teclis to return to Ulthuan, but he was determined to aid the humans. She would travel to the Empire city of Altdorf and help him set up the colleges of magic. She would work hard so that Teclis could return home all the sooner.

'I will retire now, cousin. I will leave on the morrow to join with Lord Teclis. May your sleep be peaceful,' Aurelion said, and standing on her toes she kissed him lightly on the cheek. She left the dragon prince alone. His face was cold and impassive, proud and noble. He had seen the passing of over eight hundred years, and here he was helping fight in the wars of barbarous humans. He had argued against aiding the humans. 'Leave them to their own fate,' he had said. 'Their fate is our own,' had been the reply. He hoped that was not so, for he could not see the humans of the Empire surviving many more generations before being overwhelmed. They would be gone in the blink of an eye – a decade, a century, or three centuries perhaps, and then they would be gone. They would be forgotten by history.

Still, never would he let it be said that one of the noble-born princes of Caledor would shirk his duty. The Phoenix King himself decreed that the elves would aid the humans, and Khalanos would fight with all the strength and power that he possessed to do so.

Raising his head to the dark heavens above, he gave a shrill, reverberating whistle that carried far into the air. Within minutes, he could make out a serpentine shape descending through the darkness. He would ride the skies this night.

THERE WAS A messenger waiting for the reiksmarshal when he and Stefan returned to the Empire camp. Receiving these dispatches, the pair of men retired to the reiksmarshal's tent. Stefan stood uneasily while the knight ripped open the wax-sealed parchments and spread them out on the table before him. Minutes passed as the reiksmarshal read the dispatches, turning the pages of the parchments impatiently. He swore softly.

'What is it, sir?' asked von Kessel, feeling uneasy. The reiksmarshal passed a page of parchment to him wordlessly. Stefan read over the document slowly. Reaching the end, he scanned over it again. He looked up, his face flushed red.

'The cowardly dog,' he muttered.

'The Grand Count Gruber has retreated,' said the reiksmarshal angrily. 'He has pulled his army away from the Middle Mountains, "in the face of mounting aggression from the north and fearing the plague spreading through northern Ostland", and has retreated back towards Ostermark. What the hell is he doing? He's left an open corridor straight past the Middle Mountains and into the heart of the Empire! If the army that the elf mage spoke of moves south, there is nothing to stop it,' he raged. 'An army could march straight into the heart of the Empire unopposed!'

'I cannot join the elves and leave Empire soil, reiks-marshal. To leave now would be folly,' said von Kessel.

'No, you must go. In such things we have always trusted the elves. They are wise, Stefan, and we cannot ignore their counsel. No, I must leave right away. Bas-tard! I will ride hard, commandeer his army and lead it back to the north to face the massing foe myself.'

'He will not take such action lightly,' cautioned Stefan.

'I care not how he takes it,' said the reiksmarshal. 'I'll see him dragged before the Emperor in Nuln in chains if he resists me. I'll not see us win the war in the north only for the Empire to fall due to the cowardice of one inbred, fat elector. Nor will I see civil war return to the Empire.

'No. You will join the elves, and I will ride south-east tonight.'

IT WAS JUST before dawn when Stefan entered his tent. He was dog-tired, having spent the night in preparations for the journey by ship to Sigmar knew where. The reiksmarshal had left the camp hours before, riding with around half his company of Reiklandguard. He had left the rest of the elite knight regiment with Stefan, under the command of Captain Lederstein of the Reiklandguard.

Shuffling wearily across the tent, von Kessel was ready to collapse on his pallet fully clothed, when he saw the sealed letter on his chair. Frowning, he clum-sily ripped it open and read it quickly. He re-read it to make sure he had read correctly. Standing, he moved to the tent entrance and called out to one of his guards. 'Get me Albrecht,' he said.

The tent was poorly lit when the sergeant arrived. 'Sir,' he said cautiously into the gloom, pushing open the tent flaps.

'Come in,' said Stefan from the darkness, his voice strained. As Albrecht's eyes adjusted, he saw that Stefan was sitting at his table, a letter open before him. There was a bottle of spirits on the table in front of him. He groaned inwardly. He had seen Stefan drunk before, but rarely when on campaign. He was a difficult, moody drunk, but was wise enough to know it, and would only drink alone.

'What is wrong, captain?'

'I have just received a letter from Ostermark. Sigmar knows how long it has taken to reach me,' he said. His words were said through gritted teeth, but they were clear, with no hint of slurring. Good, thought Albrecht. He would rather have Stefan angry than drunk.

'Oh? And how do things fare in our homeland?'

'Badly. Plague is slaughtering our people. The north is rife with it. Entire villages and towns have succumbed. Thousands are dead. The larger cities have closed and barred their gates, allowing none to enter. Thousands more of our people have frozen to death after being refused entry.'

'It is a bad thing indeed, this plague; not natural.'

'Not natural,' Stefan repeated. Then his voice hardened, and Albrecht was taken aback by the hatred he could hear in the captain's voice. 'Our land is suffering, and now I learn that it is led by the man responsible for it.'

'What? What are you talking about, captain?'

'Gruber is the one responsible for the spreading plagues – him and his infernal allies.'

'Stefan... You could be hanged for such words.'

'This letter I hold was sent from a Sigmarite temple in Ostermark. It bears the mark of a priest of Sigmar, and the signature of Gruber's own physician.'

'His physician? Heinrich? The physician that disappeared months ago?'

'The same. He did not disappear. He fled from Gruber. He knows the truth.'

'The truth? What, of the old man's illness? I don't understand, captain.'

'He should have died years ago! Bastard. I'll kill him myself.'

'Kill him, captain? What are you saying? What madness is this? Slow down.'

'Madness, Albrecht? Yes, there is madness here, but it is not of my creation,' ranted Stefan. 'The cur. He gave me this scar,' he snarled, indicating his face. 'He gave me this... this... *mark of Chaos*. He had my grandfather murdered, my father exiled.'

'It wasn't him, Stefan,' admonished Albrecht. 'Once your grandfather was exposed, his fate was sealed. He brought it on himself.'

'Brought it on himself. No, that was a lie, Albrecht, a lie that was fed to us all.'

'A lie? I don't understand, captain.'

'Read this,' he said, thrusting the letter towards the burly sergeant. 'Read it!' Confused and alarmed by the apparent madness of his captain, Albrecht skimmed over the letter. The mark at the foot of the page was indeed the mark of a Sigmarite priest – a hammer emblazoned with a twin-tailed comet – and he saw the signature of the physician Heinrich. His eyes widened as he read the words on the page.

...have unearthed a secret that the cursed elector believed put to rest decades ago – the truth of the execution of your grandfather, Grand Elector Piter von Kessel, a fallacy of justice hiding the true offenders – the courtiers of Ostermark, led by the grand deceiver, Otto Gruber, the true worshipper of the fell gods of Chaos...

'What does this mean?' asked Albrecht dully.

'It means that my grandfather was wrongly accused and wrongly sentenced. It means that Ostermark is being led by a treacherous fiend working against the Empire from within. No wonder Gruber has pulled the army back! He *wants* the Chaos forces to attack!'

'How can we know that this letter speaks the truth? Could it not be a trick of the enemy to sow dissent amongst us?'

'It bears the mark of Sigmar! No Chaos spawn could use such an icon of good for their own fell purposes!'

'This priest of Sigmar,' said Albrecht looking at the mark at the foot of the page, 'Gunthar. How do we know he can be trusted?'

'How do we... He is a priest of Sigmar, man! What is wrong with you, Albrecht? How can you doubt the word of a priest!' ranted Stefan, his eyes blazing.

'I've never been one for religion, Stefan, as you know. Don't get me wrong, I'll ask for Manann's favour when I board a ship, and Sigmar's boon when I go to battle, but I don't put my faith in such things. A priest is just a man, Stefan, just a man, and I don't trust any man I don't know.'

'Bah! What does it matter – this letter contains the truth. I know it in my heart!' Stefan was breathing heavily, hatred coursing through him. Albrecht sighed and put a hand to his temple, where he could feel a headache rising.

'I fear the letter speaks the truth, Stefan, don't misunderstand me. Your grandfather was a good man. We were all shocked when… Well, when he was accused. He was a better man than Gruber, there is no doubt of that. But what you are speaking of – there will be civil war, man. The Empire was almost brought down by civil war. We wallowed in it for centuries, and it almost destroyed us all. Emperor Magnus united the states. Now, while the Empire is still threatened, you want to start another civil war?'

'I cannot let him get away with it, Albrecht. You know that.'

'I know,' said the sergeant with a sigh, 'and you know that your army will follow you against any enemy – even against Gruber. But is it wise?'

'I don't know if it is wise or not, but I will kill him.'

'You would be asking men of Ostermark to fight other men of Ostermark. They would know each other. Some would be friends, or even family, and you would ask them to kill each other.'

Stefan's face hardened. 'If Gruber is truly allied with the powers of darkness, then there is no question here at all, Albrecht. He *must* be slain.'

'Aye, agreed. What of the elves, captain? As we speak, our men are preparing to take to their ships on the morrow.'

'We will not go with the elves. We cannot leave Empire soil while Gruber is walking free upon it.'

'What of the reiksmarshal's orders?'

'He was unaware of this new information. He is travelling to Gruber as we speak. We must catch up with him and warn him.'

'You know of course that we could warn him, and still go with the elves. The reiksmarshal could muster an army to face him.'

'An army from where? Stirland and Ostland are wastelands, their armies slaughtered in the Great War. The remnants of their forces have already joined with us! Talabecland? The armies of Talabecland are all but gone. Their soldiers are barely able to man the walls of Talabheim. So, from where? Middenland? Reikland? They have armies, it is true, but it would be months before they would reach Ostermark, and that would be leaving the heart of the Empire completely undefended. No, there is no one Albrecht, and I will not have the pleasure of killing the fat wretch taken away from me!'

Albrecht frowned. 'If we do not join the elves, and instead march across the Empire, what happens if the enemy attacks here? There would be no one to stand against them. Surely they would advance into the heart of the Empire?'

'There already *is* an enemy within the Empire!' snarled Stefan, his face twisted in hatred, 'and we must destroy him!'

AURELION STOOD ON the castle ramparts, watching the last trailing troops of the Empire filing away over the horizon.

'They are blind fools,' snarled Khalanos. 'They cannot see what they have done this day. Fire and darkness, and death will come of this.'

I know, thought Aurelion, but she could not help but feel pity for the scarred Empire captain. Rage burned within him, and she knew that he had learnt some terrible truth. He had made his path, made his decision as he saw it, and he would have to live with the consequences or die with them.

'You give them too much time, these humans,' the dragon prince stated.

'I pity them and their brief lives. How can they see the folly of their actions when they live so fleetingly? The captain is doing what he thinks is right.'

'You are young, Aurelion. He doesn't do what he thinks is right. He is blinded by anger. In time, cousin, you will realise that the humans are undeserving of our pity.'

'They know not the power of what the forces of Chaos seek! And we cannot tell them, for it was our duty to keep it safe!'

'What are you saying, cousin? That it is *our* fault that the humans cannot see the folly of their actions?'

'It is not truly their battle to fight, Khalanos. It is ours. I cannot loathe them for not joining you,' she snapped. She immediately regretted losing her control. 'What will you do now?'

'What I must. My fleet will leave to face the Chaos forces.'

'Without the Empire forces, you will not outnumber the Norscans, cousin.'

'I know, but they must be stopped. You know this. Pray that the actions of the human captain have not doomed us all.' He stalked from the ramparts, tall, noble and proud. As she had said, Aurelion could not loathe the humans for not doing what she had wished, and she did pity the human captain. Nevertheless, she knew that dire occurences would result from his rash decision.

She watched as Prince Khalanos launched into the air upon the back of his massive dragon. She stood atop the ramparts as the ships sailed out into the sea to hunt the hated forces of Chaos. She whispered a prayer for them, but knew in her heart that she would never see them again. A single tear ran down her perfect cheek, and she turned and left the ramparts. The white sails of the ships disappeared from view, swallowed by the dark storm clouds building on the horizon.

Carandrian, her loyal swordmaster bodyguard and his retinue awaited her. She nodded to him, and they left the castle. She would journey to Altdorf, as Lord Teclis had requested of her.

CHAPTER EIGHTEEN

HROTH ROARED, HEFTING his massive axe high over his head. The sea roiled around them, the ship rising and falling on the massive swell. Salt water sprayed into his face as the ship raced down into an immense trough. Dark grey-green clouds filled the sky, and biting rain lashed the decks. Lightning crackled and thunder boomed. More than one of the dozens of ships had been struck, the lightning shattering masts and causing fires that were almost immediately doused by the crashing waves.

Arrows strafed the deck of the giant ship, and many warriors lost their grip on the handrails as arrows slammed into their flesh, sending them screaming into the turbulent black sea. Hroth did not cower before the arrows of the enemy. He knew the Blood God was with him, and that he would protect him from the pitiful weapons of the elves. He roared again, shouting his hatred and fury at the elves he could see on the decks of their sleek, white-sailed cutters.

The Norscans struggled with the mighty ship, trying to get close to the enemy that darted through the sea. They had already rammed one of the elf ships, the daemon bound within the hull tearing into it with fury. Its crunching metal jaws had ripped apart the decking of the fragile elf vessel, smashing it asunder and sending it to the bottom of the ocean.

An elf vessel darted past the great ship, too close. With a shout, the Norse warlord, Ulkjar, ordered the chain-guns upon the deck to be fired. With the turning of infernal gears, the guns spoke and massive harpoons fired, smashing into the hull of the enemy vessel. As the massive harpoons drove through the side of the ship, reversed spikes on their tips clanged open so that they could not be removed. The chains linking the harpoons to the Norse ship began to be drawn in, clanking as they were retracted. The elf ship was dragged inexorably towards its captor.

Repeating bolt throwers at the stern of the elf vessel fired, shooting dozens of bolts towards the Norse ship, each as long as a man is tall. They skewered several of the Norscans hauling on the massive oars, pinning them to the decks. Their comrades ripped the bolts from their flesh, and those who were able returned to their duty.

Hroth roared again as the smaller elf vessel was drawn near, readying himself for battle. It had been too long since he had spilt blood for his god, and he felt his master's hunger. He stood, ignoring the arrows that flashed around him, his eyes blazing with fire. An arrow struck him in the throat, but it shattered as it impacted against him. When the elf ship was fifteen feet from him, he leapt into the air with a shout, leaping over the gaping expanse and rolling to his feet on the enemy deck.

Hroth's axe lashed out in a murderous arc, decapitating one kneeling archer and smashing into the chest of another. The elf's chest collapsed, all the bones crushed by the powerful blow. In a moment, another three elves had died by his axe, and it was then that the Norscans and his loyal Khazags leapt into the fray.

The red fury descended on Hroth, and he carved a bloody path through the elves, slaughtering left and right. The deck tipped as it rose upon the back of a wave, sending dozens tumbling into the sea, but Hroth kept his footing and carved into the enemy, his heart surging with pleasure as he slew. He killed a pair of elves before him, smashing his axe into the shield of the first. The blow carried straight through the shield and into the elf's head. He grabbed the other elf around the throat. He felt the bones and windpipe beneath his hands crush as he exerted his power, and threw the wretch over the side of the ship. He felt someone behind him and wheeled around, his axe flashing. It thudded into the neck of a Norscan, and he fell to the deck, almost decapitated. Hroth barely noticed, and would not have cared if he did. He hacked around him, slaughtering and butchering indiscriminately.

The ship suddenly began to tip as it ploughed down into the deep trough of another wave. It slammed hard against the side of the larger Norse ship, and Hroth fell to his knees, sliding across the deck. He bowled into an elf and grasped at the slight figure, dragging him down. He smashed the elf in the face with his fist, punching through bone and into the brain.

Standing unsteadily, he staggered across the deck towards the last remaining elves, fighting a valiant defence atop the higher deck at the rear of the ship. Leaping the stairs, he landed in the midst of them. One of them lunged at him, and he smashed the blade aside with a sweep of his forearm. He kicked the legs from the elf, and smashed his axe into him as he hit the ground. The axe cut through bone and flesh, and embedded itself in the wooden decking. Releasing the weapon, Hroth grabbed a spear as it was thrust towards him. He lifted the spear, and sent the enemy holding onto it flying through the air to smash against the bronze hull of the Norse ship. He slid into the water, where the blood-hungry sharks following in the wake of the longships waited. Hroth liked sharks – creatures he believed Khorne would approve of.

A blow smashed into Hroth's helmet, and searing light flared. He was knocked to one side. His head hurt, and he could feel that his helmet had been misshapen by the unexpected attack. He lifted a hand to his helmet, and with a powerful wrench and the sound of bending metal, tore it from his head. The warrior before him, his sword glowing with magical energy, took a step back as he saw that the horns on Hroth's helmet were no longer attached to the helmet itself, but rather were a part of the towering warrior. Fused with his skull, the curving horns sprouting from his brow were a part of him now, and his eyes burned with fire.

Hroth growled and launched himself at the elf captain. The elf slashed his glowing blade across the

Khorne champion's chest, cutting a bloody mark through armour and flesh. He had no chance for a second blow, for Hroth drove his elbow into the elf's throat. As he choked, his windpipe crushed, Hroth pummelled him to the deck. He stamped on the elf's head, splattering it like a melon. He lifted the sword that the elf had wielded. It blazed brightly, and Hroth snarled as the hilt burnt into his flesh. Ignoring the searing pain, he hurled it into the sea.

Ulkjar was suddenly at Hroth's side, and he deflected a swordthrust with one of his blades, even as his other sword drove into his foe's neck. Hroth retrieved his axe, and together they slaughtered the last of the elves. The butchery complete, they climbed back to the massive Norse daemon-ship, and the harpoon guns retracted. The elf ship sank under the black waves. Ulkjar looked at the horns on Hroth's head, eyebrows raised. 'The Blood God smiles upon you indeed,' he said.

'He does,' agreed Hroth. He felt powerful and strong, jubilant after the bloodshed. The sorcerer Sudobaal slunk across the deck to Hroth's side.

'We have a problem,' he hissed. 'With the sight, I have seen that this is but a diversion. The majority of the elf fleet is slipping ahead of us. They intend to get to the island first and defend it. Time is pressing. We cannot allow them to arrive before us.'

'Well, what do you suggest, oh mighty sorcerer?' growled Hroth.

'I shall summon aid from the gods,' said Sudobaal, ignoring the champion's tone, 'but I cannot be interrupted. We must move the ship away from this battle.' As if to emphasise his point, an arrow thudded into the decking between him and the Khorne champion.

'You want me to voluntarily leave battle?'

'If you want us to discover the body of Asavar Kul, then yes.' The fires in Hroth's eyes blazed, and he seemed about to say something more, or act. The sorcerer held his gaze, his unblinking yellow eyes narrowed. Finally, the chosen of Khorne shrugged his shoulders, and turned away.

'Remember your place, champion,' hissed Sudobaal, and he shuffled away to ready his dark magics.

MILES BELOW THE turbulent surface of the Sea of Claws, in the impenetrable abyssal darkness of the sea floor, an ancient and powerful creature stirred. It had swum the oceans before the coming of man or elf, and had ruled far below the surface before the coming of Chaos. For millennia, it had slumbered deep in a chasm in the deepest valleys of the Sea of Claws, where no other creature was able to live. It had felt the arrival of the gods of Chaos to the world, and sensed their power. It had allowed itself to be changed and altered by the powers of these gods, and had revelled in the new sensations and strength that flowed through its body. It became a true creature of Chaos, barely resembling its original form. For thousands of years it had been the last of its kind, or perhaps it had always been the only one of its kind. It neither knew nor cared.

Its massive flat black eyes flickered with something like lightning as it awoke. It could feel something calling to it, an irresistible siren call that pulled at its mind. A ripple of phosphorous colour shimmered down its bulbous body, and it reached its long tendril-like feelers out before it. Slowly, it remembered this place, this icy, dark world that it ruled. Yellow light flickered on the tips of its tendrils, and its giant maw gaped open, exposing thousands of long, curving teeth, far too many to fit easily in its mouth. To either side of the creature's mouth there was a cluster of luminous tendrils, waving back and forth gently. Blue rings glowed from beneath the surface of the pallid skin of long, fleshy tentacles; sharp hooks on their ends. They felt around the creature lazily, touching the craggy rock, feeling above and below. Discerning the exit from its deep-sea cave, the fleshy tentacles proceeded to pull the bulk of the creature from its den.

As it emerged from the enclosed caverns, it thrust with its powerful tail and multitude of fern-like fins. The dorsal fins of the creature flexed and fanned, pallid, thin skin stretched between skeletal spines that pumped poison as they flexed.

The secondary array of eyes of the creature opened, clumps of small blue pinpricks scattered beneath its two larger orbs. It felt the calling again, from far away on the surface of the ocean, and it could not resist. With a flick of its massive, spined tail it began to swim upwards, its clawed tentacles flowing behind it.

LATHYERIN STOOD ON the deck of the dragon ship as it planed across the water, the wind whipping at his hair. The twin-hulled vessel barely touched the water, skimming across the surface quickly, sailed by his expert crew. Other ships raced alongside, dragon ships and smaller eagle ships. Part of the fleet had turned to intercept the Chaos raiders, and he cast a mournful glance to the west. He hoped that those elves fared well, though he feared that they did not.

Dark clouds flashed with lightning in the east. The winds of the evil storm buffeted them, speeding them on their way. The clouds were an ugly green-grey colour, and Lathyerin knew that the storm was racing to ensnare them. Rain began to reach them, sharp heavy droplets that lashed at his face. He said a quick prayer for those elves who had turned into the storm to hold the Norscans at bay. The elf ships were the fastest on the seas. No other race could match the sheer speed and skill of their vessels, but the Norse were also skilled sailors, and they had a head start. Prince Khalanos had diverted part of the fleet to intercept them, in an attempt to hold them up. Lathyerin hoped that their sacrifice would be worth it.

The dragon ship swung to the east, turning to receive the strongest winds. The other elf ships turned at the exact same time, running with the fierce wind that was blowing the storm towards them. Lathyerin figured that they must have caught up with the Norse fleet, and that the island was an equal distance from both fleets. He was confident that the speed of the elf ships would make all the difference, and that they would arrive several hours before the foe. They should be able to outrun the storm if they kept this pace, but it would be a close-run thing. The swell was rising in response to the storms, and the wind was increasing in intensity and fury with every passing minute.

'Captain!' came a frantic shout. Lathyerin looked to where it had come from. It was Daralyn, a dark haired sailor who had ploughed the seas for almost two centuries. The man was gesturing wildly to the east, into the storm.

A small eagle ship was skimming across the water, touching the sea only every thirty yards or so as its sails swelled. Lathyerin could see nothing for a moment, until his sharp eyes caught sight of something that sent a shiver of fear running through him. Behind the racing eagle ship a dark shape could be seen below the surface of the water, a massive bow wave the only evidence of its passing. It was approaching the rear of the ship with great speed.

'Whale?' Lathyerin said aloud, but discounted it even as he said it. It was certainly the right size for a whale, but no whale that he had ever seen would act like this, nor be able to match an elf ship for speed. No, this was something quite unnatural, and he could sense the taint of Chaos in the air. He had witnessed several monsters of the deep in his time on the sea, but nothing that looked quite like this.

Rows of massive spined fins unfurled from the back of the beast and rose above the water, vile and pallid in colour, as if the thing had never seen sunlight. A pair of long, reaching tendrils rose out of the water before it, glowing with dull light. The eagle ship saw the approaching monster and tacked to the north, seeking escape. The creature rose fully to the surface, exposing its pallid, foul body. A pair of giant black eyes flicked back and forth before focusing on its prey. They were enormous, yards wide, and Lathyerin was horrified to see an evil intelligence in those ancient, hate-filled eyes. Below the giant eyes was a myriad of smaller, blue eyes that glimmered and shone with strange light. The flesh of the creature was sickly pale and almost translucent. Great blue and purple veins could be seen just under the skin of the beast, along with many scars up and down its sides.

It lurched to the side in pursuit of its prey, splashing with its massive fins, and it closed on the twin-hulled catamaran that desperately tacked to the south, seeking to shake its hunter. The creature was too quick for this, and it was upon the ship as it turned. A massive pair of clawed tentacles burst from the water on the far side of the elf ship, wrapping completely around the far side hull, smashing timbers and planks under its strength. Glowing blue rings pulsed with strange light under the surface of the flesh of the tentacles, and they stank with foulness.

The ship was pulled down in the water by the tentacles, the side closest to the creature rising into the air. With an unearthly screech, the creature launched itself onto the ship, its massive mouth opening. The ship was pulled completely onto its side, and the terror from the deep smashed into the hull with its mouth gaping. Its maw was bigger than seemed possible, even for such a massive beast. It was jointed in several places, and it crushed the entire hull to pieces in a single bite. Teeth like swords tore through the planking as if it was matchwood. In an instant, the ship was no more than a scattering of smashed wood and flailing bodies.

Lathyerin's hand fell, and his eagle claw bolt throwers launched their deadly missiles at the foul creature, as his ship swept around to face it. Bolts peppered the sides of the creature, and, with great satisfaction, he saw one of the missiles pierce a staring eye. The creature thrashed around angrily, hurling bodies out of the water with flailing tentacles. It dived deep as another volley speared towards it.

With a shout, Lathyerin swung his ship around. The storm was closing in quickly, and he could not afford to get caught within it.

The giant catamaran lifted suddenly in the water with a cracking sound as the creature struck it from below. The dragon ship dropped down into the sea heavily, all speed lost to the blow, and water gushed over its sides. The creature's tentacles whipped out of the water and grasped the masts. The mighty uprights groaned, but held. Rushing forwards, Lathyerin drew his sabre and rammed it into the flesh of the closest tentacle. It was thick and rubbery, but his keen blade pierced the flesh deeply. With a screech, another tentacle flew at him, the creature intending to skewer him on the clawed tip. He rolled out of the way, the tentacle ploughing into the staircase leading to the stern, and smashing it to pieces.

Lathyerin felt something touch his boot, and a stinging pain raced up his leg. Looking down, he saw a pale tendril feeling at him. He gasped, and lashed out with his blade, severing the foul, stinging tendril. It flopped back and forth on the deck. He kicked it away, and instantly regretted the action as stinging pain covered his foot.

The creature pulled itself up on the deck of the ship, making it tip alarmingly, and Lathyerin found himself sliding towards the gaping maw of the foul creature. The stench of death exuded from its foetid mouth. He saw that its teeth varied greatly in size, from more than twice the height of a man, to smaller, cruel teeth the length of his forearm. As he slid towards the mouth, he grabbed hold of some trailing rope, stopping just short of the snapping teeth. Hanging there, he knew it was only a matter of time before his grip failed him.

Searing heat erupted around Lathyerin, and he turned his face away from the sudden flames. Wind beat down upon him, but he realised that this was more than the wind from the nearing storm. Beating its wings powerfully, the dragon of Prince Khalanos hovered in the air as it breathed searing flames onto the creature of the depths. The dragon rose into the air to avoid three tentacles that speared towards it. The monster let go its grasp on the dragon ship and slid back into the water, its back black and blistering from the dragon fire. It screeched its anger and pain. The other elf ships circled the creature, peppering it with bolts and arrows, and it lashed out blindly. It managed to catch a hold of one small ship, smashing it to pieces before a series of arrows drove into its eyes, and it dived back to the depths.

Lightning struck the mast of one of the dragon ships, and the sails burst into flame. The creature may have been retreating, thought Lathyerin, but it had done its job. The elf fleet had been caught by the storm.

SUDOBAAL LAUGHED TO himself as he finally released his control of the leviathan and allowed it to return to its icy depths. The elves would not be arriving on the island first.

BOOK THREE

CHAPTER NINETEEN

'HURRY UP, CURSE you!' snarled Hroth as he climbed the ancient steps carved into the cliff face. He bounded up another set of steps, taking them four at a time, before turning to stare balefully at the sorcerer climbing more slowly behind him. Sudobaal was breathing heavily and leaning on his staff as he struggled up the stairs.

Below them, Hroth could see the Norscans on the beach battling with the elves that were landing in greater numbers. He longed to be down amongst the bloodshed and slaughter, feeling his blood pumping quickly through his altered form in response to the battle. His muscles tensed, and he clenched his hands into fists. More white-sailed elf ships were arriving, skimming across the sea at great speed. They swerved in front of the beach, their shallow draughts allowing them to approach within feet of land. Hundreds of arrows filled the air, together with the larger bolts fired from war machines mounted on the ships.

Lightning lit up the beach and thunder boomed. Rain lashed down on Hroth and Sudobaal, making the stones slippery and dangerous. They had already climbed several hundred feet, and there was around a hundred feet more before they reached the summit, and their prize and goal.

The battle was faring poorly down below, and Hroth had to repress the urge to race down into the fray. He knew that if he was there the elves would stand no chance. He knew the effect of his battle frenzy, and could feel the power of his deity coursing through him. Khorne had made his body strong, so that weapons shattered against his flesh, and he was able to shrug off otherwise fatal wounds. With the power granted him, he could tear a man limb from limb with little effort. He was taller and stronger than ever before, he knew, and all cowered before him. All could see the power of the gods within him, evident not only in his flaming eyes and the curving horns that sprouted from his head, but in the power that he exuded. All feared and respected him, except for the sorcerer, Sudobaal, Hroth thought, but soon that would change.

'The power of Chaos is strong on this island,' hissed Sudobaal in between gasps. Hroth could feel it too – he felt more powerful, closer to his god, as if the air itself was lending him strength. The island seemed to have been affected by this power too: plants writhed and twisted, toothed flowers snapping at the pair as they passed and daemonic faces appeared in the rock face, soundlessly screaming in torment.

'It is the breath of the gods. I can feel its power calling to me,' hissed Sudobaal. 'We must hurry.'

The sorcerer shuffled past the glowering Hroth, and continued up the next set of rough-hewn stairs. Hroth took a last look down at the ensuing battle, his muscles tense, before he turned and bounded up the stairs past the sorcerer.

He reached the top of the rise before Sudobaal. The rough path continued around a large rock, and down a set of stairs on the other side. Rounding the corner, he felt the power of Chaos intensify suddenly, washing over him in a stomach-churning wave. Laughter and screaming passed through his mind, and he almost staggered under the power of it. There before him was a massive fissure in the rock face. Steam seeped from the cracks in the rock around the cave entrance, like the breath of some giant slumbering beast within. The entrance was framed with craggy, sharp rock so that it resembled a gaping, gigantic maw.

A pair of stones stood on either side of the entranceway. They had once been tall and elegant, made from a luminous white stone, and Hroth could see elf runes carved up their sides, filled with gold. They had been shattered half-way up, the broken pieces of the glowing rock lying scattered around the entrance. Black throbbing veins could be seen climbing the white stones – the corrupting power of Chaos overpowering the elf magic. Sudobaal shuffled around the corner, and staggered under the sudden power emanating from the cavern. He regained his composure quickly, and surveyed the entrance with greed-filled eyes.

'The arrogance, thinking they could hold back the power of Chaos,' he spat. An evil grin appeared on his face. 'This is it: the goal that we have been working towards.' With that, the pair entered the cavern of Chaos, the sorcerer striding boldly, the chosen of Khorne walking more warily, his axe in his hands.

DOZENS OF ELF ships raced into the shallows, under the protective fire of others. Hundreds of elf warriors leapt into the surf, brandishing their spears and tall shields, their silver helms shining nobly in the flashes of lightning. The Norse met them in the knee-deep, turbulent water, and the sea ran red with the blood of man and elf.

Lathyerin leapt into the water. It came up to his thighs, soaking his long robes with its icy touch. He lowered his shining sword at the enemy, and led his men in a charge through the choppy water. The strong undercurrents pulled at him, but he fought them, struggling through the water towards the battle erupting before him.

Black fins cut through the shallow water, and he saw an elf go down thrashing as a shark grabbed him around the torso. Wolves of the sea, Lathyerin called them, and they had been driven into a frenzy by the amount of blood in the water. The foam of the waves was red as it washed over him, but he ignored his disgust, and ploughed on.

Arrows streamed over his head, falling amongst the Norscans. Most managed to raise their shields against them, but dozens dropped into the churning sea, screaming, arrows protruding from necks and exposed arms. The sharks were amongst them, and he saw one man stagger as a massive black shape grabbed his leg, dragging him thrashing out to deeper water.

With a shout, Lathyerin threw himself against the foe, his shining sword carving through a hide-bound shield and into the face of the Norscan holding it. He fell with a scream, and Lathyerin stabbed down, finishing the man off. His trusted sea guard formed up around him, stabbing and killing with their long spears. The Norscans threw themselves onto the points, dragging them down so that their comrades could close with the elves.

One big warrior of Chaos, darker skinned than the others, threw himself at the elves, ignoring two spears that smashed into his chest. With a sweep of his axe, he shattered the hafts of the weapons and leapt upon the elves who wielded them. Ditching his axe, the warrior punched one of them in the face, and leapt upon the other, his hands grabbing the elf's face and squeezing tightly, until blood spurted from the elf's pointed ears and he went limp.

Lathyerin tried to close with the berserk warrior, but the surge and flow of battle took the madman away from him. He blocked a sword thrust and sent a deadly riposte into the neck of another Norscan.

With a gust of air and an unearthly roar, the Dragon Prince Khalanos swept into the fray. His massive green-blue dragon smashed down into the Norscans, ripping and rending, and sending a great wave of water into the air. Lathyerin saw a man bitten in two, and another's arms sheared off with a flash of the dragon's claws. Khalanos himself spitted a pair of Norscans on his lance. The dragon rose into the air once again, and breathed fiery death upon a dozen other enemy. The seawater churned and boiled under the intense heat, rising in scalding steam. Those Norscans who had

ducked under the water to escape the flames rolling
towards them emerged screaming, the flesh scalded
from their bones.

'Forward!' screamed Lathyerin, and charged on,
seeking to rout the demoralised Norscans before him.
His sea guard ran at his side. Those armed with bows
sent their shafts hurtling into the enemy, striking them
down in their scores. The water was filled with dead
bodies, thrown to and fro by the relentless waves.

Lathyerin felt something large hit him, knocking
him from his feet, and the elf next to him screamed. A
massive fifteen-foot shark had him in its mouth, its
jaw clamped around his arm and torso, his shield
splintering under the strength of the creature. Lunging
forwards, Lathyerin stabbed his blazing sword into the
creature's head, driving it deep into the brain. The
creature went berserk, thrashing around in its death
throes. It knocked the wind from Lathyerin and he fell
beneath the water. He gasped, sucking in a lungful of
bloody salt water. He rose, coughing, and continued to
advance up onto the beach.

All along the beach, the elves were pushing up onto
the sand, forcing the Norscans back.

A tall warrior stood before Lathyerin, butchering the
elves around him with a pair of swords. He threw himself towards the brute, stabbing his glowing blade
towards the warrior's back as he twisted. As if sensing
the approaching blow and moving with impossible
speed, the tall Norscan spun lightly to deflect the
strike. His second sword hissed out, sinking into Lathyerin's neck, and he fell without a sound.

Ulkjar Moerk Headtaker did not pause after killing
the elf with the glowing sword, and continued to

weave a path of destruction through the elf ranks. Still, there were just too many of them, and his Norscans were being pushed back.

'Whatever you are doing sorcerer, do it quickly!' he muttered as he slew again.

SUDOBAAL TRAILED HIS taloned hand along the smooth rock wall as he descended deeper into the caverns. The rock pulsed with light and colour: blues, greens and purples. Veins of darker matter crisscrossed the smooth rock, throbbing with barely contained energy, and Sudobaal marvelled at the power coursing around him.

The hairs on the back of Hroth's neck were standing on end, warning him of the magic in this place. On the one hand, he felt closer to his god than he had ever done when not on the field of battle, but he was also wary of the strong magic that filled the caverns, ever mistrustful of sorcery. He held his axe tightly as he descended behind the sorcerer.

There was light within the cave, although it was an eerie cold light that came from the walls. The blue flames of the sorcerer's staff burned coldly, reflecting back at the pair off the smooth, reflective walls. They descended towards a bowl-shaped cavern, a circular room with walls that curved into the floor. Smoke, dark purple-red, like the colour of clotted blood, swirled around the room, coiling and whipping around at great speed.

As they neared the entrance to the room, the colour and light of the walls flared brightly, colours swirling and writhing. Through the roiling red smoke, they could see that a white stone casket, sitting on top of a rocky platform, in the centre of the room. The casket was bedecked with elf runes that were flaring brightly, white-hot. Sudobaal hissed as he saw the runes, for they burnt his eyes painfully. Looking at them gave Hroth a pain inside his head, and he gripped his axe tighter.

Sudobaal stopped Hroth from entering the room, placing one bony hand on the massive warrior's chest. Hroth looked down with disdain at the hand touching him, but halted his movement.

The sorcerer stepped to the entrance and held up his hand and his staff, as if feeling the air. The purple-red smoke whipped past him, just inches from his hands, contained within the room. He whispered some guttural words and the elf runes flared even brighter. Nodding, he stepped back, and drew out a long, curved dagger. He raised it to his face and cut a long slash down each of his cheeks. Sheathing the blade, he smeared the palm of his hand on each cut, and then stepped back towards the entranceway, raising his blood-smeared hand.

The smoke seemed to be attracted to the blood, circling within the room frantically, focusing around the sorcerer's outstretched hand. The elf runes flared brightly as he began to chant once again. He barked a harsh word, and one of the runes flared brightly and exploded in a small shattering of light. He barked the word again, and again, until each of the elf runes was snuffed out of existence.

With a smile on his face, Sudobaal watched as the last of the runes disappeared. The smoke changed colour subtly, becoming darker, and began to swirl more frenetically. The casket itself began to crack, and its white surface changed to black. Sharp protrusions sprouted from the casket, until it was ringed with rising spikes and spines that curled out of the stone.

Sudobaal closed his eyes briefly. His time had come: time to take what was rightfully his, and have his ascendancy, time to dispose of Hroth the Blooded. The Khorne champion had done what was needed, gathering an army and bringing him safely to this place, but now his use had passed, and the upstart was becoming quite a powerful champion of the gods – he was not sure how long he would be able to best him.

Sudobaal began to mouth an incantation and started to turn towards the massive warrior. In that second, he saw the axe descending towards his skull, and he recoiled backwards in shock. Instinctively, he spat a word in the language of Chaos, and a smoky black, insubstantial, clawed hand caught the axe before it struck. Hroth growled in anger, and Sudobaal scrambled backwards, putting some distance between the two. An instant later, the sorcerous claw disappeared.

Sudobaal lowered his staff, and crackling blue flames burst towards Hroth. The warrior had sensed the sorcerer's move, and had already bunched his muscles to spring, but he was too slow. The flames engulfed him as he tried to roll to the side, throwing him backwards to smash against the smooth stone wall. He fell to the ground, his body smouldering, his flesh singed and his armour blackened. He snarled with hatred and anger.

Sudobaal drew the power of Chaos into him, drawing in the magic that leaked from the casket in the next room and hung in the air. He felt it building within him, and he rejoiced in the feeling. Rarely had he felt such power, and now he would destroy Hroth with it, destroy him utterly and send him screaming into the Realms of Chaos, there to be tortured until the end of time. How dare the fool strike out at him?

His golden eyes turned black as the power in him built, and the air around him was filled with electricity. The blue flames on his staff roared, filling the room with its cold light. The blue flames flowed down over his arms and shoulders, flickering down across his body, and up over his face and hood. Within moments, his whole body was ablaze. He opened his mouth, and the flames descended down into lungs and stomach, suffusing him completely.

'How could you ever have hoped to best me?' the blazing figure questioned. 'You would never have stood a chance against my magics.'

The smouldering figure of Hroth rolled to his feet. His eyes burned too, but with fires hot and angry, seeming at odds with the cold blue flames that covered the sorcerer. 'Magic is for weaklings who cannot wield a blade, and lack the courage to face their enemy face to face, runt,' he snarled.

'Is that right?' the sorcerer chuckled. 'So what does that make you, if you are bested by a magic-wielding weakling?'

'You will never best me, Sudobaal. I'll have your soul,' snarled the Khorne champion, readying himself to leap at the sorcerer.

'Goodbye, champion,' whispered Sudobaal, and unleashed the power contained within him. The champion leapt forwards, but was not halfway across the cavern when the power struck him. It should have ripped through his flesh, rending it from his bones before sending him screaming into the Realms of Chaos, but the blue flames washed over him without touching him at all, passing around him and never getting within an inch of his flesh. Hroth could feel the heat and power of the spell that should have ended him, but it did not touch him.

With a gasp, the sorcerer fell back. Hroth emerged from the blast unscathed, but he took only two steps before he dropped to his knees, hissing in pain. His massive axe clanged to the stone floor, and his hands clawed at his neck. The flesh was bulging strangely, as if something within was struggling to escape. His head twitched to the side, and a series of brass spikes suddenly ripped through his flesh from within. Blood poured down the inside of his armour as the spikes continued to push out from within his neck, followed by a heavy metal ring. Finally, the pain gone, Hroth stood. Sudobaal crouched on the floor, staring in disbelief.

Hroth reached up a hand to touch the spiked collar that had emerged from within his flesh to encircle his neck. Then he grinned, and turned his burning eyes towards Sudobaal with a shrug.

'A collar of Khorne,' gasped the sorcerer. Bestowed by the Blood God upon some of its favoured daemons, the collar of Khorne was a powerful artefact that protected the wearer from harmful magic.

In desperation, Sudobaal spat a curse at Hroth, and a multitude of black, smoky figures appeared around the champion of Khorne, their red eyes filled with hatred. They reached towards the champion with long clawed hands to claim his soul, but they could not touch him, and recoiled from him in pain. He swatted at them with his axe as he strode towards the sorcerer, and their insubstantial forms dissipated into the air.

Sudobaal raised his staff once more, and lightning crackled around its tip, but Hroth smashed it aside with a kick. He lifted the sorcerer into the air, holding him around the neck. Holding him up to his eyes, the black robed figure's dangling feet some two feet off the ground, Hroth smiled evilly. 'You're in some trouble now, sorcerer,' he snarled.

Hroth hurled the sorcerer across the room, and he smashed into the wall before sliding to a heap on the ground. The Khorne champion walked to the crumpled figure and lifted him once again by the throat. 'I will have your soul,' he added, before hurling him across the room once again. Sudobaal slammed into the wall on the other side of the cavern.

'I don't want to kill you,' said Hroth as he walked back towards the broken form of the sorcerer, who was whimpering, 'at least not just yet.' He turned towards the bowl-shaped room, still filled with frantically swirling smoke and coiling energies.

'What happens when I walk through there? Hmm? What happens?' he asked, kicking the sorcerer when he did not answer immediately. Sudobaal coughed up blood, spitting it out onto the floor.

'It is *my* destiny, you Khazag bastard,' the sorcerer managed. Hroth chuckled.

'Well, I cannot say that you don't have spirit, sorcerer. You are lying there pathetic and bloody, and yet still you insult me.'

'I will kill you,' whispered the sorcerer, spluttering blood.

'No, you will not, Sudobaal. No longer will *I* be the dog. From now on, *I* am the master here, and I *will* have your soul. Now, I am going through into that room and claiming what is mine.'

Leaving the broken sorcerer on the floor, Hroth stepped to the entrance of the bowl-shaped room. He turned, spat at the broken sorcerer, and stepped into the Realm of Chaos.

CHAPTER TWENTY

STEFAN VON KESSEL reeled from the unexpected blow. Placing a hand to his jaw, he looked into the furious eyes of the reiksmarshal. He opened and closed his mouth, his jaw clicking alarmingly. 'Nice punch,' he muttered.

'You are damn lucky that's all I've done. You are a damn fool, von Kessel. I cannot believe you disobeyed my order.' Stefan made to say something, but the enraged knight cut him off. 'My word is the word of the Emperor, damn it! Would you disobey a direct order from the Emperor Magnus? Answer me!'

'Sir, I felt these were... extreme circumstances.'

'You have no idea what you have done, do you?'

'Sir, Gruber is a traitor! How could I let that pass? An elector count, one of the twelve most trusted men of the Empire, and he has betrayed us!'

'Aye, so you say. Off the back of one letter, you have led your army for two weeks across the Empire, disobeying a direct order.'

'But sir... I feared the future of Ostermark would be–'

'I don't give a damn about the future of Ostermark!' raged the reiksmarshal, interrupting the captain. 'All I give a damn about is the Empire as a *whole*. What good is Ostermark if the rest of the Empire crumbles around it?'

'I did what I thought was best for the Empire!'

'No, you didn't bloody think at all. Your judgement has been clouded by your anger, von Kessel. All you are thinking about is your damn grandfather and that fat wretch, Gruber! Not only did you disobey my order, I thought you might have had the sense to at least hold the ground that Gruber himself was meant to hold! But no, you have been traipsing across the Empire, leaving Ostland undefended. If the forces of Chaos return and advance through Ostland, there will be no one to defend it – they could march straight through to Talabheim and the heart of the Empire.'

'Talabheim? That great city has never fallen.'

'No it hasn't, but there are barely enough men in Talabheim to man the inner walls, let alone the massive outer walls, you fool,' the reiksmarshal said. 'If the forces of Chaos do march on Talabheim, it will be on your head, von Kessel.' The older man sighed wearily. 'If you are right, the Empire is indeed in peril from within. Damn it.' Trenkenhoff was silent for moment, his brow knotted in concern.

'Damn it,' he said again. 'Fine, I'll give you three days. Learn the truth in that time, and we will act accordingly. If you do not, you will be leading your army back into Ostland, and I pray you will not be too late.' Von Kessel still had a defiant look in his eyes, and his cheeks were flushed.

'Have your messages to Gruber got through, sir? The messages telling him to halt his retreat eastwards?'

'Damned if I know. I haven't had any response from him. My outriders have not yet returned, and the cowardly dog still runs. I don't know what he is playing at, honestly I don't. Maybe it's just the plague that is bringing Ostland, Ostermark and now Talabecland to their knees that he is fleeing from. I don't know.'

Stefan frowned. 'Fleeing the plague? Maybe–'

'Three days, von Kessel. Find your man within three days. I'll hold the army here for that time. Heaven knows the local militia could use the aid rooting out the foul creatures along the south banks of the river. Leave now.'

Stefan was still smarting from the rebuke he had received from the reiksmarshal, even now, two days after the incident. He pushed all thoughts of the episode out of his mind, as his most skilled scout Wilhelm returned, running down the steep slope through the trees. Breathing hard, he brought himself to a halt before the captain.

'Well?' said Stefan. 'Is it there?'

'Aye it is sir. Looks occupied as well. Fresh wood piled up outside the chapel doors.'

'Good. How far?'

'Not far, a half hour, elector.'

'Don't call me that,' snapped Stefan, and he kicked his steed forwards. The soldiers of Ostermark had begun to call him elector a week earlier, much to his horror. They had heard that Gruber had betrayed the Empire, and had decided amongst themselves that once the treacherous noble was deposed that the rightful heir to the position was Stefan. He had tried to dissuade them from this line of thinking, but it had proven to have no effect.

The others in his party followed the lead of their captain and kicked their steeds on up the rocky road winding into the fir-covered hills. A light snow began to fall, the soft flakes landing on Stefan's shoulders, and he pulled his cloak around him more tightly.

A dozen men rode behind him. All were competent horsemen, barring Albrecht, who hated riding. 'Horses, they don't like me,' he had stated the previous day, and Stefan had to agree with the sergeant. Nevertheless, he had flat-out refused to be left behind, despite the mutual dislike he had with their steeds. One of the horses had tried to bite Albrecht's horse earlier that day, and the mare had bucked, throwing the older sergeant to the ground. He swore that the horses had been laughing at him.

Stefan's face darkened as he approached the chapel. The mood of the journey was grim, the soldiers travelling in silence. The captain was preparing himself for the news he would hear, the truth that he longed and dreaded to hear. Night was setting in as they approached the long-abandoned chapel. Smoke drifted from the chimney of the small building attached to the rear of the retreat. The snows had settled around a foot deep, and the breath of the horses and men steamed before them.

As they approached the chapel, they did not notice the dark figures that flitted amongst the trees.

Albrecht's horse snorted, its ears pulled back close to its head, and he swore at it.

The doors to the chapel were opened, and a figure stepped into view. He was a giant, barrel-chested man. A heavy pendant hung around his neck – a twin-tailed comet, Stefan noticed with some relief. His head was completely shaved, his stony face was square, and his neck was almost non-existent – he looked like a born fighter. His nose looked as if it had been broken several times, and badly set. In his big hands he clasped a massive two-handed hammer, and he eyed the riders warily. He looked more like a soldier than a priest, but then the priests of Sigmar were well-trained warriors, as was fitting for a warrior god.

'Come any closer and feel the wrath of Sigmar, you curs,' he boomed, his voice deep and full of authority. Stefan noted that a pair of crossbows was aimed at him from the windows of the chapel, poking through the slightly opened shutters.

'Not a very warm welcome from a priest,' remarked Albrecht. Stefan threw him a dark look.

'Don't give me none of that, damn you, and you can tell Gruber that he will die a painful death by my hand one day soon. Away with you, lapdogs of Chaos!'

'We do not come from the treacherous count. I am Stefan von Kessel,' he called out. The priest squinted at him suspiciously, and then his eyes widened. He waved to the men to lower their crossbows.

'Von Kessel! Thank Sigmar! Come in, you must be frozen. I am Gunthar.' He ushered Stefan inside the chapel. 'All of you, come in. There is a small stable around the back for your steeds. There is not a lot of room in the chapel, but there is room enough for you all. Come in! Come,' he said, slapping Stefan on the back – almost knocking him off his feet with the force of the blow. Stefan felt vaguely that he had met the priest before, but could not place him.

'I thought that you were Gruber's lackeys, come here to finish me off. Thank Sigmar they have not tracked me down yet. They will, have no doubt of that. I should have moved on, left this place. I have been here for too long, but I could not leave just yet, for fear that you would arrive, only to find this place abandoned. I talk too much. There is a hot broth cooking. Come.'

The chapel was old, and had been abandoned for many years. Still, the priest had clearly worked hard to make the place clean, for the floors were freshly swept. It was austere, as was usual for places of worship for Sigmar, and the windows were shuttered. The roof was high, the rafters exposed and filled with cobwebs. There were a couple of holes in the roof that had been roughly patched over, and a slight sprinkling of snow drifted down from them. Two men were inside the chapel, although on second glance Stefan saw that one of them was little more than a boy.

'Josef and Mikael,' said Gunthar, introducing the two to Stefan. 'Mikael, be a good lad and help the soldiers with their horses, and see that there are enough blankets.' The younger man nodded his head, his red curly hair bobbing, and ran off. 'There is room enough in here for your men to sleep the night. Mikael will get you blankets. Think nothing of sleeping within the church of Sigmar – what better place for warriors to sleep, eh?'

An ancient wooden statue of Sigmar stood at the back of the chapel, the great warhammer Ghal-maraz clasped in his hands before him. The priest ushered Stefan towards a small door leading to the living quarters at the rear of the building, but the captain excused himself and approached the statue. Dropping to his knees, Stefan bowed his head and said a prayer to the warrior god. Standing, he followed the priest through into the next room.

'A devotee of Sigmar, I see,' said Gunthar approvingly, entering the small kitchen. Walking behind the priest, Stefan mused that a bear dressed in the regalia of a priest would look much the same; such was the size and power of the man. A good man to have on your side in a fight, he decided.

The kitchen was spare, little more than a solid wooden table, a couple of crates for seating and a black cooking pot hanging over an open fire. A small door led out into the courtyard behind the chapel, probably where the horses were stabled. There was another man here, an older stooped figure stirring the contents of the pot. The smell was delicious. The man turned, and he recognised him at once.

'Physician Piter,' said Stefan warmly. 'It is good to see you well.' The older man gave a weary smile. The old man had always been kindly to Stefan as a child, giving him special roots to chew on when his teeth ached, and telling him far-fetched stories when no one else would talk to him.

'I look well? Ha! My bones creak when I walk and I lose my breath climbing a flight of stairs. I am old and weary, young man, but it *is* good to see you,' he said, his voice rasping. 'It's a shame we meet under such circumstances.'

'Indeed it is, but it is good to see you none-the-less.' Gunthar sat the older man down on a crate, and ushered Stefan to sit. Then he picked up some bowls, looking ridiculously small in his massive hands, and began to serve the meal. Once he had dished out to Stefan and the old physician, he called to Josef to find bread for Stefan's soldiers. Having seen to the needs of his guests, the priest sat himself down on one of the crates.

'We have much to discuss,' said Piter. The old man sighed wearily. 'May Morr have pity on my foolish old soul. I am hunted, Stefan, you know that? I have been called a traitor and a worshipper of the dark arts. Imagine that? Me worshipping the Dark Gods! Can you think of anything more ridiculous? But I am getting ahead of myself.' The older man leant forwards, staring intently into the captain's eyes.

'This good priest here,' he said, motioning to Gunthar. 'He is as trustworthy a man as ever I have met. He is willing to sacrifice himself for the Empire – utterly devoted. You have known me since you were a lad, Stefan, and I would like to think that you trust me?'

'Of course,' said Stefan. 'As if you even needed to ask.'

'Then trust this man as you do me. Doubt not a word that he speaks.' Stefan turned towards the priest, who returned his gaze impassively.

'I will do as you ask, Piter,' said Stefan solemnly.

'Good. You may have heard of him, actually. His exploits during the Great War are quite well known, I believe.'

Stefan wracked his brain, and then his eyes widened. 'Gunthar... Gunthar *Klaus*?' The warrior priest nodded his head grimly. The man was a living legend. He had fought tirelessly during the years of the war. If the stories were to be believed, mighty daemons had been slain beneath his hammer, and armies on the point of routing had been rallied by this man alone. 'It is a great honour,' breathed Stefan.

'I am glad that you received my letter, captain – I feared that you would not. Now,' said the physician, leaning back in his seat, 'you deserve to know the truth. As you know, I have been the physician of the royal house of Ostermark for decades. I served your grandfather, not that he needed my services often, but it was I who tended to his family when they were poorly. A strong man, your grandfather. So too, I was the physician of Otto Gruber, curse his name, when he took the title of grand elector.

'Now, the man had always been ill. He had the wasting sickness as a child, you know. It is said that no one held out much hope for the boy, but he managed to pull through and get over the worst of it. Still, his health was ruined – always he was to be wracked with illness.

'When he first became elector, I thought nothing of it. He was a clever man, very cunning. He duped me as he had duped all the others. Disease seemed to be a part of him, and as the years went by, he seemed to get the symptoms of some of the most deadly illnesses that I had ever encountered. I did what I could for him, preparing tinctures and healing broths, and always he managed to pull through. At the time, I had no idea how. For a while, I deluded myself into thinking that it was my remedies, but that was just pride, I see that now.

'No, as the years continued to roll by, and I became the frail old man I am now, I began to understand that something was not quite right.' The old man paused for a moment, playing with his spoon. 'He should have died years ago. Something was keeping him alive, and it was not my doing. Nevertheless, I enjoyed the position I was in. Everyone knew that the elector had been sick for decades, but never was overcome by the illnesses, and that *I* was his physician. Counts and barons sought my services from far and wide. Again, pride.

'I finally learnt the truth. All I was doing was holding back the rottenness that was inside the man all along, and I do not mean that in any metaphorical sense – truly, the man is *rotting* from the inside out. He is rotting, but he is not dying. Indeed, I think he somehow *enjoys* the sicknesses that he experiences, comfortable in the knowledge that he will not succumb to the finality of death as a result.

'He is a creature of Chaos, Stefan, a worshipper of a foul, pestilential dark god of Chaos. I shall not speak any of its many names; suffice it to say, it is the antithesis of the natural order of things. I believe, and this is but conjecture, but I truly believe that Gruber probably would have died as a result of his wasting sickness when he was young. Certainly he would not have lived past his teens. No, I believe that to avoid this fate he sought any god who would protect him. Maybe he did not mean to turn to evil, but it was a god of Chaos that answered him. It saved him, and damned him.'

The room was utterly silent. Stefan sat motionless, his disgust plain upon his face. He cleared his throat. 'And my grandfather?' he asked.

'All I can think is that your grandfather discovered his secret. A man of true honour and purity, your grandfather would have been distraught. They were close friends. Nevertheless, Gruber must have turned upon him. Like an animal backed into a corner, he lashed out in order to protect himself and his secret.

'Your grandfather was accused of consorting with the Dark Powers. He laughed these accusations off, but, at Gruber's prompting, a witch hunter was brought in to conduct an investigation and adjudicate on the matter. This witch hunter, a vile snake of a man, "interviewed" the household servants, and the members of the court. Many screams could be heard echoing through the castle during these "interviews".

'On that last fateful night, he entered your grandfather's personal chambers and discovered a shrine to the Dark Gods. Human hearts had been left there as offerings, and blood was scrawled across the walls – vile Chaotic symbols.

'Gruber framed your grandfather, of that I am sure. So, your grandfather was put to death, your father was exiled, and you were branded with that cruel mark upon your face.'

'But… the whole court turned against him. They collaborated with Gruber's story.' Said Stefan.

The old man shrugged. 'Politicians are easily bought. Perhaps they too had been granted longevity through the worship of the Dark Gods. We shall probably never know. Long years passed. Once I learnt the truth, only months ago, I knew not what to do. I could not speak out – a physician's word against that of an elector and his entire court? Ha! I would have been flogged and hanged from the gates of the castle to be pecked over by the crows. So I fled, and here I am.'

'It is a dark tale,' rumbled the massive priest, Gunthar.

'I don't understand why he kept me alive,' said Stefan. 'Surely it would have been better for him to have killed me as a babe. If the truth came out, I would always try to kill him. Plus, as much as I dislike the thought, I am the rightful heir to the position of elector. It makes no sense.'

'Well, I agree with you on that. It doesn't make sense,' said Gunthar, 'but from everything I hear, the man lost his mind many years ago. Who can guess the motivations of a madman?'

'He did try to kill me,' Stefan said, only just realising it himself, 'but it was much later. The mission to guard the pass. It *was* a suicidal mission. Why wait so long to remove me?'

'You've got me, lad.'

'Well, there is my truth. There is nothing for it now, but to gut the wretch.'

'There is the problem, lad,' said Gunthar. 'He ain't an easy man to kill.'

Stefan frowned. 'A sword through the heart should do it.'

'That's where you are wrong. If I smashed this great hammer into his skull,' he said, hefting his massive two-handed hammer up for emphasis, 'it wouldn't kill him. I'm sure he wouldn't look too pretty afterwards, but it would not kill him.'

Stefan frowned, looking dubious. 'In my experience, staving a man's head in usually does the trick.'

'Ah, but he is not truly a man any more. It's the power of Chaos,' said the priest, giving the protective sign of Sigmar to ward off evil. 'It protects him. He sold his soul into damnation, and now the gods of Chaos protect their pawn greedily. Even with all the power of my faith, I could not kill the fiend. Damn me, but I wish I could.'

'So… how can we kill him?'

'There is something that can kill him, but it will not be easy to recover. I have learnt that...' Something rattled in the chimney, and the priest stopped talking. An object fell into the flames, scattering embers and sparks, and rolled out onto the floor. It was a metal globe about the size of fist, covered in small perforations.

'What in Sigmar's name?' boomed Gunthar, leaping to his feet. Green smoke began to seep from the holes in the metal globe, and the stench made Stefan gag.

'Back,' shouted Piter, coughing. 'Poison!' Stefan drew his sword. His eyes began to weep, and the foul smoke entered his lungs, making his head spin. Coughing, he put his hand over his mouth, and followed Gunthar through the door into the chapel. Bustling the old physician into the room, he slammed the door behind them. Piter dropped to his knees, coughing blood onto the flagstones.

'Bar the doors!' barked Stefan, wiping at his watering eyes. The soldiers sprang into action, loading crossbows and handguns, and taking up positions at the windows. Two of them barricaded the main door of the chapel, and another pair began to shift a heavy wooden pew in front of the door leading to the living quarters.

'Where's Mikael?' boomed the voice of Gunthar. 'Where is he, damn it?'

'The lad? Tending the horses,' the scout Wilhelm replied. The massive priest swore, pushed the pew out of his way with one hand, and stormed back into the kitchen.

'Damn!' spat Stefan. 'You two,' he said, indicating a pair of his soldiers, 'go with him!'

Green smoke filled the room, and the pair covered their faces with their arms, and ran into the room, following the massive priest. Gunthar slammed straight into the small door leading to the courtyard, smashing the door off its hinges with his shoulder, and burst into the fresh air. His eyes were stinging painfully, and tears ran down his face. A pair of black crossbow bolts slammed into his chest, and he grunted, but did not fall. The soldiers appeared behind him, gasping for air. There was the cracking sound of a handgun, and one of the men fell, the shot striking him in the throat.

Ducking his head, Gunthar lumbered across the courtyard and pushed his way into the stable. The horses were kicking at the doors, whinnying in terror. He saw the young lad Mikael lying on the ground in a pool of blood, and one of von Kessel's soldiers slumped against the wall. A small, black-clad figure stood above the corpses, a pair of blades held in its hands. It spun as Gunthar entered the room, its movements swift and inhuman. Gunthar saw cruel slanted eyes glinting beneath its black hood.

With an evil hiss, it sprang towards the priest, darting forwards with great speed. Gunthar had his two-handed hammer in his grip, and he swung it at the approaching assassin with all his might. The creature anticipated the move, and leapt at the wall to avoid the blow. Spinning in mid-air, the creature hit the wall feet first, and sprang off it, taking it sailing over the blow and past the priest. It plunged one of its blades into the neck of the soldier following Gunthar, as it descended, and he fell to the ground gurgling blood. He convulsed violently, and blood-specked foam emerged from his mouth. Gunthar noted that the blades the creature wielded were smeared with a dark greenish substance. As he watched, a drop of it fell to the ground, hissing and smoking slightly: poison. The creature rolled easily to its feet, crouching, facing Gunthar once more.

'Hellspawn,' growled the priest. He saw that the creature had a tail, wrapped to its tip in black cloth, which ended in a barbed metal spike. It hovered dangerously just over the creature's shoulder. It too was slick with poison.

'In Sigmar's name, I will cleanse you from this world!' He raised his hammer over his head and charged at the assassin, shouting wordlessly. The creature bared its sharp yellow teeth, bobbing lightly on its feet, twirling its blades. It leapt to one side at the last moment, but the big priest predicted this, and moving with a speed and deftness defying his size, he changed the angle of his blow. The hammer smashed into the chest of the assassin creature, and it was sent crashing through one of the wooden stable stalls. Gunthar followed it in. The blow crushed its chest, white bone splinters piercing its black robes. It looked up at him with hateful eyes for a moment before Gunthar caved its head in.

The priest left the stable and ran across the courtyard. A handgun cracked and he felt a sharp sting as the shot grazed his thigh. Ignoring the pain, he re-entered the kitchen. The smoke had almost dissipated. Gunthar quickly crossed the room and entered the chapel. Slamming the door, he helped the men block it with the heavy wooden pew.

'You're hit,' said Stefan, seeing the bolts still protruding from the warrior priest's chest. The big man grunted, and pulled the bolts from his flesh. 'Had worse,' he said, throwing them to the ground.

'My men? And the boy?' asked Stefan, reloading his pistols.

'Gone,' said the priest simply. The remaining soldiers within the chapel had taken up positions at the windows. They were firing sporadically out into the darkness with crossbows, bows and handguns.

'Here they come again!' shouted Albrecht, firing a crossbow out into the night. Stefan ran to a window as the man standing there slumped to the ground, a knife in his throat. Glancing out through the shutters, he saw a figure dart past, and fired his pistol at point-blank range. Smoke billowed from the weapon as it boomed.

'How many?' shouted the captain.

'I don't know. Too many,' came the reply from the sergeant.

'How is Piter, Gunthar?'

'Unconscious. His heartbeat is weak, but he'll live.' An axe slammed into the outside of the door leading to the kitchen, splintering the panels. The warrior priest stood with his warhammer in his hands, awaiting whatever was coming through. The axe slammed into the door again, and it was smashed to pieces. Stepping forwards, Gunthar slammed his hammer into the face of the first man. Two others leapt forwards, thrusting halberds through the doorway. Gunthar knocked them aside with a sweep of his hammer. Stefan was suddenly at his side. He unloaded his pistol into the face of one of the men, and stabbed forwards with his sword, slaying the other. It was then that he saw that they wore the purple and yellow of Ostermark state troops.

'Sigmar above,' he muttered. He was thrown aside by Gunthar as a pair of crossbow bolts streaked through the doorway. A handgun cracked and one of Stefan's men fell, the shot taking him in the back. A drift of snow dropped down into the chapel from above, and from the ground, Stefan looked up to see a pair of black-clad figures dropping from the high rafters. 'Behind us!' he shouted as the figures landed lightly in the middle of the room.

An arm flashed out, and one of the soldiers at a window collapsed, clutching at something embedded in the back of his neck. The two figures surveyed the room quickly, and their gaze snapped onto the prostrate figure of Piter. Moving simultaneously, they launched themselves through the melee, cart-wheeling over combatants and ducking beneath swinging swords. Stefan realised their target, and threw himself in between the two assailants and the fallen physician.

The captain lashed out with his sword at one of them. The figure swayed back, the blade passing within inches of its belly, and slashed out with its own weapons. It had long metal claws hooked over its hands, and it slashed at him like a rabid animal. One of the weapons scored a trio of bloody grazes across his arm, and he grunted in pain, defending frantically against the lightning-quick opponent. 'Albrecht!' he shouted. 'Protect Piter!'

The sergeant turned, and saw the other black-clad figure closing on the physician. Raising his heavy crossbow to his shoulder, he fired. The bolt shot across the room, aimed squarely at the small figure. As if sensing the approaching danger, the figure spun suddenly, a clawed hand flashing out to catch the bolt in mid air. It spun the bolt around its hand so that it held it point downwards, like a dagger, and stabbed it down into the eye of the unconscious physician, killing him instantly.

A massive hand descended on the crouching killer, grasping it around its scrawny neck. Gunthar raised the struggling creature high in the air and smashed its head against the doorframe. It went limp in his hands, and he threw it to the ground disdainfully.

Stefan was frantically defending himself against the other assassin, barely managing to keep the flashing claws at bay. He received another wound, three claws scratching across his thigh, and he stepped back, growling in pain. The black-clad figure leapt into the air, jumping to the sculptured top of one of the windows, some ten feet up. With another leap, it was amongst the rafters, and then it was gone.

Stefan knelt beside the assassin that Gunthar had slain, peeling back the black bandages that concealed its long face. Beneath was dirty, matted fur filled with lice, and he thought for a second that it was some bizarre mask, but it wasn't. The creature had a long face, ending in a black nose covered in tattered whiskers. Its mouth was open, exposing long teeth, cracked and dirty, and a purplish tongue hanging limply from the side of is mouth. One of its eyes was pale and pus-ridden. The creature was covered in open, weeping sores, and it stank like a rotten corpse.

'Shallya protect us all,' said Albrecht, covering his mouth. 'It's some kind of beastman.'

'Skaven,' said Stefan.

Another of Stefan's men by the windows fell, an arrow through his neck. A flaming brand was thrown through the window, arcing end over end and coming to a rest on the floor. More flaming brands were hurled within the structure, and there were thumps on the roof as others landed there.

'We have to get out of here,' roared Stefan. 'To the horses!' Gunthar led the charge through the door into the kitchen, leaping over the upended pew. There were two men in the room, one frantically reloading a crossbow, and the other armed with a halberd. The weapon was too big to use well in the enclosed space, and Gunthar ploughed into him with his shoulder, driving him back into the wall.

The crossbowman dropped his weapon and drew out a small dagger, intending to stab it into the warrior priest's neck. He never got the chance. Albrecht's sword pierced his chest and he fell to the ground. The sergeant spat on the fallen man.

Gunthar nodded his thanks, rising to his feet. The man he had charged into was motionless, his eyes blank and staring, his back snapped.

'Shields at the ready!' shouted Stefan, ushering his soldiers out into the courtyard. Several crossbow bolts slammed into the raised shields. Again, a handgun sounded, and one of the soldiers fell without a sound. With a curse, Stefan wrenched the shield from the dead man, and the remaining soldiers raced into the stables.

'Two crossbowmen, one handgunner. He's the dangerous one,' said Gunthar. 'He's positioned up behind the big rock on the rise, fifty yards back. A damn good shot, as well.'

'I'll go,' said one of the soldiers. It was Wilhelm, the scout that had found the chapel. 'I know where he means.'

'I'll go with you,' said Albrecht. Stefan nodded, and
the two men raced out into the courtyard, ducking and
weaving. A crossbow bolt slammed into the snow-
covered cobbles at their feet before they ducked
around the corner of the building, running for the
trees.

'Ready the horses,' commanded Stefan. 'You can
ride?' he asked Gunthar. The massive man screwed up
his blood-spattered face.

'Can't say I have a fondness for it, but aye, I can ride.'

KARL RELOADED HIS Hochland longrifle quickly and
efficiently. He had owned the weapon for almost a
decade, and he knew it like he knew no other thing in
the entire world. He cared for it more than he cared for
his wife, his friends would joke, but it was true, and
she knew it. Its range and accuracy were unlike any
other weapons he had ever held. Twice he had won the
marksman trophy within the army of Ostermark. He
had received his prize from the grand elector himself –
a golden pin showing a grinning skull with a laurel
around its head and a musket ball between its teeth.
Not that he owned it still – it had been sold long ago
for expensive ale and cheap women.

Raising the weapon to his shoulder once again, he
sighted along its long barrel. The courtyard was empty,
but he knew that the traitors were still cowering in the
stable, and that they had to come out at some point.
He didn't care – he was a patient man. He could wait.

Two of them had fled a few minutes ago, but he had
been reloading at the time, and had missed the shot. It
mattered not – the one he was truly interested in was
still inside the stable – the massive heretic priest. He

had been annoyed with himself for missing his chances so far. He should have killed him when he had run across the courtyard below, but his shot had deviated, barely scraping his leg. The other shot was a long shot, through two open doorways, and he had not been surprised when it had missed its mark. Still, it had taken down one of the rebel men of Ostermark, so it was not all bad.

His breathing was slow and measured, as was required for a marksman. He could see around a score of men approaching the stables, crouched low, swords and halberds in hand. One was slain as he watched, an arrow through his chest. The chapel was blazing, consumed with flames. He squinted along the long barrel, his breathing pausing as he saw movement. A soldier stuck his head out from the stable. Stupid of him, thought Karl as he pulled the trigger. He saw the man fall, and the spray of blood splatter across the snow. Quickly and methodically, he reloaded again, and took up his position once more.

'Come on, priest,' he whispered to himself. There was a price on the man's head, set by the grand count himself. It was enough for a man to retire with, and that was exactly what Karl planned to do. Buy an inn, and spend his years hunting for game, that was what he wanted to do. His wife wouldn't care that he wasn't around much, she was used to that, but he knew she would be happier knowing that the father of her children was a soldier no longer. He had no real desire to remain in the army. He had done his bit for Ostermark and the Empire, and if he could just manage to kill the priest, that would be it.

He knew that there were less than half a dozen men in the stables, and the crouching men were drawing ever closer to it. They fanned out to encircle it. One of them fell to the ground, his face blown away by a pistol shot. Still, those inside the stable were horribly outnumbered. They would have to make a break for it any second, probably on horseback. That was what Karl was waiting for. He was confident that he could take down the priest, but he would get no prize if those others got to him first. 'Come on,' he whispered to himself.

Killing greenskins or marauders in the north was one thing, but gunning down fellow men of the Empire made him uncomfortable. It went against everything within him to pull the trigger and kill men wearing the purple and yellow, but he reminded himself that these were Chaos-worshipping heretics, and no longer men of Ostermark, spreaders of plague, lies and deceit, and the priest was the worst of the lot. He had condemned himself. How a man could betray his own, he knew not.

Karl had seen the small, dark-clad figures moving below. They moved silently, and so fast that they barely seemed human at all. Daemonic allies of the priest, perhaps? He tried to push them from his mind.

Karl heard a sound behind him, a twig cracking underfoot. One of the clumsy crossbowmen, he thought. They were hopeless. He could never live with himself if one of those dullards managed to bag the priest instead of him. Ignoring the sound, he concentrated on the stable.

Suddenly there was a knife at his throat. 'Nice gun, you Chaos-worshipping scum,' came a hoarse whisper, and the knife slashed open his throat. A hand held him down as he thrashed around in the snow, turning it red with his blood.

Wilhelm held the man until he lay still. He wiped his knife on the purple and yellow tabard of the marksman, and looked up at Albrecht. The sergeant pointed down the slope, indicating silently that there were two men there. Wilhelm motioned for Albrecht to stay where he was, and slunk off down the slope, his body crouched low, moving like a hunting cat. Albrecht shrugged, and sat down in the snow, hefting the dead man's longrifle. Expensive things, he mused, noting the detailed engraving work up the barrel and the gold worked into the heavy stock. He wondered how much the engineer, Markus, would pay for it.

Wilhelm returned moments later, his hunting knife dripping with blood. 'Done?' asked Albrecht.

'Aye, 'tis done,' said the man. The pair of men ran down through the snow to aid their captain.

KICKING HIS STEED forwards, Stefan galloped from the stables. A pair of men who had crept right up to the stable entrance thrust halberds at him, and he swayed back in the saddle, almost falling. His steed reared, kicking out with flashing hooves. One of the men thrust forwards, burying the point of his halberd in the chest of the horse. It screamed and fell to the ground, kicking. Stefan, swearing, landed heavily. A halberd flashed towards him, but it was knocked into the ground by a sweeping blow from a warhammer. The priest reversed his strike, and crashed his hammer into the soldier's jaw, smashing it to pieces and sending the man flying through the air.

'And you were asking if *I* could ride?' he commented gruffly, just before smashing his hammer into the shoulder of the other soldier. The man's arm went limp, and he dropped his weapon. He was dispatched by a crushing blow to his head.

The captain was helped to his feet by a soldier, and he brushed himself down. There were nine men arrayed against them. 'Die, traitor,' one of them yelled out, running at the big priest with sword drawn. The priest caught his assailant's sword on the haft of his warhammer, and drove his knee up powerfully into the man's groin, buckling him. He slammed the handle of his hammer down onto the man's neck. Placing his foot up on the man's back, he raised his hammer high into the air, his voice booming out with power and authority.

'You have been duped, men of Ostermark! It is not I, nor these men who are the traitors, but your lord and master, the Grand Count Otto Gruber! I am a priest of our Lord Sigmar! Look who it is that stands beside me!'

The men looked at each other nervously. 'Von Kessel?' one of them called out, unsure of himself.

'Aye it is me, man,' growled the captain. 'Throw down your weapons. We are not your enemies.'

'No!' shouted one of the soldiers. 'He is in league with the heretic priest! Look at his face! He bears the mark of Chaos itself!' He threw himself forwards, and was smashed to the ground by Gunthar. The last of the soldiers looked around them warily as Albrecht and the scout arrived behind them.

'Sergeant Albrecht,' one of them called out nervously. 'Does the priest speak the truth?'

'He does, Kurt Nieman. Throw 'em down, lads.'

One by one, the soldiers dropped their weapons into the snow.

CHAPTER TWENTY-ONE

THE SKY OVERHEAD was black, but filled with light. Ghostly green and blue luminosity rolled across the heavens, forming what looked like giant mountains and castles high in the stars. Sometimes, Hroth thought he could see shapes up there amongst the mountains, whirling and flying through the night. The colours swirled and re-formed, creating ever more awe-inspiring shapes and dramatic colours. The blues and greens changed to fiery yellows and reds, and it was then that Hroth felt at his strongest. The realm of the gods, Hroth thought. He felt privileged to gaze upon the worlds inhabited by the great ones, if that was truly what they were. He wondered if the blood citadel of Khorne was atop one of those mountains, the castle of skulls where the god sat upon his great bronze throne.

The chosen of Khorne had been travelling across the landscape for what felt like months as days and nights blurred into one another. He could never remember the sun rising or falling, but knew that it must have. Some moments, the burning sun blazed down upon him, burning his face and making his armour blisteringly hot. The red earth beneath his feet exuded heat, and all around him he saw shimmering heat waves. Creatures flickered in the corner of his eyes, but nothing was ever there when he turned to face them.

At other times, it was the dead of night, and the green moon of Chaos hung heavy in the sky, close and throbbing with power. Icy winds ripped through him, chilling him to the core. The land itself shifted and changed, although he could never pinpoint the moment when the change had come. One moment he would be walking over red rock, the next he would be climbing strangely hexagonal black rocks that continued up before him as far as he could see. Sometimes, he walked through thin crevices of water-slick rock that he could only just fit his shoulders through. Waterfalls of black water fell from thousands of feet above him, roaring down into bottomless pits.

Always, he was driven on. He had to reach the tower of skulls, he knew that, but he had only glimpsed the massive structure in the far-off distance. He struggled on through ash wastelands, across plains of salt, walking amongst the wind-blasted skeletons of ancient, gigantic beasts.

He could feel the power of the place working on his body and on his mind. It was like a pressure in the back of his head, a pressure that built the further he travelled. He knew that if he succumbed to it, his flesh would change, alter, and he would no longer be himself at all. Give yourself up to the change, a voice within him kept saying. Give yourself to Chaos fully.

The pressure in his head built, and he could feel the struggle within. He dropped to his knees, his hands to his head. His body was resisting the change, but he felt it within him, unstoppable. His muscles twitched uncontrollably, and he could feel his organs being stretched and squeezed. His bones were shifting, breaking and reforming in stranger configurations. His backbone fused into a single solid mass, and spines burst from his skin and armour, wracking him with pain. His joints cracked, and his muscles and tendons tore and strained to contain his contorting, altered form. Flames burst up the length of his horns. With a roar, he pushed himself to his feet, refusing to give in to the mutations. He was unchanged, the same as he had been for the countless minutes or months that he had been wandering.

He fought the minions of this shadow-realm. He tore the heart out of a creature that may once have been human, but had long since changed to something *other*. It flapped pathetically on the ground, its clawed flipper-like appendages thrashing madly as he stood over it, holding its still-beating heart. Loping bloodhounds of the ether scattered at his approach, and daemonic bats swooped down at him, feeding from his life-energy.

He battled another champion of the gods who wandered in these lands, a warrior in golden fluted armour with feathered limbs and a great scythe. The champion had summoned to him a host of cackling daemons of the Great Changer, cavorting creatures whose shapes flowed from one aspect to another, giggling insanely, and assailing him with flames of change that burst from their multi-jointed fingertips. Enraged, he smashed the daemons out of his way to get at the golden-armoured warrior, but each time he slew one of the capering daemons, two smaller creatures clawed out from its skin, groaning and spitting at him. He ploughed through these fell creatures, feeling their insubstantial claws scratching at his soul, and battled the champion. The heavens moved above them, the stars sweeping over them swiftly as they fought, but eventually Hroth cut down his foe and raised his skull to the heavens in honour of his god. As he stood there, the champion rotted away to nothingness, the skin shrivelling from his bones, the bones crumbling to dust.

Hroth could not remember when he had rested last, but knew that to sleep was to abandon himself to madness and destruction. When he closed his eyes, he could see the daemons of Khorne staring at him, assessing him. He saw the bloodletters, the foot soldiers of the Blood God.

They stood before him, powerful creatures whose flesh had been flayed from their bodies, exposing the muscle beneath, slick with blood. Their elongated heads had tall curving horns atop them, and their long coiling tongues tasted him. Their eyes reflected the flames that blazed in his own. They stood before him every time he even blinked, holding their massive hellblades. They seemed to be waiting for something, looking at him hungrily with their heads cocked to the sides. Whether they waited to feast on him, or to follow him, he knew not.

Suddenly Hroth stood at the base of the great tower of skulls: his goal. It was immense, reaching up into the skies that rolled with living flame and smoke. He walked around the base of the tower, counting over fifty paces around its circumference, and it rose hundreds of feet into the air. This was the tower that the great Asavar Kul had built for Khorne, and it contained the skull of every one killed by the great man.

Closing his eyes, he saw the bloodletters watching him curiously, madness and fury held in check, for now. Stepping to the massive tower, he placed his fingers into the eye sockets of a skull, and pulled himself upwards. Using the skulls as grips for his hands and feet, Hroth the Blooded began to climb the skull tower of Asavar Kul.

CHAPTER TWENTY-TWO

WEARILY, THE CAPTAIN, the priest, the sergeant and the remaining soldiers rode towards the encamped army, bloody and tired. Stefan nodded to the Ostermark state soldiers they passed. They too looked as if they had been involved in battle. Word of the captain's arrival spread quickly through the camp, and a young soldier came running up to him. 'Captain! You must come quickly.'

'What is it, man?'

'It's the reiksmarshal. He has been injured.'

'What? Is he all right?'

'I don't know, sir. I was sent to fetch you to him.' The captain kicked his steed into a gallop, and he thundered through the snow-covered encampment towards the command tent. Leaping from his horse and throwing the reins to an attendant, he entered the tent, his heart pounding.

The tent was dark, and the reiksmarshal lay on his pallet, his eyes closed and his skin drawn and pale. His chest was bandaged, Stefan saw, and blood was seeping from a wound beneath the wrappings.

At his side was a priestess of Shallya, a woman whose face was far older than her middling years. She was dabbing at his head with a damp cloth. She turned as Stefan entered, and curtseyed briefly before returning her attention to her patient.

'What happened?' Stefan muttered.

'It was an ambush,' said a deep voice from behind him. It was the captain of the Reiklandguard, Lederstein – a tall and humourless man. 'We were sweeping the banks of the Upper Talabec, driving back greenskin tribes, when we were attacked. It was before dawn yesterday, and the lowland was covered in a thick fog. Small, hunched beastmen attacked us out of nowhere. They were all around us, emerging from the marshland and the reeds that cover the banks of the river. We fought them off, but the reiksmarshal was struck down. Shot from the saddle, he was, by a fell handgun of the enemy.'

'No natural weapon, that,' piped up the priestess of Shallya. 'A thrice-cursed shot, it was.'

'You removed the shot, lady of mercy?' asked Stefan.

'Of course I removed it. Two inches to the left and it would have struck the heart.'

'Do you still have the shot?'

'I do,' said the priestess, pulling out a small, heavy tin, and handing it to the captain. 'Don't touch it,' she said as the captain opened it. 'It is an evil thing. I have placed blessings upon it, but it is powerful.'

Inside the tin, there was a cylindrical metal rod, around two inches long. Its tip was made from a roughly-cut green stone. The stone seemed to pulse slightly, and Stefan could feel the warmth coming off it. It made his skin crawl, and he quickly closed the lid and gave the tin back to the priestess.

'It was only one shot. He will survive it, yes?' asked Stefan, looking at the reiksmarshal in concern.

'Only one shot,' the lady scoffed. 'He should make it, but it'll be a close-run thing. That shot contains some evil poison, and it had a grip on the man's heart. It still does, but he should come through, Shallya wishing. Strong as a lion, this one. He will run this fever for at least two more days, and I doubt he will be conscious for any of that time. If he is, he will not be lucid.'

'Not lucid?'

'By that, I mean he won't be giving any orders for some time, captain, and he will not be fit to fight for weeks to come. I know that's what you are wondering. You soldiers are all the same,' she said, shaking her head. She dabbed at the reiksmarshal's head once more. 'I have to leave. Five men have been struck down with plague this morning, captain. I will do what I can for them, but you must be aware that it may spread. I will be back within the hour to check on him.'

Stefan sat down heavily with a sigh. He touched the pale hand of the reiksmarshal. It was cold and dank. 'The beastmen you fought,' he said, looking up at Lederstein, 'were they… rats?'

'Aye, they were,' replied the captain of the Reiklandguard. 'Hateful rat-spawn fiends of Chaos. How did you know? You have fought them before?'

'They attacked us last night,' Stefan said, nodding, 'and I know who sent them. Captain Lederstein, would your knights be willing to join me in killing the fiend who set this up?'

STEFAN STALKED FROM the tent where the reiksmarshal lay unconscious, and ordered Albrecht to start readying the troops. 'You're going for Gruber, aren't you lad?' said the massive priest of Sigmar. 'You're going to march east to find him.'

'What of it?' snapped von Kessel. 'The man's a threat to Ostermark and the Empire. He must be destroyed.'

'Aye, he must, but I told you before, you ain't going be able to kill him.'

'Right. So what do you propose to do? Let him be? Hope that he dies of old age? No, I'll take the fight to him, and I *will* destroy him.'

'Strong words, lad. The anger's got you. That's good; it will make you fight hard, but it won't do you no good against him. I've killed some big, powerful things with this hammer in my time. Real big,' he said, and Stefan believed him. 'But I couldn't kill him – not with this weapon. I know what *will* kill him, though: a blade, forged within magical flames on the fey isle of Ulthuan. It is long since lost, but I have *seen* where it lies – Sigmar has granted me this vision. In darkness it resides, protected by the sleepless dead.' The light of faith was in the priest's eyes.

Within the hour, the camp was being dismantled, the entire army readying for war. Stefan raised a hand. In the distance, the massive warrior priest, riding uneasily, raised a hand back in salute. Thirty of the Reiklandguard knights rode at his side, as well as seventy-five other riders.

'Be swift,' Stefan whispered, watching Gunthar riding away from the army. 'I will pursue Gruber and make him face me. Within the week, I will face him across the field of battle, sword or no sword.'

Stefan lowered his hand as the warrior priest disappeared from sight.

Your time has come, Gruber, he swore. I will crush you utterly, and reclaim the honour of my family.

GRAND COUNT OTTO Gruber coughed uncontrollably. Hawking, he spat a foul mass of green phlegm to the ground. Something in it writhed, and he giggled girlishly, forgetting momentarily that he had company. Composing himself, he turned back towards his guest.

The Blind One was a gnarled, ancient creature bent almost double, leaning on a crooked staff. It wore befouled robes, and its limbs were wrapped in putrid, rotten-smelling bandages, in the manner of a leper; quite appropriate, thought Gruber. Leprosy was but one of the boons bestowed upon the Blind One. The creature's face was covered in blisters and boils, weeping down into its toothless maw. Its nose, or the half of it that remained, twitched spasmodically.

'Your skaven agents did their work, oh Blind One?' asked the count. 'The physician is no more?' The old skaven bobbed its head. 'And the reiksmarshal as well? My, my, this is a good day. Yes, a good day indeed.' The count rubbed his pudgy hands together.

'My plagues are spreading nicely. They're almost good enough to rival some of yours, I think, eh? Things go splendidly well,' gloated Gruber. 'What of our... mutual friend in the north? We must be ready to

move when the call comes... Your servants are ready to
strike, yes?'

Again, the Blind One bobbed its head.

'Good, good. We must both be ready. We have done
all the preparations. All that remains is to cast the fatal
blow. The Empire will be ours, and plague and pestilence shall reign.'

'*Pestilensssssss,*' hissed the skaven.

CHAPTER TWENTY-THREE

HROTH CLIMBED THE tower of skulls for what seemed like an eternity. He did not glance down, but had he, he would have been unable to see the ground lost in fire and smoke far below him. Skulls were crushed under his grip, but he barely noticed, intent on climbing ever upwards.

Lightning struck the tower beside him, and splinters of bone and teeth cut his face. The skulls shifted, and he held on tightly so as not to fall. Skinless flying daemons, all muscle, tendon and claws, assailed him, tearing at his hands, prying his fingers from eye sockets. He swatted them away from him, and continued his ascent.

Finally, he climbed to the top of the tower, and pulled himself over the edge, breathing hard. His arms and legs ached from the climb, and he flexed his fingers. He stood atop a plateau. Hundreds of thousands of skulls stacked neatly in piles, reached high into the sky, as far as the eye could see. The sky was afire, angry red flames ripping across the heavens.

Asavar Kul sat before him on a throne of skulls, red eyes watching him with interest from beneath his fully enclosed helmet.

The sword, the Slayer of Kings, lay on his lap. Dark power coalesced within the massive weapon, writhing as if in torment. The daemon U'zhul, straining ever to escape its bindings, Hroth realised.

Asavar Kul was a massive man, exuding immense power. His glowing red eyes bored into Hroth, and he felt humbled. He dropped to his knees before this avatar of the gods, paying his respects to one of the greatest warlords that the world had ever seen, one of the Everchosen of Chaos.

'Rise, warrior,' the great warlord said, his voice strong and loud. Hroth raised himself to his full height. Still, if the warlord stood up from his skull throne, he would have towered over him.

'Why do you seek me out here, warrior?' boomed the Everchosen. 'Why do you interrupt me?'

'Everchosen,' said Hroth, licking his lips, and choosing his words carefully. 'I come seeking power.'

'Power! Bah! Of course you seek power, it is the way of Chaos: the way of the Norscan, the Hung and the Kurgan. It is the way it has always been, and ever will be, but what is it you truly seek?'

'I... to kill, to raise a skull tower to rival yours, and to honour great Khorne.'

Asavar Kul stood up from his throne, hefting the Slayer of Kings before him. A screaming daemonic face could be seen within the blade, eyes staring out malevolently. He rolled his shoulders, the massive metal plates of his armour sliding over each other smoothly. 'A tower to rival mine, eh? That would be impressive, impressive indeed.' He swung the blade in an arc around him, and Hroth took an inadvertent step backwards. Power crackled around the blade, lightning that arced up and down its surface and over the massive warrior's armoured arms. Hroth's axe was in his hands, although he did not remember drawing it. It felt heavy in his grip.

'There is fear in you, warrior. I can sense it in your heart,' said the massive warlord menacingly. 'What is it that you fear?'

'I fear nothing, warlord,' said Hroth, his voice sounding weak in his ears.

'You fear death itself,' stated Asavar Kul. 'Death is nothing. You think that death is an end to your service to the Dark Gods? You have much to learn,' he said, leaning his head from one side to the other. 'Your service to the gods continues long after death, warrior. For what is death to the gods themselves? It is nothing. You could die here atop this plateau of skulls, and the gods would not care.' He took a step towards Hroth. The chosen of Khorne raised his axe before him.

'You are nothing, little man,' the warlord continued. 'You are nothing to the gods, and you are nothing to me.'

'I seek to continue the war that you started, the war that ended with your defeat,' growled Hroth, his anger building.

'Do you hear nothing that I say? My death meant nothing. The gods did not mourn my passing. Always, there is another to start the slaughter afresh.'

'I seek your blade, great warlord. With it the tribes will rally behind me.'

'This?' said Asavar Kul, holding the blade up. 'It is but a sword, but if you want it, you will have to best me. Little man, you think you can take it from me?'

'I will, or I will die trying,' snarled Hroth.

'As you wish it,' intoned the warlord, and stepped forwards to cut the Khorne champion down, another skull for his mountainous tower.

CHAPTER TWENTY-FOUR

STEFAN RODE ACROSS the open field, his steed stepping through the frost-covered grass. His breath steamed out before him, and he resisted the urge to blow warm air onto his frozen hands. The light was the strange cold glow of pre-dawn. Not that the sun would change much today, for the skies were bleak and filled with cloud – no sunlight would penetrate that thick blanket. Fog clung to the ground, wisping across the open field and collecting in the dips and hollows of the uneven earth.

Albrecht rode a pace behind him, as did Lederstein, the captain of the Reiklandguard. Behind them rode twenty of his resplendent knights, imposing big men riding on their massive warhorses. One of the knights held the standard of his order high in the air, and another carried Stefan's own banner, flying the colours of Ostermark.

The captain's eyes were hard and cold, staring straight ahead of him as he approached the cluster of men across the field. A massive banner flew there too, also displaying the colours of Ostermark. However, that banner bore the heraldic markings of the grand count, the leader of all the forces of Ostermark. Stefan felt bile rise in his throat at the sight of it.

'Easy, you stupid creature,' hissed Albrecht as his horse pulled at the reins.

For almost two weeks, Stefan had marched across the Empire, chasing Gruber's army almost to the foothills of the Worlds Edge Mountains. He had heard nothing of Gunthar and his mission to uncover the only weapon said to be able to kill the count. Although he hoped that the warrior priest fared well, Stefan cared not for the weapon – all he wanted to do, all that dominated his waking and resting thoughts, was to face the count on the field of battle. Today, his wishes would come to fruition.

A shout barked out, and the troop of some fifty greatswords wearing the purple and yellow of Ostermark stood sharply to attention, raising their massive weapons to their shoulders. Before them, the aides and advisors of the grand count clustered around an enclosed palanquin held on the shoulders of six men. As Stefan and his men approached, the palanquin was lowered smoothly to the ground. Its occupant could not be seen, hidden behind a gauze screen, but Stefan had no doubt that the pretender Gruber sat within.

Von Kessel raised his hand and the knights with him halted, their steeds snorting and stamping their hooves. He nodded to Albrecht and Lederstein, and dismounted to approach the palanquin. He flashed a glance over the advisors, seeing the coldness in their eyes. The copper-skinned Tilean advisor Andros regarded him with disdain, a smug smile curling the corners of his mouth. Johann, Gruber's nephew and heir, did not even attempt to hide his hatred, staring at him murderously.

A pair of men raised long horns to their mouths and blew a long blast into the cold air. 'The merciful Grand Count Otto Gruber, Prince of Bechafen, Chancellor and true chosen claimant of the title Elector of Oster-mark!' boomed one of the men that had been carrying the palanquin. Stefan's face curled in disgust.

A mechanical apparatus on the top of the palanquin whirred into action, clicking and turning as dials and cogs began to move. A small clockwork doorway opened and a miniature, mechanical drumming bear marched out, its head tipping from side to side as it struck its bronze drum. A pair of mechanised skeletons, each bearing a sand timer, walked jerkily to the front of the palanquin. One turned left and the other turned right, and they began to march across the top of the enclosed box. As they did so, the curtain hiding Gruber from view was jerked back, exposing the man reclining on a bed of pillows, stroking a dead toad. When the curtain was pulled completely back, the miniature skeletons marched back to their alcoves, and the drumming bear retreated back through its doorway. With a click, the doors slammed shut, and the whirring of gears and cogs ceased.

'Marvellous, isn't it!' exclaimed the grand count, clapping his pudgy hands together. 'Simply wonderful!' The fat man shuffled his weight. 'Welcome, Captain Stefan von Kessel. I hear that you have been performing well. I am most pleased. You do Ostermark honour with your actions, young man. Come forward, I want to see you.'

Stefan's jaw twitched and he clenched his hands at his sides, repressing the urge to leap forwards and kill the fiend where he sat. 'I would be much better, Gruber, if I had not learnt that something is rotten in the heart of Ostermark,' he managed, his anger barely contained and his voice strained.

'You will address the grand count with the proper respect, whoreson,' snarled the black-clad Johann. Gruber waved him into silence.

'Rotten, is it? You talk of the plague? Terrible thing it is, yes. Terrible,' said the grand count, a slight smile on his face, and his eyes flashing with dark humour.

'I talk of something worse than plague, *Gruber*,' snarled Stefan, casting Johann a venomous glare. 'I talk of the worship of the Dark Gods, and of the deception of the Ostermark itself: *the enemy within*.'

'You speak of your grandfather still, I see. You are fixated on it, boy. You must forget his treachery if ever you are to move forwards.'

'I do not speak of my grandfather, honest and just man that he was.'

'Honest and just, was he? He was a treacherous, Chaos-worshipping cur!' the count spat, spittle flying from his mouth.

Stefan saw that Gruber was looking far worse than the last time he had seen the man. His face was slick with sweat, and his hair had begun to fall out in great clumps, leaving bare patches on his head that were covered in flaking scabs. Both his eyes wept yellow liquid down his cheeks, and an attendant dabbed at them with a wet cloth every few moments. His mouth was surrounded in seeping sores, and his fleshy pink tongue licked at them unconsciously. The overpowering wafts of incense and scented oils could not disguise the rank stink of decay that hung over him.

'He betrayed Ostermark, he betrayed me, and he betrayed you, his cursed kin! It is thanks to him that you were branded with that hideous mark as a child, von Kessel, branded with that mark of Chaos to reflect his shame!' The count slumped back into his pillows. Stefan stood statue-still, his face reddening, but the count had not yet finished. 'You owe me your life, von Kessel! The witch hunters wanted you to burn in the flames with your grandfather and that bitch mother of yours. It was *I* who argued to spare you! And how do you thank me? By turning up before me with an army – my *own* army – arrayed against me as if for war. Grovel,' the enraged count screamed, growing increasingly red in the face, 'grovel before me, you whoreson! Grovel, or I will see you hang for your treacherous actions!'

'I owe you nothing, Gruber. Grovel before you? I think not. I would sooner die than do such a thing, you treacherous pretender.'

'I think that I can arrange such a thing,' hissed the count. 'You, man,' he said, throwing a pudgy finger towards the Reiklandguard captain. 'Take him. Do your Emperor his duty, and take him from my sight! I will see him hanged before the morning is out!' The knight made no move, his humourless face impassive. 'What are you waiting for? You are a loyal servant of the Empire, are you not? I am an elector count, knight. I *order* you to take him!'

'I cannot do that, my lord,' the knight said.

'You cannot… I will see you hang as well. Do it!' The knight stood still, his face betraying no emotion.

'So, I see you have spread your lies, von Kessel. I spared your life, you ungrateful wretch,' hissed the count.

For all his years this had made the guilt within Stefan surface, for he knew that it was true. Not now – now he was filled with a burning rage. This man had not saved him – he had condemned him to a painful upbringing of shame. He owed this man nothing.

'Will you accept your crimes and face trial?' asked Stefan, his voice icy.

'Face trial?' The count laughed, and then coughed, and hacked up a ball of phlegm, spitting it into a bronze spittoon. 'I have no need to. No one would accept the word of one shamed captain whose grandfather was burnt as a witch. I am an elector of the Empire!' He laughed at the ludicrousness of the suggestion.

'My grandfather was an elector. They believed *you*.'

'Yes they did my boy, but I was the elector's most trusted advisor, and a close personal friend of his. Everyone in his court collaborated with me, turning upon him. I, as his most *faithful* of friends, was much aggrieved by his heresies. It was with *much* regret and despair that I brought his crimes to the attentions of the witch hunters. I brought in a witch hunter myself, a close personal associate, who did his duty with efficiency and fervour. I was so upset by it all,' Gruber said with unconcealed mock sincerity. 'I brought that witch hunter here today, to witness just how far *you* have fallen, von Kessel,' he said, motioning to a figure amongst his courtiers. A tall, flamboyantly dressed man nodded sagely to the count, and stepped forwards, bowing extravagantly.

'It is with great displeasure that I can see clearly that the soul of this man is tainted with the filth of Chaos. The count stayed my hand when you were a child, von Kessel. It seems that his goodwill and mercy have been thrown back in his face. You will face public prosecution and witch trials, which will result in your death, I am afraid.' He motioned imperiously, and two brutish men stepped towards the captain.

'You could have had it all, von Kessel,' declared the count. 'I wanted you at my side, that is why I spared your life. You could have been my heir and successor. You are as foolish as your grandfather was before you. I offered him a place alongside my... friends. I offered him it all, all the secrets that I had learnt in overcoming my illnesses, but he refused them. I give you one last chance – will you stand at my side? Or will you choose death?'

Albrecht drew his sword, pointing it at the throat of one of the men approaching his captain. The knight of the Reiklandguard too drew his blade, a massive weapon, and held it in his hands before him. 'I will see you dead, Gruber. I will kill you and all your treacherous lackeys,' snarled Stefan, casting his gaze over the gathered courtiers. The witch hunter strode forwards.

'Your actions condemn you, von Kessel,' he snapped. Stefan drew one of his pistols and levelled it at the witch hunter.

'No,' he said, 'you condemn yourself,' and he shot the man in the face.

'THAT WENT WELL,' said Albrecht as they rode back to their army. Stefan's face was grim.

'Bring the army over the hill, sergeant. We end this today.'

HROTH BROUGHT HIS axe up as the daemon blade of Asavar Kul descended towards him. He blocked the blow, and lightning witch-fire exploded outwards from Kul's sword, dancing over the Khorne champion's weapon and up his arms. He staggered back under the force of the blow, his fingers and arms numb.

'You are nothing to me, little man,' said the massive warlord again, and swung at him once more. Hroth leaped backwards to avoid the blow. The blade flashed towards him again, and he rolled to the side to avoid it. It smashed into the skulls they stood upon, shattering them and sending shards of bone flying into the air.

'You think you are worthy to wield this hallowed blade?' boomed the warlord. 'You are nothing. Worthless. A pitiful, little man. You are a dog. A whelp. Nothing more.'

Something deep within Hroth broke at that point. Red fury welled up through him, filling him with anger and hatred. It fuelled his weary limbs, filling him with strength and power. The horns on his head burst into flames, and his eyes blazed with rage. With a bestial roar, he threw himself at the warlord, hefting his axe at his foe with all the daemonic strength coursing through him.

Kul met the blow head-on, parrying it and sending a brutal riposte that would have taken Hroth's head from his shoulders. The champion of Khorne ducked underneath it and rammed his axe up into the belly of the warlord, shattering armour plates and driving into the flesh beneath.

Grunting with pain, Asavar Kul smashed the hilt of his sword into Hroth's head, and kicked him away. Blood trickled from the wound down across the Khorne warrior's brow. It touched the flames on his right eye and they flared brightly. The rage was still building within him, and his muscles strained and bulged as his breathing became heavier. Growling like a beast, he launched himself at the bigger warrior, hacking and cutting.

Asavar Kul backed away from the fury of the assault, his blade flashing out left and right, deflecting all the attacks driving towards him. The daemon blade arced out, scoring a wound on the Khorne berserker's arm. The daemon within the sword writhed and contorted in ecstasy, and the wound hissed and smoked. Hroth barely noticed, and uncaring, threw himself into the attack once more, forsaking any pretence of defence. His axe was a blur as it whirled around him, and he rained countless blows down upon the warlord who struggled to match the intensity of the attack.

Hroth suffered a deep wound across his thigh, and another across his chest, but he managed to smash his axe into Kul's shoulder, ripping the armour from his flesh. Hroth's rage and power continued to build, and he could feel Khorne within him, urging him on and gifting him with furious strength. His vision was red and his mind went completely blank, utterly focused on his rage.

With a deft twist of his wrist, Asavar Kul sent Hroth's axe flying from his grasp, and it spun end over end off the side of the plateau of skulls, disappearing into flame and smoke. Without missing a beat, the champion of Khorne threw himself at the warlord, his hands reaching for the man's throat. Kul rammed the daemon blade into his chest, impaling him. Hroth, uncaring, pushed on, and the blade was driven through him, punching from his back in a spray of blood.

The champion of Khorne had his hands around the gorget protecting Kul's throat, and the metal strained and buckled under his strength. Asavar Kul slipped, dislodging a landslide of skulls. With a final push, Hroth hefted the man off his feet, and the two of them toppled off the edge.

They continued to battle as they fell, Kul twisting his daemon blade that was impaling the Khorne champion, and Hroth continuing to crush the warlord's throat. Growling like a wounded animal, Hroth drove his forehead into Kul's helmet, again and again. Blood began to pour down Hroth's face, but he did not care, already seeing only red. The metal helmet began to buckle and crumple. Tumbling over and over, they battled each other as they fell into flames.

The metal helmet of Asavar Kul was bent out of shape, and Hroth wrenched it from the warlord's head. The face beneath was bloodied and contorted in anger and pain, and he drove the palm of his hand into the warlord's nose, sending shards of bone driving up into his brain. Still the warlord fought on, even as they crashed into the skulls and bones piled at the base of the tower, hundreds of feet below.

Hroth was on top of the warlord, his knee driven deep into Asavar Kul's chest. The warlord's blade still spitted him, but Kul had let go his grasp upon the deadly weapon. The blade disappeared suddenly, and Hroth found himself kneeling over the body of Kul, his axe somehow grasped in his right hand – in his left he held the daemon blade, U'zhul.

Looking up, his vision still red, Hroth saw that Asavar Kul stood before him, arms folded over his massive chest. Looking down, confused, he saw the bloodied figure of the warlord pinned beneath him. 'You do well, warrior of Chaos,' the standing Asavar Kul said.

Then Hroth drove the blade U'zhul straight through the body of the fallen Kul with a rage-filled roar, piercing his heart. The life force and power of the great man flowed up through the blade and into Hroth, and he roared in victory. Energy coursed through him, filling his veins with power: power the likes of which he had never felt before.

Hroth the mortal was no more. Hroth the Blooded, Daemon Prince of Khorne, was born.

CHAPTER TWENTY-FIVE

ALBRECHT STARED GRIMLY across the open field. The sun had still not pierced the thick clouds overhead, and the grass was still covered in frost. In the distance, he could see Gruber's army, resplendently arrayed against them. Men of Ostermark fighting men of Ostermark while enemies awaited to descend upon the Empire, he thought. This was a bad day.

'Is there no way that we can avoid this battle?' he asked the captain, although he already knew the answer.

'Do you mean before the count threatened to hang me and I blew the head off that witch hunter? Probably. Now? Not a chance.'

'No, I know that. The men fighting for Gruber – they ain't bad men, captain. They are just doing their duty.'

'As are we,' said Stefan, his face darkening.

'One step removed and we would have been fighting on that side over there, as could any of the men fighting for you. What good will come of brother killing brother?'

'What good will come of it? Gruber must die, Albrecht. You know that!'

'Of course I know it, but surely there is some other way, a way that won't see men of the Empire butchered, regardless of the outcome.'

'If a few men have to die for Ostermark to be free, that's a price that must be paid, Albrecht. This conversation is over.' The captain stalked away from the sergeant at that point, shouting to his men, readying them for the battle to come.

Still, the words of his sergeant stuck with him, and Stefan knew that he had spoken the truth. This was a bitter day for Ostermark, and if there were some way for him to avoid the battle while still taking Gruber's head, then all the better. He had walked amongst the men for the past few hours, talking to his soldiers, showing them that he was one of them, and not some leader that would shirk battle once it was closed. Not that they needed this reassurance, for every man had seen him in battle before, leading from the front.

Why then was he so uneasy, he wondered? The answer was an easy one – because this was a battle that none would celebrate, win or lose. To gain victory, he was asking his men to kill their own kinsmen, people from the same villages and towns where they grew up. He saw the leader of the flagellants, the nameless ex-knight, seated alone on a log. He was motionless, as if his crazed fervour had finally seeped out of him. His lack of movement seemed at odds amongst the army that was bustling to be ready for battle.

'Greetings, warrior,' said the captain. The man who had once been a knight of the Reiklandguard looked up at him, his eyes glazed. The twin-tailed comet cut into his forehead was scabbed over. It had evidently been some time since he had last carved it into his head. 'You and your companions will not fight this day?'

'Fight? Today? No, we will not fight. Not yet. Not just yet.' He stared at the captain, madness clear in his eyes. 'Sigmar is not shining within me this day. He has abandoned me, and thrown me into the darkness. It is a sign. Through pain, I will cleanse my body. As day turns to night, I will cleanse myself. Through pain, I will regain his light, and then... I will be no more.'

'I see. That is... good, my friend. I wish you well,' said Stefan, and made to leave the madman with his sorrow.

'When the plagued one shows himself, we will fight,' the man called out suddenly. 'When the daemons of the Lord of Flies cavort,' he shouted, clawing at Stefan's legs. 'I will fight then! Sigmar will come back to me then!' The captain pushed the man back from him. 'He will shine his light upon me once more if I smite the pestilent ones! See! See him! He comes!' the man screamed in sudden rapture, pointing and abasing himself on the ground, smearing mud on his face. 'He comes. Sigmar himself!' In the man's eyes he saw a warrior bathed in glowing white light walking towards him, holding a blazing warhammer.

Stefan looked up to see what the crazed man saw, expecting nothing, but he saw the massive warrior priest Gunthar walking towards him, his face haggard

and drawn. Indeed, it looked as if the priest had aged
a decade – his eyes were rimmed with darkness, and
his face was heavily lined. A fresh pair of ugly scars cut
across his face, starting above his hairline, passing
down through his eyebrow and continuing onto his
cheekbone. The man on the ground continued to prostrate himself in the earth, and Gunthar knelt beside
him, placing a hand on the man's head. The man froze
for a moment, and then sat up, his eyes clear of the
madness. 'I am not our Lord Sigmar, man, but his light
shines through me. It shines in you, as well,' said the
warrior priest. The man, looking at Gunthar in awe,
stood for a moment speechless, before he ran off into
the crowd.

'Gunthar, you look terrible,' said Stefan.

'Well you ain't exactly the pick of the crop yourself,'
bellowed the massive priest before grabbing the captain in a crushing bear hug. 'At least my scars don't
cover up *all* of my pretty face.' Stefan stood rigid,
uncomfortable with any physical contact. At last the
priest pushed the captain back, holding him at arm's
length.

'I have it,' he whispered hoarsely. 'By Sigmar, I have
it!' A fierce light was shining in the priest's eyes, making him look more than a little deranged. Then the
shine seemed to fade, and the priest sagged visibly, his
massive shoulders slumping.

'We were nearly lost. I'm sorry that I return with so
few of your men, captain. The walking dead claimed
them. Evil guarded this blade, but that darkness has
been slain, and the dead have been laid to rest, thank
Sigmar.' Gunthar raised himself up, and thrust the
sword towards Stefan.

'Kill the fiend, captain. It is only right that he dies at your hand.'

'WHAT DO YOU mean, the guns are clean?' Engineer Markus asked in exasperation, running his finger along inside the barrel of one of the great cannon. He lifted up his blackened finger and held it out to the crewmen for inspection. 'For Shallya's sake, do it properly, would you? The enemy has more guns than us – these weapons must be in top condition. This cannon,' he said, slapping the barrel of the gun, 'is worth more than your lives – treat her with the respect you'd give your mothers.'

'I'd treat her with the respect I'd give *your* mother,' muttered one of the men. His companions sniggered.

'What did you say?' snapped the engineer, staring down the bigger man, not intimidated. It was a vaguely comical scene, the small and immaculately dressed though wild-haired engineer standing indignant before the hulking, soot covered men towering above him, who resolutely stared at their toes. 'Well, what was it? Some besmirching of my mother's honour, hmm? I'll have you know that the Lady Isabella von Kempt is a lady of high esteem, and is classed as a dear friend to the counts of several Imperial states.'

'I'll bet she is,' muttered another man at the back of the group, causing more muffled guffaws.

'Right! That's it, you vulgar men! I will not stand here and hear my dear mother's name smeared with your ribald foolery! I want these guns cleaned, properly cleaned mind, and hitched up to the horses *within the half hour*. That's right, groan all you like,' shouted the small engineer. 'What's the matter with you? Get moving!'

The crewmen set to their work, grumbling and swearing, while the engineer picked up his newly purchased Hochland longrifle and began to dismantle it, peering at its mechanisms and down the long barrel with intense concentration. It was back-breaking labour for the cannon crew, readying the guns for war, and they worked in silence, their faces grim – each man lost in his own thoughts.

For all their hassling of the engineer, they had merely been trying to find some humour in what looked to be a grim day. Each man was dreading the coming battle, for they knew the destructive power of their weapons, and what man would wish to light the fuse that would send explosive shells ploughing into fellow men of Ostermark? They did their duty with practiced efficiency, hitching up the cannon and mortars, and ensuring that each wagon was fully stocked with powder, cannonballs and mortar shells, and seeing to it that the helblaster *Wrath of Sigmar* was well oiled, allowing the mechanisms that spun one bank of smallcalibre cannon to the next to move smoothly without sticking.

Their tasks completed, they wrapped themselves tightly in their coats, stamping their feet to keep them warm now that they had stopped working and they smoked pipes. The engineer, Markus, would have berated them furiously if he had seen them – smoking pipes was not the cleverest thing in the world to do when standing next to bucket loads of black powder – but he had wandered off with his longrifle, so they enjoyed this vice, showing a complete disregard for the potential and very real danger. In silence, they contemplated the battle to come, feeling sick in their stomachs.

Albrecht knew from experience that this was always the worst part of any battle – the waiting. Well, apart from the getting stabbed part, he thought. He moved amongst the men, giving advice and telling crude jokes, making sure that he seemed relaxed and comfortable, although inside he was far from it. The men were tense and uneasy, mirroring his own feelings, but he continued to do his duty, putting on a front of being in control and relaxed.

He knew the effect this had on his troops – if they felt their superiors were confident and knew what they were doing, then they relaxed as well. If they saw their commanders stressed and ill at ease, that was when the feelings of uncertainty entered the hearts of the soldiers, sapping their courage and strength, and eroding their morale. That was how battles were lost, Albrecht knew. Still, he couldn't shake the sinking feeling that the enemy, better equipped with more than double the cannon and mortars that the captain had within his force, and already dug in up ahead, would blast them from the field of battle with ease.

THE SCOUT WILHELM raced through the trees, running low, covering the icy ground quickly. Bow in hand, he leapt over rotten logs and ducked under low-hanging branches, ferns brushing at his legs. He stopped abruptly; ducking down behind a moss covered rock, and glanced behind him. His team of huntsmen raced along behind him, flitting like ghosts amongst the trees. They paused, seeing that Wilhelm had halted, and crouched low to the ground. Instantly, they were completely hidden by the low ferns and mist.

Wilhelm rose to his feet and slipped around the rock, descending down a slippery slope, eyes wary. Coming to the bottom of the slope, he broke into a run once more, racing through the trees at great speed.

The land dipped down into another hollow, and Wilhelm sprinted down into it, splashing through the creek there and leaping up the bank on the other side. He threw himself to the ground, staring cautiously over the bank, before rising to his feet and continuing. Finally, he came to a halt and dropped to one knee, his chest rising and falling quickly from the prolonged exertion.

Wilhelm nocked an arrow to his bow suddenly, staring into the mist. His breathing evened out as he drew back the arrow, his powerful bow curving. For a moment, he could see nothing, but then a figure moved out of the mist, crouching low, its head moving from side to side warily. Wilhelm recognised him – a fellow scout he had trained alongside – a scout that was not part of Captain von Kessel's army. He was a good man, who had a wife and two young daughters, he recalled. Still, he had no qualms about killing him; in fact it never even entered his mind to feel compassion or remorse. He was doing his job, and that was all.

The man stepped carefully through the ferns, and Wilhelm concentrated on him, his bow still drawn. When the man was less than thirty paces away, he fired. The arrow flashed through the air and struck the scout in the throat. He fell to the ground without a sound. About fifty paces to the east, he saw another enemy scout drop silently, an arrow protruding from his mouth.

A muffled shout came from the west, and Wilhelm swore. He rose to his feet and sprinted forwards, running as fast as he could towards the sound. He caught sight of a man, running through the trees ahead of him, and Wilhelm cut off to the left, guessing that the man would turn back that way.

Branches scratched at his face as he leapt over a rock, and Wilhelm felt blood running down his face. He ignored the stinging pain, and raced on, bursting through a cluster of branches, sending a flurry of ice to the ground. The running man was just in front of him, and Wilhelm leapt upon him, dragging him heavily to the ground. Pulling his long hunting knife, he rammed it into the man's back. When the man ceased to struggle, he rose to his feet.

One of his scouts burst through the undergrowth, his face flushed. He halted as he saw the dead man. 'Sorry sir, he was too quick for me,' the man panted. Wilhelm grunted in return.

'We got them all?' he asked.

'Aye, sir. This was the only one that looked like getting away. The enemy does not know that we are behind them.'

'Good. Instruct the men to approach the edge of the forest. Do it silently. Let no man be seen. Then, await my order.' The man nodded, and disappeared into the trees.

If Wilhelm was not mistaken, they should emerge right behind the enemy guns.

CAPTAIN STEFAN VON KESSEL held the sword up, examining its long, thin blade. It was beautifully crafted, without imperfection, with delicate elf runes running along its length. It seemed to glow faintly, and the captain hefted, taking a practice swing with it. He frowned. 'It's a bit light,' he commented.

'Aye it is. Elves ain't the biggest of chaps, now, are they? But that don't matter. This blade is true death for the count.'

'Good. We cannot let this battle last long. I must kill Gruber quickly – then we can end this farce. I don't want men of Ostermark slaughtering each other – these are *my* people, Gunthar.'

'Aye, I know. You are going with your plan, then?'

'I am. Even now, my scouts have cleared the forests clean of the foe. Already the Reiklandguard knights are moving into position. I must leave to join them. You are sure you will not fight at my side? I could use your strength and your faith.'

'Me? Fight on horseback? Ha! No, my place is with my feet on solid ground, lad,' the warrior priest said. He sighed. 'It's suicide though, captain. *If* you manage to break through, you will have to fight through his greatswords to get to him, and all the while his other bodyguard regiments will be encircling you. Even if you kill him, the chances are you will be surrounded and slaughtered. You know this. It's suicide.'

'Suicide? Maybe, but maybe not. It's the only way to end it quickly, Gunthar. You know this.'

'I know I don't like it,' the big priest said solemnly. 'May Sigmar guide your blade, von Kessel. Kneel before me, lad,' he said. The captain lowered himself to his knees, bowing his head before the priest. The priest raised his hammer to the heavens in one hand, and placed his other hand atop Stefan's head. He closed his eyes, and implored Sigmar to protect this one, to fill him with strength and courage. He felt a warmth in his hand as the power of his god passed into the captain.

Stefan rose to his feet, his eyes filled with faith. 'I will not fail,' he swore.

HORNS BLASTED AND drums began to beat as Stefan's army began to move. The ground reverberated as thousands of men marched forwards. Scores of banners were held high in the air, most bearing the purple and yellow of Ostermark, but also others bearing the green and red of Hochland, and several from Talabecland, flying their red and yellow colours proudly. Gruber's army, the standing army of Ostermark, was arrayed against them. The entire force wore their traditional colours, except for a small ragtag contingent of halflings out on the northern flank, representatives from the moot, who wore an eclectic array of earthy colours.

Albrecht's heart was heavy as he shouted the order to begin the march across the frost-covered field. A feeling of inevitability and despair ran through him as he saw Gruber's soldiers, lined up on the hillside before them. They were not moving. Looking at the grand count's army, he estimated they were outnumbered three men to every two. Not terrible odds, he thought, although the enemy's cannon were far superior, and he thought that that would make all the difference.

The grand count's plan was simple and obvious. He planned to wait for Stefan's army to advance, and begin pounding them with his cannon. As they continued to advance, his mortars would join them, hammering the advancing soldiers with their explosive shells, causing chaos. Finally, the crossbowmen and handgunners arrayed on the hillside would join the attack, scything through the ranks of the advancing soldiers. That was when Gruber's foot soldiers would advance, smashing anything that remained. He reckoned that they would see the full power of the count's cannon once they had advanced about another two hundred paces up the hill. That was when the first shots of the battle would be fired.

At least, that would be what the count had planned, Albrecht was sure. The reality of things might prove very different. Stefan's cannon were hitched, and were advancing behind the main press of bodies. Once within range, they would be unlimbered, and they would begin to pound the enemy lines. Albrecht knew that the little engineer, Markus, had drilled the crews of those machines time and time again, so that the time it took them to unlimber and be ready to fire was less than a minute. The sergeant had to admit that, for all the merciless mocking the eccentric engineer suffered, his methods were effective.

With any luck, the scout Wilhelm would be moving into position in the forest behind Gruber's army, and would launch an attack upon the enemy guns, if at all possible. He would have said that such an attack was doomed to failure, but then, if anyone could succeed in such a venture, it would be Wilhelm. Albrecht did not like the hunter – he was an emotionless killer – but he respected the man's skills.

Von Kessel, leading the Reiklandguard, was also moving up through the trees, somewhere up ahead. The damn fool, thought Albrecht, trying to get himself killed with his heroics. He had said those same words to the captain's face, but the man had been sanguine about it. He had pointed out that it was the best way for the battle to be ended quickly. Albrecht could not argue with that, but he did not like it.

'There's certainly a lot of them, ain't there,' said the massive priest, Gunthar, who marched at his side amongst the halberdiers.

WILHELM SWORE AS he heard the blare of horns in the distance, announcing that the army was on the move. He crouched at the edge of the trees, staring out across the field to where Gruber's cannon and mortars were dug into the frozen earth. They were about two hundred yards off. This was within range of his longbow, but there was no way that he could fire accurately at that distance. If he was firing into a mass of enemy troops, then fine, but trying to pick out individual crewmen at such a range was folly.

To make things more difficult, the guns were defended, but then he had expected them to be. There was a block of halberdiers to one side of the entrenched guns – about a hundred men, he guessed. Also, there was a group of horsemen behind the guns. There were about thirty of them – more than the number of scouts that Wilhelm had with him. They were lightly armoured troops, wearing blackened breastplates and helms, but no other armour. They had high plumes on their helmets, and their horses looked well-bred to Wilhelm's eyes. He guessed that they were young nobles, placed behind the guns to act as a rear guard, or, more likely, just to keep them out of harm's way. He sat watching them for a moment, thoughtfully.

At last, he retreated back within the forest, and relayed his plan to his scouts. At his word, they moved off, half of them deeper into the trees, the others moving with Wilhelm to the edge of the forest. Running boldly out into the open, Wilhelm and his men covered about fifty yards before they were noticed. They halted their advance, and drew back the strings of their bows. They launched one flight of arrows towards the wheeling horsemen, and then a second, before the first had yet struck home. As the arrows struck, sending several men pitching from their saddles, Wilhelm and his men turned and fled back towards the tree line. They ran towards a small trail that cut into the trees, probably a path used by deer, or wild boar.

The horsemen galloped after them, thundering over the uneven ground. Several booming shots sounded, and two of the scouts fell screaming to the ground. Looking over his shoulder, Wilhelm saw a young noble bearing down on him with a pistol drawn and aimed. Reaching the line of trees, Wilhelm threw himself over a fallen log. The pistol boomed, and the rotten log splintered as the shot smashed into it, inches from Wilhelm's head. The horse leapt over the downed log, its hooves flashing over Wilhelm. He rose to his knees, nocking an arrow to his bow, and sent the shaft smashing into the horseman's back as he pulled his horse around, throwing him from the saddle.

Wilhelm was up, and running deeper into the trees, and he felt a shot scream past his ear. Ducking behind a tree, he peered around it. He could see the pistoliers some way back, not wishing to go too far into the trees. They spun their horses on the spot, several of the young nobles firing their pistols at the retreating scouts.

Wilhelm stepped out into plain view on the path, and launched an arrow into the chest of another of the riders. The horsemen, seeing their enemy clearly on the path ahead, kicked their steeds forwards, and they pounded down the path towards Wilhelm. About halfway down the path, the lead riders were suddenly pitched from their saddles, arrows streaking from the sides of the path, cutting them down mercilessly. Wilhelm took down another two, as they turned around in confusion. Some of the riders, realising the trap, tried to spin their steeds and gallop to safety, but those at the rear, unaware of the ambush, were still trying to advance. Within moments, all the young horsemen were shot from their saddles, and Wilhelm's scouts were grabbing the reins of their horses. Wilhelm himself was checking each of the fallen men, cutting the throats of those who were not dead.

Picking up one of the tall plumed helmets, Wilhelm placed it on his head. He picked up an unfired pistol, and shoved it into his belt before mounting one of the horses. The other scouts followed his lead, and soon they were all mounted up. They trotted back down the path towards the open field. They heard the booming roar of cannon firing, and Wilhelm swore. 'Let's go and silence those guns,' he said, kicking his horse into a gallop once he was clear of the trees.

THE FIRST SHOTS from Gruber's cannon screamed down the hill and ploughed into the advancing state troops, ripping a bloody swathe through the tightly packed men. Soldiers fell screaming in agony, their legs torn from their bodies and their chests smashed to pulp. The cannonballs bounced through the ranks, breaking limbs and crushing bones, crumpling armour and destroying everything in their path.

'Hold the line!' roared Albrecht as he felt the courage of the halberdiers wavering. 'Advance!'

As WILHELM GALLOPED towards the enemy guns, he thought that at any second the enemy would see through their deception and tear them to shreds with grapeshot. His heart was pounding as they drew nearer and nearer to the emplaced guns. The mighty cannon fired once more, and his horse struggled against him, unnerved by the ungodly sound and the strange smell of gunpowder. He kept a firm hand on the reins, galloping the horse straight towards the guns.

Reaching them, he leapt from the saddle, coming face to face with a pair of startled crewmen loading a massive shell into a mortar. They looked at him in confusion, even as he rammed his hunting knife into the first one's throat. His men leapt over the earth embankments, stabbing and killing. Wilhelm punched the other man in the face as he dropped the mortar shell, knocking him to the ground with the force of the blow. He dropped his knee onto the man's back and dispatched him with a brutal stab of his knife, and was up and moving again in seconds.

Ducking around a cannon that had just fired, Wilhelm slammed into a man shoulder first, lifting him into the air before ramming him to the ground. In the resulting scuffle, he drove his knife into the man's stomach again and again. Standing, he opened the lid of a large barrel that was full to the brim with black powder. Pushing it onto its side, he gave the barrel a shove with his heel, and it rolled down the small embankment, before coming to a halt in between two cannons. The crew of these cannon looked up to see where the barrel had come from only to see Wilhelm standing there with a pistol in his hand. Frantically, they tried to clamber away as he aimed the pistol towards the barrel, and fired.

OTTO GRUBER RIPPED aside the curtains of his palanquin as a massive explosion sounded. 'What in all the gods' names?' he asked as he saw the rising ball of fire amid his beloved cannon.

'Count, look!' Johann shouted, pointing to the south. A wedge of knights, the Reiklandguard, was charging out from the cover of the trees, behind his main battleline on the hill. They were galloping straight towards him, and closing the distance with worrying speed. At that moment, von Kessel's guns spoke, his own cannon firing up into the press of bodies on the hillside, raining death amongst Gruber's troops.

The well-drilled greatswords, Gruber's personal guard, about-faced and wheeled to confront the rapidly approaching knights. Other regiments along the battle line were turning towards the knights, but none responded quickly enough to be able to intercept them. At the front of the charging knights, Gruber saw von Kessel raise a blade high into the air, a weapon that flashed with golden light. He felt his heart constrict at the sight of the weapon, and he hissed in rising panic.

The knights slammed into the greatswords, driving deep into their ranks. Gruber saw dozens of his elite guard slain in an instant, impaled on the lances of the

knights and crushed beneath the bulk of their gigantic
warhorses. He saw von Kessel battling furiously
through the press of warriors towards him, lashing
around with the cursed, glowing blade. The advance of
the knights slowed, but they were still grinding
towards him relentlessly. They were completely surrounded, as swordsmen closed the gap behind the
knights. There was no retreat for them – either they
would be slaughtered to a man, or they would reach
Gruber.

Stefan von Kessel caught a glimpse of the elector
count's lavish palanquin up ahead, and renewed the
fury of his attack. The elf blade was light in his hand,
and he hacked down with it, slicing through helmets
and cleaving skulls. He urged his warhorse on with his
knees, forcing it further into the enemy formation. It
lashed out with its hooves, crushing another man. Stefan took a blow on his shield, the force of the strike
sending him reeling backwards in the saddle, but he
kept his seat, and lashed out with the flashing elf
blade, killing with every smooth stroke. With every
blow, he drew closer to the count, closer to fulfilling
his oath and redeeming the honour of his family.

'Lower me!' barked Otto Gruber, and his palanquin
was lowered smoothly to the ground. 'My coven! To
me!' he shouted, uncaring who should hear his words.
His courtiers, who had come to the battle to sip wine
and watch the victory, looked shocked and frightened.
    'Gather yourselves around me. Lend me your
strength!' shouted the grand count, and they moved
sluggishly into a rough circle around the fat count,

dropping to their knees. The man pulled a dead toad from within his robes, and stroked its lumpy back lovingly. He raised it to the heavens, and began to chant in a language that made all those who heard it shiver, repulsed by the unnatural sound of the language of Chaos. The courtiers arrayed around the count, his coven, began to chant along with him, speaking the language of the daemons.

FAR ACROSS THE other side of the battlefield, behind the lines of battle and beyond the advancing troops, the nameless flagellant knight surged upright, standing tall amidst the ragged fanatics.

'They come!' he roared. 'The pestilent ones come. Arise my brethren. Take up your weapons once more. The decaying ones come!'

CHAPTER TWENTY-SIX

GRUBER CONTINUED TO chant, and the sky overhead darkened. One of the courtier cultists collapsed, shaking and convulsing. A strange bulge appeared in the earth at the feet of the grand count, growing larger, like a boil ready to rupture. It grew to the size of a man's head, a foul, pallid, fleshy colour. It burst suddenly, spraying yellow pus across the ground and over Gruber's robes. There, amid the filth and the pus was a small round creature, squat and toad-like. Its cruel eyes blinked, and it opened its massive mouth to expose a myriad of rotten, childlike teeth, and a pink, fleshy tongue covered in weeping sores. It squirmed forwards on clawed feet, leaving a trail of faeces and filth behind it. It hugged Gruber's leg with its fat, warty arms, nuzzling and licking at him lovingly. More of the boils began to sprout from the earth, bubbling up all around Gruber and the chanting cultists.

A rent opened up in the earth in front of the chanting count, and a shape larger than a man was excreted from it, squeezing up, squirming and wriggling. It was held within a thin membrane of veined skin, covered in a foul smelling, yellow-brown slime. The creature within struggled frantically for a moment, before a single horn pierced the birthing membrane, tearing an opening in it. Hands the colour of dead flesh ripped this opening wider still, and the fully formed creature stepped into reality.

It stood some seven feet tall, and its flesh was covered in cuts and wounds, exposing the muscles, bones and organs within. Beetles and maggots crawled beneath its dead flesh. Its belly was bloated and fat, and there was a deep cut in its stomach through which the intestines protruded. Its massive head was dominated by a cyclopean, bloodshot eye that blinked slowly, milky liquid running from its corners. A single horn was positioned just above the eye, covered in the remains of the birth sac that it had just burst from.

Reaching one rotten, corpse-like hand to the ground, it lifted a massive, corroded blade, dripping with venom and foul poison. Raising the plague sword high into the air, the daemon of pestilence exhaled. A great cloud of buzzing flies and biting insects emerged from its lungs as it breathed out. The plaguebearer swung its large head towards Gruber, and gave him a mock bow.

Stefan paused, gagging, as the stench of decay and death came to him, an overpowering stink that made his stomach heave. The knights' horses, known for their bravery and fearlessness, baulked at the unearthly stench, whinnying and rearing. The Reiklandguard fought against their steeds, desperately trying to keep them under control. Taking advantage of this, the greatswords loyal to Gruber pushed forwards, their blades smashing knights from their terrified steeds. A glancing blow knocked one of the men from his saddle, and he fell heavily to the ground. As he struggled to his knees, a five-foot-long blade swept into his neck, cleaving through his ornate plate armour and his spine.

Stefan lashed downwards, splitting the skull of another greatsword, his horse bucking beneath him. His ears were filled with a buzzing drone, and a black cloud of insects suddenly descended on the combatants, crawling into eyes, ears and noses. They crawled through the visor slits of the Reiklandguard, buzzing and biting, and several of the knights struggled to rip the helms from their heads. They crawled down the inside of plate armour, painfully biting the flesh beneath. They swarmed over the eyes of the horses, stinging and biting. The greatswords were also assailed by the plague, and they swatted frantically at the insects as they crawled over them.

The captain spat half a dozen buzzing insects from his mouth, his stomach heaving, and raised his blade to cut down another of the greatswords that stood between him and the elector count. He paused, holding his blow as he saw that the man was desperately scratching bugs out of his eyes and swatting at the creatures crawling down his neck, the battle forgotten. Stefan could not strike down a man in this way, but he did not need to. A blade punched through the chest of the man, driven through him from behind with brutal force. The man was lifted into the air before being hurled to the ground. He lifted his face to the heavens, crying out in pain. Stefan saw the man's face begin to rot before his eyes. He was still alive as his flesh turned gangrenous and black, and his eyes turned milky-white, filled with cataracts. In seconds, the man's skin atrophied and shrivelled, and he fell to the ground, dead.

A daemon stood behind the body, grinning insanely with its lipless mouth. It opened its mouth wide, exposing crawling things within, and stepped heavily towards Stefan, hefting its filth encrusted weapon.

Nausea threatened to overcome the captain, and he felt bile rising in his throat. His steed reared up in terror, and the creature thrust its plague sword deep into the chest of the rearing horse. Whinnying piteously, it began to decay from the inside out, and Stefan was thrown to the ground. A small, pestilent creature reached towards his eyes with clawed hands, and he lashed out blindly, knocking the foul daemon away from him. Rising to his feet, he saw several of the hulking plaguebearers rearing up before him. One of them stroked the blistered and pox-ridden head of the fallen horse, fresh contagion flaring beneath its touch.

His elf blade glowing hotly, Stefan lunged forwards, driving the weapon deep into the pestilent gut of the first creature. It opened its mouth and screamed horribly, spraying out spittle, phlegm and maggots. Its flesh seemed to turn to a thick liquid, and it sank to the ground, turning into a pestilent pool of filth. Stefan backed away from the foul liquid, not wishing to let it touch him.

The greatswords and the knights were being butchered as more and more of the foul plaguebearers appeared. A rent in the earth before Stefan spewed forth another of the daemons, struggling within its birth-sac. His face curled in disgust, and he lashed out with his golden, blazing sword, despatching the thing before it could rip itself free. He felt something at his leg, and looking down saw another of the small daemons biting ineffectually at his armoured leg. He kicked the creature away with a curse, spraying blood and mucus.

A greatsword was dragged to the ground beneath a swarm of the small creatures, and they leapt upon him, biting, clawing and giggling. He saw the man's eyes ripped from their sockets, and a handful of the creatures began to fight for the morsels, spitting and striking at each other.

Stefan saw Gruber for a second, through the mayhem and the cloud of flies: the fat man was chanting and grinning madly, cradling one of the small daemons in his arms like a baby. Something was rising up behind Gruber, something enormous, but before Stefan could discern this new horror, a plaguebearer was before him, swinging its corroded blade at him. He stepped back to avoid the wild blow, treading on something that wriggled and squirmed beneath his feet. He lost his footing and fell. One of the small creatures crouched on its haunches beside his head, and it vomited up the contents of its stomach into his hair, foul liquid filled with writhing maggots and worms.

A strong hand grasped Stefan by the shoulder and pulled him to his feet. It was Lederstein, the captain of the Reiklandguard. In his other hand he held the reins of his steed. He thrust the reins into Stefan's hand and drew his ornate sabre, leaping forwards to strike at the approaching plaguebearer, and severing an outstretched arm. 'Go!' he shouted over his shoulder. 'Take my horse and pull back! We must retreat to the rest of the army. We cannot win here!'

'No!' shouted Stefan. 'We must end this now!'

The knight slammed his blade into the neck of the plaguebearer, almost decapitating the creature. Still it fought on, grinning madly as its head flopped loosely, hanging by rope-like sinews and muscles. Lederstein turned to face von Kessel. 'Your army still fights Gruber's!' he shouted. 'Stop the killing, and *then* end it! If we all die here, all is for naught!' A blade was suddenly plunged into the knight's leg, and he bellowed in pain. Smaller daemons dragged at him, pulling him down to them even as the plaguebearer withdrew its pestilent weapon, and stabbed him in the face.

Swearing, von Kessel mounted the snorting horse. Hundreds of plaguebearers were hacking down the last of the greatswords. Many of the Reiklandguard had fallen, and soon they would be overwhelmed and slaughtered by the daemons. More of the foul creatures were being excreted from the earth, and with a curse, the captain shouted out, his voice booming. 'Reiklandguard – with me!' he roared, and began to cut his way free of the chaos. Responding instantly, the knights fought their way to his side, and they rode away from the foul daemons, away from Gruber. Stefan could see that hundreds of other plaguebearers were rising all across the battlefield. They were falling on Gruber's soldiers, cutting them down in droves, spreading disease and foul contagions as they stalked across the earth. The frosted grass withered and died beneath their step, and men fell to the ground, coughing up foulness as the wind drove the stench of the daemons across the field.

Stefan's army had engaged Gruber's and the two battle lines were blurred together as they struggled to over come their foe, dressed in the same purple and yellow uniforms. They were oblivious to the horrors unfolding behind them, and continued to fight.

Kicking his steed forwards, Stefan and the Reikland-guard thundered across the battlefield, passing in between Gruber's loyal warriors. These men did nothing to halt their passage, desperately engaged in combat with the foul daemons or milling around in confusion.

Stefan angled down towards the centre of the engaged battle line and charged towards the rear of Gruber's soldiers. Many of them, hearing the thundering of hooves behind them, turned to face them, raising their halberds defensively.

'Men of Ostermark!' Stefan roared, riding along the battle line, 'Cease your fighting! We face a common enemy. Cease your fighting!'

The soldiers' eyes were drawn up the hill, towards the legions of daemons slaughtering Gruber's rearguard. They gaped in horror, and lowered their weapons. Gradually, the fighting began to cease, until it had stopped altogether. Sergeant Albrecht pushed through the press of men that minutes before had been intent on killing each other, and approached the captain.

'Sigmar above,' he breathed as he surveyed the battlefield. Pockets of daemons were fighting with Gruber's soldiers, but the hillside above was completely overrun. It was hard to tell how many of the things there were, for a massive black cloud of insects obscured them. Even from here, they could hear the sound of the flies, a dull droning that was repulsive and abhorrent. The daemons had despatched the last of the humans on the hillside, but were not yet on the move. They seemed to be waiting for something.

GRUBER STROKED THE contented nurgling in his arms, and it cooed and dribbled in pleasure. Plaguebearers capered around him, and other nurglings clamoured around his feet, seeking his attention. He continued to chant, forming the difficult words with ease. Most of his courtiers were dead. Foolish they were, to think that he would allow them to share his power. Only one was truly powerful amongst them, and he remained standing at Gruber's side, adding his voice to the count's. The olive-skinned Tilean, Andros, his eyes closed in concentration and his face awash with sweat, mouthed the powerful incantations, lending his strength to the spell.

Young Johann had looked horrified as the first of the daemons had appeared, much to Otto Gruber's amusement. A stupid boy, he had thought. He had never really liked him, and he had laughed as Johann was ripped apart by a pair of plaguebearers, and his entrails eaten by nurglings.

He had not meant it to happen like this. He had not meant to unveil himself so soon. No, he had intended to await the coming of the Chaos chosen, and reveal himself only at the last moment, when his betrayal would ensure victory for the forces of the Dark Gods. He had planned to have his army inside the besieged city when he revealed himself. He would throw open the gates to allow the attackers entry, and then the true slaughter would begin. Great Nurgle would be pleased with his deeds, and would grant him great power, and no doubt bestow even greater contagions upon him.

All this planning had gone to naught, thanks to von Kessel, and the hated sword that he wielded. Gruber had had no option but to reveal himself. Looking up at the massive daemon rising from the earth before him, he was glad that he had finally unleashed his power.

Rising to over twenty feet in height, dripping with pus and foulness, the greater daemon opened its large, gummed-up eyes and looked around in pleasure. Its massive mouth opened, displaying its rotten slab-like frontal teeth and tusks, and the thousands of smaller inner teeth. Worms and maggots writhed within its cavernous mouth, and a long tongue slithered out over its fleshy green lips. The tongue ended in a snapping mouth, dripping with saliva and filth. Horns like rotten branches rose from the daemon's head, hanging with algae and fungus. Beetles and grubs crawled over the creature's flesh, and maggots and worms buried under its skin. Flies buzzed around the face of the daemon, descending to feed on the liquid of its eyes and mouth, and the saliva that dribbled from its mouth down its front.

The creature was corpulent and massive, easily as wide in all directions as it was tall. Its greenish skin hung in folds, and great tears appeared in the daemon's rolls of fat, exposing the red muscle beneath. Ribs protruded from the chest, and entrails flopped out onto the ground from its giant, distended belly. Long, spindly arms lifted high into the air, massive hands with long, multi-jointed fingers ending in cracked talons that wept blood and pus. The lesser daemons of the Chaos god of pestilence, nurglings, infested the massive creature, nestling amongst its exposed intestines and folds of fat. They pulled themselves into the rents in its flesh, seeking the warmth and comforting fluid within.

The greater daemon gazed adoringly at these miniature versions of itself, petting them and lifting them to its bulbous shoulders. One of them poked at one of the daemon's eyes, and it flicked the diminutive creature away. One buried itself in the flesh of its armpit, clawing deep into the warm cavity, and the giant daemon plucked it up in its spindly hand and lifted it to his face. His long, worm-like tongue extended and nuzzled the small creature, which giggled, and rolled its milky eyes in pleasure.

Gruber stepped towards the towering daemon, smiling broadly. He bowed low before it, still cradling the nurgling within the crook of his arm. The tiny daemon looked up at him with love in its putrid eyes. 'Great unclean one, you honour me with your presence,' Gruber said, speaking the Dark Tongue, the language of the daemon.

The giant creature turned its gaze towards him and winked at him, forcing the flies gathered on the orb into the air. 'Little human,' it spoke, in a deep rumbling voice that sounded like sucking mud. It coughed, a foul, liquid sound, its whole body heaving. It hawked loudly, and spat a mucus covered nurgling to the ground. 'Little human, I thank you for drawing me forth… The Lord of Plagues is pleased.'

'The enemies of Lord Nurgle are arrayed against us, unclean one. They wish to kill your children,' said Gruber.

The greater daemon clutched a clump of nurglings to its breast protectively, horror on its face. 'I will not allow my pretties to be harmed,' it gargled in its booming voice. Its eyes scanned the humans on the plains below it, eyes narrowed in anger and hatred.

The great unclean one extended one of its arms, flexing its fingers. A cloud of flies and other flying insects coalesced around its hand, flying closer and closer together, forming a rough shape. They began to cling to each other, forming the silhouette of a huge blade. The fingers of the daemon clenched together, grasping the buzzing flies. The insects melted together and changed into dark, corroded metal.

The greater daemon hefted the giant blade over its head, and pointed the weapon towards the human army. It was covered in rust, and virulent poison dripped from the blade – every contagion, disease, illness and plague was contained in that poison. The daemon roared, and a great cloud of insects rose around him in response to the hideous sound. The nurglings added their own tiny voices to the roar, staring towards the Empire army balefully. The plaguebearers turned their dead eyes on the enemy, and began to lope towards them.

With massive effort, the greater daemon shifted its weight, heaving its bulk forwards on legs like rotten tree-trunks. Gruber stepped to the side, rubbing his hands together eagerly, and the daemon stepped again, eyes fixed on the hated enemy that would harm its children. It bellowed once more, and began to pick up its pace, stamping down the hill, a sea of nurglings surrounding it and the plaguebearers ranging out in front, loping towards the humans.

Cannonballs smashed through the plaguebearers, ripping apart their diseased bodies. Filth sprayed from the catastrophic wounds. Explosive mortar shells detonated amongst the daemons, sending them flying through the air, their rotting flesh ripped to shreds by hot shrapnel. The human battle line was readying itself to face the daemons, and arrows, crossbow bolts and handgun shots peppered the ranks of plaguebearers. The daemons were resistant to pain and injury, and many continued their advance even with countless bolts protruding from their flesh. Many others were slain, collapsing into pools of filth, their essence sent screaming back to the Realm of Chaos.

The great unclean one's anger grew, and it twitched as it felt every death, gnashing its teeth and spitting in fury. A cannonball smashed into its chest, piercing its flesh, snapping the ribs beneath and embedding itself deep within its body. Smoke rose from the hole, and the face of a surprised nurgling peeked its head out from inside the gaping wound. The greater daemon hissed in anger. With a roar, the daemon led its minions in a wild charge towards the army of Ostermark.

'MEN OF THE Empire! With faith in Sigmar, we shall prevail!' roared the warrior priest Gunthar, his booming voice carrying far, bolstering the terrified soldiers. 'Fear not the daemon! I faced far worse than this puissant Chaos lackey during the Great War, and I'll be damned if today is the day that I die. For Sigmar!'

Raising his hammer high into the air, the warrior priest launched himself towards the approaching daemons, roaring defiantly. Without hesitation, the halberdiers gathered around him surged forwards at his side. A great shining light surrounded the priest as he ran, glowing brightest around his massive war hammer. The daemons covered their eyes and backed away from the shining light, fearful of its intensity.

Gunthar smashed his hammer through the head of the first plaguebearer. Using his momentum, he spun around, smashing the head from the shoulders of another of the foul plague daemons.

'Sigmar, cleanse them!' Gunthar roared, and struck the earth with his hammer. A shockwave of light and power rippled out from the impact, and dozens of the plaguebearers fell to the ground, their flesh going up in flames as they were slain.

All across the battlefield, men fought desperately against the daemons. The men of Ostermark, with both Stefan's troops and Gruber's fighting together, outnumbered the plaguebearers heavily. They had inflicted a heavy toll on the daemons with war machines and missile weapons, but the daemons had closed with them, and six men or more were being slaughtered for every daemon that was felled. Where Gunthar was fighting, the battle fared well, the priest leading the halberdiers fearlessly, but elsewhere the state troops were falling back, overwhelmed and panicked by the pestilent daemons.

The great unclean one ploughed into the fray, scattering plaguebearers in its haste to join the battle. With a sweep of its blade, it sent six men flying into the air, and slew four more with its return blow. Nurglings erupted from its flesh, biting and clawing. They were largely ineffectual, but got under the feet of the soldiers, and leapt upon any man who fell to the ground. The greater daemon swept its blade before it again, and another five men were slain. The other men backed away from the creature, desperate to keep their distance from the horrific, twenty-foot behemoth, gagging and retching from its stench.

It opened its mouth wide and, with a heave, emptied its stomach contents, projecting the vileness over the press of men before it. Filled with cancerous filth, writhing worms and bile, the liquid covered thirty men, and they fell to their knees, screaming in horror and pain. Maggots burrowed into their flesh, and their eyes were burnt from their skulls by the bilious stomach acid of the daemon, the powerful liquid even eating through metal breastplates and shields. Backing away frantically, the soldiers facing the dread creature pushed against each other, and began to run from it blindly, trampling over those who fell in the press.

CACKLING AND CHORTLING with glee, Otto Gruber stood high on the hill, watching the carnage unfold as the daemons ripped through the army of Ostermark, slaughtering and killing. He yelped in excitement as the great unclean one joined the battle, sweeping everything away before it, and giggled as the men broke and fled before the horrific daemon. The day was his. True, he had unveiled his true allegiance earlier than he had wished, but it mattered not.

'All goes well, does it not, Andros?' Gruber asked, eyes fixed on the battle below. Hearing no response, he reluctantly tore his gaze from the slaughter, and saw Andros lying face down on the ground, an arrow through his neck. 'What?' he breathed, and spun around. An arrow slammed into his chest, driving between his ribs and piercing his heart. The force of the blow knocked him backwards, but he did not fall. He glared up at the small group of men that approached him, and a second and a third arrow thudded into him, taking him in his leg and chest. The force of them knocked him to his knees. Another arrowed pierced his eye, driving through his brain and into the back of his skull. Angrily, he pulled the arrow free and threw it to the ground.

'Your pitiful weapons cannot harm me, fools,' Gruber snarled, ripping the arrow that pierced his heart from his flesh.

'That right?' asked Wilhelm, stepping forwards and smashing his fist into the man's face, knocking him to the ground once again.

The scout stood above the fat count, flexing his hand. 'Seemed to work just fine. The captain will be pleased to see you,' he snarled, and smashed his fist into Gruber's face once again as he tried to rise to his feet. The nurgling that the grand count had been cradling had fallen heavily to the ground, and it clawed towards Wilhelm, baring its rotten teeth. The scout took a step backwards and raised his bow, nocking an arrow to the string. His bow was a powerful weapon, and fired at such close range, it drove right through the small daemon, pinning it to the ground. It squealed like a piglet in pain. The count tried to scramble to his feet, and began an incantation, but the scout was too quick for him, stepping forwards and smashing his fist into the man's face once again.

Gripping him by the shirt, Wilhelm drew the bloody count's face up to his, snarling. 'I'd like to gut you here and now, you sick bastard, but it seems that won't do no good. No, I'll leave that to the captain.' Wilhelm slammed his fist into Gruber's face again, the force of the blow driving the count's head into the ground. Standing, Wilhelm grabbed the leg of the unconscious man, and began to drag him down the hill.

THE ENGINEER, MARKUS, lowered his eye-glass from his eye. 'Captain!' he shouted. The engineer jumped up and down, waving his arms over his head. 'Captain von Kessel!' Not getting any response from the captain, who was wheeling the Reiklandguard around on the plains below, making ready to charge into the daemons, the engineer scrabbled inside a leather bag. He pulled out a small clay ball. A long fuse protruded from the clay sphere, and he shortened it by biting at it frantically, spitting the string to the ground. He pulled from his pocket a small brass device, one of his own devising that contained oil, and had a small flint attached. Striking it, it produced a flame, and immediately lit the small fuse. It burst into sparks, and he threw the ball high into the air. Small clockwork wings of brass unfolded from the ball, flapping frantically, but whether they aided or hindered the device was not clear. At the apex of its journey, the ball exploded with a loud bang, and light flashed like lightning.

The captain, pulling his horse around, heard the sound and looked up, his eye drawn to the flashing light. Markus leapt up and down, pointing across the field. Stefan looked across to where he was gesturing. He shouted an order to the knights, and they wheeled again before thundering up the hill towards the figure. They rode through a group of plaguebearers, smashing them aside. Markus, his eye-glass back in position, watched as one of the knights was dragged from the saddle by two of the foul daemons, his horse cut down beneath him. The man struck one of the creatures, its guts spilling out over the ground, and rose to his feet unsteadily. The creature he had just disembowelled launched itself at him, its ropey intestines trailing behind it, and rammed its single horn into the man's head. He fell to the ground, and was overcome by the foetid daemons. The other knights broke through, and galloped up the hill towards the scout dragging the unconscious Gruber.

'Engineer Markus,' came a shout, and he lowered his eyeglass to see one of the crew of the *Wrath of Sigmar* pointing, stabbing his finger down the hill. A group of daemons was loping up the hill towards their position. Markus hurriedly packed away his eye-glass, and retrieved his Hochland longrifle, hefting the heavy weapon to his shoulder. Sighting carefully, he fired, the shot smashing through the eye of the lead creature, dropping it. Marvelling at the weapon's accuracy, he lowered it, and shouted to a nearby mortar crew, gesturing at the daemons. A mortar shell was lobbed towards the creatures, detonating in their midst, tearing flesh from bones. Still, most of the daemons continued loping up the hill, despite their missing limbs and torn flesh.

'Ready the helblaster! Fire all nine barrels on my signal,' Markus called. 'Hold it. Hold. Fire!'

Once again, the *Wrath of Sigmar* spat fiery death, destroying everything in its path. Markus whooped with excitement, and began to reload his longrifle.

CAPTAIN STEFAN VON Kessel leapt from the saddle of his steed, and ran towards the unconscious count. The scout dropped the man's leg, and stepped away from him. 'He's all yours, captain,' he said, and signalled to the other scouts. They ran swiftly down the hill until they were in range of the daemons, and began to fire their longbows into the press.

As if he felt the hatred in the eyes that looked upon him, Otto Gruber blinked heavily with his one good eye as he rose from unconsciousness. Stefan stepped forwards and placed his knee on the fat count's chest. With his left hand, he grabbed the count's thin hair – in his right he held the drawn elf blade, its glowing golden tip scant inches from Gruber's throat. The count's eye widened as he saw the weapon, and he struggled in vain.

'You do not deserve a quick death, Gruber,' snarled Stefan. 'You deserve to be ripped limb from limb by horses, and for your entrails to be slowly drawn from your body. Flames should lick at your flesh, burning away the fat from your bones and boiling your eyeballs in their sockets. Your tongue ought to be ripped from your mouth, and your fingernails pulled from your fingers, one by one, but it is not to be, for I shall not lower myself to your level… This is for my grandfather, you sick bastard.'

Without ceremony, Stefan rammed the glowing blade through the fat count's throat, pushing it deep up into his brain. Gruber convulsed violently, and then his skin withered and turned black. As if all the liquid was being sucked from his body, Gruber's flesh dried up, shrivelling away to nothing in the blink of an eye, leaving just a blackened skeleton.

'It's over,' Stefan whispered. The glowing sword in his hand began to hiss, and he dropped it to the ground, the blade melting to nothing. All across the battlefield, the magic that kept the plaguebearers in existence was sucked away, and they fell to the ground, writhing and contorting, turning to foetid liquid and seeping into the soil.

Only the great unclean one remained, its power too great for the death of the magister, Gruber, to affect it. It was surrounded by the army of Ostermark, and hundreds of arrows and crossbow bolts thudded into its thick flesh. It roared in anger and pain as countless handgun shots pierced its skin. Dozens of men rushed forwards, driving their halberds into the creature's belly and back, but it fought on, smashing away its enemies as if they were insects, killing a handful of men with every sweep of its fell weapon.

It stumbled as the flagellants rushed forwards, screaming and yelling, and struck at the greater daemon's flesh with their spiked flails. The nameless ex-knight was there, exhorting his followers to do their duties, and he leapt upon the great unclean one, hacking at it with a pair of spiked maces. The daemon's flesh was torn to bloody shreds under the onslaught, and it sank to the ground. Its mouthed tongue lashed out, latching onto one of its tormentors, ripping his face from his skull. Bellowing in rage, the daemon surged back upright for a moment, and swept its weapon before it once more, the poisoned blade cutting three flagellants in half.

It slumped to the ground as Gunthar stepped before it, his huge hammer raised high over his head. With a bellow, he smashed it into the daemon's head, the blow driving through the skull and into the rotting, maggot-infested brain within.

A great cloud of flies suddenly rose, obscuring everything from view. They dispersed into the air, leaving behind nothing but a bubbling pool of poison seeping into the ground.

CHAPTER TWENTY-SEVEN

THE BLACK-CLAD body of the sorcerer knelt on the cave floor. The creature that was a part of him slithered awkwardly around the circle that the Khazag had entered, feeling at the power within. It should have been his day, thought Sudobaal. The day of his ascension, but Hroth had snatched that from him. He had been much more powerful than he had realised, and Sudobaal cursed himself for a fool.

The creature snarled with its deformed mouth, exposing the tiny teeth within. Leaning forwards on its fleshy, snake-like tail, it extended one of its tentacles gingerly towards the swirling vortex of dark smoke contained within the circle of power. As the tentacle entered the area, there was a sharp explosion of power, and electricity rippled over the creature, throwing it backwards. It smashed against the far wall, its tentacle blackened. The smell of burnt flesh rose from the injured limb.

With difficulty, leaning on its head, the creature righted itself, and gazed into the circle venomously, gnashing its teeth. Holding its wounded tentacle coiled, it shuffled across the floor of the cavern. It circled the black robed figure of the sorcerer, and began to approach the circle once again. Something was happening. The black shadows coiling within began to swirl with increasing velocity, and the creature cowered behind the body of the sorcerer, hissing.

The rocks surrounding the circle were suddenly blasted away, shattering into a thousand pieces, which scattered around the room. Dozens of these shards sprayed the sorcerer, lacerating his flesh and cutting his robes to tatters. No blood dripped from the wounds. The creature cowering behind the sorcerer began to pull itself frantically across the floor, trying to escape. The dark shadows were released from their bindings, and they screamed around the room, coalescing into shadowy, daemonic figures, before dispersing into the air.

With a further explosion of rock and earth, Hroth the Blooded, Daemon Prince of Khorne, burst from the Realm of Chaos, stepping back into reality. His blood-red wings unfurled behind him, and he bellowed loudly, the titanic sound making rocks tumble from the cave roof. In one hand, he held his faithful double-headed axe, and in the other, he held the sword, the Slayer of Kings, the blade that held the power of the daemon U'zhul. Sparks rippled over the blade of this immeasurably powerful artefact.

Turning his gaze towards the kneeling sorcerer, Hroth's daemonic, flaming eyes narrowed. He scanned the area, and his gaze came to rest on the foul tentacled creature trying to climb the stone steps that led out of the cavern. With his daemon-vision, he could see the link that bound the body of the sorcerer and this creature together, and he launched himself towards it with a powerful leap.

It screamed soundlessly and tried to get away, falling awkwardly onto its face in its haste. Hroth reached down with one of his massive, red-skinned hands and grasped it tightly. 'Get back in your flesh, familiar,' he growled, and hurled the creature across the room. It collided with the motionless body of the sorcerer, and fell heavily to the ground. Righting itself with difficulty, it threw a look of pure hatred towards the towering daemon prince, and began to burrow into the sorcerer's grey flesh.

Colour began to return to the sorcerer's skin, and blood began to weep from the wounds on his face and hands. Sudobaal opened his eyes with a gasp, as the blood began to flow. He gaped up at Hroth, who stood some twelve feet tall. Throwing himself to the floor of the cavern, he abased himself before the power of the daemon towering before him.

'Sudobaal, look me in the eyes,' the daemon commanded, and the sorcerer was powerless to resist. He raised his gaze to the flaming orbs of Hroth, his will utterly dominated. 'You belong to me now, sorcerer. Your soul is mine.'

'Yes,' stammered Sudobaal, feeling a wrenching pain within him.

'You are nothing any longer without me. I bind your soul to me; you will serve me now, and for all eternity.

In this world or the Realm of Chaos, you will serve. You will serve me faithfully, snake, for if ever you try to break my hold over you, you know that you will be tormented in the Realm of Chaos, your soul shredded over and over, but you will never be allowed release from your pain. Never will your torment cease. Oppose me, and you will reap the consequences. You know I speak the truth.'

Sudobaal knew the words the daemon spoke were truthful. He felt it deep within him, with a sinking horror. He collapsed to the ground, gasping in agony.

'I go now to deal with the elves. I will return to you once I have finished. Then we will return to the Empire, and we will finish what was started.' With that, the daemon prince left the cave, leaving Sudobaal exhausted and in agony on the ground.

A ROAR OF terrifying rage echoed above the battle, and all who fought raised their eyes to the heavens. Hroth burst from the cave, scattering rocks in all directions, and leapt into the air, throwing himself from the cliff-face. He plummeted hundreds of feet down towards the swirling melee, his wings tightly furled behind him. The wind ripped at him, and he roared as he streaked down towards the battle that was calling to him.

Lathyerin looked up with a sense of horror to see the massive daemon streaking down from the turbulent sky.

'Seaguard! Turn your bows skyward!' he called, swaying backwards to avoid a swing of an axe from a Norscan. As the axe sliced past him, an inch from his neck, he sent a fatal riposte stabbing into the man's chest.

Dozens of arrows streaked into the air, many of them striking the descending daemon in his chest and arms. They bounced from his armour, and shattered on his skin, slowing his descent not at all.

The ground trembled as the daemon landed feet first, scattering elves and Norscans alike. With a roar of pure rage, Hroth swung his axe and sword around him, cleaving through a score of elves within seconds. Blood fountained from the bodies as they fell around him, unable to match his daemonic power, frenzy or speed. Blades rebounded from his flesh, numbing the hands of the elves assailing him. Spears jarred as they struck him, doing little damage to the massive creature. In turn, he swept his weapons around, cutting elves apart, severing limbs and heads, and cutting through torsos with ease.

The daemon turned and Lathyerin surged forwards, driving his glowing blade into the back of the creature. Using all his force, the elf pushed the blade through the armour of his back, the sword tip piercing the flesh of Hroth's lower back. Despite the magical nature of the sword, the blade only penetrated a few inches into the daemon. Black blood bubbled from the wound, spitting and spluttering with heat.

Roaring in fury, the daemon spun around, lashing out with its sparking sword. Lathyerin rolled underneath the swinging blade, and came up on his knees, driving his sword towards Hroth's leg. Moving with unnatural speed, Hroth lifted his leg, and slammed his foot, a cloven hoof, down onto the shining blade, pinning it to the ground. His axe slammed down onto Lathyerin's shoulder, cutting the arm that still held the weapon from his body. Hroth rammed his daemon-sword through the body of the elf, and the daemon within the blade fed upon his soul.

Flames washed over Hroth, and a long shining lance pierced his shoulder, throwing him to the ground, crushing those he slammed into. He came up quickly, snarling his hatred, as the dragon roared overhead. Blood spat from the wound on his shoulder, and with a roar he leapt into the air in pursuit.

The dragon prince, Khalanos, soared high into the air, wheeling around, hundreds of feet above the battle. Coiling itself around, the dragon pulled its wings back and descended towards Hroth, who was screaming up to meet it. Fire roared from the maw of the dragon, washing over the daemon prince, scorching its face and chest, but it paid no heed. Prince Khalanos angled his gleaming lance at the heart of the daemon flying straight up towards him.

Hroth smashed the lance aside with a sweep of his axe, and cleaved the Slayer of Kings straight through the chest of the elf warrior. It tore through armour, flesh and bone, and the upper torso of the prince was cut from the lower body with a spray of blood, falling down into the press of battle far below. The lower part of the elf sat in the saddle for a moment, before toppling out, also falling far to the ground below. The dragon scored a series of deep wounds down Hroth's body with its powerful claws as the two creatures swept passed each other.

His daemonic blood dripping a hundred feet into the press of battle below, burning all whom it touched, Hroth turned in the air, far quicker than the dragon could, and descended towards the serpentine creature, fury driving him onwards. He smashed into the dragon as it was sweeping over the battlefield. Dropping his weapons, Hroth grappled the dragon around its long neck. His daemon sword fell, blade first, into the head of an elf, driving through his body and embedding itself in the sand. Gripping the dragon tightly, Hroth drove it down into the ground.

With titanic force, the two massive creatures smashed into the sand, crushing dozens of elves and Norscans beneath their bulks. Hroth shifted his grip as the creature thrashed around blindly, engulfing scores of men and elves indiscriminately in flame.

Hroth's massive muscles bulged, veins almost bursting with the exertion, but he refused to release the maddened creature, and the two of them rolled over and over. The dragon coiled itself around the daemon prince, and Hroth, releasing one hand from its grip around the throat, smashed his fist into the head of the dragon, feeling the skull crack beneath the force of the blow. The dragon tightened its coils, and Hroth's bones strained under the immense pressure. Still he held on, and smashed his fist into the dragon's skull once again. It thrashed around powerfully, ripping itself free of the daemon prince's grip, and uncoiled itself.

Rearing up, the dragon roared in anger, and lashed out with its snapping jaws, intending to bite the daemon in half. Hroth caught the jaws of the dragon as they descended around him, holding them at bay. His muscles strained as the jaws slowly began to close, and he roared his fury. With a burst of power, he thrust upwards, extending his arms, and ripped the jaws of the dragon open further than they were meant to go. A horrible tearing sound accompanied this violent motion, as the tendons and jawbone of the dragon were ripped apart. It thrashed around on the blood-soaked sand, its jaw hanging open loosely, emitting piteous growls and whimpers of agony and fear. It looked up at the daemon prince looming over it with hatred. Hroth held out his hand, and the daemon sword pulled itself free from the sand, flying through the air into the palm of his hand. With a single stroke, he cut the head from the long sinuous neck. The body of the dragon convulsed on the ground before lying still.

Hroth rose to his feet, hefting the dragon's head in one hand, and roared in triumph. He turned around, revelling in the victory. Dropping the dragon's head, he picked up his axe from where it lay on the sand beside him. Swinging his two weapons around him, he grinned, the flames in his eyes and engulfing his horns flaring brightly.

With a roar, he threw himself back into the fray. Within the hour, every elf on the beach was slain.

CHAPTER TWENTY-EIGHT

AURELION SAT CALMLY, her pale face displaying none of the emotions that raged beneath the surface of her icy demeanour. Her swordmaster bodyguard was arrayed protectively around her, not that there was any danger hereabouts at this moment. No, all was quiet within the forests for the time being – she knew there were thousands of creatures of Chaos here, both within the forest and *beneath* it, but she felt that they were quiet. They were waiting for the signal.

She closed her eyes, letting her spirit lift from her body. She soared into the night sky, hundreds of feet above the forest canopy, speeding to the east. She could see the pulse of Chaos across the lands, spreading like a plague both above the ground and below it. The taint was heavy across the Empire. She increased her speed, streaking through the night skies, revelling in the freedom that she felt.

Aurelion had travelled to the south after the Empire captain, von Kessel, had refused to join with her cousin, Khalanos, to defeat the hated enemy. She had travelled swiftly, passing by the Empire cities of Wolfenburg and Hergig. She had no wish to visit those crowded, dirty cities, filled with desperate and pitiful humans trying to eke out an existence in those squalid conditions. No, she had bypassed them, travelling swiftly towards the city of Altdorf in the south. At Talabheim, she had intended to board a ship, and sail the River Talabec to her destination, there to meet with Lord Teclis.

On her approach to the city of Talabheim, she had halted, feeling a familiar pulsing within her mind. Teclis! He was here! She had spoken with him the next day, and her words had been angry.

'Why do we give our lives for these humans, Lord Teclis? I felt the death of my cousin, as you must have done. Thousands of our kin slain upon the beaches to help the humans, and for what? What gratitude do they give us?'

Teclis looked at her, his ancient eyes filled with sadness and power, and she looked away. 'If we the Asur are to survive, then so too must the Empire of men survive.' She had felt shamed then, for she knew that Teclis, in his wisdom, spoke the truth.

Still, Aurelion could not forget the words that Khalanos had spoken to her before he had left. *'In time, cousin, you will realise that the humans are undeserving of our pity.'* Indeed, she did not pity them any longer. Yet the words of Teclis were irrefutable.

He had left her in Talabheim. He was travelling to the north, to try and stall the advance of the armies of

Chaos. She had expressed her concern, and her desire to join him, but he had silenced her. 'Your place in the battle is here,' he had said, and she had been powerless to disobey his order. 'The life of the man, von Kessel, is imperative, Aurelion. Remember, the survival of the Asur depends upon the survival of the Empire.'

She sped through the night sky, finally approaching the sleeping army of Ostermark.

STEFAN VON KESSEL woke with a start. He knew that what he had just seen and heard had been no dream. With horror, he knew that the elf had spoken truly, and that the forces of Chaos were within the Empire, marching southward. He still felt the accusation in the eyes of the mage, and he knew that Ostland was over-run. The feeling of guilt rose within him, and he knew that he had let his own hatred drive him on to seek the end of Gruber. That action had meant that the forces of Chaos had found what they sought, and now that it was back, more powerful than ever, the fate of the Empire hung in the balance.

The forces of Chaos were marching on Talabheim. That grand city was weak, its militia depleted. If the enemy took it by force, then no army in the Empire had the strength to take it back. The heart of the Empire would belong to Chaos.

BOOK FOUR

CHAPTER TWENTY-NINE

OLAF THE BERSERKER narrowed his eyes, staring through the trees out across the snow-covered clearing ahead. There were figures there, although there were pitifully few of them. Why they had not fled before the approaching forces, he could not fathom, but he was glad that they had not. He had enjoyed butchering the elves on the island, and now it seemed that there were more elves for him to slaughter.

Barking an order, Olaf loped into the clearing. Behind him emerged nearly a thousand Kurgan warriors, all on foot. Being one of Hroth's original Khazag warriors, one of only a hundred that remained, he held an exalted position within the massive army, and this was but one of the tribes that he now claimed as his own.

His horsemen, scouring the forest miles in front of the advancing army, had discovered the elves just hours before. They had not engaged the foe, but had swung around them in a wide loop, to determine if they were part of a larger force waiting to ambush the vanguard of Hroth's forces. It seemed that they were not, and so Olaf ordered his tribe on towards them with all haste, eager to claim the kill for himself.

Pounding through the snow, Olaf began to growl as he felt the blood rage build within him. He knew that as soon as battle was met he would lose himself completely to his berserk rage. It had been the same since childhood. The first time he had felt the red fury descend upon him, he had been but nine summers old, and he had killed two older boys, ripping their throats out with his bare hands. After the fight, once he had regained his composure, he had been shocked and horrified by his actions, at the amount of blood that coated his hands and forearms. Tears running down his face, he had run to his father. Listening to his son, the warrior had smiled, and hugged the child to his massive chest. 'You have been given a gift, my son,' his father had said. 'You will be a mighty warrior.'

His father's words had been true – he had become a mighty warrior, and thousands had fallen beneath his fury. Always it was the same – as battle commenced, he lost himself in the slaughter. He felt neither pain nor fatigue when in his rages, and he fought with the power of a bear. He had been stabbed and cut hundreds of times, but in his berserk fury he cared not, hacking and killing all who opposed him. At battle's end, he would invariably collapse, exhausted and lacking blood, but always he was the victor.

Olaf served his chieftain and warlord faithfully. He had always believed in Hroth; he had always believed that the man was destined for greatness, a greatness far beyond any that he could ever hope to attain. He was pleased to see that he had been correct in his assessment, but then he had always been a good judge of character. When not in his wild rage, Olaf was a quiet, reserved man, who preferred to sit back and listen than to be the focus of attention. His growl turned into a roar as he raced through the snow towards the elves on the other side of the clearing.

A frail figure, wearing a tall ornate headpiece and leaning heavily on a staff, stood in the centre of the small group of elves. The figure stepped forwards and raised the staff into the air. Flames began to fall from the heavens, raining down upon the Kurgan warriors. Where they struck the ground, the snow melted and the sodden earth beneath caught fire.

Fire struck Olaf, hitting his face, searing him with its heat. He ignored the pain, and ran on towards the figure, gripping his pair of axes tightly. They were chained firmly to his forearms, so that he could not drop them when the red mist of his berserk rage descended – without them, he would invariably throw his axes aside and hurl himself at the enemy weaponless, ripping them apart with his bare hands.

An explosion of heat erupted in the midst of the Kurgan, a massive column of flame that roared into the sky, instantly killing hundreds of men. Heat rolled over the other men, striking Olaf in the back and throwing him to the ground with its force. Searing hot air billowed over him, and he surged back to his feet, rage rising within him.

The centre of the pillar of flame burned white hot, and it roared outwards suddenly, catching hundreds more Kurgan in its blast, melting the flesh from their bones. Weapons and armour turned molten and dripped to the ground, bones caught fire and turned to char, and hundreds of the Kurgan warriors died screaming. As the ring of unearthly fire expanded, Olaf screamed in rage and raced on through the melting snow, intent on reaching his foe. His wolf fur cape caught fire, scorching his back.

Olaf's vision was red, and he did not feel the searing heat that began to burn the flesh from his bones. Within minutes, there was nothing remaining of the Chaos vanguard but a clearing of melted snow, the earth blackened by sorcerous flame.

STEFAN VON KESSEL stood silently on the forecastle at the bow of the massive ship, staring out across the deep water of the River Talabec. It was an hour before dawn, and a low mist hung over the river, giving it a ghostly, ethereal appearance. The morning was icy cold, winter having well and truly set in. The dark trees lining the river were heavy with snow. Stefan banged his fist unconsciously against the railing of the forecastle, breaking the ice formed there overnight.

The Talabec was a truly massive river, some thousand feet wide on the approach to Talabheim, and it travelled the breadth of the Empire, hundreds of miles long. It roared down from the Worlds Edge Mountains as dozens of smaller rivers and creeks that merged into the Upper Talabec and the Lower Talabec in Ostermark, before these two rivers merged, west of Bechafen. Leaving Ostermark and entering Talabecland, it was met by the icy waters of the River Urskoy, which flowed all the way from north of the grand city of Kislev, passing south of the battlefields where the Emperor Magnus and the Reiklandguard defeated the armies of Chaos, far in the north. These two mighty rivers converged to create the Talabec, one of the biggest rivers in the Old World. It passed through the heart of the Empire, cutting through the great forests, and leading to the city of Talabheim before continuing on to grand Altdorf, the home of the newly formed Colleges of Magic. Here it merged with the River Stir to become the Reik, and continued on to the ocean at Marienburg, feeding into the marshes that surrounded the port city.

The Talabec was one of the major routes of trade through the Empire, carrying food, livestock and precious cargo from the sea all the way to Kislev. The river was large enough for whole fleets to sail up it, enabling entire armies to travel the breadth of the Empire in a fraction of the time it would take to march. Stefan was thankful for this, for his approach towards Talabheim had been swift.

The reiksmarshal moved to stand next to him. He had recovered well, and from outward appearances, one would never know that he had been ill, but von Kessel knew that much of this was purely for show, and that he tired easily. Still, the strong-willed older man would never allow such weaknesses to show in front of his soldiers. Stefan tensed as the man stood beside him in silence. When the man had first emerged from his sickness, he had been outraged by the actions of the captain, and had exploded with anger. The priestess of Shallya had glared at Stefan balefully for upsetting her patient, and the captain had been almost more taken aback by the anger in the priestess than he was by the fury of the reiksmarshal. He had always believed that the priestesses of Shallya were calm and peaceful types, dutiful and soft natured, but this woman was formidable in her displeasure.

The reiksmarshal had given Stefan an angry dressing down, speaking of his duty to the Empire and the Emperor. For almost an hour, the reiksmarshal had berated him for his actions, and all the while Stefan was silent, accepting it all stoically. He knew that he spoke the truth, and he swore to himself not to allow his own emotions or prejudices to cloud his vision in the future. His duty to the Empire was paramount, and he vowed to do all that his Emperor demanded of him with vigour and faith.

The pair stood together for a moment longer. Uncomfortable with the silence, the reiksmarshal cleared his throat. 'That's a fearsome creature you have below deck. It damn near took a man's arm off this morning.'

The animal's grandsire had been the war-mount of Stefan's grandfather. The captain was apprehensive of the beast, but it had been brought from the menagerie with some difficulty, and so he felt that it would be improper to send it back. 'Griffons are not renowned for their gentle natures,' he replied. The reiksmarshal nodded his head, and was silent for some moments.

'I spoke the truth when last we spoke, von Kessel,' he said, eventually. 'You did not think with the Empire in mind, you thought only of your own anger and vengeance.'

'I know. I see that now, reiksmarshal,' said Stefan, his head low. The knight nodded his head.

'I know you do. You needed to hear those words, von Kessel, and you need to remember them, always, especially with the difficult role that you will need to fill in the future.'

'Sir?' said Stefan, looking at the knight, confusion on his face.

'Don't be so thick-headed, man,' chuckled the reiksmarshal. 'Gruber has no living heir, and even if he did, there is no way that he would succeed to the position of elector. You have cleared the name of your family – the Emperor himself will decree your name exonerated. You are the next in line, Stefan. You are to be the elector.'

'I… I don't want to be elector.'

'What the bloody hell does that have to do with it, eh? Any man that *did* want to be an elector is certainly the wrong man for the role. You think our Emperor Magnus *wished* to be Emperor?'

'I don't know. I've never thought of it.'

'Well, he didn't. He became Emperor because he saw that it was necessary, for the future of the Empire. Just as for the future of Ostermark, *you* must become its elector count.'

'Reiksmarshal,' said Stefan, feeling his stomach knot painfully. 'I have no understanding of politics. Nor any wish to understand them. I am a soldier, nothing more.'

'We don't need more politicians in the Empire, Stefan, we need strong leaders, and you, despite your failings, are a strong leader. Don't get me wrong, you are never going to be the type of man to inspire the populace with rousing speeches. Sigmar forbid, you would doubtlessly say something daft and cause a riot, but that does not matter. You are a soldier, a man used to action. You assess situations and respond as best as you see fit. You don't always get it right, you damn well haven't always made the best decisions in the past, but the past is the past, and the important thing is that those men that follow you trust you, and respect you. You will do just fine.'

Stefan breathed deeply, letting this information soak in. He felt sick. He didn't want this sort of responsibility.

'Here,' said the reiksmarshal. He held out a sword wrapped in a flag bearing the purple and yellow of Ostermark. 'You are not elector yet, but it is within my power to give this to you to bear in the battles ahead. Sigmar knows that you will need it.'

Accepting the proffered gift with some trepidation, Stefan held it for a moment, unwilling to open it. It was heavy, a good solid weight in his hands, and he could feel the power emanating from it. This was an ancient and powerful weapon, and he knew then what it was. His mouth dropped open.

Reverently, he unwrapped the precious weapon. A sheathed sword lay within, its hilt heavy and functional, decorative and rich in a style that was far from ostentatious, yet obviously this was a priceless weapon. The scabbard was simple black leather, with silver edging, and Stefan closed his hand around the hilt tentatively. Grasping the scabbard, he drew the Runefang, marvelling at its perfect balance.

Stefan gaped at the weapon in awe. The Runefang had been the mark of office of the counts of Ostermark since its forging by the dwarfs in the time of Sigmar, one of the twelve Runefangs forged to symbolise the alliance between the two races. It had been wielded in countless battles by generations of elector counts of Ostermark, and Stefan's own grandfather had used it to cut down the greenskins and beastmen that plagued the forests of Ostermark before his treacherous execution. Gruber had never carried the blade to battle, for he was no warrior, and it had languished in the armouries, collecting dust.

The blade of the Runefang was gleaming silver and dwarf runes ran up its length. The metal was harder than any steel that man could forge, and its blade remained as sharp as it was on the day that it was made, never needing to have been sharpened in all the centuries since that time. 'It is made of gromril,' said the reiksmarshal, 'a metal treasured by the dwarfs, one that only they know how to mine and work.'

Stefan swung the blade around him, and it hummed smoothly through the air. It felt perfect in his grasp. The hilt was long enough so that he could hold it with both hands, and it was just the right weight for him to be able to wield it with one hand comfortably. It was a wondrous sword, and he knew that there was power held within it. The old tales claimed that it could cleave through metal and stone. Holding it, Stefan, who had always discounted those stories as exaggerated wives' tales, was not so sure any more.

'This is a grand gift indeed,' said Stefan in awe.

'No gift,' said the reiksmarshal, 'it is your birthright.'

TALABHEIM WAS A massive city, rivalling the greatest cities of the Empire. Known by many as the Eye of the Forest, it was situated in the heart of the Empire. It was built within a gigantic crater, miles across. No one truly knew what caused this crater, but many believed that a great burning twin-tailed comet smashed into the ground, creating the gigantic crater walls that reared up into the sky like a circular range of mountains. Atop these crater walls were built the walls of Talabheim itself; powerful and stout, they dominated the skyline. Combined, the natural defences and the stout walls at their top formed an almost impenetrable defence against any who would dare to attack.

The city itself was situated in the middle of the crater, and was surrounded by miles of farmland. Thus, the outer walls of the city were miles and miles long, and thousands of men were needed to man them. Watchtowers and fortresses dotted the walls, and when properly manned, they allowed a view of the approach to Talabheim from every possible angle.

Just outside the crater walls ran the Talabec, forming a deep natural harbour. Around this harbour, outside the walls proper, had grown the small settlement of Talagaad. Housing some thousand or so permanent residents, it was a slum of a place that catered for the countless traders and sailors that passed through the city every day. Taverns lined the streets surrounding the docklands, filled with brawling, drunken sailors, thieves, smugglers and whores.

Albrecht smiled broadly as the ships drew near the port. 'Ah, now this is my kind of place,' he said.

'We are passing straight through, Albrecht. We will not be spending one moment longer in Talagaad than is absolutely necessary,' said Stefan sternly.

The sergeant gave a long sigh. 'Not even time for a single drink, and a hand of cards, huh. Anyone would think there was a war coming.' He winked at the captain.

'You are in good spirits this morning, sergeant.'

'Aye, I am, captain,' said Albrecht.

'Thank you for not calling me "elector", it grates on my nerves.'

'I'm in good spirits today, *captain*, because we are just about to get off this wretched ship. I hate being on the water, always have. It makes me ill.'

'Rock-hard Sergeant Albrecht scared of water, eh? I wouldn't have guessed it.'

'No, and I'll thank you not to repeat it, and I ain't scared of water, it just makes me feel queasy like.'

'Of course.'

'I'm a soldier, captain. I take my little pleasures where I can. A sunset, or the embrace of a beautiful woman – these are things to be happy about. Getting off a damn ship – it's that same thing for me – I'll take my small pleasures where I can get 'em.'

Stefan raised his eyebrow. 'The embrace of a beautiful woman and getting off a ship the same thing, huh? I think you must be doing one of them wrong, old man.'

'Old man? Don't you think that just because you have that fancy sword strapped at your side that I wouldn't knock some sense into your head if you needed it, *captain*.'

Stefan laughed, and slapped his sergeant on the shoulder. 'I wouldn't have it any other way, old man.'

CHAPTER THIRTY

ULKJAR HEADTAKER SMASHED both of his swords into the neck of the Norscan, one from either side. The blades met in the middle, and the Norscan's head toppled to the ground. Wiping his blades on the cloak of his defeated foe, the tall man sheathed his swords and bent to pick up the head. Holding it up by its hair, he turned around, showing it to all those who watched.

'I am Ulkjar Moerk of the Skaelings!' he roared, his ice blue eyes flashing dangerously from face to face. 'I am the Headtaker! I am your chieftain! This is the fate of all those who dare to challenge me!'

The tall Norscan stalked away, pushing his way through the dispersing crowd of tribesmen. Moving to a large stone, he sat down, placing the bloody head of the latest challenger next to him. He opened up the small deer-hide pouch at his side and drew out a thin needle made from carved whale-bone and a thin sinew string. Licking the sinew between his lips, he threaded it through the eye of the needle, and began to stitch up the wound at his side. He sucked in his breath as he pushed the needle through his flesh and pulled the sinew through. He repeated the movement over and over, until the wound was sewn shut. Biting the tendon off, he tied it neatly, and wiped the blood away with a soft fur cloth.

Ever since Hroth had bested him, fairly he had to admit, he had been forced to face challengers from within his own tribe. Before he had arrived on the beach that day, his men had believed that he was invincible. *He* had believed he was invincible, but no longer. He had lost this authority amongst the Skaelings, and they saw him as just a man, like them, a man who could be bested.

I am chosen, he reminded himself. How could they possibly think that they could best him? Nevertheless, challenge him they did.

Over the last weeks Ulkjar had fought off no less than five Skaelings who dared to challenge his position as their chieftain. He wondered how many more he would have to kill, and when it would end. With his death, he thought grimly. It wouldn't happen any time soon, he knew. No, he was too powerful for any of them, and that was no idle boast, but he was not young any longer. In a few years, he would be the age his father had been when he had killed him.

Ulkjar had two children back in Norsca. Within a year or two young Bjorn would be ready to join him on his raids. Would he be slain by his own son a few years after that, he wondered? He hoped so – that was the way to die – seeing your own son grow strong and proud. He would be damned if anyone else was going to do it. Still, the Warlord Hroth, a towering daemon prince, had claimed his skull for his own, and Ulkjar felt certain that he would eventually lose his life to that one. He hoped it would not be so, for if he were slain, then some other Skaeling would take his place, and his family in Norsca would no doubt be slaughtered by the new chieftain. Still, such was the way of the Skaelings.

Ulkjar rubbed the skin at his side. Nodding, he began to pull the sinew stitching back out. Gripping it in his teeth, he drew the stitching all the way out of his skin. The flesh beneath bore a scar, straight and even, but there was no other mark of his injury. Of course, he had not truly needed to stitch the wound – it would have healed of its own accord – but he found that injuries that were not stitched healed unevenly, and Ulkjar was happy to admit to being a vain man.

Putting the sinew and needle back into his pouch, he stood and stretched his side. It felt a little tight, the skin pinching, but it would pass with time. He knew that his son, Bjorn, had inherited this regenerative trait. He had seen the boy slip on the blackened rocks of the coast when looking for mussels and cut his hand deeply on the sharp rock. The boy had not wept, which made him proud, and within an hour the wound had healed completely, leaving just a jagged scar on his palm. Ulkjar had slapped his hand on the lad's shoulder. 'You are a true son of mine,' he had said. 'Some day you will become the chieftain of the Skaelings, and everyone will fear your name.'

Ulkjar grabbed the severed head of the latest challenger and stalked through the press of warriors, striding up the snow covered hill to where the daemon prince Hroth awaited him with his Khazags and the other chieftains. Approaching the gathering atop the hill, he saw that Hroth the Blooded stood in the middle of the rise, towering over everyone present. The daemon prince nodded his heavy head at Ulkjar as the Skaeling approached to join the other chieftains.

There were about thirty of them gathered there. Glancing around at the chieftains, Ulkjar saw that the black robed sorcerer Sudobaal was there too, as well as three diminutive, hooded figures. Skaven, he thought with distaste.

Ulkjar pushed several of the chieftains roughly out of his way. They turned towards him, hands flashing towards their weapons, but none drew a weapon against him. He stared down at them, for he was at least a full head taller than all present except for Hroth. There was a small pile of skulls at Hroth's side, and he tossed the head of the Norscan to join the others. 'A skull for you, Warlord Hroth, and for great Kharloth, the Blood God,' he said.

The massive daemon chuckled, the sound rumbling deep in his chest. 'Another challenger, Ulkjar?'

'Indeed, warlord. My Skaelings are mighty warriors, but they are not the smartest of men.'

The sorcerer struck his staff on a rock for silence. The chieftains stopped their conversations and turned towards Sudobaal, who stood at the daemon prince's side. He appeared even more twisted and hunched than usual, thought Ulkjar. His face was pinched and full of hatred. He was the daemon's pawn, as were they all, but he was a powerful sorcerer still.

'Our advance scouting tribe was annihilated this day,' spoke the sorcerer. The chieftains shuffled their feet in the snow, 'With sorcery. Our rat-kin friend, the Blind One,' said Sudobaal, indicating one of the hunched skaven, who bowed his head, 'brings us news that our ally in the west has been slain. He died with only part of his duty done. Although he–'

'I will feast on the failure's soul in the Realm of Chaos,' growled Hroth, interrupting the sorcerer.

'Although he did manage to spread plague and dissent across the breadth of the lands of the pitiful weaklings, with the aid of the Blind One and his minions, and cleared our approach southward of enemies, he failed to enter the city, failed in his preparations for our coming.'

'What can you expect from the weakling followers of Nurgle,' snarled one of the chieftains. Another chieftain swore, and turned towards the speaker angrily.

'Enough,' rumbled Hroth, silencing them instantly. 'We also learn through the agents of the Blind One that the slayer of our ally is even now fortifying the Eye of the Forest.'

The chieftains began to murmur amongst themselves. Ulkjar spoke the words that they were thinking.

'Our ally failed to enter the city, and his killer has begun to fortify it, ready for our attack. Why do we not alter our plans, Lord Hroth? We could bypass the Eye of the Forest, and strike out at another target, surely? Sack the cities to the south, those that have never felt the fury of our people? Else could we not head east, and take the fight to the city of the White Wolf?'

'The city of the White Wolf will fall in time, but it is not I who will lead that attack,' growled Hroth.

'The Eye of the Forest will be nigh-on impossible to take, if fully manned, warlord,' said another chieftain.

'We will rip it down, smash it underfoot, and slaughter every man, woman and child within,' rumbled the daemon, staring malevolently at the speaker with eyes of fire.

'What says the Blind One? Will you aid us to take the Eye of the Forest?' hissed Sudobaal, nodding his head to the skaven.

One of the creatures extended a hand from beneath its robes. Its fur was grey, moth-eaten and mange-ridden. With pale fingers it pulled back the hood from its face, exposing its pox-ridden features. Its eyes were milky white, weeping pus down its grey fur, and its whiskers were stubby and rotten. It opened its mouth, exposing large, chipped and yellow front teeth, and exhaled sharply several times in what may have passed for laughter. The skaven nodded its head to Sudobaal, and then again to Hroth, pledging its support.

'It is a foolish venture–' began one of the chieftains. Having heard enough, Hroth stalked towards him, the other chieftains scattering before him. He grabbed the man in his massive red hands, ripped his head from his body and threw both to the ground.

'No more talk. I hunger for battle. We attack. Chieftains: move your tribes with all speed towards the city in the crater, the Eye of the Forest. I will see it toppled.'

STEFAN VON KESSEL surveyed the defences carefully as he led the army of Ostermark through the grand portals of the fortress. Giant statues of Ulric, the ancient god of battle, winter and wolves, and his brother Taal, god of nature and the wild places, flanked the approach to the massive gates. The fortress was built into the side of the crater of Talabheim, and was an imposing and powerful structure. It guarded the only entrance into Talabheim – a tunnel half a mile long carved straight through the crater.

The engineer, Markus, gazed at the fortress with his trained eye, and could find no fault in its design. 'It is a marvel of siege engineering,' he gushed to Stefan. 'See how the towers are placed? And how the walls angle inwards? That forms the killing ground – any attackers would naturally be filtered there, and would be cut to pieces, slaughtered by crossbowmen and handgunners in the towers and on the walls – they would be fired upon from all angles. If the walls were taken by the enemy, the towers themselves would act as small fortresses – see the towers have clear lines of fire across all the walls – nowhere to hide from there, no! No square towers here, oh no! Square towers have corners, and corners are vulnerable. Destroy the corner, and the tower will collapse. Simple, really.'

'Yes indeed, engineer,' said Stefan as they passed through the gates. Looking up, he could see the pointed tips of the portcullis that would be dropped when the attack came. There were countless murder holes on either side of the portcullis, holes where soldiers in the rooms above could drop boiling oil and rocks down upon would-be attackers as they tried to batter their way through.

Past the gates, the tunnel through the crater extended before them. No end was in sight.

'Great Verena above!' exclaimed Markus, invoking the goddess of learning and justice. Stefan was equally impressed. Wide enough for two carriages to travel side-by-side, the tunnel was lit with torches every twenty paces or so. 'This must have taken a lifetime to construct!'

'It would be difficult to storm,' said Stefan, casting his warrior's eye around the heavily defended tunnel. The army of Ostermark marched through the portal behind him, and Stefan strode forwards into the half-mile long tunnel. 'Why is it called the Wizard's Way?' he asked the red- and white-clad Talabheim sergeant who had come to meet him.

'No one truly knows. Some think this tunnel was carved by magic, others that it was named for the countless hedge wizards and sorcerers who were led through it to face trial in Talabheim, but the truth? I daresay we will never know. A wizard *has* walked this tunnel in the last weeks, mind, or to be more correct, a witch. An elf, if you would believe that, skin as white as death,' said the man, giving a dramatic shiver. 'She gave me the fear, that witch. Here to aid the defence, so it is said.'

Stefan raised his eyebrows. 'Aurelion. Her powers will come in useful, I have no doubt,' he said after getting over his surprise. 'I would have thought,' he said, 'that the baron would have come out to meet us personally.'

The sergeant coughed uncomfortably. 'The young baron is ill, bedridden. No one has seen him outside of his bedchamber for months.'

Albrecht threw von Kessel an alarmed look. 'Ill, you say,' said the captain. 'What ailment plagues the Baron of Talabheim?'

'I know not, captain. Some say that it is plague. I must say, captain, that I am glad that you have arrived. Maybe now we stand some chance.'

'We will hold. I am sure that your baron has a great knowledge of the grand defences of his city.'

The sergeant laughed. 'That young fool? His father, now, there was a warrior and a leader, but the young baron? No, he is a scared young man, afraid to do his duty. Word is that he has a priest of Morr with him at all times. Expects to go at any moment, he does, so word says. No, he ain't thinking of the defence of Talabheim.'

'Oh good,' said Albrecht. They neared the end of the tunnel, and approached another fortress guarding the exit. Again, murder holes were carefully positioned in the roof, and others could be seen on the curved walls. High above, the muzzles of cannon could be seen protruding, pointing up the tunnel. Another portcullis could be dropped here, and there was another set of stout gates.

Walking through the open gates, Stefan entered what Markus pointed out was another killing ground. Balconies behind them allowed defenders to rain death down upon any who had fought their way this far, and he saw more cannon barrels. 'Grapeshot,' said the engineer. 'Those cannon will be loaded with hundreds of handgun shots, as well as all manner of nails and other pieces of metal, all wrapped up in canvas. When fired at this range, it would be devastating, shredding everything here.' He winced. 'Any force that somehow made it this far would be torn apart.'

Continuing out into the light, Stefan blinked and shielded his eyes. Talabheim proper was still some miles away. Farmland spread out before him, and he saw men tilling the icy fields, as if there was no war coming. He sighed.

'Take me to the baron,' he ordered.

CHAPTER THIRTY-ONE

BARON JURGEN KRIEGLITZ, Elector Count of Talabecland, turned over in his sweat-drenched bed, surfacing from his restless sleep as the knock on his chamber door sounded once again. His stomach churned as he came awake and reality sank in. His skin was burning with fever, and his breath seemed to catch in his throat. Coughing painfully, a dry, wracking cough that left flecks of blood on his pillow, he called out weakly.

The man was young, but his unwashed hair was already streaked with silver, and his face was haggard. His father had fought in the Great War during the previous years, leaving his only son behind to maintain his affairs. A quiet young man full of self-doubt, he was easily manipulated by the politicians, priests and advisors of his father. Not a stupid man by any count, he saw exactly what was going on, but was at a loss to know how to rectify the situation. His father was a bull of a man, a warrior born and adored by all in Talabecland. He knew how to handle the politics of court, a skill that he had not been passed onto his son. None had grieved more than Jurgen when news of his father's death had reached Talabheim. Almost the entire standing army of Talabecland had perished with him, leaving Talabheim with only a nominal force to protect the ancient city. Jurgen's face had been pale as he was made elector the very next day.

The chamber doors opened and a manservant entered, an elderly statesman in tow.

'My most honoured lord. Do you fare better today?' asked the statesman grimly. He was a true politician, his words silky smooth, but Jurgen knew that he was a manipulative snake. He also knew that he did not have the mettle to compete with the man's endless machinations. Without waiting for a response, he continued. 'My lord, the Chaos forces close upon Talabheim, but praise great Taal, for hope is at hand – a large armed force from Ostermark has arrived to aid our defence. A council of war has been called, and sits in the war room – are you well enough to attend, my lord, or shall we conduct matters as best we can in your absence?'

'I'm not well,' said Jurgen, coughing for emphasis. He drew the covers of his bedding tightly around him, and rolled over onto his side, away from the man. 'Attend to matters without me.'

'As you wish, my lord, rest yourself. All the matters of state will be attended to,' said the statesman, bowing deeply. Jurgen listened to the men back out of the room, and the door close quietly behind them.

Jurgen was dying. He would live no more than a year, the lady of Shallya had informed him, tears in her eyes. At first, he had believed his illness had come about from the pressure of his role. He hated the intrigues of his court, the politicking and the back-stabbing. He was weak, he knew. His stomach churned constantly, the acids in his gut burning him from the inside. As the months rolled by, his headaches got worse, and he had taken to bed, distancing himself from his duties. There was a cancer in his head, the lady had said. One day soon it would take him.

Closing his eyes tightly, the pain in his head a pounding throb, Jurgen hoped it would take him soon. He closed his eyes and fell into a fitful sleep.

Blessed oblivion was denied him as he heard raised voices outside his chamber doors. Closing his eyes tightly, his stomach knotting, he hoped they would go away and leave him to die in peace.

The voices got louder, and the doors to his chamber were thrown open. 'You cannot go in there, sir. The duke is an ill man!'

'Talabheim and the Empire have need of him!' came an angry, authoritative voice. 'I must speak with the elector!'

Jurgen closed his eyes tightly, feigning sleep. Heavy footsteps approached his bed, halting at his side.

'My Lord Krieglitz, you must awake and attend your duties. Your city and your people need you,' said the voice. 'Krieglitz?' A hand shook his shoulder, and Jurgen opened his heavy eyes. A man, his face horribly scared, stood before him. 'I have need to speak with you, lord.'

Wearily, Jurgen pushed himself up in his bed. His flustered manservant hopped forwards to push cushions behind his back. 'I am sorry, my lord. He burst in.

There was nothing I could do to halt him,' said the man, obviously distressed.

Jurgen waved the apology away with a weak gesture.

'It matters not,' Jurgen said resignedly. He turned his tired gaze upon the intruder, looking him up and down. 'Ostermark. Long has there been antipathy between Talabecland and Ostermark. Who are you to burst in here?' he asked, trying to sound strong, but hating the weakness he heard in his own voice.

'I am Captain Stefan von Kessel. I come to the aid of Talabheim in its time of need. The time for hostilities between our lands is long past, we are united together in the service of our Emperor, Sigmar praise his name.'

'A captain? A mere captain who bears the Runefang of Ostermark?'

Stefan's face hardened. 'I am to be elector on my return to Ostermark. It is not a duty that I long for, but it is my duty none the less. You have a duty too, my lord, to Talabheim and to the Empire.'

The sick young man closed his eyes, sighing wearily. 'I am not long for this world,' he said. 'Morr will come for me soon. Leave me in peace, Ostermark.'

'My lord, your city is but days from being besieged! Would you lie here in your bed and let it fall around you?'

'What else can I do? I am dying. Let me be.'

'You are not damn well dead yet. I met your father once. He was a proud man, a great leader and a truly heroic warrior. I mourned for him when I learnt he had fallen, but I raised my cup to his memory. A true hero of the Empire.'

'What is your point, Ostermark? Why do you come here to berate me?'

'Would you be proud for your father to see you now, man? Cowering in your bed like a child, shirking your responsibilities and letting all that he fought so hard to protect fall and crumble around you?'

'I am not my father!' said Jurgen sharply, leaning forwards. He slumped back into the cushions, sighing wearily. 'I wish I had his strength, but I do not. I will be of no use in the days to come.'

'Put on your armour, lord,' said Stefan, his voice softer. 'Your soldiers need their leader! Just to see you walk the battlements will lift their spirits! That is worth more than a thousand more troops! Show them that you will fight at their side!'

'I… I cannot. Leave me be.'

'You would leave the defence of your city to those poisonous politicians in your war room? You would bring dishonour to the name of your family like this? Does your father's sacrifice for the Empire mean *nothing* to you?'

Jurgen had closed his eyes against these questions. 'I loved my father dearly, but I am nothing next to him. Where he was strong, I am not. I cannot do this, Ostermark. Do not ask me to,' he said. His eyes opened suddenly, and he leant forwards, his face filled with sudden passion. '*You* take charge of the defence. You could do it! I know that you could. You lead my people. You would give them more hope than I ever could.'

'Your soldiers need *you*, damn it!' exploded Stefan, losing his patience with the weakling fool before him. 'Have some damned backbone, man!'

Jurgen looked at him pleadingly, silently begging Stefan to leave him be. 'I am dying,' he said weakly.

Von Kessel stared at him for a moment, his face hard. 'You want to be remembered like this? A man can be defined by the way he dies, Count Krieglitz. You could die a failure, rotting away here in your chambers. Or you could don your armour and inspire your troops. Lead them, and if you fall in battle, then you will be remembered as the elector count who gave his life in the defence of his capital, fighting alongside his soldiers. You could be remembered for all time in the annals of Talabecland as a hero who died in service to his Emperor.'

Silence hung over the bedchamber. Jurgen continued to stare pleadingly at the captain. 'I… I cannot do this,' he said finally.

'Then be damned, for all I care. Stay here and wait for death to come,' said the captain. He stalked out of the room, slamming the door behind him.

'Can… can I get you anything, my lord?' ventured Jurgen's manservant. Ignoring the man, Jurgen slumped down into his bed once more. He drew the covers around him tightly, his stomach churning, and rolled to face the wall. He waited until he heard the man leave, padding quietly across the room and slipping out the door, and curled himself into a ball, loathing himself.

THE FOLLOWING DAYS were a blur of frantic activity within Talabheim. Tens of thousands of arrows, crossbow bolts and handgun shot were delivered onto the walls, and cannon and mortars were hauled onto the tops of towers. The soldiers were posted along the walls, but there were miles upon miles of walls to cover, and they were spread thinly. Still, the main Chaos assault would come at the

Wizard's Way, and the majority of the defence was focused there. The outer fortress would face the brunt of the attack, and there would stand von Kessel's greatswords, and half of the soldiers of Talabheim. Two hundred handgunners would man the outer fortress walls, and eighteen cannon and eight mortars would rain death upon the forces of Chaos as they approached the gatehouse. Stefan was determined to hold the fortress for as long as possible, to exact a terrible toll on the enemy. The soldiers stationed there accepted their duty with stoic pride, although they knew that the chances of survival were slim.

The scouts and outriders under the grim command of Wilhelm reported on the approach of the forces of the enemy. They marched towards the city relentlessly, with more warbands emerging every day from the forest to join them, so that the Empire troops were outnumbered near four to one. But the odds were acceptable, even favourable, for the Empire troops, such was the strength of Talabheim's defences.

Still, von Kessel was uneasy, for he feared some daemonic devilry and sorcery would render all his careful planning wasted. In a hushed voice, Wilhelm spoke to Stefan and the reiksmarshal of the daemon leading the Chaos forces, which he had glimpsed from afar. His eyes contained fear as he spoke of the massive creature, and that alone worried von Kessel, for he believed that nothing could scare the cold-hearted killer. 'We're all going to die,' said Wilhelm, his face grim. Stefan knew the man well enough to know that he would not speak those words to any other than himself, and would not shy from his duty, but the certainty of the scout's words frightened him.

Talagaad, at the base of the great crater of Talabheim, was evacuated. The populace sought refuge within the walls of Talabheim, walking miserably along the Wizard's Way. Some refused to leave, and these barricaded themselves inside their homes in a vain attempt to protect themselves from the onslaught to come. Others took advantage of the exodus, looting the homes of those who had left, and there were several deaths. The richer of the villagers paid exorbitant prices to be carried away to safety onboard merchant vessels bound for Altdorf. The harbour lay empty of ships, and the streets of Talagaad were deserted.

The elf mage Aurelion and her bodyguard had been coolly distant with the humans. They had joined the defences at the outer fortress, and Stefan was glad of their support. He had seen those tall warriors fight, and they possessed skills that seemed far from natural, moving with subtle, lethal grace. They would fight to the last, he knew. He was still suspicious of Aurelion and her power, but he knew that she would be invaluable in counteracting the vile magics of the enemy.

Gunthar walked along the walls constantly, his presence doing wonders to raise the spirits of the men. He seemed to be looking forward to the coming battle, and he joked and made light with the men, who appreciated his crude stories and his booming laugh.

Albrecht worked tirelessly, shouting orders and preparing the men for the assault to come. He snatched sleep when he could, the odd hour here and there, resting in full armour on the walls. He drilled the soldiers relentlessly, making sure they knew exactly where they needed to be once battle commenced.

The Reiklandguard was to be held back as a reserve, one of a dozen flying companies that could be redeployed quickly to fill any gaps that appeared, or to stem any attack that breached the walls.

The city of Talabheim itself, about two miles across farmland from the Wizard's Way, was crowded with refugees from Talagaad. The militia that kept the peace there were kept busy as the inevitable scuffles broke out amongst the hungry, homeless and frightened people. Of Baron Jurgen Krieglitz, there was no word.

Finally, Wilhelm and the last of his scouts arrived at the outer fortress, breathless and bloody. Ropes were thrown from the walls and they ascended swiftly to report to von Kessel and the reiksmarshal.

'They come,' Wilhelm stated simply. It was then that the drumming began.

HROTH STOOD ATOP the rise, looking out across the top of his massive army towards the Empire city, his eyes burning with flame, rage and hunger. Thousands of burning torches were held aloft, thrust into the air with every beat of the drums. The sound of drumming filled the night. The relentless pounding of hundreds of drums would be terrifying to the pitiful men cowering within the walls of the city, but the sound made his daemonic heart beat quickly in anticipation of the slaughter to come. How he had longed for this time! The attack would begin. He licked his lips with his long forked tongue. Soon he would have a foothold in the very heart of the Empire, which would herald the inevitable downfall of civilisation.

Hroth roared, the thunderous sound echoing back to him from the crater and walls surrounding the city, passing over the warbands readying themselves below. The drumming stopped instantly. Hroth roared again, and his army began the assault.

CHAPTER THIRTY-TWO

FOR ALMOST A week, the attacks came at the walls of Talabheim. The forces of Chaos suffered terrible casualties, for to attack up the crater at the walls was nigh-on impossible, and the Chaos warbands of Hroth the Blooded were mercilessly slaughtered by the defenders. The dead dropped their hastily constructed ladders where they fell, to be picked up by others as they scrambled up the steep incline towards the towering walls.

To the Empire defenders, the hordes assailing them seemed countless, and the nights were filled with the hateful drumming of the foe, haunting the sleep of the soldiers, and thousands of campfires and torches burnt through the night. Night was no release from the attacks, and the Empire soldiers were dog-tired from hours of constant readiness and sporadic moments of frantic battle. They took their rest when they could get it, but it was invariably short-lived and rare. The Chaos forces attacked all around the city, striking against the walls quickly, forcing the defenders to constantly have men on all the many miles of walls.

Stefan von Kessel and the reiksmarshal knew that these were little more than diversionary attacks, for the main assault would come at the only true entrance into Talabheim, at the fortress leading into the tunnel. However, if they did not station some men on these walls, the enemy might well make a breach, and then the defence would be shattered. So, with some frustration, Stefan ordered many of the men he would have preferred to have been protecting the main entrance onto the subsidiary walls that surrounded the great city. 'Why in heaven's name make so many miles of damn walls!' he had shouted in exasperation. 'If the walls were around just the city itself, we could hold against this foe for a year!' He had not been mollified by the reiksmarshal's undeniably sensible response.

The smithies of Talabheim worked day and night to cast thousands upon thousands of handgun shots and cannonballs, and the fletchers worked tirelessly crafting great bundles of arrows that were distributed amongst the archers. The temple of Shallya was overflowing, and so the palace of Baron Jurgen Krieglitz was turned into a temporary surgery. Cartloads of the injured were carried there from the battlements daily to be tended by the priestesses of Shallya and those citizens who lent their aid. The grim priests of Morr stalked the halls, tending to those whose injuries were fatal, easing their passage from the world.

Von Kessel visited the different wall sections, bolstering the morale of the men wherever he was. The soldiers of Talabheim held him in awe, for he fought at their side as one of them, and expected nothing of the soldiers that he was unwilling to do himself. The Chaos forces made several breaches along the walls, and they surged into the open land within like a tide of insects. These breaks were but temporary, and they were crushed by the ever-vigilant Reiklandguard and other flying companies that Stefan had assigned.

The enemy was determined, it seemed, to take Talabheim as quickly as possible, regardless of the losses incurred, and Stefan could understand their need for a swift victory. The Emperor Magnus was on the march, heading towards the beleaguered city, and if the Chaos forces did not take it quickly, their army would be crushed. If they did take the city, however, something that Stefan would give every last breath of his life to prevent, it would be a very different story. If the Emperor arrived to discover the city already fallen, the Chaos force would be able to hold almost indefinitely against them.

Stefan spent much of his time fighting as part of the defence of the vital fortress leading into the Wizard's Way. The relentless barrage of cannon, mortar and handgun killed thousands. Stefan's soldiers, who were stalwart and unshakeable in their defiance of the foe, met those that reached the walls. They killed hundreds of the enemy, and kicked their corpses from the walls to fall amongst the piles of the dead at their base. The stink was horrendous, and von Kessel worried about disease. Flies descended on the bodies in massive buzzing clouds, bringing back vile memories of the defeat of the treacherous Elector Gruber some weeks earlier.

As each wave was pushed back, the Empire warriors would slump down against the battlements in silence, weary and drawn. They had been jubilant after the first attacks had been stemmed, fuelled with adrenaline, but as the days wore on, they became quieter and more reluctant to be drawn into conversation. Their eyes were lifeless and red-rimmed, and their heads hung low. They snapped upright as soon as the shout came, however, and pulled themselves to their feet to face the next wave of attack.

'They come again!' screamed a voice, and frantic battle was joined once more. Stefan von Kessel rammed his sword through the visor slit of a black armoured warrior, and he toppled backwards off the ladder. Hearing a scream to his left, the captain saw the man next to him stagger, blood streaming from the fatal wound at his throat. A heavily armoured warrior clambered over the ramparts behind him, his helmet horned and bearing hateful markings of the gods of Chaos. Roaring, the warrior lashed out with his pair of weapons, cutting down another man with a blow to the head, and slamming his spiked mace into the chest of another. Other warriors appeared behind him as the first stepped forwards, killing another as he cleared a space on the battlements.

With a shout, Stefan threw himself forwards, aiming a blow at the warrior's head. The massive figure caught the blow on the blade of his sword, and swung his spiked mace towards Stefan's chest. It impacted with his shield, throwing him backwards into another man. The warrior stepped towards him, but suddenly halted, a slender blade protruding from his chest. He fell heavily, and von Kessel saw a pair of the elf swordmasters step into the breach, their tall blades weaving around them in a blur. They moved effortlessly, gracefully swaying out of the way of blows, and striking with deadly swiftness. Several of Stefan's greatswords stepped forwards to join them, moving protectively in front of their lord. Their movement looked clumsy and slow in comparison to that of the elves, but were no less effective, their heavy swords smashing into the Chaos warriors with brute force.

Stefan climbed to his feet and rejoined the fray. He smashed his shield into the face of a marauder clambering over the ramparts. He drove his sword hilt into the face of another man as he reached the top of a tall ladder, and he fell into darkness.

The captain heaved on the ladder, pushing it backwards. It swung slowly away from the wall, taking the dozen men clinging to it to their deaths.

A bare-chested warrior leapt over the ramparts and rammed his sword into the back of one of the slender, white-robed elf swordmasters. The other elf turned towards his comrade, sorrow in his eyes, and his blade sang out, decapitating the man. A heavy axe slammed into the elf's tall helmet, smashing through the silver metal and caving his skull in. He dropped without a sound.

More ladders slammed against the fortress walls, too many to push away. Handgunners in the towers to either side of the length of wall continued to fire into the horde, smoke rising from amongst the crenellations and arrow slits. The cannon continued to boom, and the mortars fired as quickly as they could be reloaded, killing dozens with every shot, but there seemed to be a never-ending tide of warriors to step into any gaps created by the explosions.

Stefan was weary beyond belief. Attacks had been made on the walls around Talabheim for almost a week, sporadically hitting at different wall sections and towers, but the assault against the fortress leading into the Wizard's Way had been constant. The ground around the base of the walls was piled high with the dead. They were piled especially high in the killing grounds where the walls were angled back. Hundreds upon hundreds of the warriors of the Dark Gods had been mercilessly cut down by crossbow and handgun, there, as they sought to raise ladders against those tall walls, and the stench of death was almost unbearable.

A longer, protracted siege would have proven more effective had there been no threat of Empire reinforcements arriving, but the Chaos general was not a subtle commander, Stefan decided. He would wear down the defenders by throwing wave after wave of his troops against the fortress, attacking relentlessly until victory was achieved, or he ran out of men. The Empire troops had killed thousands of the enemy already, but Stefan knew that it was not enough, and that this first fortress would soon fall.

Talagaad at the base of the crater of Talabheim was nothing more than a smoking ruin, flattened by the enemy, and the harbour was filled with corpses. Those foolish villagers who had refused to leave their homes had been nailed to cartwheels, or impaled, screaming, on long spears. These grisly totems, no doubt some dark offering to the gods of Chaos, demoralised the defenders, who could see that many of the people were still alive, even as the black carrion birds pecked at them.

Massive beasts stalked amongst the endless horde of Chaos. Brutish ogres, hulking creatures dressed in crude heavy armour, roared as they charged towards the gates of the fortress, hefting makeshift battering rams under their massive arms. Trolls lumbered forwards, their gaits awkward, bony spikes protruding from the thick skin on their backs. They were mutated, evil beasts, some of them having multiple arms, or two heads sprouting from one torso. Stefan had fought trolls before, but those had been the stony-skinned trolls of the mountains, not these twisted creatures that had been mutated from their continued exposure to Chaos. Still, if they were anything like stone trolls, they would be virtually impossible to kill. This was proven when one of the creatures was struck in the chest by a cannonball. It was thrown to the ground, its chest destroyed utterly, but it pushed itself to its feet, roaring in anger. It pulled the cannonball from its caved-in chest, and launched it back at the fortress, even as the crushed bones of its body began to re-form.

Stefan killed another man with a thrust to his chest, and wiped blood from his brow. He became aware of a deep reverberation that was making the ground and the fortress itself shake, and he looked out over the sea of the enemy to discover what this new horror was. His eyes widened as he saw the giant striding forwards, a tree-trunk held in ones of its meaty hands.

The creature stood fifty feet tall, and horns curled from its massive forehead. Tusk-like teeth protruded from its jaw, and its three eyes blinked heavily. A necklace of human limbs hung around its neck, and Albrecht was horrified as he saw a cavernous tooth-lined mouth open up in the creature's gut. The giant strode through the press of Chaos warriors and marauders, breaking into a lumbering run as it neared the fortress.

Arrows thudded into the face and chest of the giant, having as little effect as insect bites. It bellowed as it ran, and the earth rumbled under its massive footsteps. It did not slow down at all as it hurtled towards the fortress wall, and men backed away from the battlements as it drew ever nearer. Lowering its shoulder, the giant slammed into the wall. Men were knocked from their feet by the impact, and the wall cracked, stones tumbling to the ground as the wall shifted.

Stefan was thrown to his knees along with the other soldiers. The giant's massive head, horrifyingly enormous up close, reached almost to the top of the walls, and it raised the tree-trunk in its fist high over its head before slamming it down onto the walls, crushing half a dozen men. It laughed crudely, spraying spittle over the crenellations, and swept its club across the battlements, smashing dozens of men from the wall to fall to their deaths below. The giant's laughter was cut short as it yelped in pain and dropped its club, pulling its hand back towards it, dripping blood, two of its fingers severed by the blades of an elf swordmaster. Its face creasing in childlike anger, the giant balled its hand into a fist and smashed the elf into the stones, pulverising it beneath his knuckles.

'Aim at its eyes!' shouted Stefan, and a flurry of crossbow bolts and arrows streaked towards the monster.

The giant swatted at the missiles as if they were flies, and ducked its head below the ramparts. It bent down and gripped the massive iron portcullis that had been dropped in front of the great doors of the fortress. Gripping the iron bars tightly in its massive hands, it began to pull at it, massive muscles straining. With a roar and the wrenching sound of tearing metal, the giant ripped the portcullis free, making stones tumble down to the ground. Lifting the portcullis over its head, the giant heaved and threw it at one of the tall towers that was interspersed between the wall sections, making part of the ancient stone structure crumble under the impact.

An arrow sank into one of the giant's three eyes and it roared in pain, staggering backwards. It stepped on a Chaos warrior, crushing the man into the ground, and stumbled. Its balance lost, the giant fell heavily backwards. It seemed to take an age to hit the ground, and the earth reverberated under the impact. A dozen warriors were caught beneath it, and were instantly slain. Arrows and handgun shots peppered the skin of the struggling giant until a cannonball ended its life, smashing its head to a bloody pulp.

Still, the giant had done its job, for the massive portcullis had been ripped clear, and already dozens of Norse warriors were charging forwards with massive axes towards the great wooden door of the fortress. Other Norse warriors ran with them, holding their shields over their heads to protect themselves from the arrows and rocks that rained down from the gatehouse above. Burning oil was tipped upon them, and many screamed in pain as the searing liquid splashed over them. Still others survived, and began to smash their axes into the sturdy wooden door.

Stefan left the walls, racing down the blood-slick stairs to the ground level of the fortress. 'With me!' he commanded, ordering a group of greatswords with him as he raced towards the gatehouse. Forty men, led

by Sergeant Albrecht, were there already, propping up
the great wooden doors with beams and timbers. The
Norscans swung their axes with great force, and it
would be but minutes before the door gave way. 'Hold
steady, men of Ostermark!' shouted Stefan.

The door suddenly exploded inwards in a shower of
splintering timbers, throwing the men of Ostermark
behind it to the ground. 'Sorcery!' snarled Albrecht,
and he led the greatswords forwards to meet their enemies as they surged through the smashed entranceway.

The battle in the gatehouse was brutal. The Norse
threw themselves at the greatswords with renewed
vigour, led by a blond giant of a man who fought with
a pair of thick-bladed swords. This man cut down men
left and right, his speed and strength far beyond that
of normal men. Albrecht hacked down several
Norscans, and Stefan and his soldiers entered the
melee, lending their weight to the crucial combat.

Ulkjar Moerk the Headtaker butchered his way
through the greatswords, his twin swords cutting and
stabbing. With one blade, he blocked the strike of one
of the men, hacking with his other blade deep into the
man's neck. Arterial blood sprayed out in a fountain.
'Blood for the Blood God!' roared Ulkjar.

Stefan drove his Runefang into the throat of one of
the Norscans, and blood bubbled up from the wound.
'For Sigmar and for the Emperor!' he shouted, and
threw himself fully into the fray.

Ulkjar heard the name of the hated false deity of the
Empire, and his eyes swung to fix on Stefan. He began
to cut his way towards him, butchering everyone in his
path. His body was covered in cuts and deep wounds,
any one of which would have been fatal to a lesser

man. He hacked the head from the shoulders of another man, and launched himself forwards to cut down the man who had shouted out the name of the false god.

Stefan stepped backwards as the swift blow arced towards his head, raising his Runefang defensively before him. The power of the blow was immense, and he was knocked backwards by the force. The second blade of the towering blond-haired devil swung in towards his gut, and he managed to get his shield in the way, but was buffeted backwards again by the force of the blow, his arm numb. Regaining his footing, he feinted a blow at the massive Norscan's head, before turning the blow in mid-air towards his chest.

Ulkjar saw the blow coming, and turned it aside with one of his swords. He was shocked at the power that was held in the blade of his foe. He could feel the dangerous magic within the weapon, and he knew that it held the power to kill him when other weapons would merely injure. He attacked with renewed fury, swinging high and low in a dizzying display of prowess, forcing his enemy further back. Lashing out almost lazily, Ulkjar slew a greatsword who was trying to aid his captain, and drove his other blade into the heart of another.

Seeing his opportunity, Stefan lunged forwards. As if he had been expecting the attack, the towering Norscan slapped the Runefang to the ground, and stabbed forwards, intending to impale Stefan. The captain twisted away from the blade at the last minute, and the sword pierced his side painfully, but not fatally. He cried out, and dropped to one knee.

'Protect the captain!' came a shout, and a heavy blow struck Ulkjar from behind. He swung around and rammed one of his blades straight through the body of his attacker.

As Stefan was dragged back by his greatswords, he cried out as he saw the fatal blow. 'Albrecht!' he shouted.

The sergeant, impaled on the Norscan's sword, turned his head as he heard his name called. Blood rose in his mouth, and dripped from his lips. His eyes met the eyes of his captain as von Kessel was bustled away from the battle. Ulkjar pulled his sword out of the sergeant, and he fell to the ground, dead.

Ulkjar bellowed in frustration at his foe escaping from him. A portcullis slammed down behind Stefan von Kessel as he was bustled into the half-mile long tunnel.

Those Empire soldiers remaining in the outer fortress battled hard, but within minutes the fortress was overrun, and every Empire soldier within was slaughtered.

CHAPTER THIRTY-THREE

OVER A THOUSAND Norse and Kurgan warriors lay dead or dying in the tunnel. The stench of blood and death was heavy in the enclosed space, as the corpses piled up on top of each other. Almost six hours earlier, the portcullis that led from the outer fortress into the Wizard's Way had been lifted, and the first men raced along the half-mile tunnel, their screams and shouts echoing loudly. This first warband, which had been given a great honour by being the first chosen to storm the tunnel, was torn apart by cannon and handgun fire. It was but one of many warbands that were determined to be the first to breach the defences of Talabheim, and for the next six hours, warriors were directed by Hroth to charge up the tunnel into the guns of the enemy.

Hundreds of monstrous warhounds were unleashed, and they raced up the blood-slick cobbles, barking and roaring in fury. They were shot down without mercy, and their blood pooled out, mingling into the congealing mess of gore. Fur-clad marauders threw themselves forwards after the hounds, and they too were massacred, hundreds of them falling under the hail of burning lead.

Great pools of gore were congealing beneath the corpses piling high within the tunnel. Fresh soldiers replaced weary handgunners, and the Empire commanders walked amongst their troops, lifting their spirits with rousing speeches. They believed that they had beaten back the best that the Chaos forces had to throw at them, that the Chaos general must pull back and attack Talabheim from a less well-protected angle. The tunnel was narrow, and only a limited number of Chaos warriors could approach at any one time, and every assault so far had been held off without any man getting within thirty yards.

Hroth was growing impatient, but he cared little about the number of his warriors that were slain, and he ordered more of his warbands along the tunnel to die. He kept his most trusted warriors, the Khazags, at his side, awaiting the right moment to throw them forwards. He knew that the end was near, and he hungered for this battle to be over.

Hroth could feel the pleasure of Khorne, for the carnage was awesome to behold. At the end of the tunnel, the portcullis and gates were open. Rank upon rank of handgunners stood there, and their weapons spat death at the never-ending horde of warriors that threw themselves towards them. As each soldier fired, he knelt down to allow the soldiers behind a clear shot at the approaching enemy, and passed his weapon back, a freshly loaded gun being handed forwards to him. A hundred shots had rung out within a minute of the first wave rushing towards the Empire soldiers, leaving scores of men in screaming agony on the tunnel floor, to be trampled by the warriors behind.

Four helblaster volley guns sat alongside the soldiers of the Empire just within the gates, and they roared their fury whenever the Chaos warriors drew too close. After the first hour, these guns had unleashed full barrages of nine barrels three times, slaughtering hundreds of the enemy. One of the temperamental guns had jammed early on, and had been wheeled back from the gates, and another had exploded catastrophically, killing its crew and a dozen Ostermark soldiers unlucky enough to have been too close. The smoke had filled the tunnel, and the Empire soldiers had fired blindly into it, fearing that the enemy was closing on them under the blanket of its cover.

Hroth leaned down to snarl in the face of the sorcerer, Sudobaal, his eyes burning with fire. He curled his lips back, exposing his sharp, dagger-like teeth.

'Do it now, *sorcerer*,' he growled, disdain in his voice. 'Prove your worth to me.'

Sudobaal, his face drawn, dark rings of exhaustion around his snake-like eyes, looked up at his lord. His back was hunched, and he quickly lowered his gaze, nodding. 'Yes, my master,' he said wearily.

STEFAN, HIS SIDE bandaged uncomfortably beneath his armour, steadied his soldiers as the evil sound of chanting echoed up the tunnel. The words made his skin crawl, and he felt the pit of his stomach knot. The words were unearthly, horrific and unnatural, the voice birthed in nightmare and madness. Still, his face was stoic, and he stalked behind the ranks of handgunners frantically reloading their weapons with shaking hands, letting them know that their captain was with them.

'Fear not the vile words of the evil ones,' he said. 'Our Emperor Magnus defeated them on the fields of Kislev, and so we shall defeat them here in Talabheim. With Sigmar guiding us, we will smite them from the face of the world.'

The daemonic chant continued, getting louder and louder, the sounds echoing eerily off the curved walls. Stefan swung towards the cool elf maiden beside him. Her face was, as always, emotionless and icy. 'Lady,' Stefan said quietly, 'what is this infernal sound?'

The elf mage, Aurelion, was silent for a moment, her thin lips pursed tightly. 'It is a plea to the Dark Gods,' she said finally, her voice musical and beautiful. 'The words bite at me, unnatural and vile. Quiet your troops, captain.'

Stefan ordered silence. The only sound was the infernal, guttural chanting that was filling the tunnel. The soldiers peered along its length, seeking out the one whose voice it was, but they could see nothing but hundreds of yards of emptiness. The only movement was the twitching of bodies.

Aurelion closed her eyes and her mouth began to move silently as she began her own incantation. She lifted her head back, her lips forming the intricate words perfectly. A fine mist began to seep from her mouth as she spoke, falling down her body to pool around her feet. The mist began to spread out around her, rolling over the cobblestones, seeking the lowest ground, and it seeped across the floor. Stefan took an involuntary step backwards away from the mist before stopping himself. The ghostly pale smoke coiled around his boots, and he felt a warmth tingle up his legs. It was not an unpleasant sensation. The mist curled around the powder barrels, and over the feet and legs of the men of Ostermark, their handguns now fully loaded, who were waiting in silence. The first man to notice it gasped. Another hissed, 'witch-craft', sharply, but Stefan put his hand on the man's shoulder, shaking his head for silence. The warriors of Ostermark looked at the smoke coiling around them with a certain amount of dread, but remained silent.

Aurelion's eyelids flicked open, exposing eyes that were now black. Her words became louder, her lyrical voice sounding somehow beautiful, haunting and frightening all at the same time. The devilish chanting faltered for a moment, and there was a choking sound from the Chaos sorcerer. Then the voice began again, the words being spat out angrily.

Aurelion gasped, and Stefan looked at her in concern. He saw a drip of blood trickle from her nose, and her voice began to sound more strained. Angry, horrible words were being barked down the corridor, and Stefan began to make out one word being repeated over and over: *Khorne*.

The word was deeply unsettling, wrong and tainted. Stefan felt anger suddenly build within him, and he ground his teeth together. His mind was clouded for a moment with images of bloodshed and slaughter, and he clenched his fist tightly around his sword hilt.

* * *

BLACK BLOOD BEGAN to run from Sudobaal's nose, and he almost faltered again over the words of his barked incantation. A force was resisting him, the power of another, and he felt fear descend over him. Hroth's fiery eyes narrowed, but the sorcerer managed to keep his stream of words flowing.

Sweat ran down the lined face of the black-clad sorcerer. He had reached the peak of the spell, the most critical and difficult part. One badly pronounced phrase, one misplaced vowel within his daemonic chant, would spell instant damnation. His soul teetered on the brink of destruction, for the forces that he was calling upon would as soon feast upon him as do his bidding. He felt the menace of the daemon prince before him. *He* would sooner feast upon his soul than allow Sudobaal to fail.

The sorcerer's legs began to shake, and he clung to his fiery staff to keep himself upright. His chanting began to increase in intensity, and his voice rose in volume. More blood ran from his nose, and it began to seep from his ears. Vessels within his eyes burst, and he closed them tightly against the pain, bloody tears running down the deep grooves of his face. He raised his claw-like hand into the air as he screamed the words of summoning.

WITH A BARKING shout, the chanting stopped abruptly. Aurelion staggered and would have fallen to the ground had her slight frame not been caught by one of her attendant swordmasters. The elves quickly backed away, taking their charge out through the courtyard, overlooked by balconies swarming with crossbowmen and cannon barrels, towards the fresh air inside the walls of Talabheim.

Just before she passed out of earshot of the captain, Aurelion regained consciousness, and called out to him. 'Beware! They come!'

WITH PLEASURE, HROTH heard the words that would draw forth the creatures of Khorne's realm, and he smiled in satisfaction. Sudobaal fell to the floor, broken and bloody, but there was an evil grin on the sorcerer's face as he passed into unconsciousness.

Half a mile along the tunnel, the blood that covered the floor began to bubble and boil. A shape rose from the gore, uncurling itself to stand taller than a man. The blood covered its muscular flesh, running off it in thick, viscous rivulets. The flesh beneath was the same colour as congealed blood, a dark, purplish, bruised red.

The creature flexed its powerful shoulders, the muscles tensing and rippling with strength. Its head was long, and great horns protruded from its brow, curling back over its head. Its mouth was filled with daggerlike teeth, and a slitted tongue darted forwards, tasting the air before it. Its rage and excitement built as it tasted blood on the air, fresh blood being pumped around mortal bodies. It opened its slanted eyes, and fire burnt there, the baleful fires of Chaos. It was a child of Khorne, one of his loyal foot soldiers and warriors, a bloodletter.

It let loose a roar of pure hatred, rage and fury. In its hand, it clenched a massive black-bladed, brazenhilted sword, one of the dread hellblades of Khorne's minions, and it hefted the weapon high over its head. Glowing runes of the Blood God were inscribed along the blade of this awesome weapon. The bloodletter roared again, and began to race down the tunnel towards the Empire soldiers.

Scores of bloodletters rose from the blood of the fallen. They had needed such a sacrifice to allow them to pass from the Realm of Chaos, and they roared their anger as they too joined the charge of the first. Soon there were over two hundred of the creatures, roaring and racing towards the Empire lines.

Hroth the Blooded bellowed in triumph, and launched himself into the tunnel, unfurling his red-hued wings. The tips of his wings brushed the sides of the tunnel, and the red mist of his frenzy descended on him. Hurtling along the tunnel, his roar boomed over the din made by the daemons of Khorne, drowning out the crackling fire of the Empire guns.

Hundreds of handguns fired, their lead shots smashing into the first wave of bloodletters. Still they came, roaring and bellowing in fury, and they charged straight through the second, third and fourth volley. More bloodletters were rising from the gore even as others were torn apart and sent back to the Realm of Chaos by the withering hail of fire from the Oster-markers. At the front of the daemons was Hroth, and he launched himself at the enemy. Most of the shots ricocheted off his armour and red skin, but several of them embedded themselves in his flesh and tore through his membranous wings. He cared not.

One of the helblaster volley guns was ignited in his direction, but Hroth barely noticed, for the fury was fully upon him. To the horror of its crew, the mechanical contraption misfired, and Hroth knew that Khorne's favour was upon him still. He descended on the Empire soldiers, and the bloodshed began in earnest.

Twelve men were thrown to the ground as Hroth landed, swinging his axe and the Slayer of Kings around him in a murderous arc. Bodies were thrown against the walls, blood splattering in every direction as he killed. His lips were drawn back from his teeth, and his breathing came heavily as the thrill of the slaughter fuelled him. He felt the daemon U'zhul, within the powerful sword, hunger for more death and destruction, and he relinquished his full control over the creature, releasing the power of the daemon within the blade.

If his fury had been great before, his hatred, strength and speed were redoubled as the daemon was released. It fought against Hroth, seeking to gain mastery over him, but he was too strong for it, and subjected it to his will. He laid around him, killing three men with every pounding heartbeat.

Men screamed in horror and pain as the unstoppable daemon slew and killed, and then the bloodletters hit them. Massive hellblades ripped through the Ostermarkers, cutting and rending, and limbs and heads flew through the air. They roared in fury, and the men screamed in agony.

'Back!' shouted Stefan. 'Back within the citadel!' He stabbed his Runefang into the throat of a bloodletter and it fell to the ground. As soon as it hit the floor, it turned to liquid, the blood that had formed it splashing out over the cobbles. He hacked and cut at the frenzied daemons that were tearing their way through his warriors. He cut his way out of the tunnel and into the citadel, pulling several of his men with him.

'Get out!' he shouted to them. 'Drop the portcullis!' Instantly it was released, the iron gate dropping from the ceiling to hold the daemons at bay. Dozens of his men were still on the other side, and he cursed himself for a fool for not pulling them back earlier. The portcullis thundered towards the ground. It would give the last of his men the time to vacate the killing ground, and ready themselves, with the last of the defenders, to face the final push of the Chaos forces. The portcullis slammed down, its heavy iron spikes driving straight through the first bloodletters, and slamming them to the ground, cutting them in two. They burst into blood, their solid forms disappearing.

The massive daemon prince slammed its full weight against the latticed ironwork, bending it out of shape, but it held. The daemon, eyes and horns blazing with fire, roared again and threw itself at the portcullis once more, wrenching it further. The bloodletters ripped through those unfortunates stuck on the same side as the daemons.

The massive winged daemon bent its knees, and gripped the portcullis in its massive fists. Its muscles strained to lift it, and it roared as the metal screeched beneath the force.

'Out!' shouted Stefan, and he ran towards the sunlight. 'Ready your guns!' He hollered up at the dozens of men on the galleries above him. The grapeshot filled cannon above would shred these daemons when they broke through. The killing ground here was long, and he knew that the daemons would fall to the guns before they managed to fight their way into the open ground of Talabheim. The galleries and windows that the guns and men would fire from were safe from retaliation – the only access to their positions was from the walls of Talabheim – a foe would have to take the walls before they could attack the higher levels of the fortress.

The captain and his men streamed from the inner citadel, blinking against the brightness of the daylight. The reiksmarshal had rallied the last of the defenders on the fields there. Stefan prayed that the guns in the killing ground would take a heavy toll on the foe. They were going to need that, for the numbers of men he had left to fight were pitifully few.

'Ready my war-mount!' shouted Stefan.

'THE END IS here,' said Markus, watching as the last of the Empire men below, the captain included, abandoned the inner fortress, the last defence of Talabheim. The engineer had organised to have the *Wrath of Sigmar*, his beloved helblaster volley gun, moved into this position above the last killing ground, alongside the grapeshot-filled cannon. He was determined that, with the last breath of his life, he would use the beautifully crafted machine to rip the Chaos filth to shreds. The guns were all set. As soon as the portcullis below was lifted and the enemy entered the final stretch of tunnel below, all hell would be unleashed.

One of the crewmen of the *Wrath of Sigmar* swore suddenly. 'What is it?' asked Markus sharply.

The crewman held up his thumb. 'Caught it in the gears, sir. Hurts like hell.'

'If that is the only thing you are worried about, then you are a braver man than me, or just plain stupid,' replied Markus in a scathing voice. 'I'd be inclined to lean towards the latter. How is Hans?'

'He's bled almost dry, but he is alive, for now,' replied the man, motioning towards the unconscious man

slumped against the wall. Blood pooled out below
him, seeping through the cloth bindings that had
hastily been bandaged around him. A misfired
handgun shot had ricocheted off the wall and struck
him in the stomach. Markus would be surprised if the
man survived. It was a shame, for Hans was one of the
more efficient of the cannon crew, but then it probably
mattered little, for the siege was rapidly nearing its end,
and the engineer was pessimistic about the outcome.

Markus believed that the enemy *would* make it across
the killing ground below. There were just too few of
them to halt the tide completely, but he knew that it
would be no easy task for them, and that they could
lose hundreds of warriors in the process, perhaps a
thousand. There was enough powder and shot to last
almost half an hour of firing. He hoped that was
enough time for von Kessel to organise his defences,
and that his guns could inflict enough casualties on
the enemy for him to stand any chance of survival
once they *did* break through.

The engineer held the captain in high esteem. He
was certainly not the brightest man he had ever met,
and was in no way a good speaker, but then he was a
soldier, and Markus respected his skills and instincts in
war as he respected none other than the reiksmarshal
himself. He knew that the captain was a battle hardened general, and that if there was a way for victory to
be secured, then he would fight hard to find it, but the
engineer was not hopeful.

The balcony where Markus stood with the *Wrath of
Sigmar* was some twenty feet above the cobbled killing
ground. Fifty feet of open ground, with eight
grapeshot-loaded cannon and the helblaster to guard

it. There were other defences: searing oil had been heated and was ready to pour down through the murder-holes, and there were several handgunners to pick off any survivors of the cannon's fury. The men waited tensely as the roars of unearthly fury echoed up to them. They had not sighted the enemy yet, but they knew that this vanguard force was not human.

The gears of the portcullis strained as the enemies below attempted to lift the massive iron gate. That was not going to happen, Markus thought, having surveyed the mechanisms earlier in the week – massive cogs and wheels that once locked in place would be impossible to shift without completely destroying them. Those below clearly came to the same conclusion, and the sound of a heavy weight smashing against the iron echoed through the tunnel. It sounded to Markus like a battering ram.

HROTH THREW HIMSELF against the portcullis again, and the metal began to buckle under the force. He took a step back and threw his shoulder against the iron latticework once more, wrenching it further out of shape.

HANS STIRRED IN his unconsciousness, the pounding and wrenching of metal piercing his comatose mind. Blood pooled out beneath him, and he groaned in pain and horror. His eyes opened heavily, waking to a nightmare. A daemon was rising from the blood pooled out before him, curving horns rising from its long head, its eyes blazing with fire and hatred. Hans tried to cry out, but his throat was dry and sore, and his weak croak was drowned out by the wrenching of metal from below. The bloodletter rose fully from the blood, *his* blood, and opened its fang-filled mouth, snarling at him. It rammed its hellblade into his guts, and then turned its gaze upon the other men on the balcony, whose backs were to it. It leapt forwards, roaring in bloodlust, and swung its deadly weapon into the back of the closest man.

Markus spun around as the hellish roar was joined by a scream of pain. Blood splashed over his face and across his silk shirt as the man besides him was decapitated. The bloodletter, towering over him, roared and cut down another two men in an instant before launching itself at the engineer.

Markus quailed and staggered backwards in horror. The hellblade slammed into his shoulder, shattering bone and cutting deep. He screamed and fell to the ground. Stepping close to deliver the fatal blow, the bloodletter suddenly staggered forwards, struck from behind by a handgun shot. It swung away from Markus, snarling in anger, seeking its foe. Fiery eyes narrowed as it saw the man frantically reloading his gun, and the daemon leapt towards him, cutting down everyone in its path. With a roar, the daemon leapt at the man, cleaving its massive blade straight through his ribcage, sending fountains of blood spraying into the air.

Markus felt his lifeblood seeping from his body and out onto the floor. He felt suddenly tired, and a strange sense of calm descended on him. All he wanted to do was to sleep. He closed his eyes.

Within a minute, every crewman on the balcony was dead. The frenzied bloodletter was finally brought down by a handgun shot, even as it delivered the fatal blow to this last defender. Still, the daemon had done its work – the deadly guns protecting the killing ground had been silenced before they had even fired their first shot.

WITH A ROAR, Hroth hurled himself at the portcullis a final time, and the iron buckled and gave way before him. Bellowing in triumph, he led the charge across the cobbled floor of the inner fortress. The bloodletters raced at his side, and behind them came the full force of the army of Hroth the Blooded. The final battle was at hand, and the fate of Talabheim hung in the balance.

CHAPTER THIRTY-FOUR

THE LEGION OF daemons burst out of the inner fortress, the heavy gate smashed into a million shards of tinder. Into the fields of Talabheim they raced, intent on slaughter and bloodshed. Stefan shouted, and hand-guns and crossbows fired, scything down many of the daemons, but still more raced towards the thinly spread Empire lines. The great beast beneath Stefan growled dangerously at the daemons, and he patted its muscular side comfortingly. She was a magnificent creature. Eagle-headed, with the body of a massive lioness, she was an awesomely powerful mount, easily capable of ripping apart fully armoured knights with her taloned forelegs and her leonine back legs. She could kill a man instantly with a single bite of her tooth-filled, wickedly sharp beak, and her large eyes stared angrily at the daemons as they raced towards the Empire lines. Fearless and proud, the griffon was a noble creature, and Stefan felt honoured that she had accepted him as her rider.

On the point of exhaustion, the halberdiers and swordsmen readied themselves for this final assault, fear in their hearts. The only defenders who seemed unconcerned by the enemy were the last twelve elf swordmasters, standing protectively around the mage Aurelion. Stefan could feel the tension and terror of his troops – in truth he felt it himself – and he called out to steady them, invoking the name of the warrior god Sigmar.

Hearing the captain's voice, the massive, winged daemon prince swung its heavy head towards him. In a voice filled with hatred and derision, it spoke. 'Your god is nothing, little mortal.'

The creature spoke in the maddening tongue of the daemon, yet Stefan and the last of his soldiers could somehow understand the words, as if they were spoken directly into their minds. 'Your god was a mere mortal – nothing more. The true gods of Chaos feast upon his soul, just as I will feast upon yours.'

Captain Stefan von Kessel felt the words claw at the edges of his sanity, and his stomach knotted in horror. A man to his left dropped his weapon and fell to the ground, clutching his head in his hands. Others swore, or made protective symbols to ward off evil. The resolve of the soldiers withered away, and every man on the field of battle knew that he had only moments to live. Stefan felt his faith in Sigmar falter, and doubts filled him. What if the daemon spoke the truth? Despair pulled at him, and he barely resisted the urge to flee.

A single figure stepped forwards to face the charging daemons. Gripping his heavy warhammer tightly, the figure of the warrior priest, Gunthar, stood defiant, his eyes glowing with righteous anger. The daemon prince slowed his charge, allowing his bloodletters the honour of cutting down this one, and they roared as they closed on the single figure, swinging their murderous hellblades.

'In Sigmar's name, begone, daemon filth!' roared Gunthar, hefting his warhammer high over his head. A halo of light surrounded him, bright and pure. The daemons shied away from the searing glow. With a shout, Gunthar slammed his hammer into the ground, and the light surrounding him exploded outwards, engulfing the bloodletters. They bellowed in pain and rage as their physical forms were ripped apart, the essence of Chaos that kept them in corporeal form melting away as they were sucked back to their native realm.

The light faded. The daemons were all gone, except the towering form of Hroth who was stalking murderously towards the warrior priest. His mortal army burst from the inner fortress, and began to pour out around him onto the field. Hatred billowed from the daemon prince like a dark cloud, and it leapt towards Gunthar, roaring in rage.

The warrior priest leapt at the massive daemon as it screamed towards him, hefting his hammer. The Slayer of Kings flashed down, meeting the hammer in an explosion of sparks. Swinging its heavy axe, the daemon slammed it into the warrior priest's chest, and the man was sent flying through the air, his armour and ribs crushed.

Hroth the Blooded raised both his weapons and roared his triumph to the heavens. The warbands behind him raised their weapons, and their bellows

and shouts mingled with his roar, and they charged
into the Empire lines, hacking and cutting.

THE TIME FOR strategy and planning was done. The day
would be won or lost on the courage of the warriors of
the Empire. The actions of the warrior priest in defying
the daemons had fired the resolve of the troops, and
they fought with a determined fury. At Stefan's
prompting, the griffon leapt forwards, beating her
powerful wings. She drove into the Chaos warriors,
screeching in joy as she ripped the head from the first
with a powerful downwards bite of her beak, and
closed her fore-claws on another, crushing the life
from him. Stefan hacked and stabbed with the Runefang at the warriors of Chaos that threatened to
overwhelm the Empire defenders.

He felt a sudden reckless abandon overcome him, a
release from the pressure of the siege over the last
week. The battle was almost over – win or lose, it
would not last longer than the day, and he felt a
strange euphoria. He blocked the thrust of a sword,
and sent a deadly riposte that punched through the
eye socket of the enemy warrior. The griffon plunged
her beak through the head of another man, his full-
faced helmet crushed utterly.

The Empire line buckled where the daemon prince
charged. Its axe and sword rose and fell, cutting and
killing with every sweep. Weapons clanged off its iron-
hard flesh, and its power and strength grew as its fury
deepened. Stefan kicked the griffon into the sky, her
wings beating powerfully. She rose from the battle
reluctantly, and dropped her last kill down into the
press of battle below.

From his vantage, Stefan could see the reiksmarshal charge into the fray, leading the Reiklandguard knights. They drove through the enemy, cutting them down in droves and crushing them beneath flashing hooves. Fully armoured Chaos warriors were spitted on the long lances of the exemplar knights, and others were hacked to the ground by their heavy blades.

Tearing his gaze from the ensuing battle, Stefan focused on the massive form of the frenzied daemon prince. His war mount needed little encouragement, and she folded her wings tightly over her back and screamed down towards the red-skinned creature.

Hroth hacked his axe into the head of a man, splitting it in half, the force of the blow driving it down into the man's torso. The Slayer of Kings lashed out, carving straight through a soldier's body and cleaving into the body of another. Hroth kicked another man, crushing his chest, before sweeping his axe through the air, and the man's head went flying into the fray. The daemon prince was a maelstrom of destruction, killing and rending with every movement.

The griffon hit the daemon in the back, knocking the massive creature sprawling. The griffon's claws dug deeply into the daemon's shoulders, and its beak flashed, ripping out great chunks of daemonic flesh from Hroth's neck. Stefan stabbed with his Runefang, the magical weapon driving deep into the back of the daemon, which roared in pain and fury. Hroth thrashed around and rolled over, knocking the griffon away, and the daemon prince rose, eyes of fire blazing.

With a hiss of pure hatred, Hroth hurled himself at the griffon, which sprang forwards to meet him. Hroth's axe swung out in a murderous arc. The griffon twisted its body to avoid the full brunt of the blow, the axe biting only shallowly along her flank. She latched onto the daemon with her talons, and her back legs raked down the daemon, tearing gouges of flesh from its body. Stefan stabbed towards the daemon's neck with his blade, but the powerful weapon was batted aside by the daemon's own blade.

Stefan swayed beneath a deadly swipe from the daemon, and thrust his sword into Hroth's bicep, the blade sinking deeply into the flesh. Hroth dropped his daemon sword, which screamed in anger. Balling his hand into a massive fist, the daemon prince punched the griffon in the side of the head once, twice. The creature staggered and fell, its head lolling drunkenly. Rolling free of the saddle, Stefan landed heavily, the air driving from his lungs. The daemon, grinning madly, stepped forwards and punched the griffon again, and it slumped to the ground.

Stefan pulled free one of his ornate pistols, and unloaded it into the daemon's face. The shot smashed the right cheekbone of the daemon, but Hroth cared not. His breathing was heavy, and he felt energy and power surging through his limbs. The bloodshed had been great this day. He could feel that Khorne was pleased. The frenzy was still upon him, and detecting a movement to his side, he lashed out with his axe blindly. An Empire soldier was torn in half by the blow. He didn't take his eyes off Stefan, and stepped towards him, ready to kill the impudent mortal.

'My Lord Jurgen!'

The baron had been trying to ignore the irritating voice, feigning sleep, but it was getting louder and more insistent, as was the pounding at his door. Coughing painfully, he rolled over and called out weakly, 'What is it?'

A frightened-looking manservant opened the door. There was a man behind him, who pushed past the attendant with an irritated look on his face. It was the captain of the house guard, Jurgen realised. He didn't know the man's name. 'What?' said Jurgen. 'What is so important that you wake me on my death bed?'

'I'm sorry for the interruption, my lord,' said the man. 'There are... strange occurrences in the city that I thought best to bring to your attention. Battle has reached the streets.'

'What? How is that possible so soon?' asked Jurgen, frowning. Why did they not just let him die in peace? 'What are these strange occurrences?'

'An enemy has appeared within the city itself, sir.'

'The walls have fallen then. The end is nigh.'

'No, sir the walls are intact. The Wizard's Way has been taken, but von Kessel is holding the breach as we speak.'

'So how is it that the enemy are here?' asked Jurgen in a tired voice, the tone of which showed he did not really care about the answer. He had already resolved to die, what happened until that time mattered little to him.

'They come from beneath us, lord,' said the man, his face stoic.

'Beneath us? What are you talking about?'

'They have emerged from the sewers, my lord, and Taal's square has collapsed. They are streaming out from the hole. They must have been tunnelling beneath us for years. Almost two thousand of them have emerged, at my best guess. And lord, they are not men,' the captain of the house guard said. 'They are... some kind of beastman. They look like... well, they look like rats.'

'I... see,' said Jurgen slowly. He wondered briefly if this was the result of his illness – that he was becoming delusional. 'I... I'm sure that you can deal with this, captain. Thank you for informing me of the rats. I will now retire to bed.'

'My lord, the ratmen are marching towards the Wizard's Way. If they hit von Kessel in the rear, then the battle will be as good as over. The city will be lost.'

'The city will be lost,' muttered Jurgen, as if weighing the words up in his mind. The words of von Kessel came back to him then – that the way you die can be the way you are remembered, or words to that effect. 'Von Kessel will perish if this attack happens?'

'Most certainly, baron. He is struggling to hold the enemy as it is. An assault in his rear will leave the army crushed utterly.'

The sick baron frowned, thinking. The captain stood awkwardly, uncomfortable in the presence of his lord. He coughed eventually, and the baron looked up at him. 'Yes?' said Jurgen.

'Shall I... take my leave, baron? Shall I lead the household guard against this foe? We will certainly be destroyed, but we may buy von Kessel some time.'

'You wish to do this, captain?'

'It is not a matter of wishing it or not, baron. It is my duty,' said the man.

'Your duty,' repeated the baron, his expression blank. 'Duty,' he said once more. He turned towards the captain, his eyes clear. 'Ready my armour and my horse, captain. I will lead the household guard.'

The captain's mouth dropped open. 'My lord?' he said questioningly.

'My armour. Have it brought here, and ready my steed.' In shock, the man nodded dumbly, backing out of the room.

Yes, thought Jurgen, duty. He was dying. Maybe before he did, he could do something that might have made his father proud. The thought both terrified and filled him with desperate pride.

SUDOBAAL GRINNED EVILLY as he pointed his staff at another Empire soldier. Blue flames flickered up across the twisted staff and burst out towards the man, engulfing him in searing heat. The man's clothes and skin caught fire, and he screamed horribly as he died.

'Ulkjar,' called out the sorcerer. 'Stay close to me!'

The towering blond Norscan flashed him an angry look, but nodded his head. The massive man hacked the legs out from underneath an Empire soldier and slammed his other sword down into his chest as he fell. The Norscan was covered in blood – both his and that of his enemies – he was covered in cuts, but he seemed not to care. Indeed, the cuts were healing quicker than they were being inflicted.

Sudobaal had been plagued with visions of his own death these last weeks. He knew that Ulkjar was the catalyst. In his visions, he was struck down by a black arrow. He had seen this in his dream-visions, but had seen in other premonitions, the Norscan step into the path of the arrow, saving him. If Ulkjar fell, then the sorcerer would be lost, of that he was certain. Thankfully, Ulkjar seemed nigh-on impossible to kill, so the chances of him falling were slim.

The time came sooner than Sudobaal had expected. The black arrow came streaking through the press of battle. A Chaos warrior ducked to the ground to kill a fallen foe, and the arrow sliced above him. It passed scant inches by the head of another, closing unerringly on Sudobaal. He knew that he was not quick enough to get out of the way. It was exactly as he had seen it in his visions. How many times had he seen the black arrow embed itself in his skull? A dozen times? A hundred? Yet he had only seen himself saved by Ulkjar a mere handful of times. In that moment, he believed that he was about to die, that the visions of the Norscan had not been true dream-visions, merely concoctions of his own mind to give him some sense of hope.

Ulkjar sliced his sword through the neck of an Empire man and spun around, driving his other blade into the chest of another. He spun again, a dervish of death, and a head went flying into the air. As he spun, he stepped into the path of the arrow, and it thudded into his lower back. He rocked forwards, but did not fall. Kicking a man to the ground, he deftly spun one of his swords in his hand and drove it down into the fallen man. Kneeling, he released his grip on the sword, impaled through the man, and gripped the arrow protruding from his back. He ripped it free, and tossed it to the ground.

It had all happened in the blink of an eye, and Sudobaal felt a surge of exhilaration. He was alive! His visions had been true!

'Ulkjar, your task is done,' he muttered.

SOME TWENTY FEET away, Hroth heard the whispered words of the sorcerer. He held the pitiful human that had defied him, around his neck, his feet dangling several feet of the ground. Hroth had knocked the Empire captain's painful sword away, and he held his axe ready to deliver the killing blow, but when the words of the sorcerer reached him, he turned instantly, and hurled his axe. It arced through the press of bodies, spinning end over end.

The axe slammed into Ulkjar as he rose to his feet. It buried itself in his chest, smashing through his armour and his ribcage. Leaping into the air, still carrying the Empire captain, the daemon prince beat its powerful wings, and landed by the Norscan, who had fallen to his knees, clawing at the massive axe embedded in his flesh.

The daemon gripped the axe shaft and pulled it free. White bones protruded from the wound, and blood pumped out over the ground. 'I said that I would have your head,' snarled Hroth, and he swung the axe into the Norscan's neck. His head rolled to the ground.

A blast of red flames struck Hroth in the back, knocking him forwards. The flames did him no harm, for he was still protected by the Collar of Khorne. Still, he turned around swiftly in anger to see who dared attack him with the sorcery he so despised. He saw the shimmering outline of an elf standing in the shattered gateway leading back inside the inner fortress.

Aurelion stood still. The mortal enemies, the warriors of Chaos, could barely perceive her. To them, she appeared as little more than a ghostly shape that could only be seen out of the corner of the eye, but she knew that to the daemon, she was clearly visible.

She cared not. For her kin to survive, the Empire must not be destroyed. She knew that Teclis had spoken the truth, and she was prepared to pay the ultimate price to ensure the continuation of her people.

The last of her bodyguard had been slain, and she stood alone. As she had hoped, the daemon threw down von Kessel, and launched itself into the air towards her. She had expected this reaction – the creatures of Khorne had always held a particular hatred for those who wielded magic, and the actions of the daemon prince were predictable.

She retreated inside the fortress, drawing the daemon towards her. She closed her eyes as she walked calmly inside, her spirit venturing forth to find the one she sought.

JURGEN WAS UNSTEADY in the saddle, the sickness having wasted his strength almost completely. Nevertheless, he battled against his exhaustion, and sat up straight, proud and defiant. His golden armour glittered in the sunlight, and the long feathers of his helmet swung in the wind. Beside him, the standard-bearer held aloft the banner of his family, the banner that had not been carried on the field of battle since he was forced to take the throne.

The men around him looked at him in awe. Despite his illness, his features were markedly similar to those of his famed warrior-father, and dressed in his full battle regalia, he resembled his father as a young man. The hearts of the house guard surged with pride as they cantered through the streets. People cheered from the windows of houses as they saw their baron riding to war. It was to be his first and final ride.

Trumpets sounded, and the two hundred knights galloped from the city of Talabheim, heading towards the battle.

THE NAMELESS EX-KNIGHT of the Reiklandguard screamed as he slew. He was the last of the flagellants, all those who followed him having been cut down, one by one, by the hordes of Chaos. Another axe struck him, smashing down onto his shoulder, and his arm went limp. He leapt on the warrior, tackling him to the ground, and drove his blade through the eye-slit in the Norscan's helmet. A sword smashed into his back, and the nameless man cried out in joy. The light of Sigmar flowed into him, and he rejoiced. Standing, he swung his sword into the head of another man before the blade was knocked from his hands. A heavy spiked mace smashed into his side, and he knew that his time had come. The blow knocked him into another warrior, and he punched his thumb into one of the man's eyes, pushing deep into his skull. A sword blow hacked into his neck, and he swayed, and slumped to the ground. Other swords pierced his body as he fell. He lay on the ground, dead, a rapturous smile upon his face.

'PROTECT THE CAPTAIN!' came a shout, and the halberdiers surged forwards to surround their fallen leader. They threw themselves at the foe with renewed vigour, and several men helped von Kessel to stand.

'A sword,' Stefan gasped, and a man thrust a weapon into his hands. He pushed away from the hands that held him upright, and barged his way to the front of the battle. The killing began once more.

* * *

WILHELM STALKED THROUGH the press of fighting, his eyes intent on his foe. Seeing his opportunity, he drew back his bow once more and fired. The arrow sliced through the air and struck the black-clad sorcerer in the back of the head. Dropping his bow, Wilhelm drew his sword and hunting knife, and ran through the battle. He leapt over a fallen man and slammed his knife into the throat of a warrior that had his back to him, felling him instantly. He ducked beneath a swinging sword and continued on, vaulting over another Chaos worshipper as he fell, a sword in his guts.

The sorcerer had fallen to the ground, and Wilhelm dropped on top of him. Remarkably, Sudobaal was still alive, and he gaped up at the scout with horror in his yellow, cat-like eyes. He tried to say something, but Wilhelm silenced him, stabbing his knife down into the man's throat. Black blood gargled up from the wound, and Wilhelm smiled down at the dying man. 'Your time is up, witch,' he snarled, and slammed his palm into the hilt of his dagger, driving the blade through man's neck. His eyes glazed over, and the sorcerer Sudobaal died.

THE REIKSMARSHAL SWORE as he saw the teeming horde of skaven approaching from the city. Walking like men, they were hideously deformed beastman-like creatures. Cowardly, except when gathered in large numbers, they were quick and vicious fighters that battled like cornered animals.

Hundreds of gigantic rats, the size of hounds, ran alongside the army. The creatures were disgusting, covered in festering sores and pus-ridden wounds, and the reiksmarshal knew that they carried virulent plague.

Looking over the horde of furred creatures, he could see a rough structure at the back, being hauled along on wheels by teams of slaves. A great brass bell hung from this structure, and a grey-furred skaven crouched there, leaning heavily on a staff. Even as he saw this bizarre creation, the massive bell was tolled, ringing out mournfully across the battlefield.

The sound vibrated within him, and he felt an unnamed horror wash over him. His warhorse, a steed that did not baulk in the face of any foe, trembled beneath him, and whinnied in fear.

That was the one that had to be slain, the reiksmarshal thought, that grey-furred rat creature. It was their leader, and he knew from experience that if it was slain, then the others would soon break and flee.

With a shout, he ordered the Reiklandguard to disengage from the enemy, and turned to face this new threat. Less than a hundred of his knights remained, and he prayed to Sigmar that that was enough to fight their way through the skaven ranks and reach the grey-furred creature. He knew in his heart that it was not, but he wheeled his knights around for the charge.

THE BLIND ONE, the plague-ridden grey seer leading the skaven force, extended one of its twisted claws, and a green wave of fog billowed out. It roiled and spread out from its extended paw, rolling through its own troops towards the charging knights. Dozens of skaven fell to the ground, gasping and choking as the virulent disease took hold, filling their lungs with black cancers and blood vessels in their brains bursting and rupturing. The Blind One chuckled.

* * *

A PALE, FLAWLESSLY beautiful face appeared before Markus, speaking to him in a sing-song, melodious voice. He tried to ignore it, but it was insistent, drawing him away from the darkness. With a gasp, he opened his eyes, pain flaring from the wound on his shoulder. He felt cold and weak, and his arm throbbed with near unbearable agony. He pulled himself upright, crying out, and saw the pale elf below him, staring up at him with her almond-shaped eyes.

With a roar, the daemon prince stalked into the chamber, hefting its massive, gore-covered axe. Its wings folded behind it, and it stamped towards the mage, eyes and horns blazing with fire.

'Time to die, elf bitch,' snarled Hroth.

Aurelion backed away from the towering creature, but her face showed no fear.

Markus flicked his gaze around – the helblaster, *Wrath of Sigmar*, was next to him, and the daemon prince was moving right into the middle of the killing ground below. Clenching his teeth tightly against the pain, the engineer hobbled around the machine, ensuring it was ready to fire.

STEFAN HACKED AND killed. With him at the fore, the halberdiers fought the Chaos warriors toe to toe, refusing to give any ground to the hulking enemy. The Chaos forces had seen their sorcerer slain, and their daemon prince was no longer on the field of battle, but they fought on regardless, fighting with brutal efficiency. The Empire soldiers fought with desperation, but still two of their own were cut down for every Chaos warrior they felled.

'For Sigmar!' shouted Stefan, and threw himself at the foe. A massive bald, black armoured warrior was before him, holding aloft a standard covered in grisly trophies. Stefan swung his sword at the man again and again. Finally, he got through the man's defences, and drove his blade into his face. He fell to the ground, and the standard fell.

THE CHARGE OF the Reiklandguard faltered, as fully half their number collapsed from their steeds as the sorcerous green fog rolled over them. Many of the horses stumbled and fell as their limbs became suddenly arthritic and filled with disease, and their lungs were filled with filth. The reiksmarshal closed his eyes and mouth against the foulness, but was thrown from the saddle as his horse expired beneath him. He rolled to his feet as the skaven warriors descended towards him in an unstoppable horde. He hefted his sword, and roared a battle cry as the enemies swamped him.

JURGEN LED THE charge, riding down the skaven between his household guard and the grey-furred creature on the back of the rolling bell-tower. They shrieked in fear and anger as they were cut down, scattering before the charge. The ground pounded with the hooves of the warhorses, and Jurgen felt more alive than he had in years. He felt joyous, even though he rode to his death. The grey-furred creature turned, blind eyes wide in panic as the knights closed on him.

Green lightning arced from the skaven's hand, killing a dozen of the knights, but they rode on. Jurgen slammed his sabre down onto the top of another skaven's head, splitting it down to the teeth, and urged his horse on. The bell-tower was only a dozen paces away, and that was when the bell tolled once more. This close, the sound resonated deep within Jurgen's body, and he could feel his organs vibrating within him. His warhorse baulked at the ungodly sound, and a skaven thrust a spear into the chest of the beast. Jurgen slashed down with his sabre, killing the creature, but his horse had been fatally wounded. Still, it kept moving forwards, and it slammed into the bell-tower structure with its full, armoured weight before falling to the ground, dead.

Jurgen fell heavily. He looked up to see the grey-furred creature topple off the structure, and drop awkwardly beside him.

In an instant, Jurgen was atop the scrawny creature, gagging at the stench of the foul thing. He had dropped his sword, and so the baron clasped his hands around the thin throat of the grey-furred rat, squeezing the life from it. The skaven panicked as the other knights slammed into their ranks, cutting and hacking at them. The bell-tower itself teetered for a moment before it fell to the ground, the bell echoing dully as it slammed into the earth, crushing several skaven beneath it.

The grey seer struggled frantically, its white, blind eyes widening as its life was choked from it. Two spears slammed into Jurgen's chest, but he held grimly on, throttling the skaven. It went limp in his hands as it died. Another spear was driven into Jurgen's body, and he slumped down over the dead grey seer. He would be remembered in Talabheim for all time, a hero.

* * *

HROTH GRINNED IN savage pleasure as he slew Aurelion, her body crumpling as the axe smashed into her. Her spotless robes of white and blue were splashed with blood, and she fell to the floor, broken. Hroth roared his pleasure, the sound echoing through the fortress and out onto the field of battle.

THE HELBLASTER UNLEASHED its fury, all nine of its barrels slamming into the daemon prince. Hroth's roar of triumph was drowned out by the booming of the *Wrath of Sigmar*, and the daemon was ripped apart by the power of the machine. Desperately, the daemon prince tried to cling to life, but its body was shattered as nine cannonballs smashed through it.

A hideous wail of pure anger screamed out as the sound of the fusillade of death faded, and the immortal essence of Hroth the Blooded, Daemon Prince of Khorne, was sent back to the Realm of Chaos. The Chaos army faltered, feeling the pain of the passing of the daemon deep inside the core of their being.

Knowing that something momentous had happened, Stefan led his troops in a desperate final push, cutting down the bewildered Chaos warriors before him. All across the battlefield, the Empire soldiers launched their counter-attack, driving the forces of Chaos back, and killing them in droves as they reeled around blindly, stunned by the death of their warlord and figurehead.

The battle of Talabheim was over.

EPILOGUE

THE FORCES OF Chaos were devastated by the loss of the daemon prince, Hroth the Blooded, his death a shock-wave that rendered them almost incapable of battle. Many of the independent tribes escaped into the forests around Talabheim, fleeing the way they came, through the Wizard's Way, but many others were brutally cut down and slaughtered by the forces of the Empire, under the command of Captain von Kessel.

The skaven forces, leaderless, scattered in all directions. Many stampeded towards the walls of Talabheim, overcoming the defences, and fleeing over the sides. Others raced back into Talabheim, killing everything in their path in their rush, and fled back into the tunnels below.

The Emperor himself honoured the engineer, Markus, and he remained in Talabheim for many years to come, overseeing the collapse of the tunnels beneath the city.

The warrior priest, Gunthar, survived his injuries and spent many years travelling the Empire, rooting out the evil of Chaos wherever he found it. He led the attacks that drove out the surviving Chaos warbands from around Talabheim, uncovered cultists in the court of the Emperor himself, and spent the last years of his long life living in an isolated temple of Sigmar in the hills of Ostermark.

The body of the elf mage, Aurelion, was transported by Stefan von Kessel back to the isle of Ulthuan, with great honour, pledges of gratitude and sorrow. A statue of her, carved from a perfect block of flawless marble, was erected in the newly formed Colleges of Magic in Altdorf.

A decade later, the scout Wilhelm killed an innocent man in cold blood, and fled into the forests, pursued by the authorities. He lived out the last of his days as a cold-hearted outlaw, preying on all who crossed his path.

The creature that was Sudobaal emerged under the cover of darkness from the shattered body of its host, and burrowed into a new body, a body that was stronger and more powerful. It stole across the corpse-littered field and recovered the daemon sword, the Slayer of Kings, careful not to touch the weapon with its bare hands. It slunk out of Talabheim, and began its long journey into the far distant north, there to seek out Hroth the Blooded, the eternal master that it was ever bound to.

The body of Reiksmarshal Wolfgange Trenkenhoff was found surrounded by the corpses of over twenty skaven. He had died fighting for the Empire, his last breath gone to secure its future, and his death was honoured with a festival across the whole of the Empire.

Stefan von Kessel became the Elector Count of Ostermark, and faced the enemies of the Empire many times in his life. He became known as a fair and honourable leader, and he always led his army from the front. He fathered just one heir, and his bloodline runs strong in the noble house of Ostermark.

ABOUT THE AUTHOR

Anthony Reynolds hails from Australia, but has
been working for Games Workshop in the UK for
over five years. Much of that time has been within
Games Development, though he currently works as
part of the Design Studio Management Team.
Mark of Chaos is his first novel.

WARHAMMER

ORCSLAYER

BY NATHAN LONG

A GOTREK & FELIX NOVEL

Check out the latest adventures of Gotrek & Felix in

ORCSLAYER

By Nathan Long

'ORCS?' GOTREK SHRUGGED. 'I've fought enough orcs.'

Felix peered at the Slayer in the gloom of the merchant ship's cramped forward cabin. The thick-muscled dwarf sat on a bench, his flame-bearded chin sunk to his chest, an immense stein of ale in one massive fist, and a broached half-keg at his side. The only illumination came from a small porthole – a rippling, sea-sick-green reflection from the waves outside.

'But they've blockaded Barak Varr,' said Felix. 'We won't be able to dock. You want to get to Barak Varr, don't you? You want to walk on dry land again?' Felix wanted to dock, that was for certain. Two months in this seagoing coffin where even the dwarf had to duck his head below decks had driven him stir-crazy.

'I don't know what I want,' rumbled Gotrek, 'except another drink.'

He took another drink.

Felix scowled. 'Fair enough. If I live, I will write in the grand epic poem of your death that you drowned heroically below decks, drunk as a halfling on harvest day, while your comrades fought and died above you.'

Gotrek slowly raised his head and fixed Felix with his single glittering eye. After a long moment where Felix thought the Slayer might leap across the cabin and rip his throat out with his bare hands, Gotrek grunted. 'You've a way with words, manling.'

He put down his stein and picked up his axe.

BARAK VARR WAS a dwarf port built inside a towering cliff at the easternmost end of the Black Gulf, a curving talon of water that cut deeply into the lawless badlands south of the Black Mountains and the Empire. Both the harbour and the city were tucked into a cave so high that the tallest warship could sail under its roof and dock at its teeming wharves. The entrance was flanked by fifty-foot statues of dwarf warriors standing in massive stone ship prows. A squat, sturdy lighthouse sat at the end of a stone spit to their right, the flame of which, it was said, could be seen for twenty leagues.

Felix could see almost none of this architectural wonder, however, for a boat-borne horde of orcs floated between him and Barak Varr's wide, shadowed entrance, and a thicket of patched sails, masts, crude banners and strung-up corpses blocked his view. The line looked impenetrable, a floating barricade of captured and lashed-together warships, merchantmen, rafts, barges and galleys that stretched for nearly a mile in a curving arc before the port. Smoke from cooking fires rose from many of the decks, and the water around them bobbed with bloated corpses and floating garbage.

'You see?' said Captain Doucette, an extravagantly moustachioed Bretonnian trader from whom Gotrek and Felix had caught a ride in Tilea. 'Look like they build from every prize and warship that try to pass; and I must land. I have to sell a hold full of Ind spices here, and pick up dwarf steel for Bretonnia. If no, the trip will make a loss.'

'Is there someplace you can break through?' asked Felix, his long blond hair and his red Sudenland cloak whipping about in the blustery summer wind. 'Will the ship take it?'

'Oh, oui,' said Doucette. 'She is strong, the *Reine Celeste*. We fight off many pirates, smash little boats in our way. Trading is not easy life, no? But… orcs?'

'Don't worry about the orcs,' said Gotrek.

Doucette turned and looked Gotrek from bristling crimson crest, to leather eye-patch, to sturdy boots and back again. 'Forgive me, my friend. I do not doubt you are very formidable. The arms like trunks of the trees, yes? The chest like the bull, but you are only one man – er, dwarf.'

'One *Slayer*,' growled Gotrek. 'Now fill your sails and get on. I've a keg to finish.'

Doucette cast a pleading look at Felix.

Felix shrugged. 'I've followed him through worse.'

'Captain!' a lookout called from the crow's-nest. 'More ships behind us!'

Doucette, Gotrek and Felix turned and looked over the stern rail. Two small cutters and a Tilean warship were angling out of a small cove and racing towards them, sails fat with wind. All the fancy woodwork had

been stripped from them, replaced with rams, catapults and trebuchets. The head of the beautiful,
bare-breasted figurehead on the warship's prow had
been replaced with a troll's skull, and rotting corpses
dangled by their necks from its bowsprit. Orcs stood
along the rail, bellowing guttural war cries. Goblins
capered and screeched all around them.

Doucette hissed through his teeth. 'They make the
trap, no? Pinch like the crayfish. Now we have no
choice.' He turned and scanned the floating barrier,
and then pointed, shouting to his pilot. 'Two points
starboard, Luque. At the rafts! Feruzzi! Clap on all
sail!'

Felix followed Doucette's gaze as the steersman turned
the wheel and the mate sent the waisters up the shrouds
to unfurl more canvas. Four ramshackle rafts, piled with
looted barrels and crates, were lashed loosely together
between a battered Empire man-o'-war and a half-
charred Estalian galley. Both of the ships were alive with
orcs and goblins, hooting and waving their weapons at
Doucette's trader.

The merchantman's sails cracked like pistols as they
filled with wind, and it picked up speed.

'Battle stations!' called Doucette. 'Prepare to receive
boarders! 'Ware the grapnels!'

Greenskins large and small were pouring over the
sides of the man-o'-war and the galley, and running
across the rafts towards the point where the merchantman meant to break through. True to the captain's
warning, half of them swung hooks and grapnels
above their heads.

Felix looked back. The cutters and the warship were
gaining. If the merchantman made it through the

blockade it might outrun the pursuers, but if it were caught...

'By the Lady, no!' gasped Doucette suddenly.

Felix turned. All along the raft-bound man-o'-war, black cannon muzzles were pushing out of square-cut ports.

'We will be blown to pieces,' said Doucette.

'But... but they're orcs,' said Felix. 'Orcs can't aim to save their lives.'

Doucette shrugged. 'At such a range, do they need to aim?'

Felix looked around, desperate. 'Well, can you blow them up? Shoot them before they shoot us?'

'You joke, mon ami,' laughed Doucette. He pointed to the few catapults that were the merchantman's only artillery. 'These will do little against Empire oak.'

They were rapidly approaching the blockade. It was too late to attempt to turn aside. Felix could smell the greenskins, a filthy animal smell, mixed with the stink of garbage, offal and death. He could see the earrings glinting in their tattered ears and make out the crude insignia painted on their shields and ragged armour.

'Throw me at it,' said Gotrek.

Felix and Doucette looked at him. The dwarf had a mad gleam in his eye.

'What?' asked Doucette. 'Throw you?'

'Put me in one of your rock lobbers and cut the cord. I'll deal with these floating filth.'

'You... you want me to catapult you?' asked Doucette, incredulous. 'Like the bomb?'

'The grobi do it. Anything a goblin can do, a dwarf can do, better.'

'But, Gotrek, you might...' said Felix.

Gotrek raised an eyebrow. 'What?'

'Er, nothing, never mind.' Felix had been about to say that Gotrek might get himself killed, but that was, after all, the point, wasn't it?

Gotrek crossed to one of the catapults and climbed onto the bucket. He looked like a particularly ugly bulldog sitting on a serving ladle. 'Just make sure you put me over the rail, not into the side.'

'We will try, master dwarf,' said the chief of the catapult's crew. 'Er, you will not kill us if you die?'

'I'll kill you if you don't start shooting!' growled Gotrek. 'Fire!'

'Oui, oui.'

The crew angled the gun around, huffing at Gotrek's extra weight, until it faced the man-o'-war, and then cranked the firing arm a little tighter.

'Hold onto your axe, master dwarf,' said the crew chief.

'Perhaps a helmet,' said Felix. 'Or a... '

The crew chief dropped his hand. 'Fire!'

A crewman pulled a lever and the catapult's arm shot up and out. Gotrek flew through the air in a long high arc, straight for the man-o'-war, bellowing a bull-throated battle cry.

Felix stared blankly as Gotrek flattened against the patched canvas of the man-o'-war's mainsail and slid down to the deck into a seething swarm of orcs. 'The real question,' he said to no one in particular, 'is how I'm going to make it all rhyme.'

He and the catapult's crew craned their necks, trying to find Gotrek in the chaos, but all they could see was a swirl of hulking green bodies and the rise and fall of enormous black-iron cleavers. At least they're not stopping, Felix thought. If they were still fighting, then Gotrek was still alive.

Then the orcs stopped fighting, and instead began running to and fro.

'Is he...?' asked Doucette.

'I don't know,' said Felix, biting his lip. After all the dragons, daemons and trolls Gotrek had fought, would he really die facing mere orcs?

The lookout's voice boomed down from above. 'Impact coming!'

With a jarring crunch, the merchantman crashed into the line of rafts, smashing timber, snapping cord, and sending barrels and crates and over-enthusiastic orcs flying into the cold, choppy water. The side of the man-o'-war rose like a castle wall directly to their right, her cannon ports level with Doucette's deck.

Grapnels whistled through the air to the left and right, and Felix ducked just in time to miss getting hooked through the shoulder. They bit into the rail and the deck and the sails, their ropes thrumming tight as the ship continued forwards. The *Reine Celeste*'s crew chopped at them with hatchets and cutlasses, but two more caught for each one they cut.

A thunderous boom went off in Felix's right ear, and one of the man-o'-war's cannon, not fifteen feet away, was obscured in white smoke. A cannonball whooshed by at head level and parted a ratline.

Felix swallowed. It looked like Gotrek had failed.

'Boarders!' came Doucette's voice.

The merchant ship had broken through the orc line and was inside the blockade, but was slowing sharply, towing the grapnel-hooked rafts and the rest of the ships with it. The man-o'-war was turning as it was pulled, and its guns remained trained on Doucette's ship as waves of roaring green monsters climbed up the lines and the sides and clambered over the rail. Felix drew his dragon-hilted sword and joined the others as they raced to hold them off – men of every colour and land stabbing, hacking and shooting at the age-old enemy of humanity – Tileans in stocking caps and baggy trousers, Bretonnians in striped pantaloons, men of Araby, Ind and further places, all fighting with the crazed desperation of fear.

There was no retreat, and surrender meant an orc stew-pot. Felix sidestepped a cleaver-blow that would have halved him had it connected, and ran his towering opponent through the neck. Two goblins attacked his flanks. He killed one and kicked the other back. Another orc surged up in front of him.

Felix was no longer the willowy young poet he had been when, during a night of drunken camaraderie, he had pledged to record Gotrek's doom in an epic poem. Decades of fighting at the Slayer's side had hardened him and filled him out, and made a seasoned swordsman of him. Even so, he was no match – physically at least – for the seven-foot monster he faced. The beast was more than twice his weight, with arms thicker than Felix's legs, and an underslung jaw from which jutted up cracked tusks. It stank like the back end of a pig.

Its mad red eyes blazed with fury as it roared and swung a black iron cleaver. Felix ducked and slashed back, but the orc was quick, and knocked his sword aside. There was another boom and a cannonball punched through the rail ten feet to Felix's left, cutting a swath through the melee that killed both merchants and orcs alike. Red blood and black mixed on the slippery deck. Felix deflected a swipe from the orc that shivered his arm to the shoulder. The catapult's crew chief fell back in two pieces beside him.

Another series of booms rocked the ship, and Felix thought the orcs had somehow got off a disciplined salvo. He glanced past his orc to the man-o'-war. Smoke poured from the cannon ports but, strangely, no cannonballs. The orc slashed at him. Felix hopped back and tripped over the crew chief's torso. He landed flat on his back in a puddle of blood.

The orc guffawed and raised his cleaver over his head.

With a massive *ka-rump* the man-o'-war exploded into a billowing ball of flame, bits of timber and rope and orc parts spinning past. The fighters on the deck of the merchantman were blown off their feet by a hammer of air. Felix felt as if his eardrums had been stabbed with spikes. The orc above him staggered and looked down at his chest, surprised. A cannon's cleaning rod was sticking out from between his ribs, the bristly head dripping with gore. It toppled forwards.

Felix rolled out of the way and sprang to his feet, looking towards the flame-enveloped man-o'-war. So Gotrek had done it after all. But at what cost? Surely there was no way the dwarf could have survived?

Out of the boiling fireball toppled the man-o'-war's mainmast, crashing towards the merchantman's deck like a felled tree – and racing out across it, half climbing, half running, was a broad, compact figure, face and skin as black as iron, red crest and beard smouldering and singed. The top of the mast smashed down through the merchantman's rail and pulverised a knot of goblins that was just climbing over. With a wild roar, Gotrek leapt from this makeshift bridge into the merchantman's waist, right in the middle of the crowd of orcs that was pushing Doucette's crew back towards the sterncastle with heavy losses.

The Slayer spun as he landed, axe outstretched, and a dozen orcs and goblins went down at once, spines and legs and necks severed. Their companions turned to face him, and seven more went down. Heartened, the merchant crew pressed forwards, attacking the confused orcs. Unfortunately, more were running across the rafts, and the merchantman was still caught in a net of grapnels, and pinned in place by the fallen mast.

Felix leapt the forecastle rail, yelling to Doucette as he plunged into the circle of orcs and goblins towards Gotrek. 'Cut the lines and clear the mast! Forget the orcs!'

Doucette hesitated, then nodded. He screamed at his crew in four languages and they fell back, chopping at the remaining ropes and heaving together to push the man-o'-war's mast off their starboard rail, while the greenskins pressed in to take down the crazed Slayer.

Felix took up his accustomed position, behind, and slightly to the left of Gotrek, just far enough away to be clear of the sweep of his axe, but close enough to protect his back and flanks.

The orcs were frightened, and showed it by trying desperately to kill the object of their fear. But the harder they tried, the faster they died, getting in each other's way in their eagerness, forgetting Felix until he had run them through the kidneys, fighting each other for the chance to kill Gotrek. The deck under the dwarf's feet was slick with black blood, and orc and goblin bodies were piled higher than his chest.

Gotrek caught Felix's eye as he bifurcated an orc, top-knot to groin. 'Not a bad little scrap, eh, manling?'

'Thought you'd died at last,' said Felix, ducking a cutlass.

Gotrek snorted as he gutted another orc. 'Not likely. Stupid orcs had all the powder up on the gun deck. I cut some ugly greenskin's head off and stuck it in a cook fire until it caught.' He barked a sharp laugh as he decapitated two goblins. 'Then bowled it down the gun-line like I was playing ninepins. That did it!'

With a screeching and snapping of rending timbers, the merchantman's crew finally pushed the man-o'-war's mainmast clear of the rail. Grapnel lines parted with twangs like a loosed bow's as the *Reine Celeste* surged forwards, straightening out before the wind.

The crew cheered and turned to fight the last few orcs. It was over in seconds. Felix and the others wiped their blades and looked back just in time to see the three orc pursuit ships smash together as they all tried to shoot the gap through the blockade at once. Roars of fury rose from them, and the three crews began to hack at each other while their boats became inextricably fouled in the mess of rafts, ropes and floating debris.

Next to the three-ship squabble, the remains of the burning man-o'-war sank slowly into the gulf under a towering plume of black smoke. Orcs from further along the line were hastily cutting it free so it didn't pull anything else down with it.

Captain Doucette stepped up to Gotrek and bowed low before him. He had a deep gash on his forearm.

'Master dwarf, we owe you our lives. You have saved us and our cargo from certain destruction.'

Gotrek shrugged. 'Only orcs.'

'None-the-less, we are extremely grateful. If there is anything we may do to repay you, you have only to name it.'

'Hrmm,' said Gotrek, stroking his still smouldering beard. 'You can get me another keg of beer. I've nearly finished the one I left below.'

The story continues in

ORCSLAYER

by Nathan Long

Available from The Black Library
www.blacklibrary.com

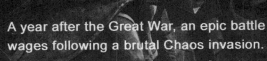

A year after the Great War, an epic battle
wages following a brutal Chaos invasion.

WARHAMMER®
MARK OF CHAOS™

The hammer drops   Fall 2006

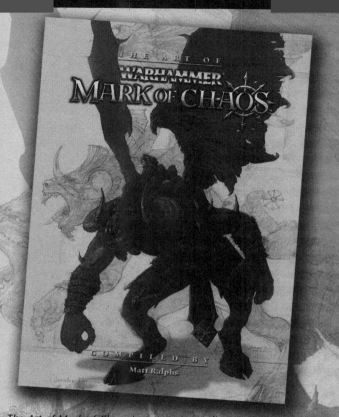

ちきゅうこうしんき

たか

MARCH ON EARTH

Volume 1

By Mikase Hayashi

CONTENTS

3   Chapter 1

43   Chapter 2

93   Chapter 3

143   The Sound You
          Make is the
        Color of Autumn

183   Afterword

WHEN WE LOST OUR PARENTS FIVE YEARS AGO...

...MY SISTER RAISED ME.

THEN SHE ALSO WENT ON TO THE NEXT WORLD AFTER A TRAFFIC ACCIDENT LAST MONTH.

Yeah.

Let's keep trying together!

YUZU, 4TH GRADE

OLDER SISTER TSUBAKI, 11TH GRADE

MARCH ON **EARTH**

YUZU TAKAMIYA-SAMA

SHE PROTECTED ME.

AND THESE TINY HANDS...

SQUEEZE

YUZU-CHAN.

THAT'S WHY I DECIDED ...

...THAT I WOULD PROTECT THESE HANDS.

地球★行進曲

CHAPTER 1

MARCH ON EARTH

TO THE VERY END, MY SISTER SAID NOTHING ABOUT HIM.

SHOU DOESN'T HAVE A FATHER.

I CAN'T WAIT TO HAVE SOME!

SEITA SAID HE'D MAKE US CURRY!

CAN'T WAIT!

"I'M HAPPY JUST GIVING BIRTH TO THE CHILD OF SOMEONE I LOVE."

RIGHT, SHOU?

IS THAT HOW IT IS...?

I still don't get it.

SEITA INVITED US OVER FOR DINNER TONIGHT.

"ME CURRY"?

WELCOME HOME, KEITA-KUN.

Ah!

BACK FROM CRAM SCHOOL?

PARDON OUR IN-TRUSION!

IN-TWUSION!

Come on in.

We love curry, right?

PLEASE

CLICK

THAT'S THE ONLY THING MY BROTHER CAN MAKE.

YAP!☆

HOW'D YOU KNOW?

Herro Kei-chan!

I'M HOME!

...ERK.

I had swimming lessons today.

I'M HOME.

← SIXTH GRADE

Gimme a break. Stupid brother.

Wah, Sei-tan's amazing!

WELCOME! ☆ AND I'M JUST FINISHING MY "SPECIAL CURRY."

...ER, WHY ARE YOU HALF-NAK--

NOOO OOO!

BUBBLE

BUBBLE

BUBBLE

Mmph!

YOU'RE THE WHA IDIOT --?

YUZU'LL FIGURE OUT MY OPERATION: LOVE UNDER ONE ROOF!!!

YOU IDIOT !!!

WHAT ?!?!

I'LL MAKE HER HEART POUND BY CASUALLY WEARING ONLY AN APRON.

WHISPER

YOU JUST LIVE IN THE SAME COMPLEX

"THAT SIDE OF HER THAT ONLY I KNOW!" THAT'S WHAT!!!

DO YOU UNDERSTAND, KEITA, WHAT'S SO EXCITING ABOUT "LOVE UNDER ONE ROOF"?

WHISPER

NOT LISTENING

UM, HEY.

SEITA.

WHISPER

REALLY NOT LISTENING.

WHISPER

8

SHOU CAN PLAY ROCK-PAPER-SCISSORS NOW!

Anyway, LISTEN, LISTEN OBA-CHAN!*

PLAY WITH OBA-CHAN*!

SHAKE!

ROOOCK, PAPERRR...

GOODNESS!

AH.

SCISSORS!

NO HEART POUNDING?!

?!

RIDICULOUS

ESPECIALLY WITH SOMETHING LIKE CURRY.

IF YOU COOK IN THAT RIDICULOUS GETUP, YOU COULD BURN YOURSELF, YOU KNOW.

SHOONK!

Welcome, Shoo-chan!

I here, Oba-chan!

...NICE DIG.

THAT'S OUR YUZU.

I DID IT!

Nm?

Why?!

WIGGLE

WIGGLE

WIGGLE

He's adorable even when he's stupid.

EEHH?!

BUT HE LOST??

YOU'RE...

SHOU-CHAN... YOU'RE...

AND I GUESS HE THINKS THAT'S PART OF ROCK-PAPER-SCISSORS...

APPARENTLY HE LEARNED IT IN DAYCARE... HE SAW ANOTHER KID GET HAPPY WHEN HE WON,

*OBA-CHAN: A FRIENDLY WAY OF ADDRESSING AN OLDER WOMAN. IN THIS CASE, MS. KUSANO.

TWO YEARS AGO, THE INSTANT SHOU WAS BORN, WE WERE KICKED OUT OF OUR OLD APARTMENT.

THEY GRUMBLED SOMETHING ABOUT NO KIDS ALLOWED.

HOW CAN YOU PROTECT THE PEACE OF JAPAN WHEN YOU CAN'T PROTECT THE HAPPINESS OF A MOTHER AND HER CHILDREN?!

I'M GONNA CHANGE THESE ROTTEN COMPANIES!!!

Just you wait, Sis!!! Shou!!!

Oho you're so manly

YUZU, 8TH GRADE

THE REALTORS DIDN'T LOOK TOO HAPPY ABOUT AN UNWED MOTHER WITH NO REGULAR JOB (MY SISTER) AND A MINOR WITH HER (ME).

MY SISTER

SELF-EMPLOYED

I'm a novice children's story author! I also work part-time!

AND THUS BEGAN MY RESOLUTION TO BECOME A LAWYER.

UNDER THOSE CIRCUM-STANCES ...

...YOU CAN ALL COME TO MY PLACE.

IF YOU DON'T MIND A 20-YEAR-OLD BUILDING...

MS. KUSANO WAS THE ONLY ONE WHO SMILED AND ACCEPTED US.

OH?

YUZU-CHAN?

I WAS SO HAPPY.

WELL, EVEN YUZU-CHAN GETS TIRED. SHE HAS SCHOOL AND HOUSEWORK, AND A CHILD TO RAISE.

YOU CAN STAY HERE TONIGHT.

Shou, you wanna play with this bus?

I yove honk honk.

Yuzu-chan, bedtime?

OH, THERE'S NOT A CHANCE. YOU DON'T HAVE THE GUTS.

WHAT?!!! WHAT'S WITH THAT LOOK, LIKE YOU KNOW EVERYTHING?!!!

Ha ha ha

Ha Heh heh heh

WHAT'LL I DO IF I TAKE ADVANTAGE OF YUZU WHEN SHE'S SO DEFENSELESS...?

REST WELL. YOU'VE EARNED IT.

...I KNEW IT WOULD BE BAD...

I'M HANDING OUT THE ANSWERS TO THE PROFICIENCY TEST.

GYAAA GYAAA

HEY, WE'RE ALL GOING TO KARAOKE AFTER SCHOOL. WANNA COME?

OH, YUZU!

IT'LL HELP YOU FEEL BETTER.

Oh.

WHAT ARE YOU GOING TO DO ABOUT THE CLASS TRIP NEXT MONTH?

UM, HEY.

IS IT ALL RIGHT IF I STAY HOME?

I DON'T THINK I'M READY TO RIDE IN A CAR YET.

I SEE ...

Natchin

BUT THANKS. I'M SORRY. I CAN'T GO.

SURE THING!

LATER!

OH. WELL, GOOD LUCK RAISING A KID.

...I'M VAGUELY JEALOUS...

...OF THEIR CAREFREE LIVES.

SOME-TIMES...

EVEN THOUGH...

...I CHOSE THIS PATH MYSELF.

WHOOOSH

BUT...

SWERVE

WHAM!

THE NIGHT OF THE ACCIDENT, WE HAD DECIDED TO GO OUT TO EAT FOR THE FIRST TIME IN A WHILE...

MY SISTER HAD JUST MET HER DEADLINE AND WAS VERY PLEASED AT WHAT A GOOD STORY SHE'D WRITTEN.

Still a secret!

What's it about?

YUZU...

ARE YOU OKAY...?

HANG IN THERE...

PLEASE...

HANG IN THERE...

YUZU...

AS MY CONSCIOUSNESS FADED FROM THE PAIN, I HEARD MY SISTER'S VOICE FOR THE LAST TIME.

...I SAW A CEILING I DIDN'T RECOGNIZE...

WHEN I OPENED MY EYES...

YUZU TAKAMIYA SAMA

EVEN WITH MY HEAD FUZZY FROM ANAES- THESIA, I COULD TELL...

...AND MS. KUSANO HOLD- ING SHOU.

I COULD TELL THAT MY SISTER DIDN'T MAKE IT.

...SHE PASSED ON, ALL BY HERSELF.

LEAVING US...

...AND SHOU AND ME.

...PRO-TECTED THE BOY WHO JUMPED OUT...

MY SISTER...

oh, you...

HIT HEAD! BUMPED HEAD!

I know I know.

COME ON, SHOU!

LET'S DO IT!

Owie!

Owie!

WAAAAAH!

FLAIL FLAIL

FLAIL

KOOOONK!

... FALL ... SIGH.

IF YOU RUN IN THE BATH, YOU'LL...

AH! SHOU, HEY!

WHAM!

OH, SLEEP TALK...

SLLLLLIDE

YUZU-CHAN.

JUMP!

HOW LONG WILL THE MONEY MOM AND DAD LEFT US LAST?

YUZU-CHAN.

WHAT IF THE AFTER EFFECT LASTS SO LONG I CAN NEVER RIDE IN A CAR AGAIN...?

I'M...

...ALL SHOU HAS.

AND SHOU...

Mad dash to get ready for the practice test.

SCRITCH SCRITCH SCRITCH SCRITCH

SCRITCH SCRITCH SCRITCH

MMM.
THANKS.

IF THERE'S ANYTHING YOU DON'T KNOW, WE'LL THINK IT OVER TOGETHER, OKAY?

SCRITCH SCRITCH SCRITCH

...IS ALL I HAVE.

RELUCTANTLY PLACED 5TH OF 402

WITH ALL HIS EFFORT PLACED 389TH OF 402

THIS IS OUT OF THE BLUE.

Hmm

THE CITY WELFARE GUY CAME THE OTHER DAY, RIGHT...?

RIGHT AFTER THE FUNERAL.

OH, YEAH.

I HAD YOU AND YOUR MOM SIT IN WITH ME...

A CITY OFFICIAL WOULDN'T BE TOO HAPPY ABOUT US LIVING ALONE, BUT I TOLD HIM...

YOU'RE SO STRONG, YUZU.

If you don't have any relatives, we can put Shun-kun in an institution...

UM!

WHA AA--?
YOU THINK SO?

Eating the lunches Kwano-chan made together.

Aim to be the brightest star in the legal world!

Yeah.

HELLO!

Welcome! SHOU-KUN! YUZU-CHAN'S HERE!

SQUEEZE

I GO HOME WITH YUZU-CHAN.

HOLD ME.

ALL RIGHT.

GET ON MY BACK.

MOMMY..... HUH......

BUT WILL YOU GO HOME WITH ME?

WE'LL GO TO THE STORE.

SHOU, YOUR MOMMY'S NOT HERE.

HE'S BEEN LIKE THIS ALL DAY...

It's unusual for Shou-kun.

MOMMY... SNIFFLE

UM...

MOM-MY'S NOT HERE.

MOM-MY!

WHAT'S WRONG, SHOU?

.....

RUSTLE RUSTLE

PA- KAP

I KNEW IT!

IT'S MY SISTER'S BOOK! ♡

YEY, A SAMPLE!

MARCH ON EART

TSUBAKI TAK

YEAH.

IS THIS...?

AH!!

WHAT NICE PEOPLE.

HMM, SO THAT'S WHAT HAP- PENED.

HEY, YUZU ...

SHOU FEELS HOTTER THAN USUAL ...

← Me on the way home...

HUFF

HUFF

...EH?

WE'LL GO ON AHEAD WITH SHOU IN THE TAXI.

YOU CAN RIDE YOUR BIKE, YUZU.

NO ...

HE'LL BE FINE WITH US.

IT WOULD BE TOO HARD ON SHOU- KUN TO RIDE THE BIKE, NOW WOULDN'T IT?

YEAH.

...

... YEAH.

THEY SAY HE CAN GO HOME WHEN THE IV'S FINISHED.

WELL ANYWAY, I'M GLAD IT WASN'T ANYTHING SERIOUS.

...SOME-THING I CAN'T LOSE.

Can you hold it?

SMILE

AH. SEITA LOOKS BLURRY.

Hey.

Waaah! Yuaa!!

...THIS FEELS BAD...

THUD

HEY, SIS. WHEN DID YOU DECIDE TO WRITE CHILDREN'S BOOKS?

...I WAS THE ONLY ONE IN MY CLASS WHO COULD NEVER DECIDE WHAT I WANTED TO DO WHEN I GRADUATED.

THE SUMMER OF MY LAST YEAR OF MIDDLE SCHOOL...

BUT I WANTED SOMEONE TO ACKNOWLEDGE THAT I CAN DO SOMETHING.

I JUST PANICKED. I COULDN'T FIND ANYTHING...

BUT FOR SOME REASON...

...I COULDN'T STOP CRYING.

I WAS LIKE, "WHAT THE HECK?"

BUZZ BUZZ BUZZZZZ BUZZZZ

BUZZ BUZZZZZ

I LIKE THAT WE'RE RELATED.

WHAT DO YOU LIKE ABOUT ME, MOM?

BUZZ BUZZ BUZZZZZZZ

SO I CALLED HOME FROM A PUBLIC PHONE IN THE NEIGH-BOR-HOOD.

HERE HER DAUGHTER IS SERI-OUSLY WORRIED AND SHE'S NOT EVEN PAYING ATTENTION.

HURRY HOME.

...TO LIVE THE WAY I WANTED.

BUT IT GAVE ME A LOT OF CONFI- DENCE...

ALL THAT HAPPENED WAS I REALIZED THAT THERE WAS SOMEONE WHO WOULD LOVE ME FOREVER.

Isn't she? She says things that are so vague, but still touch the heart.

Ah ha ha! Our mom's awesome!

But she won't say them anymore.

I'M ABOUT TO LOSE HEART NOW, TOO.

S/S...

...CHAN.

YUZU-CHAN!

Oh, she's awake!

TELL ME. WHAT DO YOU LIKE ABOUT ME?

HEY...

"HEY, SIS...

HELLO.
I'M MIKASE HAYASHI.
PLEASED TO MEET YOU.

THANK YOU FOR PICKING UP MY FIRST MANGA! I'M SO HAPPY.

THANKS TO ALL THE PEOPLE WHO SUPPORTED ME AND MY UNSKILLED MANGA. MY DREAM--THAT WAS SO HIGH IN THE SKY--HAS COME TRUE. I REALIZED THAT IF YOU WORK HARD AND DON'T GIVE UP, DREAMS DO COME TRUE. I FEEL BLESSED.

BUT! I STILL HAVE LOTS AND LOTS OF ROOM FOR IMPROVEMENT, SO I WANT TO KEEP TRYING SUPER HARD. PLEASE THINK OF ME KINDLY.

BECAUSE THIS IS THE FIRST VOLUME, LET ME INTRODUCE MYSELF.

· I WAS BORN ON SEPTEMBER 29, AND MY BLOOD TYPE IS O.
· MY FAVORITE PLACES ARE MY HOME, BOOK-STORES, ART SUPPLY STORES, THE LIBRARY, THE MOVIE THEATER, THE DEPARTMENT STORE ON WEEKDAYS, THE PARK, MY FRIENDS' HOUSES.

...THIS KIND OF TURNED INTO A FANGIRLISH INTRODUCTION (LAUGH).

MARCH ON EARTH
MIKASE HAYASHI

BUT ONE NIGHT, SHE REALIZES...

...A STORY ABOUT SISTERS WHO HAD LOST THEIR PARENTS...

SHE GETS ANNOYED WHEN THINGS DON'T GO WELL.

AND THEY FIGHT EVERY DAY.

THE HEROINE IS TORMENTED BY HER LITTLE SISTER AND HER TOMBOYISHNESS.

FLIP

...THAT SHE'S ABLE TO KEEP GOING BECAUSE SHE HAS HER SISTER.

Yeah, yeah. Go to sleep already.

Your bed is so warm, Sis!

LET'S...

MARCH ON EARTH

地球☆行進曲

CHAPTER
2

THIS BOOK IS THE LAST PICTURE BOOK MY SISTER WROTE.

IT WAS...

MARCH ON EARTH
TSUBAKI TAKAMIYA

FLIP

...A STORY ABOUT SISTERS WHO LOST THEIR PARENTS.

BUT ONE NIGHT, SHE REALIZES...

AND THEY FIGHT EVERY DAY.

THE HEROINE IS TORMENTED BY HER LITTLE SISTER AND HER TOMBOYISHNESS.

...THAT SHE'S ABLE TO KEEP GOING...

WANT SNACK!!

KAY!

YUZU-CHAN, YUZU-CHAN!

I'M HUNGRY.

...BECAUSE SHE HAS HER SISTER.

SHOU TAKAMIYA (2 YEARS, 6 MONTHS OLD)

... HUH ??

WE JUST ATE DINNER,

KA-CHAK

YUZU TAKAMIYA (AGE 15, 10TH GRADE) CURRENT PROBLEM: CAN'T GET SHOU OUT OF DIAPERS.

ALL OF MY SISTER'S BOOKS ARE TENDER STORIES.

EVERY TIME I READ THEM, I REMEMBER HER.

I STILL GET A LITTLE CHOKED UP.

HE CAN USE THEM VERY WELL.

LATELY, SHOU'S BEEN LEARNING WORDS REALLY FAST.

OPEN IT ??

ALL RIGHT!

Get in he!

POFF!

Kyaaa!

FLIP

"FAMILY" WAS VERY IMPORTANT TO MY SISTER.

WHEN SHE SUDDENLY SAID SHE WAS GOING TO HAVE A BABY AND RAISE HIM BY HERSELF...

...OF COURSE I WAS SURPRISED.

BUT I SENSED THERE WAS SOME REASON THAT SHE NEVER TOLD ME THE FATHER'S NAME.

SO, IN THE END, I COULDN'T ASK HER.

☆THE TAKAMIYA FAMILY FINANCES I INHERITED ARE MANAGED BY A LAWYER WHO WAS A FRIEND OF OUR FATHER. HE DEPOSITS A SET AMOUNT TO THE ACCOUNT EVERY MONTH.

00
370.00
190
3990
¥ 5,000
¥ 1,010

37
12.TM

DATE
12/19

GROCERIES
EGGS
MILK
BREAD
CHICKEN

TIME TO CHECK AC-COUNTS!

ALL RIGHT!

CHING

THERE ARE STILL TEN DAYS LEFT IN THE MONTH.

THIS IS GONNA BE HARD.

IT'LL BE OKAY!! WE CAN OVERCOME A TRIAL LIKE THIS!

...AND KURATA-SAN (THE LAWYER) IS SENDING MONEY EVERY MONTH...

I'M TOO EMBAR-RASSED TO TELL HIM THAT THERE WASN'T ENOUGH!!

TIME FOR HOME-WORK!

12/21 (SUN) SUNDAY

DONE WITH THE LAUNDRY!

LET'S GO OUT!

YESS ☆

FLAP

FLAP

FLAP

GOOD-NESS! HAVE FUN!

YUP! WE WERE INVITED TO VISIT HIS FRIEND FROM DAYCARE.

KA-CHAN

AH!

GOOD MORN-ING, KUSANO-CHAN!

MORN-ING!

Upsy daisy!

◄ BICYCLE

TIME FLIES.

OH, IS HE THAT OLD AL-READY?

WHAT DID YOU DO, KUSANO-CHAN?

I JUST CAN'T GET SHOU OUT OF DIA-PERS!

AH! OH YEAH!

GOOD MORN-ING.

GOING OUT?

YOU'RE RIGHT.

SHOU-CHAN WELL BE FINE.

WELL, EVERY-ONE'S DIFFERENT.

IT WENT PRETTY SMOOTHLY WITH KEITA.

BUT THAT SEITA... WE SWITCHED HIM TO UNDERWEAR AND POTTY-TRAINED HIM WHEN HE WAS TWO AND HALF.

↑ DOTING PARENT

↑ BASELESS

Ah! Yuzu!

GOOD MORN-ING!

Morning!

GOOD MORN-ING, YUZU!

BUT HE KEPT MAKING MESSES EVEN AFTER HE TURNED THREE.

He tried to destroy the evidence, but failed at that, too.

It wasn't me!

Seita, age 3

KEITA KUSANO GROWING UP RELIABLE THANKS TO LEARNING FROM A NEARBY BAD EXAMPLE. (SIXTH GRADE)

SEITA KUSANO 16-YEAR-OLD WHOSE ONE REDEEMING QUALITY IS THAT HE'S STURDY (10TH GRADER WHO LOVES YUZU)

NOTHING ...

...NN?? SEITA, DID YOU SAY SOME-THING??

I'M RUNNING LATE!

Look at the time!

AAAHH!!

N-y!

TO THINK I'D RUN INTO YOU ON A SUNDAY MORNING. IT MUST BE DESTI--

NOTHING IS WORSE THAN THAT!!

NOT INTER-ESTED?

GAH!

DON'T LOOK AT ME WITH THOSE APATHETIC EYES!!!

IT'S JUST THAT SHE'S NOT INTER-ESTED IN YOU, MY STUPID BROTHER.

YUZU DOESN'T MEAN ANY-THING BY IT.

IT'S OKAY.

Take care.

We're off!

WHOOSSSHHH

Cooold!

TWO YEARS AGO...

...WHEN MY SISTER AND I WERE HOMELESS WITH SHOU...

... MS. KUSANO WAS THE ONLY ONE WHO SMILED AND ACCEPTED US.

Kicked out of their old apartment because kids weren't allowed.

SINCE THEN, EVEN WHEN MY SISTER DIED,

AND NOW THAT I LIVE ALONE WITH SHOU...

...You can all come to my place.

If you don't mind a 20-year-old building...

KUSANO-CHAN IS THE CLOSEST TO US, AND HELPS US THE MOST.

!!!

...OH, I LOVE OBA-CHAN...♡

REALLY? OH, GOOD! ♡

HOME-MADE CAKE!!

IT'S DELI-CIOUS!

IT WAS ALL WE COULD DO TO TRAIN TOMO WHEN HE TURNED THREE. YOU JUST HAVE TO BE PATIENT AND TEACH HIM OVER AND OVER.

HM-MM.

IS THERE A KNACK FOR DOING IT RIGHT?

YES.

EH?

POTTY-TRAINING?

WOW!☆

WHAT A ☆ BIG CRISTMAS TREE!

TWINKLE TWINKLE

TWINKLE

Shou-kun, let's play!

AND THE VERY NEXT DAY, SUDDENLY HE COULD USE THE POTTY.

THAT DOESN'T REALLY HELP YOU, DOES IT?

BUT YOU KNOW, ONE DAY HE HAD A HIGH FEVER...

He cries about it every time...

Wow

I THINK I'VE HEARD THIS SOME-WHERE BEFORE...

AND THEN IT'S SO OBVIOUS THAT HE'S ALL WET, BUT HE TRIES TO HIDE IT!

HE'S ALWAYS GOING IN HIS UNDER-WEAR!

BUT, OH, THAT TOMO.

AH!

BUT IT MAKES ME FEEL LIKE IT'LL WORK OUT!

IT'S ABOUT TIME TO PUT THE TOYS AWAY AND GO HOME.

SHOU ...

THAT'S RIGHT!

THERE'S NO ONE WAY TO RAISE A CHILD.

WE'RE HAVING A HARD ENOUGH TIME THIS MONTH AS IT IS!!!

I... I CAN'T GET HIM A TOY THAT EXPENSIVE ...!!!

Darn you, Santa!
↑
MISDI-RECTED ANGER

ST OP ?

They always get along so well!

'Wow... really?!'

THE PURITY OF CHILDREN CAN SOMETIMES BE AMAZINGLY CRUEL...

CHRISTMAS SALE
TOY SHOVEL TRUCK

· · · · · · · · ·

SPIN

GLANCE
↓

STUCK TO THE GLASS →

HOW D--DARE YOU, TOY INDUSTRY !!!

CHRISTMAS BARGAINS WEEKL

CHRISTMAS EVE IS THE DAY AFTER TOMORROW...

I SEE...

This candle is so cute!

TWEE ??

SQUEEZE

WE'LL MAKE IT ALL SPARKLY AND PRETTY.

WANT TO DECO- RATE OUR TREE WHEN WE GET HOME?

SHOU ...

TWINKLE

TWINKLE

OH! YUZU!

SIGH

I WON- DER HOW MUCH THE TOY SHOU WANTS COSTS.

EVEN IF I GET A PART-TIME JOB, I'D NEVER GET THE MONEY BY TOMORROW...

AND I HAVE PRACTICE TESTS ALL DAY TODAY.

12/23 (TUE) TUESDAY

CHRIST- MAS, HUH?

THEY POSTED THE TEST RESULTS.

MURMUR

MURMUR

A--
ALL
RIGHT!
I'M
SECOND!!

TENTH GRADE PROFICIENCY TEST RESULTS

RANKINGS			
	NAME	CLASS	SCORE
1	KENICHI SAKAMOTO	2	492
2	YUZU TAKAMIYA	8	486

YOU DON'T LOOK TOO HAPPY.

HUH ??

NO, I'M DELIGHTED.

I'M GLAD IT'S TRUE THAT WORKING HARD PRODUCES RESULTS.

WOW, THAT MAKES ME PRETTY HAPPY.

PROFICIENCY TEST COMEBACK!!

↑
Score was bad last time from lack of studying.

OHHH... WHAT AM I GONNA DO ABOUT A CHRISTMAS PRESENT?

AH!

HEY!! CHRISTMAS ISN'T ONLY ABOUT PRESENTS!!

W--wait!!! I have to convey these feelings to Yuzu.....!

DRAG DRAG

Let's go.

The grammar and literature tests are in Class 1's room, right?

MUR MUR

MUR MUR

Heh. Heh.

THE PRACTICE TESTS ARE STARTING.

HEEEY, SEITA.

TWAAANG

OH...

SEITA HAS PLANS FOR CHRIST-MAS EVE.

I SEE...

I SEE.

I... I CAN'T BUY THAT!!!

CHRISTMAS BARGAIN PRICE

SHOVEL TRUCK

$125

USE THAT PHRASE...

...TO TAKE ADVANTAGE OF SHOU'S OBEDIENCE...

...NOT TO SEE HIS FACE...

...WHEN HE HANGS HIS HEAD AND DOES WITHOUT.

...AND MAKE HIM GIVE UP ON THINGS.

Kasuga Day Care

STAMP
STAMP
STAMP

MUST BE HARD TAKING TESTS ON YOUR DAYS OFF.

WELCOME, YUZU-CHAN!

HELLO!

STAMP
STAMP
STAMP
STAMP

Mmph!
Mmph!

NN?

YUZU-CHAN!

YOOK AT THIS!

STIFF

CLUNK

BA AM!

TOMOWWOW SANTA-SHAN CAN PUT MY GA-GA IN THIS!

I'VE PRE-TENDED SO MANY TIMES...

STIFF
STIFF

·····

U·HYA!

YOU'LL
CATCH
COLD.

Excuse
us.

Excuse
us!

THERE'S
NO
POINT
IN
DOING
THAT
STUFF.

WOULD
YOU
FIGURE
IT OUT
ALREADY?

Isn't it
sad to
go out of
your way
to get your
hair wet and
pretend
you were
in the
bath?

·····

ON THE INSIDE,
HER HEART
IS THROBBING
LIKE MAD
FROM MY
OPERATION:
LOVE UNDER ONE
ROOF!!!

UNDERSTAND?!
YUZU
EMBARRASSES
EASILY!!

I DON'T
REALLY
WANT
TO
KNOW.

ANYTHING
ABOUT YOU.

A
A
H
H
H
?!

WHAT
DO
YOU
KNOW
ABOUT
ME?!

·····

OBA-
CHAN.

That's
very
good!

GOOD-
NESS ♡

YOOK!
STOCKING
FO'
SANTA-
SHAN! ♡

I
MAKE
IT!

OBA-
CHAN!

They're
at it
again.

·····

·····

·····

STIFF

STIFF

. . . . .

"I'D LIKE TO HAVE A CHRIST-MAS EVE PARTY TOGETH-ER..."

WHAT IS IT, YUZU-CHAN?

TWINKLE

TWINKLE

BY NOW...

OH, YEAH.

YES ...

ACTUALLY, NEVER MIND.

...MS. KUSANO PROBABLY HAS PLANS, TOO.

...IT REALLY WOULD BE A LITTLE SAD.

AND IF SHE SAID NO...

WHAT IS IT? SOME-THING WRONG?

Tell me.

SEITA.

TWINKLE

TWINKLE

"

SEITA ...

... GH. ...

YUZU.

THERE'S NOT ENOUGH MONEY TO GET SHOU THE TOY HE WANTS.

TWINKLE

TWINKLE

TWINKLE

$20 LEFT

THUNK

NO MATTER HOW MUCH I CUT BACK UNTIL THE END OF THE MONTH

I GUESS...

I REALLY WILL HAVE TO GET KURATA-SAN TO DEPOSIT MORE MONEY.

I HATE THAT; IT'S LIKE GOING INTO DEBT.

EVEN WHEN THE SANTA CLAUS WHO GAVE THE PRESENTS CHANGED FROM MOM AND DAD TO MY SISTER...

Use it a lot, okay?

Isn't it cute!

Look, look, Shou!

WOW, IT'S THE SCARF I WANTED!

Oooh!

THANKS, SIS!

68

...I WOULD SMILE AND MAKE MY REQUEST.

AND EVERY SINGLE YEAR, WITHOUT FAIL, I GOT WHAT I WANTED.

AND YET...

...I...

SLIIIIIDE

...CAN'T DO ANYTHING ON MY OWN...

...S/S.

SQUEEZE

HERE I DECIDED I WOULDN'T COMPLAIN ANY MORE.

MUR MUR

MUR MUR

MUR MUR

11

I REALIZED THAT...

CHRISTMAS

SHOVEL TRUCK

$125

MARCH ON EA

TSUBAKI

DASH!

I HAVE AN HOUR BEFORE I HAVE TO PICK UP SHOU.

...I CAN KEEP GOING BECAUSE I HAVE HIM.

IF ALL I HAVE IS $20...

RUSTLE

SHOVEL TRUCK

$60

Merry X'mas

HUFF
HUFF
HUFF
HUFF
HUFF
HUFF
HUFF

HUFF
HUFF

CHRISTMAS BARGAIN

SHOVEL
TRUCK

$20

TOY

Merry X'mas

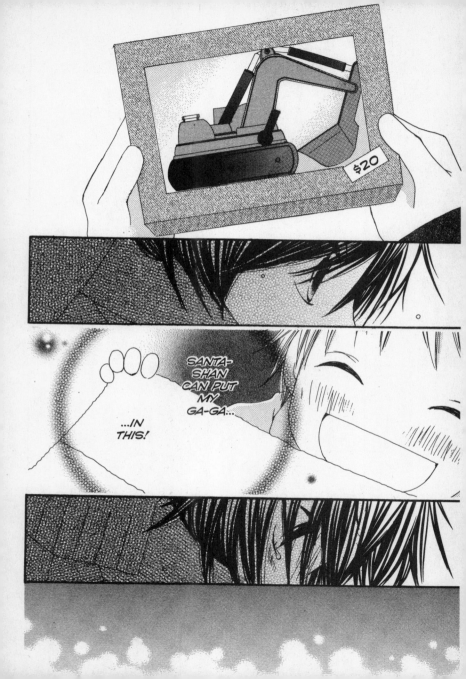

75

I HAVE A SHTOCK-ING!
HE PUT GA-GA IN IT!
......
NUMBER 8 CHOCO-LATE $30
I'M SORRY ...
I'M SORRY, SHOU.

YUZU-CHAN BOUGH' FO' ME!♡

...SHOU.

?!!

SHI_T!!

YOINK!

SHOU! YOU CAN HAVE THE CHOCO- LATE AND SANTA!☆

YOINK

YOINK

Waaah, choco!

YOINK!

84

TASTED SO WARM.

...THAT OBA-CHAN MADE.

NOW, NOW. YUZU-CHAN, SHOU-CHAN, TAKE OFF YOUR COATS.

SHALL WE HAVE DINNER?

WHAT?! YOU HAVE A PROBLEM WITH THE MASTERPIECE YOUR BROTHER SPENT ALL NIGHT WORKING ON?!

"Happy christmas party?"

What the heck is that?

GRAH!

YUZU, YUZU! DON'T YOU THINK SOMETHING'S WRONG WITH WHOEVER DID THE DECORATIONS?

TWINKLE

THE CAKE AND THE CHICKEN...

...AND OBA-CHAN WERE SO KIND.

Yuzu-chan would you like second?

SEITA AND KEITA-KUN...

AND SHOU SMILED THE WHOLE TIME, TOO.

SO...

...EVEN WHEN I WAS EATING...

...OR WHEN I WAS SMILING...

...THE TEARS...

...

WOULDN'T STOP COMING.

I REALIZED I CAN GO ON BECAUSE I HAVE HIM.

MERRY CHRISTMAS.

MAY IT
BE A DAY
WHEN
EVERYONE...

...CAN SMILE
WITH
JOY.

ON EARTH

YAKAMIYA

MARCH ON EARTH

地球☆行進曲

CHAPTER
3

WHA...??
OUT OF THE BLUE...

HEY, LET'S HAVE A CONTEST TO SEE WHO GETS THE MOST CHOCOLATE ON VALENTINE'S DAY?

Oh, boys only of course.

ARE YOU STUPID?

Look you, We're in high school now.

YOU THINK SO?

YUP! SHE MUST KNOW!

BE CONFI-DENT!

Y'know!

Poor Seita.

OH, BUT SHE CLEARLY DOESN'T KNOW HOW HE FEELS ...!!

YUZU'S TOO OBLIVI-OUS TO HIS "LOVE" ATMOS-PHERE!!

SEITA KUSANO AGE 16 AND IN LOVE WITH YUZU. SON OF THE LANDLADY OF YUZU'S APARTMENT.

I ONLY NEED CHOC-OLATE FROM THE GIRL I LIKE.

I'M OUT.

I'M SURE SHE KNOWS WHAT A GOOD GUY YOU ARE, SEITA!

YOU'LL GET IT!

How manly!

SPRINKLE

TRUFFLES

SPRINKLE

Eh! You're forming it in a lunchbox?!

POOOURRR

DEFINITELY HANDMADE, POURED INTO A LUNCH-BOX.

TO OBA-CHAN KEITA-KUN AND SEITA ♥

INCIDENTALLY, LAST YEAR, YUZU GAVE ONE CHOCOLATE TO THE WHOLE KUSANO FAMILY.

Mrs. Kusano (Oba-chan) (landlady)

Keita-kun (6th grade)

Seita

SHAKE SHAKE SHAKE

CLATTER

?!

...OOPS, AH!! I...

EH?? ME?

AH HA HA. NO.

?!

HEY, YUZU, IS THERE ANYBODY YOU LIKE?

AFTER ALL, I HAVE SHOU! ♡

... MY BELOVED SISTER ...

...AND PASSED ON TO THE NEXT WORLD FROM THE TRAFFIC ACCIDENT.

...AND THE BOY WHO JUMPED OUT IN FRONT OF THE CAR...

...PRO-TECTED ME AND SHOU...

IT'S BEEN SIX MONTHS NOW.

MORI CITY PARK

THAT SCAWY!

Mm!

Mm!

ME TOO!

SQUEEZE

YOU REALLY WERE A BIG HELP!

... HUH?

SQUEEEEZE

Whew.

DASH!

TH--

THANK YOU VERY MUCH!

ARE YOU... YUZU-CHAN?

EH?

WHEN DID YOU GET BACK TO JAPAN!?

WOW!

TAKATOH-SAN IS THE MAN WHO MADE MY SISTER'S DREAM COME TRUE-- THE EDITOR IN CHARGE OF HER PICTURE BOOKS.

AH!! TAKATOH-SAN?!

...WHEN HE SUDDENLY LEFT THE PUBLISHING COMPANY...

AND WENT OVERSEAS TO PURSUE HIS DREAM OF EXCAVATING ANCIENT RUINS, I WAS REALLY SHOCKED.

HE KNOWS OUR SITUATION...

...AND HE'D OFTEN TAKE ME TO DINNER WITH HIM...

AND LISTEN TO WHAT I HAD TO SAY.

SO...

I GOT BACK YESTERDAY.

THERE WAS A LULL IN THE EXCAVATION WORK.

MORI CITY PARK

I REMEMBERED TSUBAKI-SAN SAYING SHE LOVED THIS PARK...

...SO I CAME LOOKING IN CASE I MIGHT SEE HER.

EH?

WOW! IT'S BEEN THREE YEARS!!

WHAT A COINCIDENCE THAT I'D RUN INTO YOU HERE!!

...IS THAT...

TSUBAKI-SAN'S SON?

THE LETTERS I SENT ALL STARTED COMING BACK A YEAR AND A HALF AGO, SAYING YOUR ADDRESS WAS UNKOWN...

YES! HIS NAME IS SHOU.

I SEE...

...HUH? MY SISTER DIDN'T WRITE BACK TO YOU??

AH! WE MOVED.

I wonder why not.

...LET'S BE TOGETHER FOREVER, OKAY?

...THAT SHE'S ABLE TO KEEP GOING BECAUSE SHE HAS HER SISTER.

LET'S...

Oh, good.

It's so warm! Yummy♡

MY SISTER'S BOOK ALWAYS GIVES ME A PUSH.

IT TELLS ME TO KEEP GOING.

IT'S THE SOURCE OF MY ENERGY.

WHOOOSSSH

"WILL YOU BE BACK AT THIS PARK TOMORROW, YUZU-CHAN?"

MISTA!

Nice to see you Shou-kun!

HOP!

...PLAYED WITH SHOU UNTIL DARK.

AND WHEN I TOLD HIM...

...ABOUT THE SILLY THINGS THAT HAPPENED AT SCHOOL TODAY...

TAKATOH-SAN...

MORI CITY PARK

I FELT KIND OF TICKLED.

IT'S BEEN A LONG TIME SINCE I'VE TALKED TO ANYONE LIKE THIS.

...HE SMILED AND LISTENED.

I see you're studying hard.

TEST

AND I ENDED UP TALKING FAST ABOUT A LOT OF THINGS.

Kasuga Day Care

Ah ha ha ha

YOU'VE BEEN AWFULLY CHEERFUL LATELY, YUZU-CHAN.

DID SOMETHING GOOD HAPPEN?

I'M GONNA GO JOIN THE FIGHT, TOO!

WHOA! THIS IS INSANELY CHEAP!!

TOILET PAPER FOR 50 CENTS?!

SHE SAID TO GIVE IT TO YOU, YUZU-CHAN.

HERE. THIS IS FROM TOMO-KUN'S MOM.

A FLYER FOR THE SUPER-MARKET.

SHE SAID SHE WAS GOING ON AHEAD.

Shou-kun go to... close...

HOP HOP

JUST TOILET PAPER! YOU WAIT! TISSUE BOXES! DIAPERS!!!

OFF! TO THE STORE! ☆

RATTLE

Tee hee!

WAVE

WAVE

WAVE

GO!

YUP!

TAKE CARE.

...OH, MAN! ☆

YUZU-CHAN IS SO CUTE!

Was life that dazzling when I was young?

Age 27

It was so long ago you forgot?

Age 23

YOU SAID IT.

TAKATOH-SAN!

IT'S NO PROBLEM! ☆

THAT'S A LOT OF STUFF YOU'RE CARRYING.

LET ME CARRY SOME.

Huh? Yuzu-chan.

NO, LET ME CARRY IT.

YOUR BICYCLE IS SO UNSTEADY, IT'S MAKING ME NERVOUS.

TOTTER

TOTTER

MISTA! ♡

BOW

STARE

HEY, WHO'S THIS GUY?

HE WAS MY SISTER'S EDITOR.

AH! THIS IS TAKATOH-SAN.

HUFF HUFF HUFF

HUFF

Nn?

SEI-TAN!

OH, WE GOT REALLY INTO OUR GAME OF TAG.

WILL YOU BE ALL RIGHT?

YES!

YOU HAVE A LOT TO CARRY, YUZU-CHAN. I'LL WALK YOU HOME.

OH, YOU DON'T HAVE TO DO THAT.

EH!?

Sei-tan hold me!

HRRM.

HE WAS IN ANOTHER COUNTRY AND JUST GOT BACK THE OTHER DAY.

FLIP

I WENT TO A FEW BOOKSTORES, LOOKING FOR ONES THAT HAVE A GOOD SELECTION OF PICTURE BOOKS.

YOU CAN'T FIND THEM IN BOOKSTORES OFTEN.

WOW. YOU HAVE ALL OF THEM!

MARCH
TSUBAKI

ME SEE?

3

■MY EDITOR AND ME.
WHEN I SUBMITTED THE SECOND MANGA OF MY LIFE, IT WAS MY EDITOR WHO CALLED ME AND SAID, "I'LL BE YOUR EDITOR."
A MIRACLE OCCURRED THAT DAY.

SHIVER
SHIVER

IT'S NOT LIKE I WON AN AWARD.

MY EDITOR'S BRISK WAY OF TALKING LEFT A BIG IMPRESSION ON ME. LATER, WHEN I MET HER IN PERSON, HER VOICE SOUNDED JUST LIKE IT DID ON THE PHONE; I WAS IM-PRESSED. ...I KNOW, BUT I WAS IMPRESSED.

I ALWAYS GET STUCK WHEN I'M DOING THE ROUGH DRAFT, BUT MY EDITOR ALWAYS KNOWS WHAT I'M THINKING EVEN THOUGH I'M BAD AT EXPRESSING MY-SELF, AND SHOWS ME THE EXIT. I WANT TO WORK AS HARD AS I CAN TO REDUCE THE TIMES I'M SPINNING MY WHEELS GETTING NOWHERE!
ALSO, MY EDITOR IS REALLY, REALLY GOOD AT KARAOKE!☆
(SO IS EVERYONE IN THE EDITORIAL DEPARTMENT)◇
I'M TONE-DEAF, SO I REALLY ADMIRE THAT.

NOTE: OF COURSE SHE'S MORE BEAUTIFUL THAN THIS.

...TSUBAKI-SAN ALWAYS SAID SHE WANTED TO WRITE A STORY LIKE THIS SOMEDAY.

SO SHE DID...

...GET TO WRITE THE STORY SHE WANTED TO WRITE THE MOST.

...
EH?

YUZU...

YUZU, LET'S KEEP TRYING TOGETHER, OKAY?

I SEE.

YOU LOST YOUR PARENTS AND TSUBAKI-SAN STARTED TAKING CARE OF YOU WHEN SHE WAS IN HIGH SCHOOL, RIGHT?

THAT'S RIGHT.

WE DIDN'T HAVE ANY RELATIVES TO GO TO.

IT COULDN'T HAVE BEEN ALL FUN AND GAMES...

BUT TSUBAKI-SAN ALWAYS SMILED, AND SAID...

..."IT'S BECAUSE I HAVE YUZU."

WHEN YUZU SMILES AND SAYS, "I LOVE YOU, SIS"...

116

...THAT'S ALL I NEED; I CAN KEEP GOING AT ANYTHING...

...SHE WOULD SAY.

S/S ...

"...BECAUSE I HAVE MY SISTER."

BACK THEN, TSUBAKI-SAN WOULD SAY SHE WAS HAPPY TO GET HELP FROM THE PEOPLE AROUND HER.

BUT I'M SURE THAT WHAT SUPPORTED HER MORE THAN ANYONE ELSE WAS YOU AND THOSE WORDS, YUZU-CHAN.

...I DIDN'T KNOW.

...I MEAN, I...

FLIP

"I CAN KEEP GOING..."

MARCH ON EARTH
TSUBAKI TAKAMIYA

WHEN IT COMES TO COL-LEGE... AND MONEY...

AND WHETHER OR NOT WE CAN REALLY GO ON JUST THE TWO OF US...

YUZU-CHAN?

...I'M OKAY.

...WHEN I GET ANXIOUS THINKING ABOUT EVERY-THING...

I CAN'T TALK ABOUT IT TO ANYONE.

IT'S...

CLACK

TOO END-LESS.

...TOO HEAVY FOR A FIFTEEN-YEAR-OLD TO BEAR.

THINKING ABOUT HER PERSON-ALITY...

SOME-TIMES I GET REALLY SCARED.

THERE'S NOTHING I CAN DO TO STOP PANICKING.

...I'M SURE SHE CAN'T TELL ANYONE WHEN SOME-THING IS REALLY HARD ON HER.

...NO MATTER HOW MUCH THE PEOPLE AROUND HER REACH OUT TO HER...

EVEN SO...

Waaaaaaahh! Seita?! What's wroooooong?!

...I DON'T REALLY CARE ABOUT THE CHOCOLATE.

...AM I SO NERVOUS ABOUT GIVING HIM VALENTINE'S CHOCOLATE ...?!

MORI CITY PARK

YUZU-CHAN.

YEEEEESSS?!

(INSIDE-OUT)

JUMP!

B-DMP
B-DMP
B-DMP
Waah!
What's my problem?

WH- WHY...

WHY
...

WHY
DIDN'T
I
REALIZE?

YOU SAID YOU DON'T KNOW WHO SHOU-KUN'S FATHER IS...

BUT... WHEN WAS SHOU-KUN BORN?

It's always been Takatoh-san's dream to excavate ruins.

No! Why is Takatoh-san going overseas?

B-DMP

CHOP

CHOP

MY SISTER, WHO WANTED A STABLE FAMILY MORE THAN ANYONE...

...
EH?

...BECAME AN UNWED MOTHER.

I'm happy just giving birth to the child of someone I love.

B-DMP

AND SHE NEVER WROTE BACK TO ANY OF THE MANY LETTERS...

...THAT TAKATOH-SAN SENT.

B-DMP

I DON'T KNOW WHY.

B-DMP

BUT EVEN IF SHE NEVER INTENDED TO LET TAKATOH-SAN KNOW THAT SHE WAS PREGNANT...

...IT ALL MATCHES UP PERFECTLY.

...SHOU JUST TURNED TWO.

BUT, IF TAKATOH-SAN DIDN'T KNOW ANYTHING...

B-DMP

I...

...IMME-DIATELY LIED AND SAID HE WAS BORN SIX MONTHS LATER THAN HE WAS...

...SO THAT TAKATOH-SAN, WHO WASN'T IN JAPAN, WOULD HAVE NOTHING TO DO WITH IT.

...
I SEE.

RUSTLE
RUSTLE

I WAS SCARED.

...
THEN I...

IF TAKATOH-SAN REALLY IS SHOU'S FATHER...

BACK FROM CLUB.

YOU'RE STILL HERE?

FLUTTER

FLUTTER

FLUTTER

AND WHY ARE THE LIGHTS OFF?

YOU'LL CATCH COLD, YOU KNOW?

WINDOW WIDE OPEN IN MIDWINTER!! GOOOOOONG

Cold!

I'VE NEVER CAUGHT ONE BEFORE. I'LL BE FINE.

......

I see.

SILENCE....

...

WH OO SH

I'M COMING IN.

COLD!

PROBABLY.

PROBABLY?! DON'T BE SO CALM ABOUT IT!!

SERIOUSLY?!

GAH!

UM, HEY...

I WAS WITH TAKATOH-SAN, YOU KNOW?

... YEAH.

...BUT I...

DIDN'T WANT TO ADMIT IT, SO I LIED TO HIM.

ERK, THAT WAS SOME *REALLY BAD TIMING* ON MY PART!!!

HMMM...

?!

BUT I THINK HE MIGHT BE SHOU'S FATHER.

I JUST FOUND OUT TODAY...

...THAT SHOU MIGHT BE TAKEN FROM ME.

IT SEEMED LIKE IT WOULD BE BETTER FOR ME...

...IF TAKATOH-SAN DIDN'T KNOW THE TRUTH...

...BUT

IF I THINK ABOUT IT A LITTLE...

...TAKATOH-SAN SPOKE SO KINDLY TO ME.

HE WOULD NEVER DO THAT...

I WASN'T HAPPY SO MUCH AS SCARED ...

I BELIEVE THAT.

TOMOR-ROW...

...I'M GOING TO GO APOLOGIZE FOR LYING TO HIM.

RUSTLE

I SEE.

RIGHT NOW...

...ALL I CAN SAY TO YOU IS "THANK YOU," SEITA.

YEAH.

HA
HA

THAT'S NOT TRUE.

YOU'RE NICE TO EVERYONE, SEITA.

TWAAANG!

THUD

Waaah! Seita!!?

TOMOR-
ROW...

...WHEN
I TELL
HIM
THE
TRUTH...

...THERE
MAY BE
THINGS THAT
CAN'T
STAY
THE SAME.

EVEN
SO...

...EVEN
SO,
I...

...WILL
GO
FORWARD.

MARCH ON EARTH 1 / END

君の旋律は秋の色

THE SOUND YOU MAKE
IS THE COLOR OF AUTUMN

AKKI, THIS SEAT'S FREE.

...THIS IS UNUSUAL...

...YOU BEING IN THE LIBRARY, YOSHI-YAN.

I KNOW.

Tama-chan!

Tama-chan!

Yoshi-yan introduced us once.

You know him?!

IT'S AKKI.

AKKI?!!

Ah you're right.

UWAAH!

UWAAH!

Ooh. She's so cute...♡

WELL, I'LL BE GOING...

CLATTER

EH...?

DID I DO SOMETHING...?

He just got here...

SHUT

AH...! UM!

I...

I'M SAKU ARISAKA.

BOW

WE'RE EVEN IN THE SAME CLASS NOW.

WE'VE BEEN FRIENDS SINCE ELEMENTARY SCHOOL.

AKI* KUSANO.

BOW

*AKI IS HIS GIVEN NAME; AKKI IS HIS NICKNAME.

TEACHER
Hey, Aki-kun. Don't bottle things up inside. Tell me anything.

Yes, ma'am. But this is normal.

...SO HE WAS RAISED BY HIS GRANDFATHER, WHO TAUGHT HIM THAT MEN DON'T WASTE TIME WITH IDLE CHATTER.

HE HAS A HABIT OF SPEAKING DECISIVELY.

AKKI'S PARENTS HAVE ALWAYS BOTH WORKED...

EH?

Waaah! Sako, don't go getting depressed on me.

IT'S OKAY!!! THAT'S NORMAL!

HIS GRADE SCHOOL REPORT CARDS ALWAYS SAID STUFF LIKE...

"I WISH HE WOULD BE MORE CHILDLIKE."

Aki! What are you reading?

Kokoro.

AKKI IN MIDDLE SCHOOL

Somehow popular with older students.

BUT... HE'S VERY POLITE, AND I REALLY LIKE THAT ABOUT HIM.

AND HE KNOWS A LOT ABOUT ANNUAL EVENTS.

I WANTED TO TALK TO HIM.

CLATTER

I'M SORRY. I'M GOING HOME.

WHEN I HEARD THAT...

...FOR SOME REASON, I REALLY WANTED TO SEE KUSANO-KUN!

SO HE REACTS TO THINGS LIKE THIS.

GLANCE

UWAH! I DIDN'T EXPECT THAT.

UM, UM...

MAYBE YOU CAN'T TELL FROM HERE.

THERE ARE SWEET OLIVE TREES HERE...

Um, and...

.....

IS THAT A GOOD BOOK?

INUGAMI!?

FOR NOW.

I HAVEN'T READ IT SINCE GRADE SCHOOL, SO I'VE FORGOTTEN PARTS.

INUGAMI CLAN, HUH?

I'LL CHECK THAT OUT NEXT.

SEISHI YOKOMIZO, HUH...? NEVER HEARD OF HIM.

THIS REALLY DOES FIT KUSANO-KUN.

...MORE THAN THE KATAKANA VERSION.

Inugami Clan

AH!

HOW DO YOU WRITE SWEET OLIVE IN KANJI?

OH! I'LL GET OUT MY NOTEBOOK.

...?

金木犀

OSMANTHUS FRAGRANS

WAAAA!

THANK YOU SO MUCH!

...THERE.

YOSHI-YAN
KUSANO-KUN "AKK
IT'S SO CUTE!!!
THEY CALL EACH OTH

OH, I MADE AN AM
THE LITTLE ARBO
IS LIKE KUSANO-
VORITE "SPOT"
KUSANO-KUN'
(IT'S WRITTEN
SMELL COM

IS
AKI
ANO
KUN!!!

ALL
RIGHT!

I
DID
IT!

ACCORD-
ING TO
YOSHI-
YAN...

...THEY
USUALLY
EAT
LUNCH ON
THE
ROOF
TOGETHER.

WOULD IT BE
OKAY?

JOINING
THEM,
I MEAN.

YOSHI-
YAN
SAID IT
WAS FINE.

SAKU,
SAKU!

MOM WAS
SAYING
THAT
TODAY'S
INGREDIENTS
ARE GONNA
BE REALLY
HARD.

THAT'S
WHAT
I
SAID...

...BUT
I GRAB
THE
SPOT
NEXT
TO HIM.

TAKE
ADVAN-
TAGE
OF
THE
CONFU-
SION...

AND
GET
CLOSE
TO
HIM!!

HE
RE!

SCOOTCH
SCOOTCH

FLIP

(OSMANTHUS FRAGRANS)

RUSTLE

AH.

SWEET OLIVE.

...WE JUST TALKED.

THERE'S A TREE AROUND HERE, TOO.

BUT FOR SOME REASON...

...I ALREADY MISS KUSANO-KUN.

Wow, there are so many...

I wonder which is easiest to read.

Oh, Kusano-kun... Yeah, right.

400 LITERATURE

YOKOMIZO...

YOKOMIZO...

THERE IT IS!

SCUFF

UM, I WASN'T TRYING TO READ THE SAME BOOK AS YOU, KUSANO-KUN...!!!

BAM!

I'D LIKE TO PUT A BOOK BACK.

MAY I?

SCUFF

SCUFF

SCUFF

SCUFF

SCUFF

BOW

BOOK FROM PENALTY GAME

CLASS 1-2, SAKU ARISAKA

DATE DUE | TITLE | BORROWER

10/16 | IDEALS AND REALITY

OH...

En, Ideals and Reality...

THIS ONE'S RELATIVELY EASY TO READ.

PULL

The Witch of the West is Dead

EH?!

...I THINK YOKOMIZO IS HARD TO START OUT WITH.

EH?!

He knows everything!!?

THUNK

...WAS THE STORY OF AN OLD WOMAN SOR-CERESS AND HER GRANDCHILD.

WHEN I REALIZED HE READS BOOKS LIKE THIS...

...I WANTED TO KNOW ABOUT KUSANO-KUN EVEN MORE...

WHAT DOES KUSANO-KUN LIKE?

4

■ ABOUT LETTERS:

I READ THE LETTERS I RECEIVE VERY CAREFUL-LY AND LOVINGLY. THANK YOU SO MUCH. THEY ARE MY TREASURES! ♡

WHEN I THINK ABOUT THE TIME IT TAKES TO WRITE A LETTER AND THE EF-FORT IT TAKES TO PUT A STAMP ON IT AND PUT IT IN THE MAIL, I THINK THAT I REALLY AM HAPPY TO HEAR HOW YOU FEEL THROUGH YOUR LETTERS.

THEY ALWAYS CHEER ME UP, SO I WANT TO WORK HARD SO THAT I CAN MAKE A SERIES THAT WILL CHEER OTHER PEO-PLE UP, TOO.

AND I LOVE LOOKING AT THE PURIKURA* AND PICTURE POSTCARDS THAT ARE INCLUDED WITH SOME LETTERS.

THANK YOU SO MUCH!

I'M SORRY THAT MY RE-PONSES ARE ALWAYS SHINING WITH A LACK OF LITERARY TALENT, BUT IF YOU HAVE ANY THOUGHTS, THEN PLEASE LET ME HEAR THEM.

ADDRESS

MIKASE HAYASHI
C/O CMX
888 PROSPECT STREET
SUITE 240
LA JOLLA, CA 92037

END OF COLUMN

* PURIKURA: SHORT FOR PURINTO KURABU. THEY'RE LITTLE STICKERS YOU GET WITH YOUR PICTURE ON THEM.

I PUT A LOT OF ENTHUSIASM INTO IT! ☆

KUSANO-KUN IS HIS GRANDFATHER'S BOY.

OH... I TALKED TOO MUCH.

COUGH COUGH

SHAKE SHAKE

SOME-DAY...

I HOPE THAT SOME-DAY...

...HE'LL LOOK LIKE THAT WHEN HE TALKS ABOUT ME.

I WON'T TELL ANYONE...

...ABOUT YOUR SECRET BASE.

STARTING TODAY... CLUBS ARE CANCELLED BECAUSE OF TESTING... SO LET'S ALL STUDY TOGE--

SAKU!

AH!

Bye, Tama-chan!

SECRET BASE...?

ZA-ZOOM!

DOESN'T NOTICE

Well, let's study the three of us.

What's up with Saku?

I think I might hate Aki Kusano.

Don't cry, Tama-chan!

SLAM!

DIIING DOOONG

DAAANG DOOONG

HOW DID I RECOGNIZE HER FOOTSTEPS...?

How?

SO IT WAS ARISAKA-SAN...

SIGH

800 IDEOLOGY

IDEALS AND REALITY

LASS 1-2, SAKI ARISAKA

TITLE   SIGNATURE

REALITY

SCUFF

THE SCENT OF SWEET OLIVES...

...AND FOOT-STEPS WITH A UNIQUE TEMPO...

...AS HE DRAGS HIS HEELS A LITTLE.

SCUFF

SCUFF

SCUFF

SCUFF

WANTING TO SEE HIM...

...I WAS ALWAYS LOOK-ING FOR HIM.

SCUFF

SCUFF

HUFF

HUFF

SCUFF

SCUFF

RUSTLE

KISANO-

IT'S SO CUTE!!

THEY CALL EACH OTHER BY

THE LITTLE AR BOR IN

DISCO VERY

OH, I MADE AN

NICKNA MES.

IT'S NICE.

FRONT OF THE

THE U!! LITTLE

AMAZ ING

SHRINE IS

IT WAS THE FIRST TIME KUSANO-KUN CAME TO SEE ME.

THE SOUND YOU MAKE IS THE COLOR OF AUTUMN / END

AFTERWORD.

✳ ABOUT MARCH ON EARTH

■ CHAPTER 1

When I was telling my editor about my nephew, who lives far away, and how sweet he is, she suggested, "Then let's draw a story like that! ☆" and I thought of the basic story while she treated me to some delicious oden. (But I completely redid the first chapter's storyboard. ☆)

For Yuzu, I did my best to follow the mantra "anyway, she's and awesome girl." This is the first time I've drawn a main character who uses the Japanese "atashi" (a girly, informal way of saying "I") to refer to herself, so it was a nice change. I modeled Shou after my nephew... or so I thought, but real kids are taller and talk more, so he's a little baby-like. But wow, kids talk a lot and they really understand what we say to them; I think they're amazing. Seita doesn't really come on as a love interest (LOL), so it was pretty easy making him. ...No, I do want to be a love interest... we'll see.

■ CHAPTER 2

When my editor told me I could draw another chapter, I was so surprised my kneew went weak. I was really happy. It was for the *LALA DELUXE*＊ that went on sale in December, so I was really enthusiastic when I started the rough draft using A Christmas ☆ theme, which I'd wanted to do for a long time. But I had a really hard time drawing the character introductions in the first few pages (LOL). I thought up the scene where Seita makes the cake double-layered and made the story. After I finished the manuscript, my editor noticed some unbelievable mistakes, and I was able to fix it just in time. i had forgotten the existence of a national holiday... An important day... I was overly enthusiastic and it turned into 50 pages, but I was able to do my first color chapter cover page, and color preview, so I was really happy. Also, Shou has clearly shrunk and has bigger eyes than he did in Chapter 1.... And Yuzu's bangs got longer... I want to cut them! Her eyes will go bad.

■ CHAPTER 3

I was told I could draw another chapter... and I shook with joy. It was for the February *DELUXE*, so I thought, "Maybe Valentine's..." (I'm a simpleton.) I had always been drawing only glasses characters, so for *Earth* I had been disciplining myself (LOL), but my editor said, "Takatoh-san and Seita still look too similar, so why not put glasses on him?" and the ban was lifted, just like that... I'm so weak-willed.... And what does that say about my skill as an artist that I can't draw a character that's more than ten years older to look different? I'll do my best, really. Everyone knows by now, but I like men wearing flower print shirts (+jacket) just as much as I like glasses (LOL). I also like white coats and suits. As for girls, my heart flutters at sailor suits. (I've gotten off topic...)

When I'm working on the final draft, I have no time, so my mother helps me lay tone. I was surprised at how skillfully she cuts it. And my little sister can even erase tone (like a gradation); I was a little impressed.

＊ *LALA is a Japanese manga magazine where MARCH ON EARTH was first serialized.*

❋ THE SOUND YOU MAKE IS THE COLOR OF AUTUMN

They told me I could put a one-shot story in this book, so after wondering what to choose, I had them include this one. Never mind how well they're drawn, I love all of them. The manga from around my debut are even more incredible than what I draw now, but... still (LOL).

For this story, my editor discussed "Focusing on love more than character concepts," and I made an outline. And yet the main character (Saku) ended up with the concept that she has abnormally strong hearing and smell....

I decided on the names Saku and Aki after flipping through the kanji list in the Koujien dictionary. I completely stole the surname Kusano from Mr. Masamune in the rock band Spitz. (Incidentally, Seita and family are also Kusano...) I'm sorry... I really, really love Mr. Masamune's voice and look.... Of course, I love Spitz's songs, too. I also like Mr. Children, Bump of Chicken, and Asian Kung-Fu Generation.... Of course I like their music, but their voices... my heart flutters. ... I've gotten off topic again.

I like when boys call each other by nicknames; it's cute. It's especially good when quiet boys do it (LOL). My heart flutterings are very specific and in the minority....

The novel that comes up in the story is one from when I wanted to write a story with magic, so I bought and read all the books with magic in them that I could get at the bookstore. All the items that show up are lovely novels.
As for the sotry about magic, I didn't have the ability to express the world of the story, so I gave up on it. I practice daily with rough drafts so that someday I can write a fantasy story. The rough draft is the most trying part of the process, but I like it the most.

Thank you for reading this far.

I am truly happy to have the work that I created through my days of worry and happiness made into a book that people will read.

It is all thanks to those who read it, those who cheer me on, and those who support me. Thank you very much. I will continue to work hard.

Taneoka-sama, the editorial department, everyone who took part in the release of this book...

My family, who has no interest in my manga but cheer me on anyway...

My dear friends...

My friends who help with the final manuscripts. Kanako-sama, Nanae-sama, Akiko-sama, Yuumi-sama, Hajime Hanemura-sama...

And you, who hold this book in your hands...

I give you my greatest thanks.

MIKASE HAYASHI

THE SKY GETS HIGHER DAY BY DAY, AND TELLS OF THE END OF SUMMER.

...THE SUN WILL ALWAYS RISE AGAIN.

EVEN IF MY WORLD LOSES ALL COLOR AND I'M COWERING IN A CORNER...

FLUTTER

FLUTTER

FLUTTER

FLUTTER

FLUTTER

FLUTTER

YUP!
I MEAN, SUMMER'S STARTING. IT'LL GET HOT.

BUT IT WAS ONLY TWO INCHES.

I told you to grow it out!

EEHH? YUZU, YOU CUT YOUR HAIR AGAIN?

Mmmm, Cat. Shun-kun's car.

I'LL STEP FOR- WARD...

...SO THAT TOMOR- ROW...

...WILL BE BRIGHTER THAN TODAY.

AFTERWORD / END

CHIKYU KOUSHINKYOKU by Mikase Hayashi © 2002 by Mikase Hayashi. All rights reserved.
First published in Japan in 2004 by HAKUSENSHA, INC., Tokyo.

MARCH ON EARTH Volume 1, published by WildStorm Productions, an imprint of DC
Comics, 888 Prospect St. #240, La Jolla, CA 92037. English Translation © 2009. All Rights
Reserved. English translation rights in U.S.A. And Canada arranged with HAKUSENSHA, INC.,
through Tuttle-Mori Agency, Inc., Tokyo. CMX is a trademark of DC Comics. The stories,
characters, and incidents mentioned in this magazine are entirely fictional. Printed on
recyclable paper. WildStorm does not read or accept unsolicited submissions of ideas,
stories or artwork. Printed in Canada.

DC Comics, a Warner Bros. Entertainment Company.

Alethea & Athena Nibley – Translation and Adaptation
Hiromi DeBrun – Lettering
Larry Berry – Design
Sarah Farber – Assistant Editor
Jim Chadwick – Editor

ISBN: 978-1-4012-1594-1

DON'T MISS THE CONCLUSION
TO THIS SERIES IN JULY!

MARCH ON EARTH
Volume 2

By Mikase Hayashi. A big secret is revealed that will change everything—but will it
be for the better? Takatoh has agreed to help Yuzu take care of Shou, even though it
means putting his own dreams on hold. But Yuzu knows that's not something her sister
would have wanted and insists that he follows his original plans, even if it means leaving Japan. Meanwhile, Yuzu has some choices to make about her own future. Will she
sacrifice her dreams for Shou? Or can she find a way to do what is best for both of them?

RIGHT TO LEFT?!

Traditional Japanese manga starts at the upper right-hand corner, and moves right-to-left as it goes down the page. Follow this guide for an easy understanding.

FLIP IT!

All the pages in this book were created—and are printed here—in Japanese RIGHT-to-LEFT format. No artwork has been reversed or altered, so you can read the stories the way the creators meant for them to be read.

For more information and sneak previews, visit cmxmanga.com. Call 1-888-COMIC BOOK for the nearest comics shop or head to your local book store.